About the author

Ada Langton lives with her husband, Pete, and her eldest daughter, Indea. Together they enjoy binge TV, dry martinis and all kinds of cheese. Ada has four other children and she hopes they all find someone who will support them to be all they aspire to be. Ada loves to hide away and write whenever she can — as long as there is a good supply of hot darjeeling tea.

She was a winner of the Varuna-HarperCollins Manuscript Award, writes a sometimes blog and published two books *Sunday Best* and *After Before Time* under the name Robbi Neal. She adopted the pen-name Ada Langton for her fiction. She chose Ada in memory of her great-grandmother who tragically died of cancer aged only forty-five, and Langton in memory of her much-loved grandfather who was the inspiration for Reuben in this novel.

The Art of Preserving Love

Ada LANGTON

mira

First Published 2018
First Australian Paperback Edition 2018
ISBN 9781489246721

The Art of Preserving Love
© 2018 by Robbi Neal
Australian Copyright 2018
New Zealand Copyright 2018

This is a work of fiction. Names, characters, places, and incidents are either the product of the author's imagination or are used fictitiously, and any resemblance to actual persons, living or dead, business establishments, events, or locales is entirely coincidental.

Published by
Mira
An imprint of Harlequin Enterprises (Australia) Pty Ltd.
Level 13, 201 Elizabeth St
SYDNEY NSW 2000
AUSTRALIA

® and TM (apart from those relating to FSC®) are trademarks of Harlequin Enterprises Limited or its corporate affiliates. Trademarks indicated with ® are registered in Australia, New Zealand and in other countries.

Cataloguing-in-Publication details are available from the National Library of Australia www.librariesaustralia.nla.gov.au

Printed and bound in Australia by McPherson's Printing Group

MIX
Paper from
responsible sources
FSC
www.fsc.org   FSC® C001695

This book is dedicated to
Asher, Seth, Indea, Zane, Maia and Pete
with all my love.
P.S. Pete — every hero is a version of you.

Half an inch, half an inch, half an inch shorter,
The skirts are the same for mother and daughter,
When the wind blows each of them shows,
Half an inch, half an inch, more than she oughter.
— *The Triad*, a journal devoted to literacy, Sydney, July 1928

Part One

One

Edie

*Early in the morning of Sunday, 5 November 1905, in Ballarat,
when the sun has just woken, wiping sleep from its eyes.*

Edie had a plan. She'd written it in her notebook and once something
was written in her notebook, Edie knew it would happen. The
letters had curved and spun on the paper as she wrote, as if they
were threading themselves into the ordinary moments of life,
quietly breathing their magic and putting things into place while
no one was looking.

Edie's plan wasn't a big majestic plan that would up-end govern-
ments or bring love sweeping in like the gust of wind that roared
up the wide main thoroughfare of Sturt Street to the big intersection at Doveton Street, where it would swirl like a tornado and
whip women's skirts up around their thighs, throwing them off
balance and into the waiting arms of lonely miners.

Edie had made a modest plan. A carefully thought out plan.
A plan for a love that would be gentle and soothing like a freshly
brewed hot cup of tea first thing on an icy morning.

The dim morning light wove its way through the trees into Edie's room and turned the leaves of the rose-patterned carpet from olive to chartreuse, gently announcing the day.

Edie had woken before the sun and now eased herself up onto her elbow. She tugged hard at her nightdress, which was caught under her hip, and reached under her pillow. Her notebook had slept there, safely tucked under her dreams, and now as she held it in front of her the sun lit up its gold-embossed initials. She loved the feel of the leather cover and ran her fingers over her initials on the front. When she held it to her nose the warm musky smell filled her heart. Her father had given it to her on her birthday. It had a leather loop at the side to hold a small pencil. She opened it to her latest entry and read it over:

Fifth November Five
I am nineteen years old.
Plan — Marry (try to make it Theo Hooley).

She always wrote the date out in words, it looked more permanent than numbers. Then she put the notebook on her bedside table, threw the blankets aside and jumped out of bed. She was ready to put her plan into action.

Now, Edie wasn't an ugly girl, not by anyone's standards. She didn't have skin that was cratered like the moon or a nose that was long enough to hang a coat on. She wasn't too fat or too tall. But her looks were unremarkable; men didn't turn to drink her in when she walked past. She was ordinary, as are most girls who don't have older sisters to show them the ropes. No one had shown Edie what suited her or how to attract a man's attention.

She didn't know how to tease with inviting words or how to catch a man's gaze for just long enough to pique his interest before quickly pretending disdain so he would come scurrying after her.

Just yesterday her mother Lucy had said, 'I think the problem is, my love, that none of the men match your intelligence and spark,' and passed her a cup of tea exactly how she liked it.

'You say that because I am your only child,' Edie replied. 'You have to say something to make me feel better.'

'Plainer girls than you have married,' said her father, jabbing his umbrella at an imaginary jury. 'Your mother is right — you are just too intelligent for them.' Paul Cottingham swirled his umbrella in the air as if it was a magician's wand, only just missing the glass lightshade. 'Edie darling, if I could click my fingers and conjure a devoted and loving husband from thin air I would do it in an instant. You know I will give you anything within my power,' and he bowed to her to show that he meant it.

Then she saw him dismiss her problems from his mind and focus instead on the stitching on the umbrella, as if it was far more important than she was.

Her father had been even more distracted than usual for the past month. He didn't really seem to listen when she talked about how Essie had got engaged to Vincent Jessop. More importantly, Essie was two years younger than she was — did you hear that? Two years younger. He would nod absently as she went on to tell him how Marjorie Hollings already had a baby that was six months old. He used to give her optimistic hugs and carefully kind words, but these days he mostly gave her preoccupied murmurs and inattentive nods. Edie had watched him, longing for him to think about her again. She knew, and she knew her father and mother knew, that now she was nineteen the chances of her finding a husband were dwindling fast. This was an urgent matter.

'I think they've got the stitching uneven here,' said Paul, and had held the umbrella out for inspection. 'Does that look like an even quarter-inch spacing to you?'

Edie ignored the umbrella and said, 'Well, if I can't find a husband I might as well find work. Perhaps what you can give me is a job in your rooms?' She knew the reaction she would get to this. Her mother had sighed and leant back in her chair and fussed over a drop of milk that had been spilt on the table. She'd whispered quietly to any spirits watching, 'Here we go again.' She had seen Paul and Edie have this same conversation many times.

Paul had snapped his head up quick smart, his eyes dark and blistering, and said what he always said, 'No daughter of mine is going out to work as though I am too poor or too negligent to support her.'

'You're so, so …'

'So what, Edie?' he demanded.

'Oh, I don't know — impossible and … and old-fashioned,' and she'd stormed off as she always did, leaving the perfect cup of tea lonely on the table before he could lecture her on his role as a father to provide and her role as a daughter to be provided for. She already knew his views on her working but as for his distractedness with that stupid umbrella — she really didn't know what was going on with him these days, and put it down to a problem bothering him at work. It certainly couldn't be a problem at home.

Her home — or rather, her father's home, because that was how she, her mother Lucy, and their maid Beth thought of it — was a home with fine filigree cast-iron lacework and great leadlight windows. The house had its roots buried deep in the soil and it sprawled into four bedrooms and a sun-filled sitting room, a reading room, a formal dining room, her father's study and the maid's room. Its wide verandah stretched from the front right-hand corner of the house around to the far left-hand corner of the rear of the house, where it met the maid's bedroom and the laundry. Jasmine clambered over the verandah railings and took its moment in spring with vigour, filling the house with gusts of perfumed air that promised anything was possible. There was an expanse at the side of the house large enough for two horses and carts to come right up to the verandah if they were so inclined, and there was a brick path that wound through the garden from the front gate to the verandah steps and up to the front door. The house was her father's gift to her mother and was full of the sweet voice of her mother singing for her father.

Edie thought about the fabric that had built the home she lived in, she thought about it hard, the love her father and mother shared, and she yearned to share that love with someone of her own. She now sat cross-legged on the carpet, still in her nightie, hacking away at her best Sunday skirt with the enormous haberdashery scissors she had taken from Beth's sewing drawer. Her fingers ached with the cold. It was chilly and every now and then she shivered, but she was too intent on what she was doing to notice the goosepimples on her arms and legs, her head filled with the cruel words of the women at church.

Edie had tried to convince herself that she didn't care what the women said about her and tried to harden her heart, but she did care and her heart was soft and the women's barbs pricked at her heart like a splinter she couldn't scratch out.

'I'll show them,' she said to the skirt crumpled unhappily in her lap.

Even though she tried not to think of them, the most hurtful scenes repeated themselves over and over. Edie saw Vera Gamble, who still had a little-girl voice she had chosen never to grow out of, whispering to Marjorie Hollings. Could you even call it whispering when everyone within ten feet of her heard? Vera had looked around her, not to make sure no one was listening but to make sure everyone was listening, then she'd leant over and in a big show of whispering confidentially had said to Marjorie, 'What hope has Too Girl got of catching a husband with her looks?'

Edie had rushed home and stared at herself in the mirror for a good hour, wondering if she really did look that bad. There was no sister to tell her that Vera Gamble knew Edie could hear her rotten whispers that were bitter like mouldering oranges or that Vera was just being nasty for the sake of it to give herself a little thrill. Ever since that whisper Edie had accepted that at best her looks were unremarkable and at worst downright unpleasant to men.

She slashed at the material of her skirt with the scissors. She cared very deeply. It gave her a physical pain in her chest when she thought about it. And it wasn't just Vera Gamble.

Missus Whittaker always nodded her head disapprovingly when she looked Edie's way, and Missus Blackmarsh had stood in the church kitchen doing the washing up and waved a soapy teacup in the air and said to Missus Turnbull, who was drying up, that the problem with Edie Cottingham was that she had no idea what a man needed in a wife.

'Edie,' she'd said, 'is full of toos. Too stubborn, too outspoken, too liberal — you can thank her father for that — too ordinary, too modern.' And Missus Turnbull had laughed with a strained noise that sounded like a cow mooing and Edie, who had been about to go in and offer to help, had heard it all from the hall. From then on Missus Blackmarsh had called Edie the Too Girl and then all the women started calling her the Too Girl, even though they had no idea how the nickname had started.

But Edie was going to change everything. She would make the men notice her and she would show Missus Blackmarsh what modern really was.

Edie had got the idea for her plan from *The Delineator: A Journal of Fashion, Culture and the Fine Arts.* The magazine had all the latest trends. It took those trends a good two years to reach her from Europe, but apart from Edie, the people of Ballarat were happily ignorant that they were at least two years behind the rest of the world. Edie ripped a piece of material away from her skirt. She'd be the very first girl in town to have a skirt like this.

Her father would die when he saw it. God only knew what he'd say.

Edie worked away, cutting and sewing. When she finished the skirt, she would have to adjust her petticoat to match. She heard Beth get up and start clanging china and pots in the kitchen as she set about breakfast and preparing lunch for after church. She heard the clock ring out six chimes.

Edie kept pulling at stitches. She kept cutting away cloth. She heard the clock chime seven and then eight.

Finally the job was done.

She stood up and held the skirt out in front of her. She shivered at her daring and smiled proudly as though she had created the entire garment herself. Then her father knocked on her door. It was as though he knew she had done something mischievous. He always knew when she was up to something.

'Damn it,' she said. Then she reminded herself that she wasn't a little girl any more and her father couldn't see everything she did. He couldn't see through the thick wooden door.

'Edie, are you all right?' he asked, and she thought she could hear suspicion in his voice. 'Are you coming to breakfast, Edith? You better get a hurry-on.'

She felt her cheeks burn as if she'd been caught out, even though his voice sounded far away, muffled by the thick closed door. She had to remind herself again that he couldn't see her through the wood. She ran and put her weight against the door so he couldn't come in. Blimey, he'd have a fit when he saw what she'd done.

'Edith?' her father said, expecting an answer.

'I had breakfast earlier,' she lied, and the lie sat uneasily in her chest. Her father was a man of principle, the sort of man who could gaze into your soul and know immediately if you were guilty or innocent, especially if you were his only child. It was a talent that stood him in good stead in the courtroom and had frightened Edie when she was little.

She listened to her father's steps recede down the hallway and relaxed when she heard the murmur of his voice talking to Beth.

She waited for Beth to settle her father and serve him breakfast and then when the clock struck nine she rang her bell for Beth to come and help her dress. She'd have to rush now, to get dressed in only an hour, and she thought how good it was that she hadn't had any breakfast — it would make her waist look smaller.

Edie sat on the edge of her bed and pulled on her stockings, clipping them to the garter, and then she laced her short boots with the buttonhook, because once she'd got her corset on she wouldn't be able to bend over. She had the latest — a new health corset, imported from England and designed by a lady doctor to protect a woman's vital organs. But once Edie strapped her body into the corset she'd be nearly immobilised.

Beth knocked on the door and Edie called out, 'Come in, Beth.' She stood up as Beth walked in. 'Sometimes I envy you, Beth, that you're not expected to wear a corset,' she said.

Edie didn't notice the jealous frown that Beth threw at her expensive clothes, but she did notice that Beth yanked harder than she needed to on the lacing, and Edie's breasts were thrown unnaturally forward into the world, while her hips were pushed back and her spine was warped into an S shape, bowed like wood left out in the rain.

'Not too tight,' gasped Edie, 'I'm getting too old to expect miracles from corsets.'

'Do you want me to measure?' asked Beth. The corset had its own agenda and was aiming for a sixteen-inch waist.

'No I do not. I'm hopeful, not delusional.' She handed Beth the bust bodice, which, with the help of clean white handkerchiefs stuffed down it, consolidated her breasts into one impressive structure that presented a united front to the world.

Beth reached for the five-gored petticoat lying across the bed.

'I'll be right now,' said Edie. 'You go and change for church or you'll be late.'

She didn't want Beth to see what she'd done to her skirt. Not yet.

When Beth had shut the door behind her, Edie put on her silk chiffon bodice with its leg-of-mutton sleeves and boned lining, and finally the matching pale blue silk chiffon skirt. She tied the satin ribbon around her waist. She pinned the pompadour frame on her head and brushed her hair up over the frame, pulling the brush through strands that wouldn't grow past her shoulders; thin wispy fibres that, now she looked at them through Vera Gamble's eyes, she had to agree refused to speak of beauty. Edie might not have an older sister but she could read and she had learnt some tricks from *The Delineator*. She reached for the extra hairpieces she had purchased to make her hair appear abundant and secured them in place with hairpins, and then pinned on her hat. It floated high on her head, a cloud of ostrich plumes. She had bought the new plumes especially for today, on special at the milliner's, only seven and six for fifteen inches. The advertisement said they were an indispensable aid to beauty. Edie wasn't taking any chances; she'd take all the aid she could get.

Only now, when she was completely ready, could Edie bring herself to look in the mirror. She gasped at how short her skirt really was. She hadn't quite expected to remove that much material. For a moment she wondered if she had the courage to go through with it. But she was desperate. Without a husband she'd never have a home of her own. She'd always be a child in her father's house. She'd always be the Too Girl. She would have nothing to do, her father wouldn't ever let her work and her mother looked after their house and didn't need her help. As much as she loved her father, she had to escape, she had to have her own home and her own life. She stood back a little and pretended she was Missus Theo Hooley.

Missus Blackmarsh always tugged her hair, black like her name, so tightly into a bun like a doorknob on the back of her head that her eyebrows were pulled up and her skin was stretched over the harsh pointy bones of her face. Her eyes became tiny dark slits through which she peered disapprovingly at the world. She had seen Edie through her slit eyes gazing at Theo one Sunday and said to herself, 'Well, well, well, fancy that.' And then she had turned to Missus Whitlock and said, 'Too Girl is far too loud to ever catch quiet Mister Hooley.'

'He'd never say another word,' added Missus Whitlock. And laughed as they looked at Edie, who knew they were laughing at her and blushed. Since her interest in Theo had been noticed, the other girls, who might not have thought of him before, thought that if Edie was interested in Theo he must have something worth being interested in and were now considering him a viable option. Edie had seen them flitting and fluttering around him. She'd seen Vera Gamble fluttering just last Sunday, giggling like a schoolgirl at every word he said, which, given Theo, wasn't many. Edie couldn't flutter or flitter or flirt. She gazed at the mirror to see what sort of an impact she could make on him, if it would be enough to whet his appetite.

Edie waited behind her door until it was time to leave for church. That way she could put off the inevitable hullabaloo over her skirt. Her heart pounded against the bones of her corset. Her fingers began to sweat as they gripped her umbrella too tightly. It wasn't the possibility of her father being angry that made her nerves jangle, it was knowing that this was her very last chance. She had thought through all the available men in the district and there were no other possibilities. There was no one else for her if she didn't get Theo.

Two

The Cure

In church, where the air sits still and lazy around people's heads, making the women faint and the men sleepy.

Now Theodore Hooley wasn't a boy in his twenties whose chest was puffed with arrogance and newly discovered clout. Oh no. Theo had been to the African war and come back. He'd had the clout well and truly knocked out of him. At least he'd come back in one piece, and Edie thought that made him worth loving alone. Besides being physically whole, which was undoubtedly a huge plus, Theo Hooley had also come back quieter, hollowed out and embracing the ordinariness of life. He seemed content living with his mother and playing the church's newly imported organ on Sundays. The men occasionally commented that Theo hadn't decided on a career since getting back from the war. Many returned soldiers opened a shop or went to the mines, but Theo hadn't done anything except eat his mother's cooking and play hymns.

Missus Blackmarsh told everyone Theo didn't need to work because he had brought back gold from Africa hidden in the seams of his greatcoat, and the quantity grew each time she told the story.

When Edie had mentioned Missus Blackmarsh's theory to her father, Paul had laughed and said, 'Well, as I manage the estate for Missus Hooley I think I would know if there was golden treasure involved.'

It didn't bother Edie that Theo seemed content with an uncomplicated life. It was precisely why she knew that, even though she was now nineteen, she might have a real chance with him. She could just slip into his life almost unnoticed; she could fill a hollow space and the two of them would be comfortable.

She took one last look in the mirror and a deep breath for courage.

'Edith — we're leaving.' Her father's voice called out again and suddenly, full of the possibility of Theodore Hooley, Edie did feel brave and 'so what' if everyone was going to be outraged by her short skirt. She flung open the door and it banged against the doorstop and shuddered like a washboard. The jasmine filled her lungs with hope, she stepped into the entrance hall with its glistening tiles and frowning portraits. She smiled broadly, trying desperately to keep everyone's attention on her face and not on the shortness of her skirt. By jiminy her father would go berserk seeing his only daughter — his only child — scantily clad. Her father was always so intent on setting a standard in the community and expected Edie and her mother to follow suit.

'I've never seen you so happy about going to church before,' her father commented dryly, seeing her expectant face; then he tapped his fob watch, swung his umbrella in little circles and said, 'Righteo.' He was bound tightly into his three-piece suit; it was pulling at his middle, which was slowly expanding with age.

Edie was perplexed. In truth she was a little annoyed. He hadn't even bothered to look at her skirt. He was so vacant these days. She looked questioningly at her mother, who was leaning against the wall. She had dark rings under her eyes and a large loose cape over her dress. But Edie didn't notice her mother's tired appearance and looked back at her father, who was still tapping his watch, timing their departure perfectly, and then she looked at Beth standing a few feet away in her linen skirt, waiting to see if she was family or servant today. She was always fluctuating between the two, sometimes an intimate, at other times an observer; the tide entirely depended on the family's mood.

Two years ago Beth had been lost and empty, living with her oldest sister Dottie's family and working for Mister Scully at his bakery. She knew she wanted something different but she didn't know what that something was. Beth at thirteen was the youngest of four sisters; Dottie was the eldest and was fifteen years older than Beth. Dottie liked to remind the other sisters that she was the practical one, like their mother, but Aggie (who was two years younger than Dottie) said Dottie was just plain bossy and it had nothing to do with being practical or being like their mother. Beth bit her lip when Aggie said this because she couldn't remember their mother; whenever she was mentioned the other three sisters looked uncomfortably at each other and changed the subject. Florrie was one year younger than Aggie and Dottie called her Aggie's shadow — not to her face, of course. Florrie and Aggie worked at the Bunch of Grapes where they poured warm beer into cold miners' stomachs and didn't come home until four in the morning. Dottie said the two of them were as useless as their father, who had upped and disappeared when their mother died. Beth said nothing because she couldn't remember their father either. Dottie's husband was called Laidlaw, but even Beth couldn't tell you his first name. He worked down the mines and when he got home and collapsed into his chair at the end of the kitchen table the whole house became noisier as his laughing voice boomed its way around the kitchen and up the hall. If Dottie's two kids had been asleep, they were soon awake. When his voice filled the house, Beth knew there was no room left for her.

Every day Beth came home from Scully's bakery with her clothes covered in flour, but one night she came home and the flour was imprinted with Mister Scully's fingerprints fluttering all over her like flies she was forever trying to brush away. Dottie had stopped mashing potatoes and looked at her good and hard but she didn't say anything. The next night her mother's friend Nurse Drake had turned up at the door and spent a good half-hour whispering with Dottie in the entranceway. Beth had stood and watched them, leaning against the hallway wall. She knew they were whispering about her because they turned at regular intervals and gave her long meaningful looks, and after much nodding of heads Dottie had turned and said to Beth, 'Get your things, Bethie, you have a new job. Nurse Drake is going to take you there now. It's live-in.'

'You mean I won't be living here?' said Beth, and added point-edly, 'With my family?' just to make Dottie feel guilty, even though they both knew there was no room.

'It's an opportunity,' said Nurse Drake. 'Don't look a gift horse in the mouth, missy.'

Well, it just so happened that Beth liked opportunities. She liked to spot them and jump on them because you never knew where they might lead, and as long as they led somewhere, she didn't mind taking a risk on the unknown.

So Beth had gathered her other dress, her hairbrush and her stockings and underthings and shoved them into her small tattered suitcase with someone else's initials inscribed in the worn leather and followed Nurse Drake up the street. Nurse Drake nattered all the way, filling Beth's head with noise, which was annoying because she wanted to take in where they were going.

'They're a good family; you've really landed on your feet, missy. I'm doing this for your poor mother because I said I'd watch out for you. Don't waste this opportunity, young lady.'

Beth had no intention of wasting the opportunity to get away from Mister Scully's fat clammy fingers and Dottie's full house, where Beth had to share her bed with Aggie and Florrie who woke her as they clambered in tipsy, giggling, and loudly sshh-ing every night.

And the Cottinghams were good to her. Miss Cottingham told her she would be treated like one of the family and they were true to their word — most of the time. Missus Cottingham taught her how to iron Mister Cottingham's shirts the way he liked and how to use the hot meat fat to make sure the potatoes crisped. She was a patient teacher and now Beth could do it herself. She ate the same food as the Cottingham's at the same table at the same time, but she prepared all the food and served it and cleaned up afterwards. She had her own bedroom and her own bed, but hers was a wooden bed in a tiny room at the back of the house, whereas Edie had a brass bed in the front room with bay windows and velvet curtains. The Cottinghams provided her with everything she needed so she didn't need the wage they paid her of a sovereign each week. She always changed the coin into two half sovereigns when she did the grocery shopping and took one half to Dottie and stashed the other half in a washed golden syrup tin, and when she counted how many sovereigns she had at the end of each month she always had to wash her hands afterwards because the coins were sticky. But all in all Nurse Drake had been right. Mister Cottingham never tried to flutter his hands over her as though he was grasping for gold dust, and Missus Cottingham was kind and quiet and like the mother she never had. Edie gave her all her old dresses and sometimes it was almost like they were sisters. The risk had paid off.

Edie stood in the hallway, gave a little nervous laugh at absolutely nothing, and fidgeted with her hat. Then she saw her mother frowning at the bottom of her skirt.

'Don't look at me like that, Mama,' Edie leaned forward and whispered, 'I haven't killed a Chinaman.'

She watched her mother's face closely. She was expecting a lecture but Lucy only sighed and leant back against the wall. A shiver ran down Edie's spine, a sense of foreboding. Nothing was happening as it normally would. Her mother should have said something to alert her father, she should have said, 'Father, see what our Edith has done to her Sunday best,' not just sighed as though her mind was elsewhere altogether, concentrating on things more important than Edie. And her father should have noticed and demanded she go and change. Edie had always been the focus of their attention. But suddenly it seemed that her mother and father weren't interested in her any more and she felt immensely put out. She looked at her father again, demanding his attention with her gaze, but he was still tapping away at his watch as though enough taps would give him control of time. His brow was furrowed and his thoughts were far away.

Edie sulked; she didn't care now what they said about her skirt. They could say what they jolly well liked if they were going to treat her like a piece of glass. She looked from one to the other and what was really only a minute or two seemed to stretch into the future. But her father stayed focused on his watch and her mother's eyes gave nothing away.

'What are you hiding under that cape, Mama?' Edie fingered the fur trim and wondered why her mother insisted on wearing it when the morning had become quite warm. It was past ten and they would be back from church well before the afternoon chill set in at four. Lucy didn't answer; she just looked at Edie with watery eyes. Edie failed to see how drawn and pale her mother was, as if talcum powder had been smeared over her cheeks.

Edie turned her attention to Beth and said, 'Lovely skirt, Beth,' even though it was the same skirt Beth wore every Sunday.

'You'd be a hit at the Bunch of Grapes in your skirt,' said Beth, thinking of the miners who her sisters said could be filled up with beer but could never get enough loving to sate their appetites.

'Really?' asked Edie.

'Oh yes,' said Beth, thinking of the miners.

'Righteo,' said Paul. He had given up tapping his watch and instead swung his black umbrella, which doubled as a walking stick, in a figure eight and tapped it on the ground three times. Then he went back to his watch, like a boy that couldn't leave something alone for one minute. 'Righteo then, we better be off,' he said finally. And without looking back he led the way out the front door that was framed by the reds and greens of the flying rosellas in the leadlight windows.

The windows cast rainbow beams that bounced off the walls, lighting the entranceway like children's wishes. When Edie was a child she had sometimes sat in the coloured beams, letting their magic play over her skin, and as she sat there she would ask God for the things that she wanted. God had always seemed to answer. So as she passed under the beams this morning she quickly asked for a husband and if God was in a good mood could he make it Theo Hooley.

Paul was already walking smartly down the verandah steps and the timber boards bounced under the weight of his determined footsteps and the tapping of the umbrella. The three women scurried to keep up with him. He stepped out onto the driveway and the gravel crunched under his shoes.

The women followed.

'Men!' Edie said to Lucy as they walked down the steps after him. He hadn't even looked at her skirt once. How could he not even notice her hours of hard work?

'Which man?' asked Lucy absently, putting her arm through Edie's and giving a little squeeze.

'Father of course — look.' And Edie stuck out one stockinged foot showing the new length of her skirt, as though her mother hadn't already seen it. Her ankle poked out, sitting right between her boot and the new bottom of her skirt, clothed only in a black woollen stocking.

'But what about a dust ruffle? Beth will be constantly washing it.' Lucy was a practical woman.

'Me and whose army,' muttered Beth.

'I don't need a dust ruffle now that it can't drag on the ground,' Edie pointed out.

Her mother raised an eyebrow.

'Fashions change,' said Edie.

'Not if your father has his way,' said Lucy and they looked ahead to where he strode in front of them, leading the women of his family down Webster Street to Drummond Street and on towards the church in Dawson Street as though he was leading a regiment.

'*Onward Christian soldiers*,' sang Edie.

Edie sat in the hard pew, bored senseless by the monotone preaching of weedy Reverend Whitlock, whose high-pitched voice sounded like a child whining for a treat. His sentences were shrill

but he always dipped on the last two words, which he drew out
like a Gregorian chant. She shifted her weight from side to side
and looked about for a distraction to occupy her mind for the
next three-quarters of an hour. A good Baptist sermon has three
main points and lasts for twenty minutes exactly, but Reverend
Whitlock was a man who liked the sound of his own voice and
rambled off his points regularly. As far as Edie could tell his main
point was always a warning to the young women to stay away
from the miners whose hands were so used to the dark they could
find their way to any secret place. Many of the miners had wives
and kids back home in Ireland that they forgot to mention to the
single young ladies in town.

Theo was sitting up the front of the church at the organ he'd
played every Sunday since he returned from Africa. Edie could
only see the back of his head, his hair smooth and shiny with
oil. She watched him for a while, willing him to look at her,
but he didn't, and soon even the back of Theo's head lost its
appeal and she turned and watched her mother. She studied the
wrinkles around her mother's eyes and began to notice that Lucy
was slumped in her seat, whereas normally she sat straight and
dignified. Her eyes were puffy and dark and she'd definitely put
on weight, and when Edie really thought about it she couldn't
remember the last time she had heard her mother singing.

Edie wondered why she hadn't noticed all this before, why
she hadn't worried more about her mother spending so much
time in her room. Edie felt she should have realised sooner and
prescribed some remedy. She was a bit of a whiz when it came
to medical knowledge, you could learn a lot from reading the
advertisements in the local papers. If she hadn't thought of her
plan, and hadn't written in her notebook that she was going to
marry Theo, she might have learnt nursing, though her father
would never permit it. Paul thought work was something only

the poor did, or rich men like him did for a hobby so they didn't get bored with life. Edie knew she would make a darn good nurse. She knew a lot about bodily functions. She knew the Swiss-Italians in nearby Hepburn pined for feathers of crisp snow during the Australian summer heat and that sometimes in the middle of January they sweated until they hadn't an ounce of moisture left in their shrivelled bodies and lay down on their cane divans on their verandahs and died of 'nostalgia'. She'd read that in the paper: *Mister Pedretti, father of fifteen, died on Monday in Hepburn of Nostalgia.*

Edie also knew that for a child's hacking cough at night Wood's Peppermint Cure was guaranteed, and for gravel and bladder problems Warner's Safe Cure was concentrated and would restore complete health within a week. Edie shook her head at her mother's puffy fingers. Must be her bowel; nearly all health issues, particularly those of women, could be attributed to fermentation in the bowel. She'd get some of Dr Sheldon's Gin Pills first thing in the morning. They'd fix anything, and better late than never. She wondered at a world that could turn gin into pills, so even those who abstained from alcohol could still reap its medicinal benefits. Of course Lucy's ill health could be 'women's failures' or 'the change' or old age, but either way Gin Pills would be sure to do the trick. Edie took out her notebook and smiled at Missus Hooley sitting just over the aisle, who assumed she was so engrossed in the sermon she was taking notes. Edie opened to a fresh page and wrote:

Fifth November Five
Plan — Heal Mama. Buy Gin Pills from Connell's Chemist

Satisfied that she'd considered all the possibilities of her mother's ill health and arrived at a sensible diagnosis and remedy, she glanced towards Theo sitting at the organ and was filled with pangs of an unrecognisable feeling that made her want to leap across the pews and rip Vera Gamble's hat from her head. The hat was so small it barely constituted a hat. It sat cheekily on the side of Vera's hair and a few coloured flowers poked out of the band; it was picnics and sunshine in that little hat. Edie looked at Theo again and then back to Vera and back to Theo. There was no doubt he was gazing longingly at Vera Gamble, who sat just a few pews ahead, her curled blonde hair piled on her head in luxurious pillows of softness. A halo of sunlight through the windows touched Vera's hair with magic, turning it golden and glowing as though it was filled with stars.

Edie's heart sank as she realised her plan was in ruins.

Three

The Seduction

Under the vigilant eyes of Reverend Whitlock.

Theo turned around on his organ stool. He pretended he was considering the enormity of Reverend Whitlock's words as he gazed out the stained-glass window. He did that so that no one would realise he was really trying to find Edith Cottingham in the congregation. Finally he spotted her sitting in a pew halfway down. She was on the end and next to her was her mother and then Beth and then her father. When he thought it wouldn't be obvious, he twisted further around so he could properly take her in. Out the corner of his eye he saw Vera Gamble smile at him and he smiled back to be polite but his gaze was drawn back to Edith. He watched her as she fidgeted, looked at the ground, looked at the ceiling and then took out her notebook and wrote something. Obviously she was as bored with the Reverend's sermon as he was. She crossed her legs and swung one foot out into the aisle and he caught — was it a glimpse of ankle? No, it was more than a glimpse, it was her stockinged ankle laid bare for the world to see. Theo nearly fell off the organ stool.

He was shocked. Then he was spellbound. His emotions swirled in his chest and he grasped it tightly to stop the tornado inside him. He wanted to savour that ankle, to look and look until he was completely familiar with its curve and its softness. It was a fragile, slender thing that he could encompass in his hand. He reached out his hand to touch it, to run his finger along its arc, then he remembered where he was and quickly gripped the organ stool. He wanted to run down the aisle and claim that ankle as his own and cover it up. He felt urges that weren't right to feel in church and quickly pulled the hymnal off its perch on the organ. It fell to the ground with a thud and the Reverend stopped mid-sentence and waited and watched, and the entire congregation waited and watched with him, while Theo leaned over, picked up the hymnal, checked it for damage and then laid it over his lap. There were stirrings in his blood that he hadn't felt since looking at naked black women in Africa. Despite himself he couldn't tear his eyes away and gazed blatantly at Edie's ankle until he felt Reverend Whitlock boring holes through the back of his head. Theo glanced at the Reverend. The Reverend glared back at him and the sermon spilled out of his mouth once again. Theo felt his cheeks burn hot with embarrassment as Reverend Whitlock's eyes settled accusingly on the hymnal in Theo's lap.

Theo turned his back on the Reverend and stared at the organ. He turned the hymnal over and opened it to the next hymn, 'How Great Thou Art', and slowly placed it back on its stand. Reverend Whitlock finished his sermon and sat down behind the pulpit. Theo struck the opening chords; the notes blurred in front of his eyes and he played from somewhere inside him where he knew the hymn by heart, his brain filled with hot blood and images of Edith. Before he knew it, the congregation had stopped singing but he wasn't with them, so they had to wait for him to finish the last bars, which he did, thumping the keys as though he was finishing with a crescendo on purpose. After Deacon Blackmarsh gave the announcements, the congregation stood to sing the final hymn, 'Abide With Me', and Theo played the introductory bars thinking how lucky he was that his fingers could again dance over the keys from memory, as the notes in the hymnal no longer wrote the song, but formed the word Edith, over and over, as if they were reading his heart.

Edie thought he maybe was looking at her after all. It was hard to tell. Just in case he was, she gave him her good side to study. She kept her head at an angle with the sun warming her cheek to a pink glow and she gave him a few minutes to admire her before she turned and gazed at the ceiling so he could see that she was thinking about God and Reverend Whitlock's words. Then she lowered her eyes, crossed her legs and put her ankle out into the aisle for him to see. She willed him to look down and notice it, but he didn't seem to and she wondered if all her planning had been for nothing.

These secretive looks were seen by everyone — well, they were seen by the women, and soon the men would know because their wives would tell them.

The women whispered, 'Nothing will come of it. Vera Gamble has much more hope. She's embarrassing herself, really.' While Reverend Whitlock bellowed the final prayer Missus Blackmarsh turned to Missus Turnbull next to her and said that if Theo was interested in Too Girl then maybe he had just spent far too long in Africa and perhaps any white woman looked good to him now.

Missus Horlick sitting in the next pew leant back and muttered that Theo might be getting on, but he still had the pick of any handsome young girl who'd be happy to marry him.

Everyone whispered, *What on Earth could he see in Too Girl?*

'Blowed if I know!' they answered.

And then they stood for the Benediction and the gossipers smirked as if they knew more about Edie and Theo than Edie and Theo did.

If Theo hadn't had the clout knocked out of him, he might have told the women exactly what it was about Edith Cottingham that made his heart feel as though it was going to fly away. Her lips, for example, were always curled at the ends, ready to smile. And Edie bounced when she walked, as though she was always dancing; yet when he listened to her talk she was down-to-earth and not giggly at all. Her chin was always held too high, too defiantly for a woman, and he liked that about her; she wasn't afraid of life. To him, Edie was straightforward. She didn't worry and fret continuously like the other women he knew, like his mother did. Edie was still so young and trusting and he felt so very tired and so very old after the war. He felt worn out and dusty, as though the slightest knock could make him crumble away to nothing. When he saw Edie he felt the warmth of her heart on his skin. It was as though she was bathed in light, as though the sun had blessed her and never left her.

Theo had never told this to anyone because all the words got shot out of him by the booming canons in Africa. Those canons made him stone deaf for a good six months. And even though his hearing had come back, he'd had trouble with words ever since. Words came to him slowly, taking their time to form in his mind, and often by the time they were ready to be said he found it was too late, and the words died away before they found life.

Finally the Reverend marched to the entrance of the church like he was the king himself and the congregation began to shuffle out. It was only after Edie turned to help her mother from her seat that Theo was able to force his eyes away from her. He turned to the organ and played out the notes, the music he was supposed to play while the congregation filed out of the church. Theo's hands kept moving over the notes but he watched over his shoulder as Edith carefully put her hymnal on her seat and filed out after her family into the pleasant midday sunshine.

As soon as she had gone Theo abruptly stopped playing, closed the lid of the organ and quickly walked out of the church. Old Mister Tonkins, who was stacking hymnals back onto the shelves in the foyer and was unable to look anyone in the face because of the perfect stoop of his back, tried to waylay Theo in the vestibule.

'Lovely playing today, Theo,' he said, his voice worn to a failing breeze by the years. Theo shook his hand furiously, making Mister Tonkins almost topple on his toes like a wobbly toy, and kept walking instead of asking how he was getting on as he normally would. Mister Tonkins was left reaching for the shelves to steady himself.

Theo squished past the people shaking hands with the Reverend and his wife on the church porch and looked around at the clusters of people standing at the front of the church. Then he saw her. She was standing next to Beth at the other end of the porch and for a moment it looked like she was praying.

He saw the women muttering at her skirt and casting glares at her mother and father for allowing it. He saw the groups of men smiling and saying how much they liked the new fashion — though not for their own wives or sweethearts, of course. Theo watched as Reverend Whitlock, having shaken everyone's hands, walked past him, and he saw Edie's father walk up to the Reverend, take his arm and engage him in some obviously serious conversation from the look on Mister Cottingham's face. It was probably about Edie's hemline.

Theo smiled; he liked the length of Edie's skirt. He'd seen skirts that length in Europe, on his way back from Africa. The girl had gumption. He liked that. He felt he had lost all of his. In his head, he'd rehearsed what he was going to say to her. He had spent the week thinking about it. Now he took a deep breath and he was ready.

This time the words would come.

'The first Sunday of November and it's a beautiful day, Miss Cottingham, Beth,' Theo said as he took off his bowler with one hand and pointed to the sky with his cane, as though Edith needed direction to find the sky. He sighed with relief. He had got the words out.

'It is,' Edie agreed.

'Hello Mister Hooley,' said Beth and she surprised him by giving him a little curtsey as she looked up at him from under her lashes. He'd seen a lot of those looks from women in Africa.

'What was that for?' Edie said. 'You never curtsey, Beth.' Beth giggled into her hand. Beth was certainly young and pretty and Theo didn't miss the thunderous look she got from Edie; it made him smile.

'The Reverend's sermon was inspiring this morning, don't you think?' Theo said.

It was clear to him that Edie didn't have a clue what Reverend Whitlock had said as she answered, 'Oh yes, I was taking notes.' He teased her by waiting for more and seeing he wasn't going to save her she said cleverly, 'What do you feel were the main points, Mister Hooley?'

'Well …' said Theo.

She was watching him carefully, and he tried frantically to think of something the Reverend had said, to arrange some words in his mind, and as usual they just weren't coming. 'His — he, he …'

'He spoke about the workers' claims. He said that a man who doesn't work doesn't deserve to eat,' said Beth.

'Did he indeed?' said Edie, her temper flaring in an instant. 'How can he say that from the pulpit? What about those men's children and wives? What good Christian should suggest that the children of these men go hungry? I believe in protection of our trade which will of course protect the workers, just like my father, just like Alfred Deakin. My father worked hard to have Mister Deakin back as leader of this nation.'

And then he saw the realisation spread across her face; she had been too outspoken, too vehement, too unwomanly. Did she think that maybe he wasn't a Deakin voter or a protectionist? He saw her face immediately lose all its light and she looked for a moment, just a splinter of a moment that was shorter than a single breath, as though she had lost her entire world. And his heart leapt into the clouds with joy and hope. She cared what he thought of her. He mattered to her. He tried to stop the smile that was forcing its way onto his lips.

Edie looked to Beth in a panic and Beth, a quick girl whose older sisters had taught her all the tricks, clumsily pretended to lose her balance on the edge of the porch and she fell in Edie's direction and pushed Edie into Theo.

Edie reached out and grabbed Theo's cane-holding arm and as she fell she flung her leg unreasonably high in the air, taking advantage of Beth's clumsiness and giving him the opportunity to notice the shortness of her skirt and the fineness of her ankle once more.

It was her last hope.

He caught her swiftly.

'Steady there,' he said putting his hat back on, amused by her efforts.

'Thank you, I don't know what happened, my shoe must have caught on a stone,' said Edie as she removed her hand from his arm. He immediately felt stung by the removal of her touch.

'No, it was my fault, I fell,' said Beth quickly, but neither of them took any notice of her.

So she shrugged and said, 'I'll just see where Mister and Missus Cottingham are,' and walked off.

Theo scratched behind his ear. His hat wobbled on his head.

'Did you kill anyone in Africa?' Edie asked seriously. 'It would be awfully exciting and mysterious if you did.' Then she scolded herself and whispered, 'Stupid stupid — too forthright.' She looked miserable, sure she would lose him now, and his heart leapt higher.

'I'm sorry, I'm too forthright — just ask Missus Blackmarsh — she'll warn you soon enough,' she said and stared at the ground, willing it to open up and swallow her.

Yet this was a question Theo got asked frequently by curious people who had no idea what war was. He had an answer prepared: *A man does what he has to do for his country and his king.* But that answer wouldn't do for Edie. She was a person who demanded honesty. He looked down at his arms and wondered what it would be like to wrap her up in them. He knew what it was like to wrap up a naked woman, to cover her body with his own, to feel her warmth and softness, to know that a woman could make everything else in the world disappear. But he also knew that Edie Cottingham was a well-bred young woman who would know nothing of these things. She would not know these needs of men. For her men were respectable and reliable like her father. They kissed you when you were engaged to them and you set up a home together. She would know nothing about sex and its blistering hold on a man. He loved her for it. It made him feel new.

To anyone looking on at that moment, they were a picture of misery: she waiting to dissolve into the ground and he unable to find any words to give her.

Theo stepped closer and Edie felt his warmth envelop her and dared to look up at him.

'I wonder if I could …' Theo began and scratched behind his ear. When he could stretch his scratching no further he added, 'A …'

'A word in private?' she finished for him.

Theo took Edie by the arm. He led her down the steps of the porch and up the dusty street a little way, where they wouldn't be overheard. He saw her look over her shoulder at the intense gazes of the churchwomen. Missus Blackmarsh looked as if this was the best entertainment she'd had in years; Missus Whitlock had her face screwed up like she had sucked on a lemon; Missus Horlick looked as though there was nothing between her ears and Vera Gamble looked smug and very pleased with herself.

'Don't worry about them,' he said quietly in her ear. 'Let them think what they will.'

Theo walked her over to a tree still struggling from the cold frosts that had come during the winter. It cast a pitiful shade that wasn't enough for them to stand under.

He scratched behind his ear some more.

'You didn't bring back lice from Africa, did you Mister Hooley?' she laughed.

'What? No,' he said and thought he must stop the scratching and concentrate on getting something out of his mouth. He motioned to her to come closer and when she was close enough he bent to speak to her, his spine curving over her in an arch like the trees that arched over the road and listened quietly to the whispers spoken in the houses.

Her breath was hot on his neck. It burnt the ends of his fingers. He took off his hat and ran his fingers through his hair. 'I want to ask for your permission to speak to your father,' he said almost whispering.

She laughed nervously and whispered back in his ear, 'Well Mister Hooley, you can speak to whomever you want without asking my permission.'

'No, Miss Cottingham, you know what I mean,' he said, looking unswervingly at her.

Her eyes were glorious, so steady and firm. He couldn't measure how much he wanted her — it went on forever.

She took an enormously long deep breath as she absorbed his meaning and let it become real. He felt he was waiting forever, he could feel his heart had completely stopped and until she answered he would never be able to move from this spot under the sickly tree.

He stood and waited some more.

Finally she said, 'Of course I give my permission and I am sure he'll say yes and if he doesn't I will throw an almighty tantrum.'

'All right then,' said Theo.

Everything in his life had just suddenly fallen into place. He put his hat back on, straightened and standing tall, tapped his stick on the ground a few times as if he knew there was something else he should say or something else he should do but it just wouldn't come to him, so he strode away while Edie stood, her eyes closed waiting for his kiss, the kiss that would seal him to her. The kiss that would show the world she was worth something because someone named Theodore Hooley wanted her for his own. And the churchwomen, watching her standing with her eyes closed and her head held up and her lips waiting as Theo walked away, laughed and nodded at Vera Gamble. Edie Cottingham was just Too Much.

Four

Paul

A seed is planted but may not grow because the sun at
its most spiteful burns any vulnerable thing.

Paul Cottingham had Reverend Whitlock pinned up against the
cold bluestone of the church wall.

'Reid is a joke,' said Paul vehemently. 'All he managed to give
this country is Empire Day — one lousy holiday, a holiday we
already had and he gave it a new name and everyone acted as
though he was the workingman's hero.'

Reverend Whitlock's hair bristled and his thin eyes narrowed
until they disappeared.

Paul was furious with the Reverend's sermon and had hauled
him off to have it out with him. Reverend or not, the man
was a top-class idiot. Paul had swung his umbrella about as if
it was a sword and Whitlock had retreated in the face of Paul's
advance until his back was up against the church wall and he
stood pinned like a dunce in the corner of a schoolroom.

Whitlock's cheeks turned beetroot.

'Now, Reverend,' Paul took the Reverend's fine slender hand
firmly in his own broader one and held it tightly.

The Reverend winced. He hated to admit it but it hurt. He wouldn't ever tell anyone that. He might say, *Oh, that Cottingham's got a handshake like a bear,* but he'd never say it hurt.

'Do you think it's reasonable to denounce a man in his absence?' Paul put the question as though Whitlock was on the witness stand and he was addressing Judge Murphy.

Whitlock knew exactly what he was talking about; Cottingham made no bones about his political commitment.

'Well now, if Mister Deakin wanted to lead this country again, then surely he put himself forward for public scrutiny, wouldn't you say, Mister Cottingham?' The Reverend thought he defended himself quite nicely. 'The trouble with the protectionists,' he went on, gathering confidence, 'is that they want too much too fast.' He nodded in agreement with himself. He didn't like change. Change brought conflict and conflict unnecessarily churned up your gut and pushed acid into your throat and you could taste its bitterness. That couldn't be good for you. He felt the need to burp and stifled it. If only Paul Cottingham would keep his blasted opinions to himself. But he could see the wretched man wasn't going to, and after all, he never had. Obstinate fellow. The daughter was painted with the same brush. No wonder she was still single. He'd seen the outrageous shortness of her skirt. That would be the topic of next week's sermon. He'd put a stop quick smart to such sluttiness before it caught on.

'Yes, in the public arena,' said Paul, 'but your words from the pulpit are considered to come from God. We are building a new nation, Reverend Whitlock. Do you honestly believe that God would have us build this nation on the backs of starving families? This town we live in, Reverend, is gloriously built on the backs of the miners. Look at this very building, at St Patrick's Cathedral opposite there; look at our immense Town Hall with its glorious clock that chimes every hour. It's mining money that's purchased those bluestone blocks and the carved organ they house. It's the hard labour of ironwork that has decorated the buildings, but do you see the miners living in fine buildings? No sir, only the mine owners, who never get their hands dirty, can afford to buy their way into heaven with bricks and mortar. We must pray that Mister Deakin remains prime minister of this nation for many a year so he can protect our trade and our workers as much as possible.'

Surely, thought Paul, this supposed man of God should care first and foremost for those who had little.

'Mister Deakin! Well! We all know exactly where that man got his ideas from. Mister Deakin is a Satanic spiritualist,' the Reverend spat.

'Mister Deakin is a staunch admirer of Bunyan and what finer Christian example could anyone wish for?' snapped Paul.

'I hear tell,' the Reverend said slowly, producing his trump card, 'that our honourable Mister Deakin claims he channelled the words of his book from the great man Bunyan himself. There is only one place spiritualism comes from, Mister Cottingham, and it isn't our Lord Jesus Christ.' Reverend Whitlock smiled, then he leant in close and whispered, 'Because I am a man of God and don't spread another man's sins far and wide I won't say this too loudly, but — I think you're a bit of a radical socialist, Mister Cottingham.'

Paul laughed, loudly and deeply, rolling back on his heels. The stupid man thought he had insulted him, when in fact Paul was proud of his socialist beliefs. To him it was the only Christian option.

'Don't you take anything seriously?' the Reverend sneered.

Paul stopped laughing and grinned, as though Whitlock was a bit slow on the uptake. Then Paul spoke slowly, as if he was explaining to a child — obviously the Reverend had the social intelligence of a six-year-old.

'We have, Reverend, a choice between free trade and protectionism; one dependent on chance, the other on care. Do you leave the wellbeing of your flock to chance, or do you care for it?'

Paul's gaze scorched the Reverend, who had to look away, and as he did so, his eyes widened. Paul turned to see what the Reverend was gawking at and saw Edie standing under a tree with the Hooley lad.

'That girl of yours is being very forward with the church organist. If they stand any closer they'll be fornicating in public view.' The Reverend raised an eyebrow. 'But I'm not one to point out another's sins. It's not my style, Mister Cottingham.'

Paul had already forgotten the Reverend and murmured absently, 'You may step down.'

Paul watched his daughter closely. Hooley whispered something in her ear and after a while she whispered back. Then she lifted her face as though she expected Hooley to kiss her, right there in public, for goodness sake. But Hooley put on his hat and walked away.

Oh no, thought Paul, *the stupid fool has cast her aside*. He got ready to rush over to comfort Edie but then when she turned in his direction he saw she was triumphant, her eyes filled with everything she had ever hoped for. She took out her notebook and wrote something and then she rushed over to him.

'Oh Papa, it's like I'm walking on a sunbeam, can you see it? Can you see all the pieces of me just floating around in the sun?'

He looked hard at her. Excitement was building and twirling in her head and her heart; it was bubbling so furiously it was threatening to spill out in front of everyone. She reached out as if to catch the sun, to catch her dreams and hold them tightly in her hands forever.

'Steady, steady,' he said.

Edie took a deep breath. 'He didn't kiss me but that doesn't change anything. Not really, does it?' Paul saw her tuck away that first tiny disappointment. 'He's going to ask, Papa,' she said. 'That's all that matters. He's going to ask you.'

'What's he going to ask me?'

Edie twirled around. 'Look. I wrote in my notebook.' She held the book open and he saw she had written:

Fifth November Five
Plan — Papa will give permission.

'What shall I say? Not on your sweet Nellie, I suppose.'

Edie dug him in the ribs.

Then she burst into laughter and ran, triumphant, in front of Missus Blackmarsh and Missus Turnbull and twirled in front of Missus Whitlock and they all tutted and glared at Paul as if it was his fault that his daughter had finally lost her marbles, and Theo, who was watching her from where he stood with some of the men, smiled. She was everything he wasn't.

Edie ran to Beth and grabbed her hands and jumped on the spot; soon she'd be an engaged woman. She turned to her mother and threw her arms around her, and her mother held her tight. Lucy was still not sure what all the excitement was about and looked questioningly at Paul as he walked over to them.

'We're off home now, girls, we're not staying for morning tea this week,' he said. 'It's time that scandalous skirt was put back in a cupboard where I hope it will spend the rest of its life. It's done enough damage for today. Maud Blackmarsh will be telling stories about it for many years to come and the skirt will get shorter every time she tells it.'

'Oh no,' said Edie, 'this is the best skirt I've ever had.'

All the way home they tried to keep up with Edie but failed, so she was waiting at the front door for them.

Paul stopped to catch his breath and reached into his pocket for his key. He looked at Lucy, who was pale and winded.

'You look done in,' he said as he helped her through the door. She leant against the cool wall. 'It was probably the brisk walk home,' he added with no conviction. If only it was just a brisk walk that was causing Lucy to look so ashen. He stood in the rainbow beam and wished Lucy would be all right; only then would he be able to breathe properly again and lose the constant constriction he felt in his chest.

Lucy took deep gasping breaths. 'I'm just going to have forty winks. I won't have lunch, Beth.'

'Beth can bring you in a tray,' Paul said, hoping she would eat.

'No, thank you all the same. I don't think I can eat.'

'But you must eat, you must keep up your energy.' Paul felt his chest getting tighter and the air becoming heavier. Lucy didn't reply, she took another deep breath and walked to her room, using the wall for support.

'I'll come and check on you in a while,' he said after her.

'Mama's all right, isn't she?'

Paul looked at Edie. He knew there was something important happening with Edie but for a moment he couldn't remember what.

'Papa? Mama's all right? She's not sick or anything?'

'She's just a little tired, nothing to worry about; the vigorous walk home from church has done her in. She's just having forty winks.'

Paul took Edie by the arm and walked her into the dining room, and they sat at the oval blackwood table. Beth made several trips to the dining room, carrying the lamb, then the potatoes and gravy, and finally the peas and carrots.

Edie lifted the lid covering the roast lamb and it seemed a live thing staring back at her; it looked just like Missus Blackmarsh who had said she was Too Plain. *He won't come, he won't come,* the Blackmarsh lamb taunted as its heat hit her face and she quickly put the lid back on to shut it up.

'I can't eat — when do you think he'll come to ask, Papa?'

'I expect given his age — what, he must be thirty at least — I'd say he's as eager as you are, dear,' said Paul. 'Now pass me the vegetables.' He didn't want to bother with this fellow wanting his daughter at the moment.

'You'll be the bridesmaid, won't you Beth?' Edie asked, ignoring her father's jibe at Theo's age.

'I don't have a dress,' said Beth.

'That's easily fixed,' said Edie. 'Besides, you have to be my bridesmaid, you're practically my sister.' Edie grinned at her father and kicked her feet feeling her skirt brush against her ankles. She put her hand in her pocket and felt her notebook resting snugly there. Her plan had worked. Without a little extra incentive Theo might have spent the rest of his life considering whether or not to ask her. She may not be pretty but she knew how to make plans and solve problems.

Just as well I pushed her into him, thought Beth as she tried to avoid the peas and only pick up carrots, *or he'd never have had the courage to take her by her arm and ask.*

Paul sliced up the lamb as though he was slicing up the Reverend. The pulpit was not the place for politics and Paul had pressed his point home with the Reverend, a man so spineless it was no wonder his compassion was so thinly spread. Without the pulpit as a fortress for his thoughts, the man was feeble-brained. After lunch Paul would go and tell Lucy how the Reverend had whispered in his ear, 'You're a bit of a radical socialist', as though he'd just cleverly unmasked a secret.

Paul had felt like patting him on the head when he came out with that, the way you pat a child who has just worked out a simple equation or how to spell c-a-t. 'Good boy, Reverend, good boy,' he'd felt like saying, 'you're starting to figure things out by yourself.'

Of course Paul hadn't said anything; he was too busy laughing at the man's incompetence.

'Compromise is not the same as defeat.' He hadn't realised he'd said it out loud.

'Sorry?' asked Beth.

'It's what I always tell my clerks,' said Paul. He put a slice of lamb on Edie's plate, ignoring her protest, and a slice on Beth's. He put two slices on his own.

Of course what had really got in the way of his little talk with the Reverend was Edie. He looked over at her; she was playing with her food.

'For goodness sake, Edith, stop chasing that pea around the plate.' She looked at him. He'd hurt her, he shouldn't have snapped at her like that. 'Chase all the peas you want, love,' he said and got up and took yesterday's papers from the paper basket and buried his nose in *The Courier*. It was four broadsheets and took up a good deal of space on the table — he had to push his crockery out of the way — and if he read he didn't have to think about Lucy. *Oh Lucy*. But he couldn't help thinking about her. If she was at lunch she'd be giving him her look for reading at the table. But she was lying down, and it was his fault and he'd check on her soon. But he turned to the page with the cablegrams and pretended to be more engrossed than he was, building an invisible wall of 'don't disturb me', because he knew that Edie badly wanted to interrupt him.

'Papa?'

'Hmmm,' *here it comes*, he thought. He'd never get his few moments of relief with the paper. He watched as she swallowed the last of her stewed apple whole, gulping it down like a dry piece of steak.

'Papa,' she said again.

'If it's about Hooley, you don't need to prep me,' he said.

'Well, what are you going to say to him?'

He sighed. He just wanted to read his paper. He didn't want to think about his only child being claimed by that tall, too quiet man who was nearly half her age again. Edie's chin was out, that was a bad sign. He'd never get any peace. He folded the paper and put it on the table.

'I suppose that first of all I shall warn him about your persistent temperament, your stubbornness, the way you put your nose in the air when you're cross — which you are too often, and the way your chin juts out when you're determined to have your way — which you always expect. I shall warn him that unlike most women you always speak your mind whether it's needed or not, and that if he persists in marrying you he shall never have a moment's peace.' He smiled at her worried face and added, 'And then I shall say it's up to you because you've never listened to anything I've ever said anyway.' He stood up, dodged her swipe at him and pushed his chair into the table. 'I've got to go to the office for a few hours.'

'Working on a Sunday?' asked Edie. 'What if Theo comes by?'

'Theo already, is it? Then send him down to the office.'

'What are you going for?'

'I have to go and prepare my speech for tomorrow night's meeting at the Mechanics Institute,' he said, thinking he might also finish the paper. 'If we're to build a new nation, Edith, it must not be built on the backs of factory workers and miners — they're a sorry bunch, being paid tributes instead of decent wages. As if you can feed families on tributes! I had a fair mind to walk out of the Reverend's sermon this morning, I was that riled. I can only hope the rest of the congregation took as much notice of the Reverend's words as you did, Edie.' And he ducked another swipe. 'Well, you know where I'll be,' he said.

'But what about Theo?'

'What about him? I already said — send him down to the office.'

'But Papa, he might not want me if he has to walk to the office,' she said, sounding six years old.

'If a three-block walk puts him off, Edie, then he's not worth having.'

'Four — it's four blocks.'

'Well, if it's four blocks then we can test his commitment and stamina at the same time.' Paul picked up *The Star* from the basket, rolled it and *The Courier* together and tucked them under his arm as he walked to the door. Damn that man for wanting his daughter. He'd miss her terribly when she was married.

Paul stood at the door of his wife's bedroom. She was asleep, lying in her clothes on top of the made bed, her arms flung above her head, her dress falling over the side of the bed in a waterfall. He watched the tides of her body rising and falling. It was quiet. Not a sound except her breathing. He knew she was too old to be going through this and the guilt made his chest begin to hurt as if a bluestone block was sitting on top of it. She was so thin, she hardly showed. He'd seen her body through the bathroom door; she was like a twig bending under the weight of an emperor gum's cocoon. The shame made him slump against the door.

She opened her eyes and looked at him.

'I was just going to the office,' he said, 'but I can stay here with you.'

'What about Edie's beau?'

'He can come down to the office. I'll only be sending him back to Edie anyway. If he's serious he won't resent a little running around for our daughter.'

'Well go on then, I'm only going to sleep anyway. You go, dear,' Lucy said, but he didn't move.

'I don't want to leave you.'

She tried to laugh but only a small wheeze came out. 'I'm not going anywhere in this condition. Going to church has done me in for the day.'

'I would have thought Edie would have worn you out for the day. If I'd noticed she was going to church practically showing her undergarments I would have locked her up. But all I've been thinking about is you.' He walked over and put his hand on her forehead. Dear God! She was burning up. Paul lay down beside her and put his head on her belly. Her clothes, damp with her sweat, wetted his cheek. The growing baby inside, feeling the presence of its father, somersaulted in its wet cocoon. He remembered reading once about the underground houses the opal miners built in the middle of the desert to stay cool in the searing heat. Lucy felt the heat so badly and the summer was coming. He wished he could give her one of those houses.

He stood and bent to kiss her cheek, taking in the sweet smell of her perfume and the warmth of her neck. She turned her head towards him and her soft black hair, speckled with grey and released from its usual bun, fell momentarily across his cheek. He was reminded of the first time he had loosened it with trembling fingers, pulling each clip out slowly as if pulling out fragments of her soul. When her hair was free he'd buried his face in it.

The first time he saw her she had been wearing a white summer dress and a wide-brimmed hat with a pale blue ribbon that lifted gently in the breeze. She was holding her baby sister in her arms and singing to her, and her voice was tender like whispers on the wind. The hat cast a shadow over her, as if she and the baby were in a separate world created by her song, and he wanted desperately to enter that world. His own was full of rules and precedents, claims and litigation; he knew he needed her quietness, her voice to lull him to a place of gentleness.

She was sixteen when they met, eighteen when they married, and they had hoped for so many children. But till now only Edie had come.

He kissed her cheek again and said, 'I can stay,' but she shook her head and said, 'Go, go.' So reluctantly he left her room.

'I'll be back by five,' he said, but she was sleeping again. Every time he left her it felt as if it would be the last, and it was like a kick in the gut.

'I'm off now, Edith,' he called and closed the front door behind him.

He stepped out into the afternoon sun, looked up and swore at it. 'You're a bloody problem you are!' The sun smirked and grew hotter, and the hotter it got the more he could feel Lucy slipping away from him. It was as though she was melting away to nothing.

Last year the summer heat spawned bushfires that ate up farms and took jagged bites at the edges of the town. The heat and smoke from the fires filled everyone's lungs. Women dissolved in their skirts and corsets, and men put on brave faces. Lucy had wilted like a plucked wild daisy. Watching her, Paul's heart had seared and stung. Then winter had come and she had picked up for a while, but now it was warming up again and she was dwindling away. There seemed to be nothing he could do to help her. He jabbed his umbrella at the sun seven times and then sighed and set off.

It was a comfortable stroll to the office. He always said to his clerks that it was important for a man to be on his own between work and home to make the transition from the duty of work to the duty of home. A man's life is a matter of keeping these two responsibilities in equal balance so that neither is neglected nor put upon by the other. That's what he told his men and what he lived by. His walk was his space, and he banged his umbrella along the fence posts making a racket the way schoolboys do with sticks. By the time people looked out their windows he was gone, so they ran to their front gates and shook their fists at the boys who were kicking tin cans down the street. He got to Drummond Street and decided to cross the main road and walk down Dana Street. It was steeper but it was downhill and his office was right on the corner of Dana and Armstrong in the centre of town, just a block from the Town Hall. The Town Hall clock sounded as loudly in his office as if he was standing under it.

His mind turned back to Lucy. He might have a son this time. Not that he cared, as long as Lucy was all right. He hadn't missed having a son; he always told people that 'You don't pine for what you've never had.' But thinking about it as he walked, his umbrella now tapping on the road, he thought it might be nice to have a son, someone to leave the business to. But his bones ached with worry and his chest refused to take in a decent amount of air. If Lucy didn't survive the coming summer there might not be any baby at all, and even worse there might not be any Lucy. He thought of the miners who worked beneath the very streets he walked on, working away in the dark coolness. The idea grew in him and gave him hope.

'Why couldn't I?' he said to himself. What was to stop him? Not money. 'Why bloody not?' He smiled.

He turned the key in the office door, pushed it open and secured it with the boot scrape so a breeze could blow in. It was silent inside. Dead silent. No tapping typewriters, no chatting staff, no clients making demands. He was surrounded by the woody, responsible smells of oak and teak and he let them seep into him. He propped his umbrella in the stand and he went to his desk behind a glass partition at the back of the office. He was protected there. Clients had to get past his staff to get to him and he could see everything from where he sat. There was his pipe, patiently waiting for him. He took it and filled it with the Havelock that he kept in his top drawer. The tobacco, the wood, the oily polish seeped decency and steadiness into his pores.

He dipped his nib in the inkwell and thought of what he wanted to say at tomorrow night's meeting. Most likely his audience would be a bunch of rowdy miners and some council members, not to mention hecklers. If he was lucky there'd be some like him who were concerned about the future of the nation. He should mention Eureka. He thought of Eureka as Australia's first war. Most of the miners could cite an uncle, a father or grandfather who had been part of the uprising fifty-odd years ago. It had taken place just a few blocks from his office. The town had memories of rebellion that sat rumbling and fermenting in its bowels. He wrote:

I have never come across a miner who would take tributes if he could take wages and the miners of this town only take tributes because they CANNOT get wages! What man would work for piece rates instead of a wage? The chance of a miner coming across a block that will give him twenty pounds a fortnight is as likely as winning one thousand pounds in Tattersalls sweeps …

Paul paused to collect his thoughts. He looked at his watch and the time surprised him. Already it was past three and here was Beth coming in to see him. He smiled.

Five

The Gift

Which is unwanted and cannot be returned.

It took Paul a moment to realise that Beth was in a panic. She leant on the clerk's counter, her whole body heaving. Beads of sweat wet her hair and tears stained her cheeks. He jumped up and ran to her.

'You must come. Edie sent me and said to come immediately,' she panted.

Paul didn't ask any questions; he was too afraid of the answers. He kicked the boot scraper away from the door too hard and it toppled over and he had to kick it again to get it out of the way. As the door swung shut he caught it and held it open for Beth. He told himself not to panic until he knew what he was panicking about, even though he knew full well what he was panicking about. His pulse was racing and he could hear his breath coming in short ragged gasps. He grabbed his umbrella and bowler hat. Beth stepped into the street, still breathing heavily and holding her waist and he wondered how quickly she'd be able to get back home in this state.

'What's happened?' he asked at last, bracing himself. But Beth just looked at him.

'Go on,' she said, 'hurry.'

And he did. He ran home, his heart thumping furiously, his thighs burning. What had seemed a short walk now seemed like an expedition. Finally he got to his house, which buckled and bowed, its iron lacework drooping like melting ice-cream as moans and sobs escaped its walls. He gasped for air. His lungs had shrivelled and the air he needed wouldn't come.

'Oh house,' he said, 'what shame are you hiding?'

He went in through the back door that was always open and in the kitchen his heart froze at the sounds of pain echoing down the hallway. He dropped his umbrella on the kitchen table. It rolled off and clattered onto the floor but he left it and ran up the hallway to Lucy's bedroom and stood in the doorway. Edie was bent over the bed, mopping her mother's forehead with a flannel. He saw his wife, her skin clammy, her body heaving. Sweat trickled down her forehead.

Edie was crying. 'I don't know what's wrong. She collapsed in the hallway. There's blood. If you call Doctor Appleby he's more likely to come than if I call him. He'll think I'm just a panicky woman.'

'I think this is normal. This is what happens. It's just too soon, that's all,' he said.

'What's normal?' Edie cried, terrified. 'What's too soon?'

He tried to answer, but the words suffocated in his airless lungs.

'I'll call the doctor,' was the best he could manage.

He went to the telephone on the wall beside the hallstand and put the call through.

'There's no answer,' Doris the operator told him in her I-don't-care voice. He looked accusingly down at the earpiece and slammed it into its cradle. He went back to the bedroom door. He wanted to go to her and sweep her up in his arms but it was as if there was an invisible barrier that he couldn't get past — women only.

'He's not there, we should get your mother to the hospital, I'll call the ambulance cart,' he said.

'I don't need the hospital, call Nurse Drake,' said Lucy from the bed. It didn't sound like her voice; it was harsh and rasping instead of supple and inviting. She hardly sounded alive. He watched with sudden horror as she heaved herself out of bed, stumbled to the door, leant her weight against it and shut it in his face.

He was on his own now. Shut out of their world. He heard Lucy cry out again and he had never felt lonelier in all his life than he did in that moment. The hallway that he walked up and down each day was now alien and cold. Another cry stabbed into his heart and he shivered. He had to do something, take some kind of action no matter how futile, so he went to the telephone again and commanded Doris to try this Nurse Drake.

'I would,' said Doris curtly, 'but p'raps you should remember that most of us isn't made of money and most of the town hasn't got a telephone!'

He slammed the telephone down. Useless contraption. He swore and thumped his fist against the wall, not knowing what to do. He paced the hallway, past the portraits that looked at him accusingly and the landscapes that beckoned and he struggled to breathe. Fears swirled inside him and gave him a splitting headache. He fretted for Lucy, for his unborn child, for his daughter who was unmarried and knew nothing about the birthing of babies.

'Well, I suppose she's about to learn,' he laughed out loud to himself in a brief minute of respite but then the fears grabbed him again and he had to do something so he picked up the telephone again.

'Try for Doctor Appleby again!'

'I have!' Doris said.

'Well, keep trying until you get him!'

Doris told him that she didn't need reminding to keep putting the call through thank you very much and disconnected him
before he could hang up on her again.

Eventually Edie appeared, white faced and stony, and he
watched her walk straight into her bedroom and emerge with the
scissors she had used on her skirt that very morning. She walked
past him as if he was a shadow she could walk through and into
the kitchen. He followed uselessly and watched as she got a pot,
filled it with water and put it on to boil. Then she threw the scissors in.

'Who told you to do that?' he asked.

'Mama.'

He stood there for fifteen minutes watching her watching the
clock. Neither of them said anything until Beth burst through
the door.

'What's happened? Has the doctor come?'

He shook his head and thought that Beth was looking at him
accusingly, as though it was his fault the doctor hadn't shown up.

'What about a midwife then? Nurse Drake's real good, she
delivered me and my sisters,' said Beth, thinking they were useless
without her around to organise them.

'Where's this Nurse Drake live?'

'Eddy Street,' said Beth, 'off Peel down near Grant. I sometimes see the boy that lives next door.'

This was news to Edie and Paul but it went by without even
a wink. Their minds were congested with fear for Lucy. Paul
shook his head again. He watched Beth join Edie standing over
the stove. The two girls stood studying the boiling scissors as if
it was the only thing happening in the entire world. He wanted

to join them at the stove but felt outcast. Then when the hands on the kitchen clock ticked over again Edie grabbed the scissors with the dish towel and, with Beth behind her, hurried back to Lucy's bedroom. The door closed in his face.

Slam.

He couldn't stand it so he went outside into the front yard. The children next door were playing cricket using a rubbish tin as a wicket. He called, 'Arthur, Arthur, I need you to run a message for me.'

The boy came over to the fence, followed by his two younger brothers Geoffrey and John. Paul thought Arthur was about eleven, certainly old enough for responsibility. Paul fished in his pocket and pulled out a coin.

'Do you know where Eddy Street is? I need you to run to Eddy Street, off Peel. Find Nurse Drake, she lives there. Tell her she's wanted here — no, tell her she's needed here immediately.'

He looked at the younger boys, 'You two, go and tell your parents what Arthur's doing for me.' He handed Arthur the coin. 'Well, go on Arthur, quickly — a life may depend on it.'

The boys scurried off, the younger ones jealous that only Arthur got a coin. Why weren't they getting a coin when they were also delivering a message? It wasn't their fault it only had to be delivered to the kitchen where their ma and pa were having a pot of tea and what they called 'a discussion'.

Paul walked in circles and prayed to God to save his wife and child, but if a choice had to be made he'd have his wife. He prayed until he heard Edie calling him. Then he rushed inside, where the door of Lucy's bedroom was wide open. He blinked at the scene before him, trying to make sense of it.

Beth was picking up bloodied linen and cloths.

Edie stood still against the wall, her back pressed against it hard, as if she wished hard enough it might swallow her up and take her back to the beginning of the day and they could all start again. Her father looked at her and his soul filled with pity. Her day had started out so bright and was ending up so black.

'Edie,' he called.

Edie didn't hear him. Her ears were filled with buzzing and she was wringing her hands. Her white, tense knuckles knocked against each other, her fingernails dug into the skin and a drop of blood spilt to the floor. She hadn't even noticed. The pain in her heart was so great. She didn't know yet that her mother was dying, but she did know that this baby that had appeared out of nowhere was an evil thing. It had been here no more than a few minutes yet had brought nothing but sorrow and pain to those she loved. Imagine what horror it would wield over the course of a full life. All her fear, all her shock over learning where babies come out, was dissolved in her hate for it as quickly as sugar dissolves in hot tea. She would drown it later, like an unwanted kitten.

Her brain was hurting, the blood tearing through her veins at impossible speeds, and with it, shards of her heart.

Paul wanted to comfort his daughter but his wife needed him more and he needed her. He went to the bed, bent over her and kissed Lucy and saw the new baby, wrapped in a thin tea towel, cradled in her arms.

'She's heavy,' whispered Lucy.

The baby was so tiny and scrawny he wondered for a moment if it was even alive, and decided that it wasn't. It was so small it couldn't be. But Lucy was alive and for that he was grateful.

'Beth, get me a knee rug,' he said, and he ran a trembling finger through the river of sweat on Lucy's brow, saying 'Sshhh' over and over. When Beth brought the rug he reached to take the dead infant from Lucy's arms and it screwed up its face. It was alive.

He wrapped the baby in the rug. It was wet and damp, covered in the fluids that had aided its birth. He pulled up a chair and sat next to his wife, clutching his new child in his arms as though it was made of fairy floss and would float away and disappear.

The room was filled with silence. Everything was shocking and new.

Paul was so wrapped up in his new child and his wife that he didn't hear the knock at the front door or see Beth leave the room.

'Beth, let me in,' said Doctor Appleby, suddenly appearing far too late. 'The operator said you tried to ring.'

Paul moved to stand up, but the doctor motioned for him to stay where he was as he strode into the room.

'The doctor's here,' Paul said to Lucy, but she barely opened her eyes. He looked at Doctor Appleby and could read the worry in his face. Paul felt his heart lurch as he registered that look.

Doctor Appleby lifted the blankets and murmured, 'A lot of blood loss.'

Lucy's eyes were closed now.

Paul watched as Doctor Appleby picked up Lucy's fragile wrist. He knew somewhere inside him that Doctor Appleby was taking her pulse but routine actions seemed out of place in a world that was churning and turning. The doctor leant over and whispered in his ear so Edie couldn't hear.

'This happens with the change of life ones — always a risk. Not much I can do here for the moment.'

Paul stared vacantly at the meaningful glance the doctor was giving him. He knew what the glance meant but he wouldn't acknowledge it. He'd prove the doctor to be an unreliable witness, guilty of perjury, even. Paul could feel Edie looking at him, her panic rising. To restore some normality he said, 'Would you like a cup of tea, Doctor Appleby?'

'I just got back from lunch at the Tonkins'. I could do with one. I like it white with two sugars.' And Doctor Appleby looked meaningfully at Beth, who knew she had to make the tea but made no motion to leave.

Paul needed the doctor out of the room. He needed to be alone with his wife and children.

Beth didn't want to go. She was part of the family, wasn't she? That's what they always said. Lucy was the closest thing she had to a mother. Paul nodded in the direction of the kitchen, so she motioned grudgingly for Doctor Appleby to follow her.

Paul could never remember when the realisation hit him that Lucy was going to die. It might have been when he saw Edie's blood drop to the floor, a single tear that fell from her clenched hands and burst on the polished mirror of the floorboards. It might have been when Doctor Appleby came back into the room, balancing his tea cup on its saucer, and leant over and whispered in Paul's ear, 'There's nothing I can do for her. I'm sorry.' It might have been when Lucy opened her eyes, looked over at him and whispered, 'Name her Grace,' with her last ounce of energy and closed her eyes. But whichever moment it was, it was as if someone ripped his heart and soul from his body and tossed them carelessly aside.

Half an hour had passed since the doctor had left the room for an arrowroot biscuit and a second cup of tea. Paul clutched baby Grace as though she was his anchor, the only thing able to hold him back from following his wife as she slipped through the tides of life. Death was in the room, bringing its awful odour with it. It was an odour that curled the corners of the soul if you were living, but perhaps if you were dying it was rose petals and the sea because suddenly Lucy smiled and sang — just a few words of the song that had ensnared Paul's heart at the very beginning.

'*Dear Child who me resemblest so, it whispered, come oh come with me, happy together let us go, the earth unworthy is of thee.*'

Her voice was as light as the first day he heard it and it gave him hope.

'Mama,' called Edie and rushed to the bedside.

With an enormous effort Lucy looked into Edie's eyes and reached out and gently touched her cheek with her finger. Edie burst into heartbroken sobs.

'You must be her mother now,' whispered Lucy.

'No, you must stay,' cried Edie.

'Promise me,' pleaded Lucy, her hand touching Edie's hair. But Edie was crying too much to answer.

It was hard work for Lucy to stay in this world, even for a few minutes. It was only love that was keeping her. She looked at her new daughter, wrinkled and pink in the rug in her father's arms.

'Gracie,' she whispered.

Paul nodded. 'I'll agree to any name you wish, if only you wouldn't leave.'

She looked at him and tried to send him all her love as she sang, '*When one is pure as thou art now, the sweetest day is still the last.*'

The baby Gracie, wrapped in the knee rug Lucy had crocheted, was quiet as she turned her tiny face. Then she twisted and turned her body. Paul jumped, surprised to feel such strength in such a spindly newborn, and wondered what the baby was trying to do. Then he realised she was turning to see her mother.

'Go on, look at your mother,' he whispered in her ear, 'for you will surely follow her and stay by her side.'

Gracie focused her brand-new eyes, still filmy, on her mother's face, reached out her tiny fingers, and smiled. That first smile filled Paul with peace.

It was Gracie who sent her mother on her way. Lucy, having received all she needed in that one tiny smile, lay back on the pillow and left them. The room was filled with icy silence, aside from the muffled weeping of Edie.

And the broken heart of Paul.

After a long while Edie spoke. 'I don't want her, send her back to God and exchange her for Mother!'

Paul considered his girl. She sounded like a five-year-old child. He looked at the baby and suddenly he knew what to do to push his and Edie's grief to somewhere controllable.

'Come and welcome your sister,' he commanded, 'she is so small she may not be with us for long.'

Edie didn't move.

'Now, Edith!'

Edie shuffled across the room, her face red, wary and angry with grief. She didn't want to look at the thing that had just taken her mother's life. She didn't want to see what had spread blood and pain through her home. Paul moved the baby so Edie had to look at her, then he placed her in Edie's rigid unwilling arms. Edie turned away. Her father might put the child in her arms like a parcel, but that didn't mean she had to acknowledge it. So Edie missed it when the baby girl smiled, and everything turned and shifted in their house once more.

Doctor Appleby stood in the doorway wiping crumbs from his face with his white monogrammed handkerchief. He coughed.

'I see you need me now — to sign the death certificate.' Feeling he should offer more, he said, 'It's all right, I've already rung Reverend Whitlock and he's on his way.'

Down in Eddy Street, a narrow street with only a few sparse trees and small struggling gardens, Young Arthur thumped on the front door of Number 12.

Beatrix Drake and her fella George hid under the blankets.

'Shhh,' she giggled, 'whoever it is will think no one's home and bugger off.'

Arthur thumped for as long as the coin Mister Cottingham had given him was worth, then put his hands in his pockets and wandered slowly home.

Theo, waiting at the front door of the Cottingham house, felt the house shift and the world turn and was filled with sorrow.

Six

The Decision

*Which comes after hot soup and thick slices
of bread and a restless night.*

The mines meandered under the houses and streets of the town, twisting this way and that under the hills and paddocks and under the great Town Hall clock itself. Countless icy tunnels of dank suffocating air that swallowed men and boys in the dark mornings considered whether or not to spit them back up in the afternoons.

At four o'clock the Town Hall clock, with its eight bells weighing four and half tons, each tuned to a different note, cried out its song four times.

When they heard the clock, the mines breathed a sigh of relief that the working day was over and great gusts of cold, icy wind rushed out of their mouths. The chilly air rose from the tombs of the mines that held the bones of gold and men and filled the town like a rising mist. Women ran for pullovers for their children, men lit fires with damp kindling and everyone rubbed the goosebumps on their arms. The mines could not be trusted for much — they teased men with promises of wealth and played with their lives

62

according to their mood — but they could always be trusted to send out their cold-hearted draughts at four in the afternoon. They were as regular as the chimes that rang out over the town: the cold arrived, regardless of how pleasant the day had been.

The clock chimed and the air turned nippy and Theo Hooley continued to stand outside the Cottingham front door. If his mum could have seen him she'd have snapped, 'Your arms are goosepimply, son. You'll catch your death if you're not careful!'

But Theo hadn't noticed the frosty air; his hand was raised, ready to knock on the front door when it opened and Doctor Appleby stepped out.

'How long have you been standing here, Hooley?'

'Not long,' said Theo.

He'd been standing watching the house as its beams groaned and shifted for hours.

'No use going in there, son, they've got other things on their minds just now,' the doctor said.

'Edie's all right, isn't she?'

'Edith's fine, the baby's fine for the moment, everyone's fine except the mother.'

'What mother?' asked Theo, confused by the doctor's strange words.

'Yes, yes, the mother — Missus Cottingham. She just died giving birth to a scrawny, underweight daughter. Let's just hope she fills out and survives but I don't hold out much hope. Not at all.'

Theo stared, trying to take this in. Missus Cottingham was gone, dead, and there was a baby. It was hard to believe and he didn't know why or how yet, but he knew this would change everything for Edith and him. A stone had been thrown into the pond and the ripple had reached the edge where he stood and wet his toes. Dampness crept over his heart. He somehow knew that his chance at happiness had just disappeared. The knowledge hurt and Theo dropped his cane and clutched his chest.

'Are you all right son? Your lips are blue — where's your coat?' Sometimes it felt to Doctor Appleby as if his work was never done. 'Son, did you hear me?'

But Theo just looked blankly at him and Doctor Appleby thought, not for the first time, that Hooley might have got a bit of brain sickness over there in Africa. The place was too damn hot. Just like the blistering summer that was coming again here. Heat was a nasty thing that bred germs on your skin and then the sweat of your body turned the germs to liquid and the liquid seeped into your pores and worked its way to your brain. He had begun as a doctor in his twenties and for thirty-five years Doctor Appleby had seen miners fresh from Cornwall turn mad from the Australian heat. Looked like Hooley had got a germ in his brain over there in the African heat. After all, heat was heat. Didn't matter which country you got it in.

Hooley still stood, looking vacantly at the door.

'It's a fine house, isn't it son? That's what you can buy with a barrister's wage.'

Theo looked at him as if he was the one that was mad, and Doctor Appleby saw the sorrow in Theo's eyes and realised it wasn't the house he was mesmerised by but what was inside it.

The doctor sighed. 'I'm only a country doctor; I can't keep up with advances from the city. I watch miners die of silicosis before they're forty, I watch women die giving birth, I watch children die of diphtheria. I can't cure any of them. If the truth be known I can only cure folk of illnesses they are likely to survive anyhow. But I also know I can't cure you of standing there gazing at that grand house like a cockatoo that has lost its mate.'

Theo remained silent.

'They mate for life you know — cockatoos,' the doctor continued. 'They mourn if they lose their mate. Maybe I should have been a veterinarian — might have been easier.' He felt the weight of a bad day's work. He couldn't cure anything today.

Theo watched Doctor Appleby walk out the front gate, his short stumpy body on long legs like a spider, his bag swinging at his side. The doctor's house was twice the size of the Cottingham's and housed three servants.

Theo looked up at the sky. The sun had exhausted itself and disappeared. Grey clouds filled the sky. There was no warmth left in the air at all, and there was nothing to do but walk home.

'It's over with Edith,' Theo said to Lilly, his mum. He fell into the kitchen chair, put his arms on the table and rested his head on them. He could speak with his mum; his words came freely when it was just the two of them. With her it was like he had never gone to Africa and lost his voice and his insides. It was like he was always a child, the voluminous warmth of her being soaked up his hollowness and kept him safe. She didn't have one harsh edge to make his words bounce back at him; his words soaked into her motherly softness and found a place to belong.

He watched as she poured soup into a bowl, balanced it on her stout middle and carefully walked to the table with it, trying not to spill any on her apron.

'I didn't know it had begun with Edith,' she said. Lilly had been in the church kitchen after the service getting morning tea ready. She'd made a sultana cake and two-dozen rock cakes, and had cut the cake into thin triangles to get twelve slices out of it, as these would be the first to go, the boys would pounce and gobble them up. She hadn't seen Edie and Theo under the tree. She thought he was interested in that awful Gamble girl.

'Yes, I was going to ask for her hand this afternoon but everything has changed.'

'It's mulligatawny soup, your favourite — not too spicy, though. I know you like it spicy but I can't eat it as spicy as you, Theo.'

'How could it change in such a short time?' he said, and put his spoon into the bowl and left it there. It slid down the side of the bowl and under the soup.

'Oh dear,' said Lilly, 'you fish that out and I'll get another spoon.'

Theo put his fingers carefully into the hot soup and grabbed the tip of the spoon and tossed it over the table like a cricket ball. It dropped into the kitchen sink with a loud clatter and clang. She handed him the fresh spoon and pushed the bread over to him.

'Here,' she said and reached for the butter and started spreading a slice for him. 'Hot soup and a nice slice of bread will cheer you up.'

'Missus Cottingham has died,' said Theo, and now it was Lilly's turn to drop her knife. 'And she's left a baby, apparently, though Doctor Appleby says it will die soon.'

'Oh, oh! The poor poor man left alone with a tiny baby.' She knocked her soup bowl and the soup sloshed from side to side and onto the tablecloth, leaving a greasy stain.

'Sorry,' Theo said, even though it wasn't his fault.

'Would you like some scones? I've made some scones for you. No, no, you'll want them after with jam and cream.'

'No thanks, Mum,' he muttered to the soup.

'How do you know it's over with her? Have you spoken to her father? Did he say no?' Lilly wriggled to get more comfortable, to position herself right in the middle of the chair so she spilled evenly over each side.

'I don't need to speak to anyone. I just know. Everything has changed.' He swirled the soup round and round into a whirlpool. 'I could feel it. The whole house groaned with it and Doctor Appleby said not to bother her. He said it like it meant ever — don't ever bother her.'

'Well son, I know you don't want to hear from me but I'm going to tell you anyway. You don't give up, you just give her a bit of time. She just has to come to terms with things, she needs time to adjust. Then you start again. You'll see.' And she took scones out of the old biscuit tin with a rosella on the lid and piled them high on a plate like the Leaning Tower of Pisa.

Well, well well, she thought. *The Cottingham girl.* She hadn't expected that but she was pleased it wasn't Vera Gamble he liked. Edie Cottingham had more substance, she had a kindness about her that came from inner strength. And she could talk the hind leg off a donkey which could only be an asset to her son. Lilly wanted to do something for her son. She wanted to make the Cottingham girl love him above all else if that was what he wanted. But she couldn't, she could only feed him good food to fatten his bones so the fat could absorb his aches. He had come back empty from Africa and she did all she could to fill him up. She took the top scone and broke it in half, piled jam onto it and a mountain of whipped cream on top of that and she handed it to him. Theo put it on the tablecloth beside his untouched bowl of soup and his untouched bread. Then, sighing, he took the bread and tore it apart, dropping chunks into the soup like islands. They soaked up the soup and turned it into a grainy mush; the butter formed tiny oily pools that sat on top.

Lilly smiled as he put a spoon of bready soup to his mouth. Later she would get out the lemon cake for supper and if he didn't want that she had also made a date roll and if he didn't eat them she would sit and eat them for him, as though he was still inside her and her body could nourish his.

That night Theo slept badly, suddenly waking at 2 a.m., and again at four and at six, each time instantly aware that he'd lost Edie. By morning he'd made up his mind. His mother was right. He, Theo, was not going to be a quitter. He didn't survive the African war just so he could give up on the rest of his life. Of course Edie would need time to grieve her mother, plenty of time — six months, at least. He could give her that. Six months was not a long time; once a long time ago he had waited for far longer. He knew how to wait and he was going to wait for Edie.

He knew his mother had baked a pie before he got to the kitchen. The hot pastry wrapped around what was secreted inside and the smells promised rich gravy and salty meat and made him hungry and he pulled his dressing gown tighter around his chest. It was sitting in the middle of the table just aching to be broken open and he reached to break off a piece of the buttery pastry but Lilly slapped his hand away.

'It's not for you, it's for the Cottinghams. It's mutton and mushroom. I'm going to take it over later.'

'I'll take it when I'm dressed,' he said firmly, the matter decided. He thought his appearance with the pie, as if he had baked it himself, would let Edie know he was there waiting, not forgetting her and not to be forgotten.

Seven

Theo

In 1881 when Theo is a much-loved runt of a boy aged five.

Theo was eating toast dripping with melted butter that trickled through his fingers and down his arms into little pools around his elbows on the table. Theo's father, Peter, who was thirty years older than his mother, kissed him on the forehead. His moustache prickled Theo's skin but Theo didn't mind. Then Peter took his mother in his arms and twirled her around the kitchen, narrowly missing the corner of the table and nearly sending the aluminium teapot and its bakelite handle flying. Lilly was giggling and Peter looked over to Theo with a secret grin and then swooped her backwards over his arm and kissed her long and hard. Theo smiled and clapped his buttery hands at the pantomime they were putting on solely for his enjoyment — or so, being only five, he thought. Peter pulled Lilly back up to vertical and reached over and scooped Theo into his arms and they had all laughed. Peter laughed so hard he coughed and had to bend over with his hands on his knees to catch his breath.

'Just a mo,' he croaked between coughs, his finger in the air, holding time still for them all. When the coughing had stopped he stood up and grinned and said, 'That's how it's done, son. That's how you kiss the woman you love good and proper,' and Theo nodded in agreement even though he had no idea what his father was talking about. The only woman Theo loved was his mother and he certainly couldn't bend her over his arm the way his father had done.

Peter put Theo down and picked up his leather satchel, adjusted his collar and necktie, put on his bowler and kissed Theo on the forehead again. Then he put his arm around Lilly's waist, pulled her to him and kissed her.

Lilly grabbed the dishcloth and wiped Theo's hands clean, leaving them damp and sticky and smelling like week-old dishcloth, which Theo didn't like, and they followed Peter out onto the front verandah and watched him walk down the path. When he got to the gate he turned, smiled and blew them a kiss. Lilly caught the sadness in his eyes and for a fleeting moment she wondered about it and felt afraid, but Theo only saw the smile on his father's face. Lilly was holding Theo's hand too tightly and he wriggled free and climbed up onto the verandah rail so he could better watch his father. As Peter disappeared down the street Theo leant over so far to watch him he nearly toppled into the garden. He wasn't sure what his father did at the bank but his mother had told him that his father was the boss and all that mattered to Theo was that other people knew just how important his father was, because to Theo there was no one in the world more important.

Every afternoon around four o'clock Theo sat on the third verandah step from the bottom and waited for his father to come home from work. It was autumn and the weather was pleasant and Theo scratched a kingdom of castles and moats into the dirt by the stairs with a long stick.

'It's too early, Theo, he won't be home for ages yet,' said Lilly the first time he'd sat waiting, but Theo had shrugged and sat and waited, so Lilly brought him biscuits to eat and milk to drink while he sat there. She knew she shouldn't take him food because they would have dinner as soon as Peter got home, sausages and mash and fresh beans from the backyard, and Maud Blackmarsh was forever telling her that she fed Theo way too much. But Maud had no right to be giving child-rearing advice since she and her husband hadn't had any children yet. And besides, no matter how much Lilly fed Theo, he never seemed to grow any fatter.

The night before, Peter had picked up his crumbed chop, leaned forward and said to Theo, 'Son, I'm thirty years older than your mother. I don't know why she married an old codger like me — a beautiful young girl like her could have had anyone. People thought she was mad, they tried to stop her, oh yes they did, but she ran off with me anyway.'

'Oh, stop filling his head,' said Lilly.

But Peter ignored her. 'I was fifty when I found your mother.'

'And I was barely twenty,' said Lilly quietly.

'There was never anyone before her but she was worth waiting for, son. Every minute was worth it. So you wait, son — you wait for the right woman,' and he waggled the chop and some of the crumbs fell off. 'Oops,' he smiled and popped the crumbs into his mouth.

In the mornings Theo and Lilly stood on the verandah and waved Peter off to work, and Peter always stopped at the gate to wave and blow them kisses before he set off down the street. Theo and Lilly would fill their days together with household chores, Lilly cooking and washing or ironing, and sometimes Theo helped and sometimes he played until it was time for him to sit on the third step from the bottom and wait for his father. Sometimes he took paper and pencils with him and drew on paper instead of in the dirt, but the drawings always had lines in them where the pencil got lost in the cracks between the wood. Sometimes he took his

teddy bear to talk to and sometimes he took his marbles, but he
had to be careful not to lose any of them through the cracks.

Lilly brought him pound cake and milk on a little tray that had
a hand-painted windmill on it, just like she always did.

Today Theo waited and waited for his father. His father would
normally be home by now and he wasn't and it was so extraor-
dinary that Theo didn't know what to think. Lilly came and sat
next to him and Theo could see the dark grey clouds in her eyes
as they waited together. Then darkness came and Lilly began to
cry soft quiet tears and she said to Theo, 'You be a good boy, you
just sit there for a moment.'

Theo nodded and wondered why adults told him to be good
when he never considered being anything other than what he was.
He watched as Lilly pulled her cardigan tightly over her chest.
Then she walked down their path and up Missus Blackmarsh's
path and knocked on their door. Mister Blackmarsh opened the
door and Theo could hear the muffled sounds of their conversation. Lilly came back and sat next to him again and she was crying
harder and it made Theo feel like crying too. A few minutes later
Mister and Missus Blackmarsh stood in front of him looking hard
at him and Lilly but not saying anything. After a while George
the policeman appeared and said he and Lilly would have a few
quiet words alone. Lilly patted Theo's hand and walked a few feet
away from the steps and she and George had their quiet words.
Then George walked over and ruffled Theo's hair, which Theo
hated, and said, 'You look after your mum, hey,' and Theo nodded solemnly. He knew policemen were serious people and you
had to do what they told you. George had a few more words with
Lilly and Lilly cried out and collapsed onto Missus Blackmarsh's
shoulder and Theo heard Missus Blackmarsh say, 'I'm sure there's
another explanation — Peter wouldn't —' and she looked at Theo

and changed her mind about what she was going to say and added, 'Besides, in this small town we'd know about it, men can't hide anything like that.'

That night Lilly let Theo sleep in her big bed where his father normally slept and Theo buried his face in the pillow that smelt just like his father. The next day when he woke up Aunty June and Uncle Cliff were in the kitchen eating huge slices of cake and whispering with his mother. They stopped whenever he walked in and his mother continued to cry.

'No, no, no,' said Uncle Cliff, 'I just don't buy it. I don't buy it at all. Not my brother.'

In the afternoon Theo went and sat on the third step from the bottom and waited for his father because surely his father had simply forgotten to come home, or had lost his way, and tonight he would come. Lilly brought him drop scones with jam and cream, and some warm milk. When it got dark, Uncle Cliff came and picked him up.

'Come on, mate,' he said. 'It's too dark out here.' He carried Theo to his mother's bed where Lilly fed him warm soup and Auntie June and Uncle Cliff sat on the end of the bed and watched. When the soup was finished Lilly laid him down and held his hand and Uncle Cliff nodded at her and Lilly said, 'He's not coming home tonight, Theo.' Theo looked at her hand that completely covered his. Her hand was soft and smooth and fine. His dad had said, 'Look, Theo, look what lovely slender hands you mama has, hey? You've got her hands, they're piano hands, son.'

'I know,' said Theo because he thought that's what Lilly wanted to hear him say. Then he turned over and buried his head in the pillow.

When Theo woke in the morning Aunty June and Uncle Cliff were still there. Uncle Cliff was reading a letter out loud and his mother was crying and Aunty June was holding the teapot in mid-air like a statue. Uncle Cliff stopped reading when Theo walked into the kitchen, so Theo shrugged and wandered off to do all the things he would normally do until the afternoon. Then he went and sat on the step and waited for his father until his mother finally came and took his hand and pulled him up saying, 'He's not coming home tonight, Theo.'

The next day Aunty June and Uncle Cliff went back to their house in Humffray Street with lots of 'Are you sure you'll be okay? Are you sure you don't want us to stay longer?' And Theo mimicked their words to his teddy bear.

That night, lying in the big bed, Theo asked, 'Where's he gone, Mum? He's coming back, isn't he?'

'I don't know,' she said brushing his hair from his face. 'I hope so. We just have to wait and see.'

'Wait and see,' Theo said to his teddy bear.

Theo thought that if waiting was what he had to do to get his father back, then that was certainly something he could do. Waiting was easy; waiting was sitting on the step each night, no matter how long it took, until his father walked through the front gate.

Peter hadn't planned to walk away from his home, his job and his young wife in her rosebud dress and her curls that fell across her face even when she tried to pin them back and her laugh that was like sunlight bursting from a raindrop. He hadn't planned to walk away from his son, a funny skinny little thing who thought the world would only ever bring him kindness and love. But the further away he walked, the more convinced he was that leaving was the right thing to do. He knew there wasn't much hope for him. He couldn't burden them with what was to come or sit back and wait until everything good in their lives had been ripped up. He wasn't going to let Lilly and Theo watch him disintegrate to nothing before their very eyes. He wasn't going to burden Lilly with his care that could go on for months, or have her doing the most intimate things he would need as though she was not his wife but his mother. He didn't want his son to remember him as a sick, shrivelling man. He had no choice but to disappear. This was the kinder path. This was something he had to do and pray to God they would one day understand.

Peter had passed by Maud Blackmarsh's house and as luck would have it the devil herself was collecting her milk. Peter kept his head down and said good morning from under his bowler and made sure to keep walking so she was left with her hand in the air and her voice trailing, 'Ahhh Peterrrr ...' after him.

'Morning to you too, Mister Hooley,' she snapped to the milk bottles and wondered again what an old man like him was doing with such a young wife, and decided he must have money. She saw Theo about to topple over the verandah railing into the wild daisy bushes below and she pointed to him to alert Lilly, who she considered a lax parent at the best of times. She hadn't seen the tears that stained Peter's face as he scurried down the street.

Peter was expected at the bank at 8.30 a.m. but instead he walked to the train station where he handed over 13 shillings and twopence for a first class ticket. Then he walked to the end of the platform, away from the café and the newsstand where he might bump into people he knew, and sat on the bench, pulled the bowler down over his head and waited for the morning train to Melbourne, which was due in at eleven. He had the carriage to himself and he sat in the corner, his head against the window, and for the three-and-a-half-hour journey he stared at the passing landscape. When he arrived at Spencer Street Station he walked to Little Bourke Street and booked a room for one night only at Gordon Place. As he threw his bag on the bed he realised what he had done and a moan escaped from deep within him. He sat at the desk and wrote a letter to Lilly begging her forgiveness and explaining where he was, what he was doing and, hardest of all, he explained that he didn't know if he would be returning. Then he wrote out a cheque and put it in with the letter. The letter would take three days to reach her.

In the morning he walked to Collins Street. Starting at the Spring Street intersection, he began the first of six consultations he would have in Collins Street over the coming week.

He saw Doctor Thistlebaum first, a man so doddery he could barely walk to the other side of his desk, let alone examine his patient. Nonetheless he was considered a specialist on the matter and with much murmuring and clearing of his throat he told Peter the same thing Doctor Appleby had said: 'Your problem, sir, is failure of the organs. The upside is you can expect a speedy death.'

'That's the upside?' said Peter.

'Oh yes, it won't be drawn out — it will be fast, so go home and put your things in order,' said Doctor Thistlebaum, and he looked at the door and Peter knew the consultation was over. He settled the outrageous bill with Doctor Thistlebaum's nurse and went on to the next expert, Doctor Fickett, who was slightly younger than Doctor Thistlebaum but three times as wide.

'Are you going to examine me?' asked Peter.

But Doctor Fickett didn't like to get out of his very comfortable chair unnecessarily and to that end he had ensured it was a good swiveller. He said, 'You're here for an opinion, aren't you?' And he pointed Peter to the chair on the other side of the desk.

'Yes,' said Peter.

'Well, sit down then, I don't need to examine you to give you my opinion on the matter. I imagine you've seen Thistlebaum, he's the expert, and if he's confirmed your diagnosis I'd be mad to suggest it was something else.'

'Well, yes,' said Peter, though he wasn't sure at all.

'Well, in my opinion it's hereditary.'

'Hereditary?' asked Peter.

'Absolutely, we see it in families all the time. What did your father die of?'

'I don't actually know,' said Peter.

'Exactly,' said Doctor Fickett, bored with having to explain medical facts to his patients. 'I don't doubt for a second it was the same ailment that you, sir, now suffer from.' And he looked at the door to indicate it was time for Peter to settle his bill with the nurse sitting starched and straight in her crisp white dress and cap behind the counter outside.

Peter saw Doctor Bigsby next and then Doctor Whitehall and Doctor Simpson, who all said they confirmed Doctor Thistlebaum's opinion before they even knew what Doctor Thistlebaum's opinion was.

In addition — and this advice they each gave freely for the good of mankind — he shouldn't waste his money by seeing Doctor Le Sueur. Well, he'd have to be a foreigner with a name like that and he was a bit of a scallywag, wet behind the ears, a bit too willing to go where no respectable specialist should go. Well, what could you expect from these European types with their new ideas that have no basis in medical fact? No, they told him, don't waste what little time you have left with the likes of Doctor Le Sueur.

As it happened Peter had made an appointment to see Doctor Le Sueur, who had his room in Little Collins Street, not Collins Street proper. Little Collins Street was small and dark, whereas

Collins Street was a wide and regal passageway to Spring Street, where the grand home of federal politics sat. Collins Street was carriages and the tramway and contented women in pale skirts and large hats with arms full of shopping parcels and bellies full of Devonshire tea. Little Collins Street was bustling and shoving and pushing, it was spilled barrels and rubbish brushed up against the paths. Paul walked straight to Doctor Le Sueur's rooms from Doctor Simpson so he could cancel the appointment without any delay. He got to the building, which sat next door to the Hunt Hotel. The hotel spilled drunken men and whooping and the stench of spilt beer out into the street. Peter walked back and forward for half an hour tossing up between saving his money, which Lilly would need if he was gone, and thinking that one last opinion couldn't hurt. In the end he decided to sleep on it and in the morning he realised it would be rude to cancel at this late stage and so he went to get the opinion of this doctor who was in all likelihood a quack. He walked into the foyer of the doctor's building and the board said *Doctor Le Sueur — Second Floor*. He took the elevator and walked down the narrow dark corridor until he found the glass panelled door with *Dr Le Sueur M* in large black lettering.

'Your D is missing,' said Peter as he walked through the door. He was expecting to see a nurse and a waiting room but the door led straight into the consulting room, and the man he presumed was Doctor Le Sueur sitting inside it. Peter thought he looked more like a farmer than a doctor: he had a ruddy outdoors complexion with boyish freckles and pale blue eyes. Perhaps he wasn't even a properly trained doctor. Perhaps he was a herbalist or a homeopath or a veterinarian.

'The D is only missing on the door, I assure you I am indeed a medical doctor. Now, now don't sit down. I want to examine you before I say anything,' said Doctor Le Sueur and pointed to his examination gurney that had seen better days. Peter took off his jacket and his shoes and lay down. Doctor Le Sueur tied an operating mask over his mouth and nose, then he took his stethoscope from where it hung on the wall and listened to Peter's chest for a long time, getting him to sit up and lie back down again, now sit up, now cough lightly, now cough hard, which threw Peter into a fit of uncontrolled coughing and made Doctor Le Sueur stand well back and look at Peter as if that was exactly what he was looking for and now he knew all he needed to know to give his diagnosis. Only when Peter had completely finished coughing did Doctor Le Sueur remove his mask and motion for Peter to sit at the desk.

Peter felt ill in his stomach. He shouldn't because he already knew what the problem was, there weren't going to be any surprises, he'd seen enough doctors now to know the original diagnosis from Doctor Appleby was spot on.

'It's not good; I can't pretend it is, so I won't. No, it's not good,' said Doctor Le Sueur and as soon as he said that Peter relaxed.

'Ridiculous,' he said, 'that hearing that should make me feel better.'

'Well, sir, we feel better when we know what we are dealing with. It's the unknown that scares the hell out of a man.' He stood up and went to the corner of the room where a filing cabinet stood next to a table with a washbasin and jug. The doctor poured water into the basin, washed his hands, dried them and then fossicked in the filing cabinet.

'Ahhh,' he said finally and pulled several pieces of crumpled paper from the back of the cabinet. He then proceeded to try to smooth out the paper with the flat of his hand on his desk. After several attempts he gave up and the paper stayed crumpled.

'See here,' Doctor Le Sueur said, jabbing his finger at the paper. 'Oh, this is so terribly exciting, see this scientist here, Robert Koch, he injected rabbits with the — well, in layman's terms with the tuberculosis germ — and he found it's contagious, terribly contagious. Do you have any family, Mister Hooley? Well, if you do, for their sakes stay away from them. But it's not all bad news because this other doctor, Doctor Trudeau — and you won't hear this anywhere else, Mister Hooley, and you may well get advice saying this is utter rubbish, because that's how the medical profession responds to new information, but let me tell you this — Doctor Trudeau had your complaint himself. His older brother Jim died of consumption and he then caught it himself but — this is the important part,' Doctor Le Sueur leant forward over his desk and looked clear and straight at Peter so that Peter felt like he was in the headmaster's study and shuffled a bit and sat up straight so the doctor would know he was giving him his full attention, 'this Doctor Trudeau cured himself.' And Doctor Le Sueur threw his hands in the air at the sheer miracle of it.

'But I've been told my situation is hopeless,' said Peter.

'Well, it might be,' said Doctor Le Sueur, leaning back in his chair. 'I'm not God so I can't tell you, but I can tell you that this Doctor Trudeau,' and he waved the papers in the air, 'cured himself with fresh milk — he took four big glasses a day — three healthy meals a day and as much exercise in fresh cold mountain air as he could manage, and by exercise I mean at least brisk walking.'

'Cold fresh air, exercise, milk and healthy meals — that's all?' asked Peter, expecting there to be some secret.

'That's how he did it.'

Peter thought about it. If he was going to die anyway, what was there to lose? 'Well, it's worth a try. I could go to Daylesford. Do you think that it's cold enough and high enough?'

'If you like, I expect if you took the waters as well as Doctor Trudeau's other recommendations that would be a very good thing. I certainly don't see how the waters could do any harm. But remember, Mister Hooley, you are very contagious — this is now a proven fact so there must be no contact with family members. If you follow Doctor Trudeau's advice you will be creating your own private sanatorium, Mister Hooley, if you have the means.'

Peter did have the means. He had been single for thirty years before he met Lilly, he'd had no one to spend his salary on until he met her and it was a decent salary. He thanked Doctor Le Sueur profusely and Doctor Le Sueur said, 'I won't shake your hand if it's all the same, as you are contagious, but I do wish you luck and do let me know how you manage. If you're successful in beating this I would be most interested in knowing.'

Peter walked to the motel in Little Bourke Street and got his briefcase and checked out. From there he walked to Georges in Collins Street, where he purchased a suitcase, a pair of trousers, a shirt, socks, undergarments, pyjamas, a dressing gown, a coat, and, most importantly, a woollen scarf. He chose the scarf he thought Lilly would have chosen, green with a red check running through it. Then he walked to Flinders Street where he took a coach to Trentham and then the train to Daylesford and a coach to Hepburn Springs. He walked into the Savioa Hotel and, pulling the scarf up over his mouth and nose as if he was cold and making sure to stand well back from Missus Gervasoni, he signed for a room.

'I need the room indefinitely with all meals delivered to my door with a knock — that's all, just a knock. I won't bother anyone to bring the food in or lay it out and I'll light my fire myself, thank you, if you just leave me kindling and wood each day.'

'But our lovely dining room is just ...' said Missus Gervasoni.

'No, I won't be attending the dining room at all — you can take that for a fact but I would like to sit out on the front verandah each day to breathe the air, but I don't want to be disturbed.' And so Missus Gervasoni told her husband Angelo that they had a very reclusive guest who was sure to be someone famous or at least important and so they must follow his instructions exactly and make sure to bring up a bottle of their wine from the cellar for each meal and to make sure he had plenty of wood for the fire because he obviously was from a warm climate — maybe Cairns or Darwin — because he felt the cold so badly he was using a scarf in this warm weather.

The room was pleasant, the fire was lit and through the window Peter looked out at the dense bushland behind the hotel where lazy kangaroos grazed. He wished Theo was there to see the kangaroos. He felt a pain in his chest and the pain started the coughing. Peter bent over until it stopped, then he put his few clothes in the drawers and pulled back the rose-patterned cover on the bed and lay down and stared at the timber ceiling. He wondered if this room was the room he would die in, and that the ceiling would be the last image to fill his eyes, or whether Doctor Trudeau's treatment would work. It seemed too simple.

As agreed, the Gervasonis left a meal outside his door with just a knock, and when he heard the footsteps retreat down the hall Peter collected his food and tried not to think about the pain in his chest that was not the consumption but the spaces that were usually filled by Lilly and Theo.

When he woke in the morning it took him a moment to remember where he was and why. Then it all came back to him so he got out of bed and started his regime. He wanted to return to Theo and Lilly and the only way he could do that was to get well. He went for a long walk, down the main street, around into the mineral water reserve, down to the sulphur spring and back to the hotel. When he got back breakfast was waiting for him. Fat bull-boar sausages and scrambled eggs and, as ordered, a large glass of milk. He ate, washed and went for another long walk. He only allowed himself to rest for two hours in the afternoon when he sat out on the verandah and wrote long letters to Lilly which he dared not post in case he contaminated the paper. He asked Missus Gervasoni for old milk bottles and collected mineral waters from the natural springs every day and drank them down even though they smelt like rotten eggs, and he sucked the fresh air into his damaged lungs. When winter came he purchased another coat and another woollen scarf and gloves and still walked and when it snowed and he really couldn't walk he sat rugged up on the verandah breathing in the still purity of the air. He had meals of freshly made macaroni from Lucini's over the road with Angelo's sauces and fat sausages smothered in rich gravy with mash and osso buco and he learnt the names of the different types of macaroni and every day he thought of his Lilly and Theo and convinced himself that he was doing the right thing — Doctor Le Sueur had told him to stay away and stay away he must. He wasn't out of the woods. Doctor Le Sueur had told him he would most likely get worse before he got better.

One day, about eighteen months after Peter had walked out the front gate, Lilly received a letter that made her cry. She sobbed loud retching sobs and Theo ran over to her and put his head on her shoulder. He was surprised when she smiled at him through her tears and said, 'It's all right, Theo, these are happy tears,' and then wiped her face on her apron and sat at the table and scrawled out her own letter and she and Theo together put it in the letter-box for the postman to collect that afternoon.

At four o'clock Theo waited for his father on the third step from the bottom as he always did, wearing his coat and a scarf because it was September and cold and his mother brought him a bacon and cheese sandwich and warm milk. The next afternoon she brought him lemon delicious pudding and the afternoon after that she brought him golden syrup dumplings with custard, and anything Theo didn't eat she ate for him — one way or another she would fatten the boy up and make him healthy and strong.

On the fifth afternoon as Theo sat on the third step from the bottom, he hadn't touched the cinnamon scroll Lilly had made. Lilly came and sat with him, bringing a rug for their knees.

'I'll finish that off for you, shall I?' she said and he passed her the windmill tray with the cake and the empty glass white in patches from the milk he had drunk.

'I should stop waiting for him, shouldn't I?' Theo asked. After all, he was older now and he knew that sometimes you just had to accept the way things were.

'Oh no,' said Lilly, 'never stop waiting for what you truly want.'

Lilly was wearing her dress covered in red rosebuds; she washed it each night and hung it to dry by the fire and put it on again the next day. About a year ago she had let out the seams, and then again six months ago. Now the dress stretched uncomfortably over her middle and her breasts, pulling hard at the seams, but she couldn't bear to throw it out. She wore a thick woollen cardigan over the light summery dress. Theo studied the rosebuds, he touched them one after the other with his finger. It had been his father's favourite dress, he knew that because his dad had said, 'She's my rosebud. Your mum agreed to marry an old codger like me when she was nought but a sweet young rosebud.'

Theo didn't know why he looked up at that moment but he did and there he was, standing at the gate.

And that was how Theo learnt the art of being quiet and waiting.

Eight

The Hole

Saturday, 11 November 1905, when the neighbours
are cantankerous and the sun bears down turning
men's brains to mush.

Young Arthur's mother and father stood at their kitchen window, their brows furrowed, their eyes wide and their mouths scrunched as though they had eaten a fruit salad made out of lemons. They looked through the spaces in their side fence where palings had once been; they could see everything going on in their neighbour's yard whether they wanted to or not.

'Let him be. He's just lost his wife, for goodness sake,' said Jack Puce.

'Wife or no wife, he can't be taking our fence apart,' said Daphne Puce.

Egged on by his wife, Jack leaned out the window and called, 'What are you doing to the fence, Paul?'

Paul ignored him so Jack looked back at his wife and shrugged his shoulders. He'd tried, hadn't he?

Paul had scavenged discarded planks of wood and old pickets from where they had hidden, happy and undisturbed for years

85

against the corner of the garden shed. When he realised the old timber wasn't enough to do the job, he had viciously pulled the palings from the fence, creating gaping holes between his and the Puce's back gardens. On and on he pulled paling after paling from the fence and Daphne said to Jack, 'Well, when are you going to do something? The entire fence will be gone soon and then what?'

But Jack wasn't keen on disturbing Mister Cottingham even when Mister Cottingham wasn't grieving his wife. The man had a way of seeing right through you when you were trying to convince him that the fence boundary was three feet out in his favour when really it was in yours. To disturb him when grief and the searing sun had got into his brain was asking for trouble Jack couldn't be bothered with, so he told Daphne he'd have a word. And he did have a word. He said hello to Paul on his way to the pub. When Jack came home from the pub, feeling much better about life after four pots too many, his improved optimism was shot to pieces by the sounds of hammering ricocheting through his head and their house. The rhythmic thumping made the walls shudder as if the house was wrenching itself up from its foundations, and the effect made Jack swear he was done with drinking. The hammering went on well into the night. Jack and Daphne turned and moaned in their beds and Daphne said, 'For Godsakes, Jack, do something to shut him up,' and Jack snapped, 'Just what do you expect me to do, Missus Puce? You tell me and I'll do it pronto.'

Paul's mind was filled with such a vicious tornado and his soul was so broken into dust that he wasn't able to think about anything other than hammering. So on and on he went, nailing plank after plank over the windows and then the door of her room. He would entomb her bed, her chaise lounge, her pictures and books, her linen, her summer skirts and bodices. He would seal up the nights they had shared together in that room, wrapped in each other's arms, keeping each other's souls safe from the rest of the world. He would seal it all up forever. He couldn't bear to look at it and he couldn't bear to have anyone else gaze at the site of their intimacy. He drove each nail through the wood cruelly. He banged and thumped and crashed about.

Beth tried to sleep with a pillow over her head.

Edie couldn't stand the noise any longer and clambered out of bed and stood a little way away, out of range of the flying splinters of wood, and watched her father in his frenzy. Finally he hit his thumb with the hammer.

'It was bound to happen,' she said.

Paul shook his finger in the air and then kept on hammering. The pain seared through him but it was an insignificant pain compared to the pain in his soul. He wasn't even aware of Edie standing there and he hadn't heard her speak.

'Father,' Edie said. 'Papa!' she cried.

He turned then and saw Edie shivering in her nightgown and bare feet even though it wasn't cold. She looked like a lost little girl, hungry and cold, brought into the court to be admitted to the orphanage. For a moment he started to drop the hammer and go to her. *She has no mother*, he thought, and the grief consumed him again.

He bent and picked up the next nail. A big dirty one that he'd yanked out of the wall of the garden shed. It was a permanent sort of nail, it was nasty and strong and convincing and once he got it in, it wouldn't be easy to yank out again. He needed it for the door, it would stop people entering this sacred place. He held it up to the light so Edie could see it.

But she looked unimpressed.

'This'll do the job,' he said.

'Papa, I've been standing here hollering, I called umpteen times but you've been making such a racket. Papa, are you listening to me?'

He wasn't listening. He couldn't hear her words as he banged the nail into position. He stood back and looked at the door.

That would do it.

Job done.

'Papa, I need some sleep,' she pleaded. '*Are* you going to bed now?'

He didn't know what he might do next, he might go to bed — he might not. How could he know what he wanted?

He saw Edie was frightened. It was he who had frightened her and this brought him back to himself.

'Oh, no, no, no,' he said, and he went over to her and wrapped her in his arms.

'I've just lost my mother and it looked like I'd lost my father as well,' she said. *And it's all the baby's fault,* she thought.

Nine

The Lake

Wednesday, 13 December, when secrets are kept hidden.

If you went down to Fairy Land and stayed very still, you might see a platypus. Fairy Land is at Lake Wendouree and Lake Wendouree is a marsh that humans with shovels turned into a lake, but it refuses to cooperate. In blistering summers, it regularly drains itself when people need its cool wetness the most. The wealthy rowers who live in the houses around the lake curse and fuss when it dries up because they can't hold their regattas, and a dried-out lake will devalue their properties. The poor miners who live a good mile's walk away laugh because the lake's cratered dusty bed has become an eyesore that the wealthy are forced to look at — and that has to be a good joke on them. But the town is proud of the lake they created from a mosquito-ridden swamp. When it has water, musk ducks bicker in its shallows and swans chase children for their picnic lunches — or the children terrorise the swans back into the water. On Saturday and Sunday afternoons the town's population comes out to walk around the lake whether it is dry or full. They walk with umbrellas to protect them from the sun's

89

harsh glare when it is warm and with umbrellas to protect them from the icy wind and rain when it is chilly.

The lake was full when Edie was walking the baby around it in a pram, though the town's engineers were saying the way the weather was going it would be dry by March. At first the baby had been a quiet peaceful soul and Edie wouldn't even have known it was in the house if it hadn't killed her mother. But now, at five weeks old, Gracie fretted, whimpered and squirmed and she got worse as it got hotter. Nothing would console her. She knew the sun had evil intentions and she was frightened. Paul had said a walk in the pram might settle her and Edie had replied that she had things to do. Paul had raised his eyebrows knowing full well that Edie didn't have anything she had to do — which Edie thought was another issue in itself. She didn't have anything to do, no occupation and no Theo. Theo, who hadn't come around to ask her father, and for this she could only blame the baby. This baby had ruined everything.

'Edie, I must ask that you get Gracie out in the fresh air before it becomes too hot,' Paul persisted.

'Beth can do it,' said Edie. She could hear her father's demanding tone and was purposefully ignoring it. She didn't want anything to do with the baby if she could help it. If she had her way it would be where it belonged: in the orphanage. Beth was folding a pile of nappies on the kitchen table.

'Because Beth doesn't have enough to do already,' said Beth, holding out her hands.

'Edie, I'm asking you to do it. Beth has enough on her plate now there are nappies to wash and bottles to be boiled, not to mention her regular work.'

'I suppose I could drown it while I'm down there,' said Edie.

She saw Beth and Paul look at each other.

'Oh, I didn't mean it,' said Edie, and laughed a fake, empty laugh. But she did mean it. And now she was walking around the lake having to put up with people stopping to coo at the baby. *Oh, isn't she beautiful?* they said, pushing their heads into the pram. *Oh it's such a shame her moth—* *Oh, she's a mixed blessing, isn't she?* And they would stop short and pop their heads up like a jack-in-a-box and look at Edie, waiting for her to forgive their tactlessness.

Well, Edie wasn't giving out forgiveness for carelessness, not today, and she said goodbye to the baby cooers and said she must get on before it got too hot to be out, and deliberately pushed the pram close enough to brush their clothes and make them stand back.

Edie pushed the pram to the area of the lake called Fairy Land, where the platypus sometimes came out to play and where there were tall native grasses that could hide all sorts of sins. Edie looked in on the baby. It was grizzling and squirming. She looked up at the sun, which was working its way up into a fiery frenzy that would send everyone inside in the afternoon. The baby looked at Edie and Edie picked it up and she stepped through the tall marsh grasses towards the murky deeper water, not minding the mud getting all over her boots and her dress. She held the baby out over the water.

'It's so easy,' she said to the baby, 'just to be done with you here. After all, you are a murderer, and it's a fitting punishment for your crime.'

Beth thought if it was hot outside it must be fifty degrees hotter in the kitchen with the wood-burning stove. There was no choice but to have the fire going, they had to have sterilised bottles for the baby and warm milk and bathwater and Beth didn't really mind doing anything if it was for Gracie. There was something about the baby that soothed Beth. When she held Gracie in her arms the world seemed a better place; when she sang to her, the baby seemed to sing along in sweet tuneful whispers. And when Beth held Gracie close to her chest, her heart was open.

So Beth couldn't understand why Edie seemed so uninterested in Gracie. Sometimes Beth even thought Edie seemed to hate the baby, like this morning when she said she could drown it. Beth thought Paul looked like he was going to have a heart attack when Edie said that, as though he thought Edie might really do it. She never expected such venom from Edie, who was normally so kind and guileless. Beth was making chamomile tea for Gracie, which she would feed her in tiny teaspoons like an injured bird so that she didn't choke. In the evenings when it had cooled a bit Beth would take her in the pram all the way down to Eddy Street, where she would rock the pram back and forward over the bumpy road while she chatted to her fella Colin. And at 8 p.m. Colin would walk them both back home to Webster Street and she would hand Gracie over to Paul, who would pace up and down the hallway with the baby until an exhausted Gracie finally fell asleep.

She boiled the water and poured it over the dried chamomile buds. She wanted it ready and cooled for when Edie brought Gracie back from their walk. Beth set the bowl of hot brewing tea aside and placed a doily over it. She had sewn tiny coloured beads around the edges of the doily to weigh it down so flies wouldn't find their way under it. Later she would strain the tea from the buds. Beth's mind played Edie's words over and over in her mind and each time she became surer that Edie wasn't joking. 'Surely she was joking,' Beth said out loud. She thought about it again. Edie could be a very determined person when she got something into her mind.

'Has she come back yet?' Paul stood in the kitchen doorway. Beth looked at him and their minds collided on the same path.

'Come on,' said Paul, 'just leave whatever you're doing. Let's hurry.'

Beth and Paul ran up Webster Street and crossed over Wendouree Parade to the lake. There was a path that ran around the circumference of the lake but they didn't know which way to go.

'We'll split up — you go that way,' said Paul, pointing to the left.

Beth nodded and ran, her eyes scanning everywhere, stopping anyone she knew to ask if they had seen Edie, which they hadn't, or they might have but wasn't that at least an hour and a half ago? Beth's mind spun furiously, losing more control with each spin. She saw all the possibilities and all of them were awful and becoming worse as she walked further and further and still couldn't find Edie. Half an hour later she saw Paul walking towards her and she held out her hands full of nothing and he shook his head.

If something had happened to Gracie or Edie, Paul knew it would be his own fault. He'd been so consumed with his grief he hadn't really considered Edie's loss at all. He hadn't noticed, not until now, when it all came flooding back to him. It was always Beth who bathed the baby, Beth who fed her, Beth who changed her nappies and took her out in the cooler evening air. And it was he who rocked Gracie to sleep each night and he who cooed lullabies to her. Edie never had anything to do with Gracie if she could possibly help it. Paul remembered the times he had seen Edie looking at Gracie as though she was the Devil's baby. They were just fleeting looks, so afterwards Paul would think he had imagined it.

Paul was puffed from the run from the house to the lake. It was only a short distance, just four or five houses, but he hadn't been able to breathe properly since Lucy died, the air just wouldn't come to his lungs. He had walked furiously around the lake, trying to gasp in the air to fuel his pace; he had gone halfway around the lake when he saw Beth walking towards him, her arms held out. She hadn't found Edie either. He stopped and they both stood still. He didn't know what to do next. Around them were a few picnickers, mothers with their children; it was a Wednesday and the men were at work. Children were chasing swans, and some of the birds came and hid behind him to escape the bullies. He looked at the houses that gazed down on the lake, and then towards the area of tall grass and caught a glimpse of a woman's straw hat. Edie's hat. He ran towards it, pushing his way through the marshy grasses, spraying brown mud over his trousers, shirt and vest until he came to a standstill next to Edie.

He stood in silence. He knew he needed to be careful or they might all drown. Beth stood on the other side of Edie and Paul put his finger to his lips and Beth nodded.

Edie was holding the baby in her arms but Paul couldn't see if Gracie was okay because she was covered with a cotton sheet. Edie looked at him but didn't say anything. Her face was unreadable and he didn't know if Gracie was alive or drowned. He hoped the cotton sheet was to protect her from the sun. But the baby was quiet, and that was a worry.

'Ssshhh,' Edie said finally. 'If you look hard you can see a platypus. There is a yabby he's been trying to catch. It comes out first and then he comes after it. Ssshhh.'

The only thing Paul wanted to see was Gracie alive and well. Then Edie pointed at a yabby scurrying for its life through the water and after it the hungry platypus, an odd creature from another world, gliding effortlessly through the water like a strange ugly bird. The animal's grace filled them all and they stood in awe. Too soon the platypus captured its prey and disappeared.

They let the moment wash away slowly and carefully and embedded it in their memories. What they would remember was not the platypus but the mystery of another world touching theirs.

Finally Edie turned and walked out of Fairy Land. Paul and Beth followed and at last Paul asked, 'Is she okay? Gracie, is she okay? Are you okay?'

'Of course,' said Edie and pulled back the sheet to reveal the sleeping baby.

Then she looked up at him and said, 'She smiled at me, Papa, and everything changed.'

'I know,' said Paul. 'She does that.'

Ten

The Doctor

If he has to give bad news it might as well
be with a nice piece of orange cake.

Anyone who has had a baby knows the slightest change of wind is enough to wake it, and when a baby wakes its first instinct is to bellow and let the world know it has been rudely woken. The moment Edie placed Gracie in her crib she woke, looked crossly at the three faces staring down at her, noted their concerned looks and began whimpering, which then built momentum into wailing. Paul, Edie and Beth stood over her like the three wise men.

'It's the heat,' announced Edie, as though she and Gracie had discussed the matter, and she picked the baby up and muttered soothing *there-there-theres* to her. She had carried Gracie back home from the lake, leaving Beth to push the empty pram. Every now and then she had looked at Paul and said, 'She's just so beautiful,' and Paul thanked Lucy that their eldest girl had come to her senses.

'We'll shut her in the bathroom,' said Beth. 'That's what my sister does with her bub. She says it's the coolest room in the house.'

'Perhaps we should try the bathroom,' Paul said. So they laid Gracie on a towel on the bathroom tiles to see if that would turn her off. But still her flesh turned prickly and spotty. Rashes formed in the trapped moisture that gathered in the folds of her baby skin as the hot sun stole its way through the bathroom window to suck at Gracie's life.

'It's not working,' Paul said and wished again that Lucy were here. She would know what to do with a baby in the heat. 'It's cool in my study. I can take her in there and wait for Doctor Appleby's visit.'

'Oh, with the walk around the lake this morning I completely forgot he was coming,' said Edie.

'Well, he'll have to make do with drop scones today,' said Beth.

'If you're sure, Papa. I have some writing to do,' said Edie, patting her pocket.

'It's never a problem to have you, Gracie, is it?' he said. As he took the baby he felt Edie's reluctance to give her up.

Paul's study was a small room that replicated his office at work. He had an oak desk inlaid with a leather writing area, his swivel chair, his bookcases and a window that provided him with a view of the front gate so he could see who was coming and going. All that was missing was his pipe, which he had never smoked at home because Lucy hated the clouds of reeking smoke that wandered through the house and settled into the corners of the rooms. Paul sat at his desk, Gracie squirming in his arms, and remembered that Edie liked to be laid across an arm when she had colic. So he laid Gracie across his knee. Even at nearly six weeks Gracie was so small she lay easily on his lap. She made weak mewing noises that sounded like the pain in his chest.

'Cry for her, my darling,' Paul whispered. 'Cry for her all you like, for I certainly do.' And he put one hand against Gracie's tiny chest, covering it entirely, and the other hand against his own aching chest, creating a circuit linking their hearts and their loss.

'There will never be anything of her,' said Doctor John Appleby as he stood in the doorway ten minutes later with his cup and saucer in one hand and his bag in the other.

The doctor had come in through the back door, straight into the kitchen so he could grab a cup of tea and a slice of cake or a biscuit from Beth.

'What have you baked for me this morning, Beth?' he asked, and she scowled like she always did. She needed to know her place, that girl, she needed to know that she served not only Mister Cotting-ham but Mister Cottingham's guests if they so desired it, and she could wipe that forced smile off her insolent face too, he thought.

'How do you think the bub is doing, Doctor?' she asked, pass-ing him a plate of drop scones smothered in jam and snowy peaks of cream. He was a bit disappointed, he couldn't help it, he really liked her orange cake best and a piece of that was just what he needed this morning.

'We've had a busy morning,' said Beth, thinking of their anx-ious flight to the lake. 'I didn't have time to make a cake. So what about baby Gracie, what do you think?'

'Ah well, that's a conversation I need to have with your employer,' said Doctor Appleby and off he trundled up the hall-way, his teacup rattling on its saucer and spilling tea onto the drop scone that balanced on the edge, a plate of four more drop scones on a plate in the other hand, his satchel hanging from his arm. Beth took the kettle off the stove — they were both steaming.

Every Wednesday afternoon Doctor John Appleby made time to come by the Cottingham home to check the baby. Really, he just wanted to make sure she was still breathing. There was little he could do, but he hoped his visits gave Cottingham and his daughter some comfort, and Beth's cooking was a nice little fringe benefit. He stood in the doorway to Paul's study. Paul was sitting to the side of the desk looking over books on his shelf. John could see the baby lying restlessly on Paul's lap; Paul had one hand on her chest to stop her falling off.

'She's always going to be fragile; it will be touch and go for many months to come. I don't know if she's going to make it.' He felt Paul needed to know, bluntly, so there could be no confusion about what he was in for. One death on top of another was not going to be easy for him. John knew the best thing was to prepare him.

'I didn't see you come in, John,' said Paul, and John saw the aching etched in the other man's face.

'You can breathe a sigh of relief if she manages to reach the age of say … hmm … seven years,' he added, feeling maybe he had been too harsh after all and perhaps he should offer a shred of hope. He walked over and put the cup and saucer on Paul's oak desk and it balanced uneasily where the leather met the wood. He put his bag on the floor, unclipped it and pulled out his stethoscope and put it against the baby's back. 'Hmmmm,' he said noncommittally, then added, 'Babies dehydrate quickly and get brain sickness, especially in this merciless heat,' and he flipped Gracie over while she was still on Paul's lap. He listened to her chest and put his hand against her head. 'Is she lifting her head?'

Paul nodded no.

'Is she holding her own weight at all?' and again Paul nodded no. This was a concern.

'Has she lifted her head at all?

'I told you already John, no, she's so tiny. I don't remember Edie at this age. Maybe it's too soon for head-lifting.'

He could hear the panic in Paul's voice and said calmly and quietly, 'Well Paul, it could be just that she's small and she was early. But I've seen this before in the early ones.'

'Come on, John, spit it out,' said Paul.

'There's nothing to spit out — not at this stage. We just need to wait and see, but she could be damaged from the early birth.'

'You're wrong,' said Paul emphatically. 'She's perfect.'

'I hope so, Paul, I really do.' John left his cup and saucer on the desk, picked up his bag, put his stethoscope in it and walked to the doorway.

Doctor John Appleby turned to leave and as he always did he stopped and carefully put his bag on the ground as if he had just thought of something very important. He took out his handkerchief and wiped the sweat from his brow. By God it was hot this year. He rested his hand against the door jamb to harness its strength and said, as though he had only just thought of it and it was the very first time he had ever made any comment on the subject, even though he said the same thing every week and Paul had become so accustomed to the words that he mouthed them in unison with him:

'Don't you think it's time, Paul, to take the ugly timber boards off her mother's room?' He tried to say it in his kindest voice, knowing he was picking at an open wound.

Paul snapped, 'No John, I do not!' As he always did.

So John shrugged his shoulders, as he always did, because what else was there to do?

The sun fuelled itself on Paul's anguish and aching and by afternoon it was blistering the tar and scorching the trees, incinerating the leaves to dust and showing no mercy to the gasping earth or the people who tried to live on it. It dried up the mines and shrivelled their walls, making them brittle and chalky. Choked dry by the sun, the mines no longer breathed their cold air into the town in the afternoon. At four o'clock the men emerged coughing mine dust from their lungs, their eyes red and stinging with grit and their clothes drenched in sweat.

Paul had to keep the sun out. It sucked the breath out of his lungs, and if the heat got into the house any more it would suffocate him and kill the baby. He felt that every breath he took was a breath stolen from Lucy, a breath denied to her. He couldn't lose Gracie as well, no matter what the doctor said. He couldn't lose the last gift Lucy had given him and something had to be done. The doctor was right, the heat could kill a tiny infant and Gracie even more so because she was weak and ill. But Paul couldn't say any of this to John. Paul looked away from the doctor and stared out the window at the hazy air.

John Appleby sighed. The man was losing his brain. His wife dying and a sick child was too much for him. Such a shame in a fellow who had once been so smart and quick.

'Have you ever been to Coober Pedy, John?' asked Paul, looking back at him.

'No, can't say that I have.' Yes, the man was losing it. If that baby survived, which it wouldn't, it was likely to be an orphan.

'No, neither have I,' said Paul.

John sighed, picked up his leather bag, shut his concerns safe inside, secured the clip and set off.

Paul watched from the window as the doctor walked down to the front fence, his bag swinging in one hand, the other hand wiping the sweat from his neck with his handkerchief.

When the doctor had reached the letterbox and headed off down the street, Paul dipped his nib into the ink and wrote:

I am advertising for four miners and I am willing to pay good wages.

He leant back and looked at what he had written. That would do it. That would get him workers straight off. He had never come across a miner who would take tributes if he could take wages. He kissed Gracie's soft downy head and scratched out what he had written and started again.

Wanted.
Four Miners.
Immediate start.
Full day's pay — no tributes.
Monday 18th, 7 a.m. Cottingham Residence, Webster Street.

Then he crossed out the four and wrote eight. Tomorrow he would get his clerk Jensen to pick it up, copy it and run over to *The Star* and *The Courier*.

Eleven

The Miners

18 December 1905, when it is agreed that
Mister Cottingham has lost his marbles.

They wouldn't come down the pathway even though he'd gone out and beckoned to them from the front verandah. They just shook their heads and then one of them called out that they were right to wait where they were. Paul, Beth and Edie stood watching them from the study window, Gracie in Paul's arms. There were about twenty despondent men standing in groups of three or four, sharing smokes and occasionally kicking at the dirt. Men with uneven home haircuts, whose shoulders hunched and limbs hung gloomily. They were men whose egos were battered by never having enough to stand tall.

'That one's my brother-in-law,' said Beth.

'Which one?' asked Paul.

'Oh, you'll know him,' said Beth, 'he'll be the noisy one.'

'They've been out there since five. What do you need with them?' asked Edie, looking at the clock. It was now seven.

'I have a renovation in mind, but I want to keep it a surprise.'

'Well, don't you want builders — not miners?' asked Edie.

'No, I need miners — you'll see.'

He took his cup of tea in one hand, and with Gracie still nest-
ling on his other arm, quietly crying as she always did now, he
walked down to the front fence, settled his cup of tea on top
of the letterbox, gently jostled Gracie into a better position and
interviewed the men in his slippers and housecoat right there on
the street.

'Who has children?' he asked. 'No, no, don't all answer at once,
put up your hand if you're a father.' The younger men smiled —
he was going to send the old fellas home for sure and they would
be taken on.

'Okay, those of you that aren't fathers can go,' he said, and the
younger ones grumbled as they wandered off. Paul counted how
many were left. Ten. He had halved the number so that was a
start, but he really only needed eight strong men. He looked at
the men before him: sad, bedraggled-looking humans. He wondered what their kids looked like, whether they were skinny and
underfed, whether their shoes were patched with wads of paper
and leather straps.

'I'll take all of you,' he said. He couldn't bear to send any who
were fathers away. They were older-looking miners, the ones
with several children and a wife to support; men with dirt in their
pores that would never wash out, men with clothes that were
patches on patches.

'Two sovereigns a week for six days; you don't work Sunday
because I am sure like me you will all be in church.' The men
chuckled uncomfortably and Paul continued, 'Plus overtime. All
up that's got to be at least double what you'd hoped for, and a darn
lot more than the one sovereign a week you'd have got before
tributes were brought in.'

On hearing this good news the men seemed to grow taller.

'But don't go thinking you can drag that two sovereigns out for the next six months. I want this job finished in two weeks, one if you can, even if you have to work around the clock in shifts,' he said.

'Yes, judge,' they chorused, as though they were at school.

'I'm not a judge, not yet — sir is fine,' he said. 'I hope to God that the good wages I'm going to pay you goes home to your families and not to the Bunch of Grapes.'

'Yes, judge,' they murmured, wondering how much they could get away with spending at the Bunch of Grapes without sending their wives flying off the handle. The wives would hear how much they were getting paid; there was no hiding anything in this town.

'You have to start immediately, as in right now,' Paul said knowing full well they were ready to do so and had nothing else to do.

'We're on it, judge,' Laidlaw said in his booming voice, and the others all put in, 'Yes, judge — right on it.'

'What's your name?' he asked the loud one.

'Laidlaw, sir,'

'Laidlaw, ah yes, our Beth's brother-in-law. Well, you seem to have the loudest voice, you're now the foreman. You get an extra sovereign a week.'

The others all wished they had had the balls Laidlaw had and had spoken the loudest.

'But I won't stand for any bullying. Any bullies will get their marching orders on the spot. Well — get going. I think you'll find all the tools you need in the garden shed. Anything else — well, let me know what you need and I'll get it. I'll explain to Laidlaw what I want done and then he can direct you as he sees fit.'

The men went to the garden shed and began pulling out tools while Laidlaw stayed behind to find out what the judge wanted that was so special he was willing to pay double rates. Paul pulled an old newspaper article out of his dressing gown pocket to show Laidlaw and Laidlaw stepped back, his eyes wide, considered the enormity of what the judge had just shown him, and then nodded his head.

'It's like bloody Noah building the ark,' said Laidlaw to the other men after he had explained Cottingham's plan, "cept the other way round.'

'Do ya reckon he's gone mad on account of his grief?' asked Paddy.

'What's it matter to us? As long as we get paid,' said Barrett, 'and right on bloody Christmas.'

Paul gave Gracie to Edie. He hadn't said a word about the doctor's concerns about Gracie having come so early. He would just make sure that the child had everything she needed; he would give her the best chance possible. He dressed for the office, downed a cup of tea and a slice of toast and butter, grabbed his briefcase and umbrella and went back outside. Laidlaw told him he had sent Simpson off for more tools.

'Well, I should have given you some money to purchase them.'

'No need, judge,' said Laidlaw, 'some of the fellas have the tools at home already. I'll let you know if I need to order something special and when we are going to need those supplies I mentioned.'

The rest of the men had started pulling palings off the bottom of the house.

Paul stood and watched.

Edie came out into the garden, Beth following close behind. 'Papa, what's going on? It sounds like Armageddon.'

Paul watched the men, but his uneasiness grew and his chest constricted, God's giant hand was clasping tighter and tighter, squeezing the breath out of him. He gasped at the air. Something was wrong but he couldn't think what. He tapped the tip of his umbrella against his head and then jabbed it into the ground. This was his plan, his idea, and … his Taj Mahal. This was his last love letter to Lucy. It had to be made with his love.

'Edie, ring the office and tell them I won't be in for the next week or so.'

Paul threw off his jacket and handed it to Beth. 'Well, go on, Edie, they can do without me for a week or so.' And with that Paul picked up a crowbar and stepped in with the men and wrenched at the palings.

An hour later Paul had removed his vest and shirt and stripped down to his singlet and braces like the rest of the men. He looked about him. Mounds of dark brown earth were quickly growing into small hills. Bluestone blocks and timber palings were being loosed from the bottom of the house and scattered in piles about the garden.

'Papa, what are you doing, besides giving us all a headache?' Edie jostled Gracie in her arms.

He touched Gracie and left a muddy fingerprint on the white skin of her arm.

'Hmm,' was all he said, and as Edie stood and watched he walked off and jiggered at another block of bluestone with the crowbar.

Jack and Daphne Puce stood at their kitchen window in their pyjamas, Daphne's hair tied up in knots of fraying cotton cloth.

She looked at her husband and said, 'This is all your fault. You should've done something to stop this sooner.'

On Wednesday 20 December, the men are still hard at work.

The men muttered and swore and sometimes slapped each other on the back as they dug away under the house. Soft soil meant the job was a good lark and they nodded to each other at their luck landing the job and congratulated themselves on being sensible enough to respond to the advert in the paper; when they struck hard soil and stone they grumbled in each other's ears that they should have asked for more.

At ten-thirty Paul would put down whatever tool he had in his hand and invite the men in for morning tea, but they would look at their boots and Laidlaw always said, 'Nah judge, us blokes are right out here.' So Paul would go into the kitchen and Beth would have his favourite apple cake and tea waiting for him and then most days she would say, 'Well, when are you going to tell us what's going on?' Most days Paul would smile, lift the cake in the air and say, 'Best apple cake as always, Beth.' Then any leftovers he would take out to the men.

When Paul went inside for morning tea Barrett would turn to the others and say, 'I reckon Cottingham is mad or greedy. The old bugger is looking for gold under the bluestone stumps of his own family home.' And he would grind the stub of his cigarette into the dirt with his boot and light up his next.

'Nah, my missus says he's gone mad with grief for his wife,' said Johnno.

'I reckon we should all shut the fuck up,' said Laidlaw, drinking tea from his thermos lid. 'This is the best fucking work conditions we are ever likely to get.' And the men couldn't disagree.

All the men except Laidlaw whistled at Beth when she hung the nappies on the line, despite Paul's stern looks and reminders that each and every one of them was married, and despite Laidlaw reminding them that Beth was his sister-in-law. They tipped their hats when Edie walked outside but she hardly noticed, her mind was a scurry of worry for her father. Had the heat cooked him? Like the Swiss-Italians, would he suddenly collapse and die? She checked on him often and would stop him mid-digging and put her hand on his sweaty forehead, her face screwed up with anxiety.

'It's just good honest sweat, Edie,' he would say and bend to shovel more soil or yank more planks and bluestone.

She spent hours holding Gracie, who fell into her arms like she belonged nowhere else, and looked at the excavation happening in their yard and shook her head. Her father really had lost his marbles.

On Friday 22 December, it's getting awfully close to Christmas.

Paul told the men they wouldn't be working Christmas Day — nor Christmas Eve, given it was a Sunday and he never let them work on a Sunday. Edie handed them each a basket of fruit and Beth handed them each a fruit cake as a gift to take home to their families for Christmas lunch. Paul shook their hands and said he would see them 6 a.m. sharp on Boxing Day and gave them each an envelope with an extra two shillings and said, 'Buy your children and wives a treat.' The men thought of the Bunch of Grapes and saw Cottingham looking at them like he knew exactly what they were thinking and Laidlaw quickly said, 'We're off to the milliner's for ribbons, lads.'

On Tuesday 26 December, it's getting awfully close to 1906.

On the Tuesday at 6 a.m. they were back on the job. The underbelly of the house had become more than a rabbit hole; it stretched

out and in just a few days the space had become big enough for
Paddy, the smallest of the workers, to fit inside. Paul purchased
supporting beams which were delivered by lumbering Clydesdales that came right up to the end of the driveway and the men
dragged the beams from the cart under the house and the space
under there became wider and deeper and then two of them could
work under there, then four, then eight and finally all of them
could work under the house and so doors and timbers for archi-
traves, mantles and skirting boards were delivered and carried
under the house. The underbelly of the house took shape and
formed itself into passages and rooms and the men were convinced the old bugger was indeed mining for gold under his own
house but obviously had some stupid rich man's idea of what a
mine looked like.

As cartloads of earth were lugged away by the Clydesdales,
Paul began to notice that the air he sucked into his lungs stung
less. As rooms and passages grew he was able to breathe more easily, and he became more enthused.

'I want a spiral staircase,' he said, 'up to the house! I want a dining room, a sitting room and a hallway!'

That was when the men realised he wasn't digging for gold at
all, he had some other mad plan to build a house under a house.
They didn't care what deranged thing he asked for, as long as it
kept them in work.

More earth was lugged away.

'I want a doorway with a glass pane directly out onto the garden, so we can take her straight out to wander among her mother's grevilleas in the evening when it's cooler.'

The men rolled their eyes and patted their pockets full of
sovereigns.

'I want it to duplicate the house upstairs except for the kitchen,
as that is where the staircase is,' he said and he dragged Laidlaw,

who quickly threw off his boots, barefooted and muddy through the house to show him the layout and Laidlaw went down to tell the men they would be working through the night to change the walls they had already built. When the walls were built and Paul had approved them the men rendered them and then painted them with off white just like the walls upstairs.

When the walls were finished, timber flooring was laid, the electricals installed and then it was done — all in three weeks. It had taken longer than Paul had wanted as his plan kept growing, but now the result was exactly what he wished for.

On Monday 8 January the men said a sad goodbye
to their good luck.

Paul had created an underground house as his last gift to Lucy. A sanctuary away from the summer with its suffocating heat and sweat and bushfires, each wall built with Paul's longing and loss.

Paul looked at the miners standing around him, their faces filled with amazement at what they had created. As the enormity of what they had accomplished took root they started to congratulate themselves and Paul and shook everyone's hands till they nearly fell off.

Congratulations done, Paul needed Beth, and found her in the kitchen washing preserving bottles.

'Beth, you can look now,' he said.

She dropped her tea towel. 'Really?'

'Most assuredly,' he said, 'Come on,' and he took her outside into the garden and down the path they had cut that sloped down into the ground to the door of the underground house.

'What am I looking at?' she asked peering into blackness.

He pulled the cord and the electric lights flickered to life and he watched her face fill with wonder.

'Bloody hell,' she said. And then, 'I'm sorry, sir.'

He laughed and it didn't hurt his chest and he took her hand and led her down the steps and into a small entranceway, and then he took her through each of the rooms he had created.

'I want you to clean it,' he said. 'Give it the best clean you have ever given anything in your life — make it gleam. Let me know when you have finished.' He took her up the spiral staircase and opened the door they had built in at the top and she found herself looking at her own kitchen.

'And I thought you were just putting in a pantry,' she said.

'Now I'll wait while you clean downstairs for me.'

Paul paced in the garden, Gracie whimpering in his arms. The men sat on the grass enjoying the break and sharing smokes. Beth brought out a broom and mop for the floor and cloths for dusting and oil for the woodwork and a bucket of warm soapy water. She cleaned the underground house till it sparkled under the electric lights. She called Laidlaw when she needed the water changed and he brought her a fresh bucket, the soap suds bubbling over the top. An hour or so later Beth announced she had finished and Paul said, 'Just wait, not much longer.' So the men lit up new cigarettes and Beth got glasses of water for everyone and they waited in silence, awed by what Paul had created.

'Ah, right on time,' Paul said as horses pulled a cart piled with furniture up the drive. Edie came out at the sound of the horses; she expected they were delivering more building materials.

'Can I see what you've done to our house?' she asked.

'Not quite,' said Paul, passing Gracie to her.

Paul directed the men to carry the furniture into the underground house and showed them where each piece must go, directly under its mirror upstairs: a new bassinet, easy chairs, a bookshelf, a bed, a change table.

Paul walked through the rooms. Yes, it was perfect. Then he took Edie's hand, ignoring her wide eyes and stunned face.

'Follow me,' he said, and with Gracie in her arms led her through his underground house. Immediately the coolness of the earth enveloped them and he felt Edie shiver. It was hard to believe it was so hot out and so cool down here. Paul walked to the bedroom that had been built directly under Lucy's.

'Go on,' he said, 'lay her down.' She laid Gracie in the bassinet Paul had had the men put there in the cool, and at last the baby fell asleep.

Now his love letter was finished he said, 'Okay, I'm going to call in this Nurse Drake. We're ready for her now.'

Twelve

The Nurse

*Wednesday, 10 January 1906, when Nurse
Beatrix can't believe her luck.*

'It's a fact that lawyers and doctors are all richer than they deserve or need to be,' said Beatrix Drake to her fella George, who had recently been promoted to First Constable, 'and that's why, Georgie, last September, when Missus Cottingham turned up at my door to see if I could midwife at the birth, clever me — Nurse Beatrix Drake,' she said pointing at herself, 'knowing Missus Cottingham was a lawyer's wife, I quoted triple my usual figure and she never bat an eyelid.'

Beatrix sat on the edge of the bed and pulled on her stocking, 'Where's the other one, George?'

George laughed and looked among the sheets that were tangled about his legs. 'Here it is, love,' and he waved it in the air just out of reach so she had to lunge over him to get it.

And now, thought Beatrix, putting on her other stocking, Missus Cottingham had gone and died, God-bless-her-soul, and they'd need to put the child somewhere. A new baby, only a few weeks old, a rich baby.

114

'I could ask a sovereign a week for the care of the Cottingham baby, I reckon,' she said and George slapped her bare bottom and readily agreed. He said her bottom was like two warm loaves of bread, soft, doughy and pliable. He said she was so comfortable that a man just wanted to plunge himself into her and forget all his worries, which he did every Wednesday afternoon at two when he should have been walking the streets.

She thought about the last kid she'd taken on. It was only last week she'd got rid of her, so the Cottingham baby had come along at just the right time. The mother of the other kid had turned up on her doorstep looking all mournful and in a hurry and offered her half a sovereign a week for the kid's keep and said she was off to Hamilton to work as a housemaid. Beatrix had looked hard at the kid, trying to assess whether she was a brat or not, whether she'd be more trouble than the mother was willing to pay for her keep. The kid looked at the ground like she wanted it to open up and suck her into a different world. She looked hungry, Beatrix could see that much straight off, she looked like a half-drowned kitten.

'All righty,' Beatrix said to the mother, 'I'll keep your pup as long as you keep paying. On time. I ain't a charity.' The mother looked relieved. Beatrix wondered what was really waiting for the mother in Hamilton — it'd be a fella for sure. A fella that didn't want some other dog's pup to look after.

'Up front,' said Beatrix. 'I need the first eight weeks right now.'

Those eight coins were the only ones Beatrix Drake ever saw. When she'd had the kid for another six weeks without a brass razoo arriving, she did the only thing she could do in the circumstances and made an application to have the kid committed to the orphanage. She'd hauled herself to the courthouse in Camp Street, dragging the silent three-year-old girl along behind her and waited for three hours on a hard bench in a dreary corridor until a clerk finally yelled out their names: 'Beatrix Drake and Constance Hardy'. Beatrix took the girl's hand and dragged her into the courtroom where Judge Murphy sat behind his huge high desk looking down on everything and everyone.

Beatrix had a good mind to give that Judge Murphy what-for for keeping her waiting so long out in the corridor when she saw him at mass the next Sunday without his wig and robe and he looked just like the rest of us. It was a waste of her precious time, it was.

Judge Murphy was absorbed in a mountain of papers when she entered the courtroom and the clerk had motioned for her to sit down in the front row. She'd lifted the girl up onto the bench and looked over at her fella, George, who was sitting with the other coppers who had to give evidence in the other cases. He smiled at her.

The only sound was the child's sniffling.

'I've heard of this practice of leaving children in the care of so-called nurses,' Judge Murphy's voice sliced through the silence, echoed down the corridor and made them all jump.

'I'm registered!' she'd said much too loudly and her voice ricocheted around the room. It was as if she was on trial when it should be the girl's bloody mother.

'I'm aware of that, Nurse Drake, and in future you should make full enquiries before taking a child.' The judge put down his gavel and peered hard at her. 'This practice of leaving children in the care of nurses and not paying for their keep is now the vogue way in the city to have a child placed on the state by negligent mothers who have decided there are more exciting things to do in life than raise their offspring. This isn't the city and for that I thank God. I don't want the practice creeping into our community. If I place the girl in care I am condoning the mother's behaviour and before you know it every mother in town that's doing it a bit tough or is

a bit bored with being at home with children and fancies them-
selves a bit of a flibbertigibbet is going to be on your doorstep.
I'm more inclined to make you her legal guardian,' said Judge
Murphy.

Beatrix looked at George open-mouthed; it had never entered
her head that she could be stuck with the kid.

Then Constable George Stephens stood up and certified to her
good character and, despite the city influence creeping into the
regional town, Judge Murphy made the kid a ward of the state,
to be delivered to the orphanage. Beatrix Drake wasted no time
in carrying out the judge's direction and walked straight from
the courthouse in Camp Street down to Victoria Street to the
orphanage with the kid trotting along behind, struggling to keep
up with her.

There would be no risk factor with the Cottingham child.
They had money. Beatrix prettied herself up. She put on her Sunday best. Her white shirt with the lace down the middle and her
gored A-line navy cotton skirt. She pinned her hair into a tight
bun and, even though it was too hot, she put on her jacket. She
wanted to make a good impression on the Cottinghams for when
they handed the baby over.

'Of course,' she said to George, 'the father is not going to want
to keep the baby that killed his wife. It would only be a painful
reminder of his loss. I'm amazed he didn't get rid of it straightaway.' She grabbed her bag and stood for a moment looking at her
fella, splayed out over her bed, the sheets still tangled in his legs.
He was plump with satisfaction; she'd done that to him, made
him soft with her loving. His white belly wobbled as he sat up
against the pillows, and she leant over and kissed the bald spot on
his head. 'You look like a Roman emperor.'

'Feed me some grapes, slave, and satisfy all my desires,' he
commanded.

'Toodaloo then,' she said, and as she left the hot northerly wind grabbed hold of the front door and ripped it from her grasp, slamming it behind her. She walked to Sturt Street, holding hard to her hat, which threatened to fly off, and hailed Jones's cab, which she couldn't afford but she wanted the Cottinghams to think she was better off than she was. She didn't want them to think she needed the child. They had to think she loved it. It would appease their consciences as they handed it over.

Beatrix stood at the gate of the Cottingham house. 'My, my, my,' she said. The Cottingham house made her cottage look like one of the Chinese-ie tents that used to pop up on hillsides in clusters like white mushrooms. She and the other children were alternately warned to stay away from those Chinese-ie encampments and threatened with being dragged off to them if they didn't toe the line: *'You kids bloody behave yourselves or you'll be boiled up by them Chinese-ies with the miners' washing!'*

She wiped the sweat from her brow. By God it was stinking hot. She tucked some stray hairs behind her ear, walked up the path and pressed the bronze doorbell. Today her life would change. Today she would set herself up for many years to come.

The door opened and Beth stood looking at her. The girl could look downright insolent if she wanted to.

'G'day Beth. Haven't seen you hanging round with Young Colin next door in a while.' Beth must run rings round that simple boy. Beatrix could read people and this girl was determined to do something. Beatrix couldn't get a handle on what that something was, but she knew it probably wouldn't include Young Colin.

'I been busy helping with the baby,' said Beth. Beatrix noticed that Beth had turned out a particularly pretty girl with lovely thick dark hair, a face like a pixie and big brown eyes. She must be at least fifteen now. Beatrix stepped into the foyer without being asked and ran her fingers over the ornate hallstand; she'd always wanted one of those. She took in the huge gilded mirror and the family portraits, all looking sternly down on her, the intruder.

'Come in,' said Beth pointedly.

Beatrix heard the tone. Beth was cross because she hadn't waited to be invited and was already well into the foyer.

'Where the hell did they get a mirror that size?'

'It's imported,' muttered Beth, reaching for Beatrix's hat.

'You're a lucky girl to land a job here, aren't you, Beth? Lucky you had me to step in,' she said, holding her hat on her head. She would take it off when she was good and ready. 'You could be working in a pub pulling pots for smelly miners like those sisters of yours, specially after your ma died and your pa disappeared. This is a lark — all thanks to yours truly.' That would put the young miss back where she belonged.

'Can I take your jacket and hat?' asked Beth coldly, reaching again for the hat.

'Not yet.' Beatrix slowly unbuttoned her jacket. Given the heat, she was more than pleased to be rid of it. She took her time, taking the opportunity to have a good look at the place while Beth stood impatiently waiting.

'This town is full of single miners that'd be happy to have a wife as pretty as you, Beth,' Beatrix said.

'I'm quite happy with my Young Colin,' said Beth.

Beatrix leaned towards her and said conspiratorially, 'Some girls look like a mallet hit them. I've heard that said of Miss Cottingham.'

'Nurse Drake.'

She turned and saw the Cottingham girl standing in the doorway directly off the foyer.

Blimey, did Miss Cottingham hear what she'd just said? She quickly whipped off her hat and hung it on the hallstand. 'Well, where's this beauty of a bub then?' she said too cheerily, trying to smother her previous comment before it could breathe.

'Come this way,' Miss Cottingham said.

Beatrix noted that Beth skipped a quick step to wedge herself between Miss Cottingham and herself as though Beth was Miss Cottingham's protector and Beatrix thought yes, there was something vulnerable about the Cottingham girl, something yearning in her.

The portraits watched Beatrix suspiciously as she followed the two girls past the hallstand, past shut doors, past one door she couldn't help but notice was boarded over with ugly planks of wood as though a child had clumsily hammered them up.

'Well, I'm guessing that room's out of bounds — I suppose there's a dead body in there, is there?' she laughed, but the two girls completely ignored her. They led her past the dining room and she tried desperately to peek in on her way past. From the glimpse she got it looked bigger than her entire cottage. She kept following as the two girls led her into the kitchen.

'Down here,' said Miss Cottingham, opening a green door. Before Beatrix had time to have a good look at the kitchen the girls were disappearing down a spiral staircase into utter darkness.

'This is the dungeon, is it?' Beatrix said. 'You not going to tie me up and murder me or anything are you?' she tried to sound jokey but truth be told she was getting edgy. These rich folks were just too strange.

'Well, I'll be blowed,' she said when she got downstairs. She slapped her hands on her ample bottom. She was no longer hot. In fact she was rather cool and a shiver ran down her arms. She touched the cold rendered walls, she stomped her feet on the floorboards and the girls both said, 'Shhhh.' She looked at the soft glow of the electrical lighting that flickered like fairy lights and cast a blue hue that turned the space into a dream.

'It's an underground house, walls, floors, doors, the lot.'

Flickering or not, that electrical lighting must have cost a bloody fortune. My God how the other half live! Just wait till she told George about this. He'd never believe it.

She didn't bother to hide her gawping; she didn't wait to be invited. She looked into every room, touched every wall and each piece of furniture until the Cottingham girl took her arm and firmly guided her into the only room she hadn't inspected. Beatrix saw straightaway that this was the nursery. There was a wooden Noah's ark and two of each of a menagerie of animals on the mantle. There was a soft goat's hair rug on the timber floor and a pram in one corner, a bloody expensive-looking pram just like you'd expect, chairs in two other corners, and in the last corner was the bassinet. Beth began folding a pile of clean cotton nappies from one basket and putting them in another basket.

'It was the only way to keep the baby cool,' said Miss Cottingham. 'She seems to really feel the heat just like Mama did. So Papa built her an underground house — like they have in Coober Pedy.'

Beatrix tried to take all this in.

'Mother mentioned you before she passed away and that's why I've called for you. Of course Doctor Appleby comes by once a month now but he doesn't tell us how to manage the nitty gritty of looking after a baby.'

'Where's your father, Miss Cottingham?' Beatrix asked. She walked over to the bassinet and peered at the sleeping child that was sucking contentedly on her thumb. She was a scrawny little thing, and snuffled as she slept. Asthma, thought Beatrix, sickly and asthmatic.

'Mister Cottingham's at work, he's left all this to me to organise,' said Miss Cottingham, and she sat down in the big leather easy chair. 'And please call me Edie.'

'Oh, I can understand that — him not wanting anything to do with the arrangements for the child. I'm sorry for your loss, Miss Cottingham,' Beatrix said, trying to sound sympathetic. *Of course he hated the child that had caused his wife's death*, she thought. She'd seen the reaction before in other fathers.

'Edie, please,' and the girl held out her hand and so she leant over and shook it awkwardly. What a manly sort of girl, plain and wanting to shake hands as if they were about to conduct business like men.

'The baby?' Beatrix asked too quickly and immediately worried she'd given the impression that she wanted to grab and run. 'Her name, I was just wondering about her name.'

'It's Gracie,' said Edie.

Beatrix held out her hands to pick the child up but Edie surprised her by quickly leaping out of the chair and taking the child in her own arms, holding her to her chest and making cooing noises. It was as if the Cottingham girl didn't trust her with the baby.

'Now what I want, Nurse Drake,' said Edie, glancing up from the baby who was now awake and gurgling in her arms, 'is for you to teach me all you know about infant care. I know a fair bit about medicinal care, but not when it comes to babies, you see,' and the girl sat down again, her attention still mainly on the baby in her arms, not realising that it was Beatrix who should be getting her attention so they could work out the particulars. Beatrix had learnt her lesson when it came to arranging the care of children, she was going to make sure every detail was sorted before she agreed to anything; she didn't want Judge Murphy foisting some kid on her permanently.

'May I sit?' asked Beatrix pulling up the only other chair in the room, an uncomfortable wooden one. 'Are you asking me to move in here as a nanny?' This was better than expected. She could get out of her rented miner's cottage with its gaps in the timber walls and the leak over the stove that was turning the cooktop rusty. She could move out of her street where the houses were so jammed together she could hear every word Ginny Eales hollered at Colin Eales Senior when he happened to be in town, usually over his wages and why he always misplaced most of them at the Bunch of Grapes on his way home from work. Moving in with the Cottinghams as full-time nanny would be hard on George but she'd negotiate an afternoon off once a month, and on her new wage she and George could go to a hotel. She'd tell him it was quality not quantity that mattered, which would make him laugh if nothing else. Full-time nanny — that'd have to be worth at least two sovereigns a week.

'Heavens no,' said Edie, almost jumping in her chair.

Beatrix was nonplussed for a moment, but then she realised. 'Oh of course — you want me to take the child in to my place. Either way it's the same cost.'

'Heavens no,' said Edie, even louder, 'we just need someone to teach us the proper methods of raising a child.'

Then it dawned on her that they were planning to keep the child. Beatrix saw her sovereigns flying out the window (if there had been a window in the room).

'But you aren't ever going get a husband with a child under your feet!' she blurted before she could stop herself.

She saw Edie stiffen. The girl's face turned stone cold. 'But that's hardly your concern, Nurse Drake,' she said and her chin jutted forward. 'Besides, what do you suggest I do? Put my own sister in the orphanage?'

Now Beatrix was taken aback. 'Well, I should take her. I'm sure it's what your mother God-bless-her-soul meant to happen. That's why she mentioned my name, I'm sure,' she said, her voice becoming quieter under the dagger glare she was getting, and she realised that Edie had taken control of the whole situation. This was something Beatrix, who was always the boss, wasn't used to and she sat up primly in her chair as though in fact she was overseeing everything. Under her breath she muttered, 'Your dada might be rich but you need me, young lady.'

Beth heard her mutter and glared at her, so she glared right back.

'Medical knowledge is of great interest to me. I'm fascinated but I also know my limitations, and caring for infants isn't my area of expertise — yet. We will pay you a worthwhile sum if you will teach me and Beth all we need to know.' Edie nodded at Beth.

'Hmmm,' said Beatrix, biding her time and looking around the room at the carved oak tallboy and the two gold-framed pictures hanging on the wall. One was of Jesus caring for the little children and the other she assumed was a portrait of the child's mother as a young woman, which personally she thought was a bit macabre but rich people were odd, everyone knew that, and this lot took the cake. Her mind ticked, counting the possibilities.

'Now,' said Edie, 'what do you think?' and without giving Beatrix a chance to answer, the girl continued as if she'd known all along that of course Beatrix would take the job because of course she was desperate for the money. 'The first thing is a shopping list. Mother wasn't expecting to deliver for some time, you see, and we only have things that a few kind people have lent to us and the things Papa bought for in here.' At this Beth pulled out a pencil and notepad from her apron pocket.

Beatrix sighed loudly, as if this was such a burden for her given her busy schedule. She dug in her bag and put on her nurse's cap. The best way to get respect was to look the part. She wriggled in her seat as though she was still considering, thus giving the proper air of authority and letting them know her expertise didn't come cheaply.

Finally she began. 'Two sovereigns a week,' said Beatrix. She saw Beth's eyes pop open but she ignored her and went on, 'I'll come on Mondays and Wednesdays and Fridays. On Tuesday, Thursday, Saturday and Sunday you can manage on your own but you can call for me if need be. Now, for the proper care of an infant you need three dozen nappies, two feeding apparatus, seven matinee jackets, fourteen nightgowns, seven pairs of booties, seven caps, one cot before she is six months old, one perambulator, which I see you have already managed to obtain and a very nice one at that, or is it on loan as well? Four blankets, one cot lay-out, one perambulator lay-out, one bassinet lay-out, one layette, seven baby frocks, one bottle of Doctor Sheldon's Colic Remedy, one jar of rash ointment, one bottle of Scott's Emulsion, you can get a free sample if you send them four pence for postage, you'll need to buy Castlemaine beer for her asthma — yes, she has asthma, I spotted it at once — some Lloyds cocaine toothache drops for when she teethes, and I assume you've already got infant formula and an Indian rubber teat or the baby wouldn't be here with us today. Have you got all that?'

'Beth, did you get all that?' asked Edie. 'Never mind you can tell Beth anything she's missed later.'

Knowing she'd impressed the girl with her knowledge of child raising and finally got the respect she deserved, she continued. 'Now, these things are essential,' and she counted them off on her fingers, 'One — the baby must be swaddled tightly, which you haven't done at all. You can't just let her lie about, arms and legs akimbo. If you neglect to do this and let her lie loosely in her blankets as I see she presently is, she will undoubtedly grow up to be of an insecure and nervous disposition, not to mention her hips and knees can dislocate given she is unable at this young age to control her limbs.' She looked at Edie sternly and waited for her to tighten the baby's wrappings. But the girl just sat poised for the next instruction, and realising she'd be waiting till the cows came home she said firmly and pointedly,

'Two — the baby must not be cuddled as she presently is, this is most serious, and if I were her permanent nanny I would insist you put her in her bassinet immediately. Where does she sleep at night, by the way?'

'Down here, in the other room — in bed with me,' said Edie, as though this was perfectly normal.

'Oh heavens! No, no, no.' No wonder these rich women all have nannies; they have no idea of how to bring up an industrious child. 'If you cuddle her more than once a day you will bring up a spoilt, rebellious and demanding child who will be the bane of your lives! Now, three — she must not be fed more than one bottle every four hours. This is most essential otherwise she will be fat and greedy and no one will want to marry her.' Beatrix realised too late the tactlessness of what she'd just said, given Edie's own situation, and quickly went on.

'Now, let me see her. Come on, give her over, I'm a nurse for heaven's sake, I'm not going to hurt her,' and she took the baby out of Edie's reluctant arms and laid her on the change table. 'Come on, come on, you both need to see this,' and when the girls were standing nearby she looked up at Edie to make sure she had her full attention and felt chagrined that the girl was still looking at her as though she was likely to injure the infant. Beatrix opened the shawl smartly and removed the baby's nappy. She didn't look at the child's face so she didn't see her smile. She was concentrating on the other end, and hoisted the baby's legs in the air, raising her bottom well off the table.

'Here, here and here are where she'll get a rash, you need to open the folds of skin and powder every day. I find Cashmere Bouquet the best. If the rash appears, use ointment straightaway, don't delay or it will only get worse.'

Beatrix put the baby's bottom back on the table and inspected her own fingers. Her forefinger had the shortest nail so she shoved it in the baby's mouth. Gracie sucked furiously. Beatrix poked her finger around and explained, 'I'm feeling for teeth, don't look shocked. I myself have delivered a baby born with a full set.'

Beatrix wiped her finger on her skirt. 'Beth, you can put her in a clean nappy and put her in her bassinet now,' but Beth ignored her and Edie stepped forward, put a clean nappy on Gracie and then cuddled her close to her chest.

Beatrix sighed. This was going to take some work. She picked up her bag and said, 'I'll come thrice weekly, as I said, to check how you're getting on and to give you further instructions as she grows. I'll charge the two sovereigns a week I mentioned.' She waited. She looked at Edie and waited again. She said, 'In advance.'

An outrageous sum, she knew, but she sensed she might have the upper hand here given both girls' complete lack of knowledge. Still, she gave Edie another moment to haggle. It took her a full three minutes to realise Edie wasn't going to, so she filled the space with a cough and went on.

'For that you can call me any time you have a problem. Just send Beth down. Oh, and one last word of advice,' Beatrix leant over to Edie, 'and I'd take this most seriously if I were you. Never bother your father with the infant. When he comes home make sure she is shut up tightly in the nursery. She will only remind him of your poor mother's untimely death and no good will come of that.'

With that Beatrix left, her purse jangling with coins and her last words hanging in the air. She made a bet with herself that Miss Edith Cottingham would not last much more than a few months and the novelty of playing babies would wear off. That baby would soon be living with her and she'd be four sovereigns a week richer if she played it right. Normally she'd have given someone like Edie only two weeks but she'd seen in an instant

how determined Miss Cottingham could be. She fossicked in
her purse to feel the four half sovereigns she had been paid in
advance. She might catch one of those new electric trams down
Sturt Street; she hadn't ridden on one of them yet. She'd only ever
ridden a horse-drawn tram and, well, that was just an oversized
carriage. An electric tram ride would be a little treat to celebrate
the regular wage she'd be getting as of now. She couldn't help
it; she was a tad anxious as the conductor helped her onto tram
number 12 at the Drummond Street stop. He was very nice, he
reached down and put his hand under her elbow and lifted her up
into the tram and she took a seat next to the window so she could
see for herself just how fast the houses flashed by. She heard it was
so fast they became a blur. Everything in the tram was new: the
shiny red leather seat that she kept slipping off, the timber panel-
ling polished so she could see her reflection, the clear glass without scratches. The conductor took her threepence, clipped a ticket
and gave it to her and then pulled his rope. As he did, Young
Colin Eales and his smart-alecking mates leapt into the carriage
hooting and shouting. She knew these boys, Young Colin who
lived next door and Jimmy and his string-bean brother. So much
for her peaceful tram ride. The three boys were grubby and grimy
from the mines, they looked like they hadn't washed in years and
their skin was stained with streaks and crusts of dirt. Their veins
stuck out on their scrawny necks, dark brown instead of purple.
Their eyes were grey smudges, but she had a pretty good idea
they'd also been drinking. They normally went to the Bunch of
Grapes, so something had brought them to a watering hole up this
end of town instead. They sat right opposite her, whispering with
one eye on her, hoping she couldn't hear them, laughing inanely,
slapping each other and cooking up some lark.

The conductor stood in front of them, waiting for them to
stop larking around and hand over their fares and they made a big

show of fossicking in their pockets looking for coins. The conductor looked over at Beatrix and rolled his eyes and she looked at the boys sternly. Finally Young Colin pulled two coins out of his pocket and held them high in the air for the world to see — well, Beatrix and the conductor.

'Sorry, sir,' said Young Colin Eales, as though he genuinely cared about the predicament he was causing the conductor, 'it's all I got.'

So the conductor took Young Colin's sovereign and gave a handful of change back to him. Then without saying a word String Bean held out his coin, which was also a sovereign, and took every last coin in the conductor's change bag. Jimmy also only had a sovereign, which he sheepishly held in the air. That was when Beatrix stepped in and said, 'Had a good day down the mines, did we boys? Tributes paid off for once? Well, you know what, Jimmy, your friends have got plenty of change, they can pay for you. And they can pay for anyone else who hops on, seeing the poor conductor has been robbed of his change. If you don't, I'll be having a word to Constable George.' All their skylarking flew out the window and they sullenly stared at the shiny new floorboards of the tram.

When the tram pulled into the next stop, two couples got on and Beatrix was true to her word. 'It's all right, loveys,' she said loudly so everyone could hear, 'Young Colin Eales has had such luck down the mines that he's offered to pay everyone's fares,' and she glowered at Colin, who handed over his money because otherwise the old busybody would have a word in his mother's ear, and his father's ear too if he ever showed up, not to mention a word in the ear of her fella George, who could cause you trouble you didn't want. Colin handed over his money and saw pots at the pub disappearing as each new person hopped on.

Thirteen

Pumpkin Mash

Monday, 9 July 1906, when everyone
faces the dark after dinner.

When Edie woke the water was frozen in the taps and over the puddles, the trees bent under a thick layer of white frost. The weather promised snow later in the day, but in the end would only deliver nasty sleet and rain. Until the sleet and rain arrived the boys ran with sticks cracking the ice on the puddles with as much whooping and splashing as they could manage. But that was later in the day, and now it was still early. Beth had also only just woken and she got out of bed onto the cold floorboards that made her shiver and rugged herself up in a scarf, coat, boots and finger-less gloves. She rubbed her hands together and shoved them under her armpits as she walked across the grass covered in ice, brittle like glass, to the wood shed. The neatly stacked wood was damp with cold and she held it out from her chest as she took it inside. She opened the door of the cooker and took a stick to poke at the grey ash inside until she found a tiny ember. She blew on the speck of red that had survived the night and her breath brought it to life; she fed it with paper, and when the paper caught she put in the kindling, and when that had caught she added the wood, which sizzled and steamed as the moisture cooked out of it. Later, when it was warmer, she would need to let the fire burn down and empty the ash out onto the broad beans and start a new fire. Every few days the ash built up and stopped falling through into the grate pan. She left the door open so that the fire began to do its work, heating up the kitchen until it was cosy and warm and the water in the tap started to run.

By the time Nurse Drake arrived at ten-thirty the fire was singing, steam from the kettle and a pot of boiling pumpkin was filling the room, and there was hot tea in the pot. Beth topped it up as often as she could and when the tea leaves had no more flavour she made a fresh pot. Paul had escaped to his office to avoid having to talk to Beatrix, and Beth, Edie, Grace and Beatrix all felt safe and cosy inside as the weather beat against the windows.

Edie watched the pumpkin boil. It looked like lumpy orange soup. She had cut the pumpkin into pieces, making sure to remove all the hard skin.

'Now you must boil the pumpkin for a good hour minimum to draw out the goodness,' instructed Beatrix as she looked in the pot. She was holding Gracie, naked, plump and pink and now eight months old. The kitchen was so deliciously warm Gracie was wrapped only in a towel around her fat bottom. Edie looked at the boiling pumpkin as it turned to mush. Then she looked at Gracie as if to say *This mush is meant for you.*

'Oh, I could just eat you up,' Edie said, nuzzling Gracie's fat thigh, and Gracie chuckled her awkward baby laugh and hoped the pumpkin wasn't what they expected to feed her.

'It needs longer,' said Beatrix, moving Gracie to her other hip, and going to the enamel tub sitting on one half of the kitchen table. Edie watched as Nurse Drake tested the water in the tub with her elbow, nodded to herself and lowered the baby into it, and she laughed ungraciously when Gracie began splashing the water as soon as she could reach it, splashing it straight into Nurse Drake's face and up her nose and all over her clothes.

'I warned you,' laughed Edie, smiling at Beth. Edie and Beth loved it when they were proved right about anything to do with Gracie.

'Keep checking that pumpkin,' snapped Nurse Drake, wiping the water from her face, 'it needs to be liquid.'

Edie raised her eyebrows at Beth, who was at the sink washing glass jars ready for the pumpkin, and the girls shared a secret smile as Beatrix tried to brush soapy water from her cardigan. Beatrix took Gracie out of the bath and dried her off on the tabletop.

'I'm sure you are feeding this child more than I have instructed,' she said, and held Gracie's feet in the air, moving them in circles, making her thighs wobble like jelly. Gracie chuckled more as Beatrix inspected Gracie. The child had put on weight, so that was something to be grateful for, though she was still small for her age and had an occasional cough.

'So what are you feeding this fat child, girls?' she asked.

'Oh,' said Edie, 'we try to follow your instructions to the letter, don't we, Beth?'

'Of course,' lied Beth.

Beatrix wrapped Gracie tightly in the towel, picked her up and came over to peer into the pot again. 'See, this is the consistency you need in order to bring the goodness out of the vegetable and to make it possible for her body to absorb it. Boil it for two hours if you must — the longer you boil it the more goodness you draw out of it.'

Edie looked at the orange slop in the saucepan and thought she wouldn't feed it to a dog.

'That's good food in there, Miss Cottingham, a darn sight better than any of us got as babies in our day,' said the nurse sharply.

'You need to put the pumpkin in a jar until you're ready to use it. Do it while it's hot so it seals hygienically.'

Edie poured the pumpkin into the jars and Beth quickly screwed the lids on. Then Beatrix dressed Gracie in her baby dress and wrapped her tightly in two blankets, trapping Gracie in a straitjacket and wiping the smile from the baby's face. 'Now I'm putting her in her room, there's a fire ready, isn't there, Beth?'

Edie looked at Beth and she nodded.

'Well,' said Beatrix, 'remember: no picking her up for four hours,' and she looked at Edie, and Edie knew Nurse Drake considered her the most likely culprit to break her rules.

As soon as the last plume of Nurse Drake's overly decorated and ridiculously large hat had disappeared up the street Edie ran to the nursery and clutched Gracie to her breast. Gracie had short soft curls like lamb's wool all over her head and her eyes had turned from baby grey to sky blue. Edie followed none of the nurse's rules. If Gracie was hungry she was fed, regardless of the time of day or when she had had her last feed. If Gracie cried, Edie carried her around, resting Gracie's colicky tummy over her arm. Edie sang to Gracie so she would know she was loved more than any other baby in the world and she cooed for her smiles. In the autumn months she had let Gracie's arms and legs hang free so she could feel the warmth of the sun as it came through the dining room windows on her soft duck-down skin. Now it was cold Edie sat on a rug by the cooker with Gracie in her arms and they played with the offcuts of wood that Paul had cut small enough for Gracie's fingers and then sanded until they were smooth and shone so Gracie could see her reflection.

Edie's days revolved around Gracie's needs and her nights around Gracie's warm and powdery smell. Gracie had filled up Edie's life. It had been this way for her since the day at the lake when she had stood, her feet in the mud, ready to drop Gracie into the water

below. Gracie had been barely balanced in her hands, all it would
have needed was a twist of her arm, a movement from Gracie, or
for Edie just to take one hand away and Gracie would have plum-
meted down. But Gracie had smiled at her and Edie remembered
what her dying mother had asked of her. So now Edie knew deep
in her soul that her task in life wasn't to be a nurse or to be a wife:
it was to be Gracie's mother. The underground house had helped
them all through the mean summer.

'Your underground house saved Gracie's life,' Edie said to her
father on many occasions. And Paul smiled; they both knew it
was true. But the summer had passed, the autumn had passed,
and Gracie no longer slept downstairs in the underground house.
She slept in Edie's bed wrapped up in Edie's arms. Except for
when Nurse Drake was due. When Edie heard her at the door she
would call for Beth to let the nurse in while she ran to the nursery,
put Gracie in her cot and whispered, 'Shhhh, not a word, you've
been here the whole night, haven't you?'

And Gracie would smile to show she understood their secret.

Paul would arrive home from work at precisely six. He'd done
this ever since Gracie was six weeks old, so Edie was always ready
and waiting for him. When it was warm she would wait on the
verandah, now it was cold she would wait at the study window
with Gracie in her arms so they could see him as soon as he walked
through the gate.

'I just can't bear to work any later these days,' he told Edie, and
she knew that it was because he wanted to get home to Gracie.

This evening he put his umbrella in the stand, took off his coat
and hung it on the hall stand, and then took off his boxer, which
he hung over his coat, and finally his scarf and gloves. As she
watched him, Edie thought he seemed so much older than he was
before her mother died. Something about him was frailer, his hair
and eyes seemed greyer. And she thought how just eight months

ago she had been a girl concerned with no more than making a man fall in love with her. Now she was a woman, aware of life and death and how they walked hand in hand. Edie put Gracie into Paul's arms and Gracie smiled up at him. Then they went to the dining room and sat down to the dinner of lamb stew with dumplings that Beth had prepared and Edie tried to feed Gracie the pureed pumpkin and they all laughed over the amount of pureed pumpkin that was on the outside of Gracie rather than the inside and instead they fed her bits of stew from their own plates.

After dinner Beth took the dishes to wash in the kitchen, then she soaked the oats, squeezed the juice and simmered the fruit in syrup for breakfast the next day. She ironed Paul's shirt ready for the morning and finally collapsed exhausted into her bed. As she did every night.

As he always did, after dinner Paul lifted Gracie out of her high chair and Gracie waved goodbye to the teddy bears painted on the tray. Paul carried her to the sitting room, where he flopped into his leather chair that caressed every groan and creak in his body and read, resting a monstrous law book on one arm of the chair, while cuddling Gracie with his other arm. Gracie was contented. She lay back in her father's arm and occasionally kicked her chubby legs. Sometimes she leant over to suck the corner of his book.

After dinner Edie sat beside them knitting a jumper for Gracie, who grew quicker than Edie could knit, until Paul fell asleep in the chair with Gracie still in his arms. When Edie was sure Paul and Gracie were both fast asleep, she gently picked Gracie up out of Paul's arms.

'Papa,' Edie gently shook his shoulder. 'Papa, time you were in bed.'

'Mmmmm,' he said, blinking his eyes sleepily. 'Oh yes, I've fallen asleep again.'

And he reluctantly lifted himself out of the chair. He looked so sad and lost and she knew he missed her mother, but she didn't know that of all the times he missed her, this time, at night, was the moment he loathed the most. It was now he had to face his large, empty bedroom and his cold, empty bed. There would be no visits from his wife in her nightgown, her hair falling to her shoulders like clouds visiting the earth. This was the time of day when he had to pass her room, the boards still nailed over her door, knowing there was no point taking those boards down, she wasn't Sleeping Beauty, waiting in there for his kiss. It was the room he no longer visited later when Edie was asleep; he no longer listened to the whisper of her song that filled his soul. His life was now full of no-longers. He envied Edie that she could take Gracie to bed with her and drift off to sleep with Gracie's plump smell warming the brittle night air. He sighed and wandered off to his room.

Edie put Gracie in her bed, where she slept with the baby nestled in close to her bosom.

'Gracie, you are so perfect I couldn't imagine ever being anywhere but with you,' Edie whispered into the silence of the night. And in the dark, baby Gracie smiled.

Every night after dinner Theo played Chopin's *Prelude in E Minor* and the melancholy notes seeped into the walls, the furniture, and Lilly's skin and made her weep. It was a fine piano that Theo played: a Beale piano with the new Beale-Vader all-iron tuning system that Octavius Beale had patented in 1902. The frame was hand-strung and the timber panels were wet sanded so they shone like a mirror. It had cost him £45 after the 25 per cent discount for buying direct from the manufacturer. Every string in that piano and every piece of ivory that his fingers touched wept as the notes filled the house. Theo played every night for precisely two hours and as the last note drifted off into the world, he would gaze at his reflection in the piano and wonder who he was now. He knew that his life was no more than a series of perfunctory actions, as though he was acting until his real life could begin — his life with Edie.

'Two hundred and forty-six days,' he whispered to his reflection, 'five thousand nine hundred and four hours, three hundred and fifty-four thousand two hundred and forty minutes, twenty-one million two hundred and fifty-four thousand and four hundred seconds, twenty-eight million and three hundred and thirty-nine thousand and two hundred beats of my heart.'

That was how long he had waited for Edie Cottingham so far.

Theo could wait and even though he had told his mother he would wait for six months, he had waited eight. In the four weeks he had watched Edie come to church, her skin stricken with grey in her black mourning clothes and a dismal grey hat that bleached the colour from everything it touched, unable to speak to anyone and looking only at the ground. It was Beth or Mister Cottingham who pushed the baby in the pram and who made an effort to smile when the women, including his mother, cooed over it. Then suddenly one Sunday it was Edie with the baby and no pram. She carried the baby like it was the most precious thing in the world and she smiled at everyone and was wearing a white hat with blue ribbons instead of her mourning hat. He saw how tiny and dependent the thing was in her arms, like a bald pink joey peeping out from the safety of a pouch. Then last Sunday Edie had thrown off her mourning clothes altogether and worn crimson like a rose and he knew that was the sign that her mourning was over and she was ready for him. He saw the baby in Edie's lap playing with a knitted giraffe. The baby had grown so much, it probably didn't need Edie now. But he did. Now she was no longer mourning, he would ask her father for her hand.

All this time, for all these months, he had said no more to her than 'Good morning, Miss Cottingham' and gone on his way. He couldn't bear talking to her as though nothing had happened between them. So not being able to step back and not being able to step forward he just hadn't spoken to her at all.

Lilly disturbed his thoughts. 'Penny?' she asked, putting her hand gently on his head and leaning in close as if he was still six years old.

'Nothing, Mum.' He closed the piano lid and walked into the kitchen, sat at the table and opened the paper.

Lilly got the apple upside-down cake she had made that afternoon out of the rosella tin and cut them each a thicker-than-respectable slice. Theo nodded at the paper spread out in front of him.

'I just don't see how all these legislative changes that occur in the middle of the night in the celebrated Parliament House in Spring Street actually affect real lives down here in Ballarat. The miners are just as poor and badly behaved as ever; the rich are still cosseted in their big houses near the lake. I just don't see why these pollies get these big fat wages to sit around and yell at each other,' he said.

Lilly knew he wasn't at all interested in politics and was really thinking of the Cottingham girl. It was a worry, the way he was so set on her when he could have had someone else by now. He could be settled and starting his own family and making her a grandmother — oh, wouldn't that be the sweetest thing.

Theo felt her gaze on him and spotted another item that might distract her from the subject of Edie Cottingham, which he could see she badly wanted to raise.

'Listen to this, Mum: "Wireless communication successfully sent across Bass Strait,"' he read out. Lilly cut him another slice of cake.

'I should be a porker with the amount you feed me, Mum. But I'm not, it just doesn't seem to stick, does it?'

She worried for him, nothing had ever made him fatten, she was sure his innards had dried out so much in the African heat he could no longer absorb any nourishment at all. The worry of it made her cut another slice of cake and put it on her plate.

Theo folded the newspaper and leant over and tucked it in the basket for fire lighting, as though he could neatly fold up time and tuck it away. He wondered, as he had many times before, if he should not have come back from that war, whether he should have died over there. War was a bad thing, it emptied a man out. His feet didn't seem to stick to the ground any more and that was why he needed Edie; she would tie him to the earth.

There's nothing to him, thought Lilly, *he needs something to weigh him down.* And she took the last piece of cake.

Fourteen

The Rose

Sunday, 15 July 1906, when Theo does a simple thing, really.

Theo sat at the kitchen table. He had pushed his plate of roast lamb to the side to make room for the paper, which rose and fell like a mountain over the loaf of bread. He turned the next page and read that if you hung roses upside down you could dry them and that way keep them forever, but they would lose their colour and the petals would separate. He thought of his mother's rosebud dress and his father who had finally succumbed to consumption, having survived far longer than Doctor Appleby Senior had said was possible, passing away when Theo was twelve. His father had said that Lilly was his rose, so Theo knew that a rose was a true symbol of love. He wasn't interested in drying roses if they lost their colour. Colour and wholeness were of the utmost importance to him. The article went on to describe how to dry the roses keeping the bud intact and maintaining most of the colour. It was interesting information but he didn't want a rose to preserve and he didn't want just any rose. He wanted a rose that was of the deepest crimson. He wanted a rose that made you want to become one with it, in the same way he wanted to be one with Edie. He closed the paper and left his roast lamb unwanted on the plate, so Lilly finished it for him.

'I'll be back,' he said to Lilly and he walked into Missus Blackmarsh's garden next door. She had many rose bushes meticulously placed in her yard like children lined up at school and he examined each one, looking at its roses and its leaves and half an hour later he chose the rose he wanted. It had the richest blood-red petals and stood out from all the other roses. He went back inside and said, 'Mum, where are your scissors? Quick.'

She didn't question him, just put down the knife she was using to chop the celery, wiped her hands on her apron and fossicked in her drawer of kitchen utensils. She handed him the scissors and went back to chopping celery.

Theo returned to Maud Blackmarsh's garden and tenderly held the stalk, supporting the flower in his hand as he cut it from the branch.

Maud, her hands on her hips, watched through the front window and turned to Milton Blackmarsh and said, 'I think Hooley's finally lost all his marbles, he just stole my best rose. That was my show rose. I was going to win with that one.'

'Well, you won't be winning with it now I expect,' said Milton.

Theo put some water into an empty milk bottle and put the rose in the bottle, carefully resting the stem against the rim, and put it in the middle of the kitchen table.

'I'm going out, Mum,' he said and went to see Missus Johnson whose two boys were due to come for piano lessons that afternoon and explained he wouldn't be available and their lesson was postponed.

'Indefinitely?' asked Missus Johnson, but Theo was away in his future, the present made no impression and he didn't answer.

Theo walked home quickly.

'Mum, I need you to iron and starch my best shirt.' She washed the onion juice off her hands and got out the ironing board and put the iron on the stove. She liked it when the onion juice made her cry; she had a lot to cry for, it got very tiring being cheery all the time, being able to cry was as good as having a nice lie down. She didn't know what Theo was up to but he seemed to have perked up and that had to be a good thing, and he had put a rose — heavens knows where he got it — on the kitchen table and that was really sweet of him. Maybe he had even put on a skerrick of weight — or maybe she was imagining that bit. She inspected the shirt for creases and, satisfied it was good enough, left it hanging on his doorknob.

Theo stood in front of the hall mirror and filled his hair with oil and twirled the ends of his moustache. He had put on the shirt and his new good suit and polished his boots. Then he called out, 'Mum I'm just popping out for a bit.'

'What, again?' she said.

'Yes,' he said and picked up his rose and kissed her on the cheek and was out the front door and on his way. He walked from his mother's house in Ligar Street, cutting across the railway line and over Doveton Street to Webster Street to arrive at Edie's door at precisely three in the afternoon.

Theo thought about how he had stood before this very door some eight months earlier, full of hope for their future together. He looked at the door and felt dwarfed by its unyielding size; it was a tangible barrier between him and Edie. The last time he had stood there for hours, never knocking.

'Come on, Hooley,' he said to himself. 'You faced more daunting things than a wooden door in Africa.' He breathed deeply and knocked loudly and waited. He supposed it would be Beth the maid who would answer. So he was ready when she did; he'd practised his lines so they wouldn't get stuck in his head.

'I'm here to see Edith,' he said with rehearsed coolness so the servant girl wouldn't see his desperation.

Beth raised an eyebrow at him and stood there like she could see more than he gave her credit for.

'Well, go on, go and get her, that's what you're paid for, isn't it?' he said, thinking her eyebrow was mocking him and surprised at how well he just handled her.

Beth glared at him and yelled through the house, 'Edith!'

What an impertinent creature, he thought and knew immediately that the battle lines had been drawn and the trumpet sounded.

'If you were in my Company,' he said slowly, 'you'd be punished severely for insubordination. I said go and get her, not yell at her.'

He saw her looking at him as if she would teach him not to muck with her. But maybe he was tougher than anyone thought, tougher than he thought. He sighed loudly, letting her see his exasperation, and reminded himself that she was just a servant and not worth getting too upset about.

'How do the Cottinghams put up with you?' he said, and that made her turn on her heel and stomp off, leaving him alone to wait for Edie. He wasn't sure who won that fight — he suspected she had. Perhaps he had been a little too harsh, he thought, and tapped his foot on the stone front step in time to his heart as he waited for Edie to appear.

It seemed to take longer than all the months just past. Surely she wouldn't leave him standing there? Surely she would come?

Finally Edie was before him, with the infant over her shoulder. He looked at the chubby legs kicking under the lacy baby dress. He didn't think of babies as human and he felt an urge to reach out and touch those fat pale kicking things, they looked so foreign to him. He thought the infant looked like something that should be kept pickled in a bottle, like a museum exhibit.

Then he saw that Edie was gently patting its back over and over, as though the child was part of her. She seemed completely natural with the baby, as if she was simply twiddling her thumbs or absently rubbing her elbows. And he realised with a terrible shock that the child had become part of Edie. His heart lurched as he wondered why it couldn't be *their* infant. If it was theirs it would bring them together, whereas this child had forced them apart, and he hated it. Then he realised that Edie had been gazing at him for some time, waiting for him to speak as she rocked the baby.

He removed his hat in readiness to give his prepared speech. On the way over he had decided that he needed to take things slowly. Begin again, as it were. Work his way up to asking her to marry him.

'I was wondering, Miss Cottingham, if you would accompany me on a stroll around the lake next Saturday afternoon. There's a prediction of fine weather,' and he looked at the sky as if he had a contract with it, already in place for Saturday afternoon. Then he quickly looked at the ground, not daring to read her face in case he saw something in it that wasn't hopeful. It seemed to take another forever before she answered. His heart thumped so loudly he wondered if she could hear it.

'Everything has changed, Theo, there's Gracie now. Gracie and my father need me,' she said slowly and he looked up as she made to shut the door.

He thought at first that he hadn't heard her properly, but when he saw her beginning to shut the door he knew he had. *That's it,* he thought. *I waited eight months for you and you say the baby needs you more than me! How could anyone need you more than me?* And his frustration fuelled his determination.

'I know what death does to people,' he said quickly, putting his polished boot in the doorway, making her step back a little. 'I've seen death, I saw it when I was a little boy of twelve and my father died and I saw plenty of it in Africa. I know death has a way of crippling you so you can't go on with life. I know what it's like and if I have to wait till forever for you Edie, I can do it. I'll wait till you're ready, Miss Cottingham. I've waited this long. What will a little longer cost me?' Edie didn't say anything so he stepped back and placed the rose that he had hidden behind his back on her doorstep.

'I am waiting, Edie. I'll wait forever,' he said, and really believed in his heart that he could. He walked off down the path, elated that he had finally found his voice. From the study window Beth watched him go.

Edie clutched Gracie tighter to her chest as though the baby was the anchor that would stop her running after him and keep her where she knew she belonged.

Later that night Edie took out her notebook, which she hadn't opened since the day at the lake, that awful day when she had planned to do a terrible thing until Gracie stopped her. How could she forgive herself? Edie would make it up to Gracie, she would love Gracie above all else for the rest of her life — after all, loving Gracie was an easy thing to do. Edie turned to the last entry and ran her fingers over the words.

Wednesday Thirteenth December Five
Plan — Always keep the promise Mama asked of me. The promise I should have said yes to when she asked.

She took out her pencil and added:

Sunday Fifteenth July Six
Note — He said he would wait forever.

Fifteen

At the Door

*Sunday, 10 November 1907, when Theo has
been wooing Edie for nearly eighteen months,
he discusses the Harvester Case with Beth.*

Everyone in town knew that Theo never gave piano lessons on a
Sunday afternoon any more and hadn't done so for the past eighteen
months, so there was no point asking him. For eighteen months, every
Sunday afternoon, he had put on his good suit and walked to Edie
Cottingham's house. He would stand at the gate for a few minutes and
check his watch and at precisely three o'clock he knocked on her door.

Beth always answered. She always rolled her eyes at him as if he
had just ruined an otherwise perfectly good day.

Then, having set the pattern for their relationship in their very
first conversation, they bickered. If he said it was warm out today,
Beth said that in fact it was cold. If he said it was going to rain, she
said there was a drought coming. If he said the child was looking
healthy, Beth said she had been quite ill of late. They exchanged
curt, cross words with each other.

'What do you think of the Harvester Case?' asked Theo, knowing she would know nothing about it.

'Do I look like a farmer to you?' she said, putting her hands on her hips.

'The Harvester Case is a legal ruling, Beth, made just this week. It means a minimum wage for every workingman. It's a great step forward.'

'Well, you seem not to have noticed but I am not a working-man. So tell me something that helps the working woman, Mister Hooley. Can you do that?'

He tried to think of something, anything, that would top her, but no words came to him and their war raged on, each waiting to see who would become exasperated first. He saw the smirk on her lips and the victory in her eyes.

She turned and hollered, 'Edie,' and her voice bounced off the walls like ping-pong balls as it echoed down the hallway.

Theo put his fingers in his ears and said, 'Just shrieking this week? Normally you stomp off on me.'

'Oh, I don't like to disappoint you,' she mocked and she spun on her toes and her dress flounced in the air like it was dancing and she stomped off.

A few minutes later Edie appeared at the door. Theo asked her to go for a turn about the main street. 'Or would you like to take a ride on the trams? Or we could go for a picnic, or a steamer ride on the lake?'

And she answered as she always did: 'I'm so sorry, Theo, but my father and sister need me. I can't possibly entertain anything that would take me away from caring for them.'

Her face, which had been so open to him that day by the tree when he had asked her to marry him, was now shut and bolted. He couldn't tell if she still loved him or if he was a weekly annoy-ance that she hardly thought of.

This made Theo more determined than ever to win her. He admired her perseverance and dedication to the child and her father, but sometimes he wanted to shake her, to make her see that he needed her more than they did. But he knew women didn't like to be yelled at, or shaken, and he had never yelled at anyone let alone a woman, so as she closed the door he stooped and left the rose on the doorstep for her.

Just as he had done. Every Sunday afternoon at three. For the past eighteen months.

Sunday, 17 November 1907, when Lilly has a thing to say.

Theo arrived home after his weekly walk to Edie's house, where he had been turned down yet again, and where he had left a rose on her doorstep yet again. He was hoping to go unnoticed to his bedroom, but as he passed the kitchen Lilly said very loudly, 'I'm not saying anything more about it and you're a grown man, Theo, and you can do what you like with your life and far be it from me to tell you what to do now that you're an adult when you never listened to me when you were five years old but the way you moon over that woman at church and the way you go up there week after week isn't healthy. You could have a wife by now. Someone prettier and younger than Edie Cottingham, too. But far be it from me to say anything.'

Theo stood in the doorway, his hat in his hand, and said quietly, 'You don't have to say anything, Mum. I know exactly what you're thinking because you always tell me.'

'So you know just what I'm thinking, do you?'

'Yes,' he said, 'because you just said it all.'

'Well, go on, I'm listening to what I think.'

'If it takes years I will wait for Edie. She needs time to get over the shock of her mother dying and feeling she has to look after the baby. When she feels free then she can marry me.'

'And when will that be?' Lilly asked.

He thought for a moment. 'When the child turns six it can go to boarding school or to a nurse and it won't need a sister for a foster mother any more, so Edie will be free to marry me.'

'Is that so?'

'Yes!'

'Fat lot you know about babies and children and mothering,' she said.

Sunday, 24 November 1907, when the children have a pleasant walk.

As soon as the town's children had forced down their greens they asked to leave the Sunday lunch table and ran to Ligar Street to wait outside Mister Hooley's house. They had been doing this for months. When it was cold their mothers made them rug up first in their pullovers, but now it was November and it was hot, so their mothers made them wear hats. In the beginning it had been just a few of his piano students who had waited outside Theo's door. But as the weeks and months went by the band of children had grown. Lilly heard the noise of children's voices growing louder in the street outside as if it was lunchtime at the school. She peeked out from behind the curtains to see how many had gathered and saw that the street was crowded with a good hundred or so children. The girls stood in huddles and the boys tossed stones on the road while they waited for Theo to appear.

'There's more of them every week. You're the Pied Piper of Ballarat.'

Theo ignored her disapproving tone as he adjusted his hair and straightened his jacket in the hallstand mirror.

'Well, you encourage them, Mum,' he said.

She opened her mouth in a perfect O. 'Oh, I do not!' she said.

He kissed her on her forehead, 'Yes you do, come on,' and then he went out the front door with his rose. He had no shortage of roses to choose from these days. *'Oh Theo, I have beautiful red roses if you want to have a look and see if any suit your purpose,'* the mothers of his students said. *'Oh Theo, I have grown the most beautiful red rose bush just for you,'* said the women who stopped him in the street. But Maud had Milton Blackmarsh move her best rose bush into the backyard behind the tool shed where it was safe from Theo's eyes and his mother's scissors,

Lilly followed behind Theo with the tray of honey jumbles she had made for the children. Thank goodness she always cooked more than she needed.

'Just one, just one each or there won't be enough to go around,' she said as little fingers grabbed for the biscuits.

Theo didn't speak to the children. He just straightened, adjusted his collar, looked again at the rose in his hand and the children knew that was the sign they were off. The children followed him all the way to Edie's. The girls skipped and jostled to be nearest to Theo, the boys tumbled and ran and kicked at stones on the road. Women came out of their houses and stood in their front gardens, waving their fans to cool their faces and chatting to their neighbours as they waited for Theo to pass by. As he passed they called out hello and dreamt of having a man so devoted to them that he would visit every Sunday for years and years.

The men sat on their front porches drinking beer and they raised their glasses to toast him and wished him good luck as he passed. When he was out of earshot they complained to each other that he was ruining everything for ordinary blokes like them whose wives were going to expect roses from them now.

When he got to the front gate of Edie's house the children stopped. Theo wouldn't let them follow him to the door. It was all very well for them to come on the walk but what he said to Miss Cottingham was private. The children always moaned as if he was cutting them out of the best part and then they waited on the street for him. If it took him a while to knock on the door they got bored and the boys played mock fights and the girls dreamt that they would get to be flower girls when Mister Hooley finally won his love. Some of the older boys lost patience altogether and wandered off to swim in the lake.

Theo checked his watch and knocked on the door. The girls, leaning against the letterbox watching, put their hands over their hearts. Maybe this week Miss Cottingham would come running into his arms.

Beth answered the door. 'You again?'

'You knew it would be me,' he said, 'so don't pretend to be surprised.'

'You and all the town's ratbag children.'

'It's going to be a hot summer, don't you think? It's already sweltering and we haven't even hit December yet.'

She leant out the door and peered into the street. 'You better make sure those boys don't ruin Mister Cottingham's garden throwing those sticks around like swords.'

'Are you going to holler for Edie or stomp off in a sulk to get her for me? The day you behave properly, Beth, will be the day hell freezes over.'

'Some men appreciate a little waywardness in a girl,' she said and slowly looked him up and down, sizing him up. 'But you wouldn't.'

He thought of the women in Africa. It had been so long ago. He wanted to tell her that he amounted to more than she saw, that he might not have a lot to say, he might not be one of those men with silky words but he knew how to bring out the waywardness hidden in a girl's soul. He saw her waiting for him to take the bait. But this wasn't Africa and he wasn't that person any more and Beth wasn't the girl he wanted.

'Are you going to get Edie for me or do I need to holler myself?'

'You? Holler? You can barely speak, Mister Hooley.' And she laughed too hard and saw that he knew she was putting it on and she turned and went down the hallway to get Edie.

For once Edie didn't have the child with her and it gave him hope.

'Miss Cottingham, I thought a walk around the lake? Or if it's too hot for you we could stick to the botanical gardens?'

Did he see pity in her eyes? He prayed not, because if there was pity there was nothing.

She took a deep breath and held tightly onto the door jamb; he could see her knuckles turning white. 'I can't, Theo, I really can't. Because you see I know and you know it's not just an afternoon that you're asking about. Not really. You don't just want a walk with me. You want a lifetime.'

He was sure he could see tears welling in her eyes — or were they welling in his own? His heart wanted to crack open but he wouldn't let it. He would keep waiting. The child was walking now, but in not so many years she would be off to school, gone, and he would have his desire.

Later that day as the sun loosened its bite and began to set, Beatrix and George sat on her front verandah drinking beer.

'It's like the Stations of the Cross at Easter,' Beatrix said, 'the way he walks up there every week with all those children in tow.'

George reached over and grabbed her plump bottom and pulled her closer and she giggled and said, 'Next week you better turn up with a rose or else.'

'Or else what?' he laughed. 'Let me give you a bit more or else.'

A little further away, sitting so that busybody Nurse Drake couldn't see them, Beth and Colin were on the verandah steps next door.

'It's truly beautiful,' Beth said to Young Colin Eales as she pulled at the brown dry grass, 'the way he is so devoted to her. She doesn't deserve him.'

And further away still, in the underground room, Edie lay on the bed with two-year-old Gracie asleep at her side. She wrote in her notebook:

> *Twenty-fourth November Seven*
> *Gracie is two years old and she calls me BeeBee. It makes me laugh every time.*
> *He has the bluest eyes, even bluer than Gracie's — endless like the sky.*
> *Plan — I will stay true to my promise to Mama.*

Theo continued to visit every Sunday afternoon at three. He never missed and every week he left Edie a rose on the verandah step. When the summer came, the sun in its fury cooked the oil out of the rose and the petals became a crisp brown sacrifice, and when the winter came, the morning ice froze the petals and then the afternoon rain turned them to crimson slush, as though they had been bled out. And in all weathers each Monday Beth came out with a bucket of soapy water and a scrubbing brush and washed the rose stain from the porch. It took her hours and she wondered about a man whose love left such persistent stains.

Sixteen

Colin

*Friday, 8 May 1908, when the rain falls
day after day as if it will never cease.*

Beth's bloke, Young Colin Eales as everyone called him, was wet, cold and red in the face.

'The rules say us miners only have to work six hours a day in a wet shaft,' he yelled and the men agreed with him. He looked around at their faces, pleased they were letting him do the talking even though he was the Young and not the Senior Eales. It was his dad who usually did the yelling, but not this time; this time it was his turn and his ability to bellow on behalf of the men must mean he was being taken seriously.

No one messed with his dad so they probably thought that now he was no longer a boy, they better not mess with him. He was glad, he was tired of being a boy. Growing older couldn't come quick enough for him. He didn't know what might be waiting for him when he was older, he just knew it had to be better than what he had now.

The men stood in a huddle outside the mine entrance that stared at them like a gaping mouth ready to devour anyone stupid

enough to walk into it. They were in a stand-off with management, who stood in front of the mine, invisible swords drawn.

Young Colin was at the front of the miners. They were forlorn,
really, their bones were brittle and shivering, their livers were bil-
ious and yellowing and their cheeks were hollow. The dust from
the mine floated around them, scratching at their eyes and making
their clothes stiff as the wet cloth turned it to clay; their trousers
chafed their balls.

The manager, Mister Bladcock, and Darby, his accountant,
rubbed their chins thoughtfully and muttered together in their
crisp black suits until finally Bladcock stepped forward and said,
'Yes, but how wet is wet?'

Young Colin Eales kicked at the dirt, sending a splosh of mud
onto Bladcock's woollen suit pants and said, 'Bloody hell!' And
the men standing around him swore too and nodded their heads
as if that explained everything.

Mister Bladcock rocked on his heels in his muddied suit, which
he ignored, so as not to give Young Eales the pleasure of knowing
he'd annoyed him, and said, 'Local by-laws don't clearly define
what a wet-shaft-sink is. How deep is the shaft Mister — ah ...'

'Eales,' said Young Colin, knowing the bugger knew exactly
what his name was. 'I reckon it's maybe ...'

'About four hundred and fifty feet I'd say,' put in Davo Conroy,
Young Colin's dad's best mate, who up until recently Colin had
called Uncle Dave.

'Yeah,' said Young Colin, 'I reckon that'd be about right.'

'Hmmm,' said Mister Bladcock, 'four hundred and fifty feet.
Your dad works the mines too, doesn't he? Where's he gone?'

'I don't exactly know at the moment,' mumbled Young Colin.
Bladcock and Darby smirked and the men looked at the ground,
embarrassed. It was a cheap shot. Everyone knew Young Colin's

dad was off with his other family in Hamilton. Jeez, everyone also knew that Alice Hardy had dumped her kid at Beatrix Drake's and run off to join him.

'Local by-laws state that nothing under five hundred feet constitutes a wet shaft. You're fifty feet short,' announced Darby.

The men swore some more. Who made these laws up? Bloody government employees with brooms up their arses who'd never set foot in a bleedin' mine.

'We're constantly bucketing water out,' said Young Colin vehemently.

'Constantly?' asked Mister Bladcock, raising an eyebrow.

Young Colin nodded and said, 'No amount of bucketing is gonna get rid of the water and working in clothes soaked to the skin constitutes wet in my book. If you want to bring an official down here, Mister Bladcock, you go and do it, but we ain't doing more than six hours a day in these conditions.' Young Colin stood as tall as he could and threw his chest out like a barricade. He wouldn't be broken by men in suits.

Mister Bladcock stepped back and had another private, mumbled word with Darby, then he nodded and stepped forward again and said to the men, 'So you're having to bucket water out all the time?'

'That's what I said, ain't it,' said Young Colin.

'Hmm, yes,' drawled Mister Bladcock, and Young Colin began to feel edgy, as if he was about to be done over. His shoulders began to slump.

'The removal of water,' Mister Bladcock said slowly, as if explaining to idiots, 'constitutes shaft-sinking and shaft-sinking is paid on an eight-hour shift at six shillings. You'll be paid after your expenses have been removed of course — unless you'd rather tributes.'

No miners wanted tributes, where they were paid a portion of the value of the gold they mined. Tributes were inconsistent and didn't keep families fed.

'But our normal pay is seven shillings,' stammered Young Colin.

'But that's for normal labour which you yourself said is not what you are doing at present,' said Bladcock smugly.

Colin glared at Bladcock, but couldn't think of anything to say. The bugger had got them on a technicality. Slowly he walked off towards the mouth of the ruddy mine followed by the men.

Mister Bladcock sighed. His was a tough lot and he wasn't paid anything like he ought to be. Some days, he felt he was taking his life in his hands dealing with these uneducated miners. Nothing's to say there wouldn't be another Stockade if they got it into their minds, most likely led by Eales Senior, who wouldn't have been such a pushover as his son.

The Eales cottage was Number 7 Eddy Street. It was a small low cottage with just one step up to the verandah. The front door was plumb in the middle of the front of the house and sat there sullenly wishing it was the entrance to something much grander. Either side of the door was a window that let in very little light. When you went inside you stepped into the narrow hallway that ran right through the middle of the cottage and straight out the back door. Next to the Eales cottage was a narrow grassy laneway and then Beatrix Drake's house at Number 9, which lorded it over the Eales cottage with its ornate cast-iron lacework at the corners of its verandah posts and its width, which was a good half as wide again as the Eales cottage.

Young Colin told Beth all about the meeting with management that night as they sat out of the rain on the verandah. He told it so that he was a hero, like Peter Lalor, and he could feel in his bones that he really could be a hero.

'Mister Cottingham's always trying to help the miners,' she said. 'You oughta talk to him.'

'We can work this out ourselves,' said Young Colin, who mistrusted anyone who lived around the lake. Bored with talking about work, he noticed the inviting rise and fall of Beth's chest as she breathed, and whiteness of her breath as it floated like wisps of smoke in the chilly evening air. He thought how much better his head would feel lying on that pretty chest with her breath settling on him, so he said, 'How 'bout you and I go up the lane and work something out?'

'It's raining, Colin,' she said.

'I can find us somewhere dry and we can keep each other warm.'

'Yeah, and what if your nosy neighbour catches us? She knows where I work, doesn't she,' said Beth. 'And we ain't married, remember.' She waggled her ring finger in his face.

Young Colin pushed his hand under the thick wool of her coat and rested it on her breast. He nuzzled his head into her neck under her scarf and she giggled because it tickled, which wasn't the effect he was after. Frustrated that he still couldn't persuade her to go up the lane he sighed and stood up. Nothing was going his way today. He walked to the other end of the verandah.

'Sulking now, are we?' she asked, and he was relieved when his mother called them both in to tea because he was sulking but he didn't want to admit it. Sulking wasn't manly.

'When's your dad coming back then?' asked Beth as they resumed their spot on the verandah after dinner. Colin shrugged.

He didn't like talking about his dad going off and leaving him and his mum with five younger nippers to feed.

'I dunno, Mum reckons he's most likely gone to Hamilton and maybe his girlfriend's gone up there with him, but I reckon he's just gone on a bender and can't find his way home. Or maybe he's in a lock-up till he dries out. But he's been gone a good long while,' he said as he tried to get his hand up her skirt.

'You're not getting any,' said Beth. 'Not here with that old busybody Nurse Drake looking out her window.'

'She's got her own fella,' said Colin, 'so she shouldn't be throwing no stones.'

Beth pulled away from him. 'Go on.'

Colin sighed, he didn't want to have to bother telling her about Nurse Drake's business. He was over talking for the day, a man had other things he'd rather be doing. Now he wished he hadn't said anything because he knew she'd persist till she got it out of him.

'What'll you give me if I tell you?' he asked, smiling.

'Come on, tell me.'

'What'll you give me then?' He threw out his hands like he had nothing in the world until she filled them with her something.

'You tell me or you won't ever get nothing again!' she said, walloping him on the arm.

'Oww,' he cried, making out he was hurt. She hit him again, this time harder. 'Oh all right, before you beat the living daylights out of me. She's a married woman, right, and her husband's a miner in Bendigo and she has a boyfriend on the side. One of the local coppers. He comes round thrice a week regular as clockwork. Saturday, Sunday and Wednesday arvo.'

Beth almost couldn't believe it. Nurse Drake committing unholy adultery? Colin lived next door to her so he'd know if it was true.

Colin could see she was in two minds about believing him, so he said, 'Hey these ain't houses like the Cottingham's round the blasted lake, there ain't no gardens and bushes planted just so your neighbour can't see your dirty deeds.'

There were no secrets here. He watched her look at the space between the houses. She looked disappointed now that she believed him. Now she knew this piece of news it didn't seem as exciting as when she didn't know it and could still imagine all sorts of possibilities. He saw his chance of getting a bit of comfort fly away.

'Come on, it's dark and too cold to be sitting out here any longer. Walk me back to Webster Street,' she said, opening her umbrella. 'And pick me a rose on the way like Mister Hooley does for Edie.' She slipped her arm through his.

Young Colin's face darkened. She was always on about Mister Hooley. Mister Hooley this and Mister Hooley that. 'Blimey I hate that geezer!' he said.

'Why?' asked Beth pulling away from him. 'How could anyone hate Theo Hooley?'

'Think about it,' he said. 'How are the rest of us blokes ever to live up to his antics? A rose a week on her doorstep. All the kids following him up there, the women mooning over him as he passes their houses. I ain't getting you no rose, Beth. You have to just take me as I am.' And he stood tall, pleased he'd put it to her like a real man, a grown man who wouldn't put up with any ruckus from his missus.

But it cost him because Beth removed her arm from his and sulked after that and he got wet from the rain because the umbrella wasn't large enough for the two of them unless they stayed close. Beth looked longingly at every rose bush they passed and he seethed because he was green to the gills at the way she always went on about Theo Hooley.

Reading his fiery thoughts and unable to step away from the flame, Beth said, 'Mister Hooley told me how to preserve rose petals.'

'What're you going to do with them? Serve them up with custard?'

And she laughed and forgave him for his moodiness and put her arm back through his and he patted her hand and thought how he loved her and could spend the rest of his life listening to that laugh. His mum said laughter was the secret to a happy union, which meant he and Beth would be real happy.

Saturday, 9 May 1908, when Young Colin makes a decision.

The next day Colin got up at 3 a.m. like he always did. He put on his clothes that were stiff with cold and rubbed his hands together to bring his fingers to life. His mum had packed him some bread in a tin case and tea in a thermos and it was waiting on the kitchen table for him. The rest of the family were still asleep. Davo Conroy, who lived in Number 3, was waiting out the front and they walked to work together.

'Uncle Davy, think I'll marry Beth when I'm twenty-one.'

'You've got a four-year wait if you're going to wait till twenty-one, mate.'

'Beth seems to like a man who can wait,' said Colin bitterly.

Seventeen

Beth

Sunday, 29 October 1911, when secrets are made and kept.

The laundry was outside, a little room that sat on the far edge of the back verandah. Inside it there was a large copper and a concrete double sink with a wringer that perched between the two sinks; there were shelves, neat and evenly spaced like railway tracks that went all the way up to the ceiling. Normally the shelves held the glass preserving bottles. If the preserving had just been done, the jars would sit on the shelves like autumn, filled with the shades of burnt orange and lime green of peaches, pears, figs, grapes and apricots. Over winter these would slowly disappear and be replaced with clean empty bottles waiting for the next year's fruit. The laundry door was usually jammed ajar with a wedge of firewood. That way Beth could easily carry the laundry or the bottles of preserves in and out without having to bother with the door latch. Now the door was not only shut and latched, it was bolted and locked. Beth wouldn't let anyone in the laundry, and what was even more concerning to Edie was that she was doing all the laundry in the kitchen, by hand, without the wringer or the copper, and wouldn't explain why. Even more mysteriously she wouldn't let anyone inside the laundry, they couldn't even peek in. Beth was immovable. No one was allowed to look inside the laundry.

'Oh, come on, Beth, you can tell me. Why you won't let us in the laundry?' pleaded Edie.

'I don't understand why you are doing the laundry in the kitchen,' said Paul. 'We have a perfectly good laundry and there is nothing wrong with it. I think I should demand that you use the laundry properly and whatever you have locked up in there needs to see the light of day.'

But Beth turned on her heel and said, 'Well, Mister Cotting-ham, the day you feel I am not doing a good enough job is the day you can give me the sack but the laundry stays locked.'

Beth remembered the exact date that Theo told her about the roses. It was Sunday the fifth of January 1908.

Beth had said to him, 'You and your roses. It's all very well to leave a rose on the porch each week Mister Hooley but who do you think it is that has to clean up the mess it makes on the porch?' And as soon as she said the words she wished she hadn't. She had been too mean. Her words had cut his heart. She could see the grey wash over his face, his eyes became dull and his skin paled as if she had brushed away his life with no care at all. He was devastated that Edie left his roses on the porch to wither, and Beth had to clean them up.

'I had hoped Edie would have collected the rose after I'd gone,' he muttered.

'She's not the sort of girl that would do something romantic with them, Mister Hooley,' Beth said softly, trying to close up the wound. 'Her mind is filled with caring for Gracie, and besides she's a practical girl.' *Not like me*, she thought. If they were her roses she would put them under her pillow so their magic would make her dream of love.

Beth watched as he gathered himself together, stiffened and put his pain away somewhere she couldn't see. He said light-heartedly, 'Well, that's a wicked waste, you could at least use the petals for tea,' and he had told her how to dry roses by hanging them upside down.

'Of course they lose their colour, shape and perfume,' he'd explained. 'If you want them to stay whole you have to get glue. You must carefully, with a toothpick, put glue at the base of each petal. Then you must smear the glue down the stalk to where you want to cut it. About, say, two inches. Then snip the stalk where the glue ends, fast but carefully so as not to disturb the bloom, and seal the end of the stalk with the glue. Then when the glue has dried get a container, like a tin, and fill it with two inches of sand, then place the bloom upright in the sand and put it somewhere safe to dry out for four weeks. It will dry as a complete bloom that you can carefully lift out of the sand when you want to.'

'Who would want to bother with all that nonsense?' she'd said.

At first she collected the roses because she thought that one day Edie might change her mind and want them, and then she began to collect them for herself. To her, the roses Theo left on the porch were the seeds of undying love. She had even thought that maybe she could feed Colin rose tea from the petals and make him love her with the same passion that Theo loved Edie; but she never did. Maybe because somewhere deep inside, some-where she wasn't yet willing to acknowledge, she was dissatisfied with Colin. But she didn't know why, and when that feeling eked into her consciousness she would push it away and remind herself that of course she loved Colin. If she had spoken about it to her sister, Dottie would have laughed and told her that if she had to remind herself she loved Colin, then she obviously didn't. 'We'll marry one day, Beth,' Colin would say after he had taken her up the laneway and frantically plunged himself into her and her heart would sink, because marrying wasn't necessarily the same as undying love.

Each Sunday after Theo's visit, Beth carefully gathered up the rose and carried it, hidden in her apron, to her bedroom. There she jammed the door shut with her bedside chair. From her drawer, she got the glue she had cooked on the stove and sealed in a jar and the toothpicks she had purchased and very carefully followed the instructions Theo had given her. When the glue had dried she placed the rose into a clean preserving jar already filled with sand from Gracie's sandpit.

She used a different glass jar each week. If it was a half-pint jar she cut the stem shorter and left it longer for a one-pint jar. She always made sure to have a jar clean and thoroughly dry and filled with sand ready for the next week's rose. Sometimes when there wasn't a spare jar she would look in the pantry for one that was nearly empty and when Edie and Mister Cottingham weren't around she would quickly tip the syrupy fruit into the compost and wash the jar and dry it ready for her rose. She thought of them as her roses now. Even though he brought them for Edie. When she had carefully placed the bloom in the jar, she cut a strip of brown paper, wrote the date on it and glued the label to the jar. She then carried the jar to the laundry and put it on the shelf. She kept the jars in order, putting the date on them the way you did with anything you were preserving so that you knew how long you had had it. Beth knew that she had one hundred and ninety-nine jars of dried roses filling every inch of the small laundry. Beth had soon used up the three dozen jars the Cottinghams owned and so had to scrounge jars from everyone she knew. 'Oh, do you have a few spare preserving jars I could borrow?' she asked the women at church and her sister Dottie and when they looked at her and waited for an explanation she said, 'Oh, I'm making preserves for the church fete.'

'Well, you are thinking ahead,' the churchwomen said, but Dottie had dropped her head to the side, scrunched up her lips and looked hard at Beth and Beth knew Dottie didn't believe her and was waiting for the truth. But Beth couldn't tell anyone what the jars were really for. She knew she couldn't keep borrowing jars, especially from Dottie, and so she used her saved sovereigns to purchase more. They came in a box of a dozen and after the first two boxes Mister Turnbull, with his wife staring over his shoulder, said, 'What on earth are you preserving, Beth, that you need so many jars?'

And she said, 'Body parts, Mister Turnbull,' and looked pointedly at Missus Turnbull so that she stepped back and pretended she was busy making up bags of tea.

Beth preserved as little fruit as she could get away with. She felt that using the jars for fruit was a waste, they had a more important purpose. So she only served preserved fruit when the Cottinghams asked for it, and most of the time they didn't think about the fact that the fruit always seemed to be stewed now.

Eventually Beth could no longer move in the laundry without the risk of knocking the jars over and she didn't want to do that — the longer the roses sat preserved in their jars the more sacred they became. So now she did the washing in the kitchen.

Eighteen

The Birthday

Sunday, 5 November 1911, when there is
no remedy for what ails Beth.

The summer heat was returning but it was not going to be like the year when Gracie was born. The sun was muted by calm breezes and unable to yell out fiercely.

The days were cool in the mornings and cooler again in the afternoons, which everyone felt was the proper way of things for Ballarat. During the day the warm northerly breezes teased the women's skirts as they crossed the Doveton Street intersection and made them flounce deliciously. The skirts were getting shorter and rising well above the boot, making the old women scoff at the state of the world and making the miners smile, thinking things might at last be turning in their favour. The afternoons were pleasant and the lake was full and on Saturday and Sunday afternoons the townspeople ambled around it, agreeing that life would always be like it was right now and what more could anyone ask for.

In the early hours of Sunday morning, Beth and Gracie both lay awake in their beds. Beth's bed had timber slats that had lost their varnish and no longer shone. Gracie's bed was a brass one that had ceramic balls atop each of its posts with hand-painted pictures on them of ladies on garden swings with bluebirds flying around their heads. Beth and Gracie were each lying perfectly still, though Gracie had her arm around her doll named for her mother Lucy. Gracie thought Lucy was the most beautiful doll she had ever seen, she had eyes that opened and shut and if Gracie used her little finger she could touch the tiny white teeth inside the doll's smiling mouth. The doll had a white dress trimmed with lace and she had soft brown hair that curled slightly at the ends.

Gracie could hardly move as her body was in a commotion, every part of her tingled with excitement. She felt it down in her toes and she stretched them to see if the tingling disappeared but it didn't and it coursed all the way up to her head, where her hair was tied in cotton rags to keep its curl. Gracie wanted to savour the tingling and she smiled because today was special but tomorrow wouldn't be and so the tingling wouldn't be there tomorrow when she woke up. It was here for today only and she was going to make the most of it and make the feeling last as long as possible. It was here because it was her birthday. She wondered for a moment what her birthday presents would be and if Beth had made her a cake. But mostly she enjoyed knowing that today would be a perfect day because it was her birthday.

As soon as Beth opened her eyes, she knew it was a special day. Her body tingled all over with expectation. She lay with her hands by her sides, under the bedclothes, and felt the trembling begin in her toes and swim this way and that up through her body as she tried to think of why it was a special day. Gracie had grown from a sickly baby into a robust child and today she was six years old. But Beth knew that wasn't it. There was something else, something that was hiding itself from her.

Beth's thoughts drifted to Colin Eales and she absently twisted
the engagement ring he had put on her finger a few weeks ago.
'There you are, Beth,' he'd said. 'You're mine good and proper
now. Next year you and I are twenty-one and we'll marry.' He
hadn't asked her and he hadn't waited for an answer, he'd just
assumed they belonged together. Round and round she turned
that ring while she thought of his needy kisses and the way the
silly blighter would quickly peck her on the cheek over and over,
trying to get the kissing done as quickly as possible so he could
throw his hand down her blouse to grab hold of her breast. And
when he did grab hold of her breast he held tight like he had just
got the best toy and was going to hold on so the other boys didn't
come and take it. Sometimes he would get his other hand up her
skirt and once he got that far she would give in and let him have
what he wanted, which he would take quickly, as though he had
to gulp her down before someone took her away. But more and
more lately she would push him away and he would say, 'But
we're engaged, Bethie.'

'Engaged isn't married,' she'd say and walk back down the lane
and stand where Nurse Drake could watch them through her
window.

Beth's thoughts travelled to Theo Hooley, and how he stood on
the porch waiting patiently for Edie. For over five years that man
had been waiting. How did he have such constancy? She wondered if his lovemaking would be slow and careful like his life.
They said he could never find his words but he never had trouble
finding a few choice words for her when he came to the door.
He'd lecture her on her rudeness, or tell her she knew nothing
about reading the clouds for a weather forecast, or that she should
be more informed about what was going on in the world if she
really cared about women's rights as much as she claimed she did.
Or he'd tell her of the punishment she'd receive if she was a digger

in the army and tried that rudeness on a superior. But while he said all these things there was a curve to his lip and she didn't know if he was serious or just teasing her.

Ass, she thought. But then she thought again of how long he had waited for Edie. Colin never waited for anything. Beth thought it was awful the way that Edie wouldn't even walk out with Theo Hooley.

'You could leave Gracie and your father to my care for an hour or so,' she'd said, and Edie had replied, 'I can't possibly leave Gracie and Papa alone.'

I'd be here, thought Beth, feeling the bitterness she always felt when it was brought home to her that she wasn't really family.

Then Edie said quietly, as though they were closer than any real sisters could be, 'He doesn't just want me for an hour or so, Beth — he wants me for life, and if I step out even once, I am saying yes to making my life with him. He and I both know that. But my life belongs with Papa and Gracie. It's just the way it is. It's just the way life has turned out and you and I both know why.'

Beth imagined she was Edie basking in Theo's unfailing slow love. Sometimes she put a rose in its glass case under her bed so its magic could change her life and bring her something — she didn't know what, but something else. Last night when the others had gone to bed she had carefully carried in a rose. She had chosen one that was smaller than the others, but redder. She unclipped the lid and sweet smells filled her head, then she placed the rose under her bed. She imagined the magic wafting up through the mattress, through the sheets and into her pores. And when she woke this morning she felt warm with sun coming through the window, and now she threw off the blanket and let the sun kiss her body sprawled on the bed. Drowsily she pulled her night-dress up over her legs, past her belly, and let it slide gently over her breasts and then she rose slightly so she could pull it over her head. Her body was smooth and fresh and the sun's gentle touch on her skin warmed her just the right amount, making her feel golden and immortal. The sun, an old hand, knew what he was doing. First he gently warmed Beth's hair until it shone, next he lulled her into sleepy laziness by warming her young face till her cheeks were pink, then he moved lower down and allowed his beams to tickle her nipples, warming them to little peaks. Slowly, slowly he rose higher in the sky and cast his warmth lower down on her body. The sun moved his heat now between her legs and she lifted her hips to soak up more of him. She moaned quietly, deliciously — no one suspected her and the sun except the rose under her bed. Its alchemy grew stronger in the warmth and its sweetness filled the room. The sun was clever, he could have taught Young Colin a thing or two. A smirk fell across his face and gently he caused the slightest cool breeze to blow in through the louvre windows and Beth was consumed by licks of fire that burnt her toes and fingertips.

A few minutes later the walls of her bedroom slowly came into focus; her bed, her wardrobe, her dresser and the sad picture of Jesus on the wall that gazed mournfully at her no matter where she was in the room. Sometimes she shut Jesus up by throwing her shawl over his face. She felt sure she had just been dreaming and it was time the stove was lit. She sat up and suddenly the world was a cold place compared to where she had just been. Beth got up from the bed and the room spun and she held her hands to her dizzy head. Maybe she'd got a sickness and needed to get Edie to give her a double dose of Boomerang Tonic for good measure, or maybe she had just spent too much time lying in the warm morning sun. She felt her abdomen murmur uneasily and she rubbed it gently. Then she felt her forehead for fever and decided she was definitely a bit hot and then her head went blank and she gripped the bed to steady herself. It was as though her head had been pulled up into the cloudy mists on top of Mount Buninyong and was lost in grey-white rain clouds. Her brain was full of nothing and everything at the same time, and she suddenly remembered it was a Sunday, the day of Theo Hooley's visits.

There would be another rose.

Beth breathed deeply until she felt she could stand up without fainting, then grabbed her skirt and bodice from where they hung over the end of her bed. She remembered that Edie had recently given her another hand-me-down and she pulled it from the walnut wardrobe and put it on instead. She slipped her feet into her boots and tied them. Then, down on her hands and knees, she pulled the preserved rose from under the bed, clipped the lid shut and carefully carried the rose back to the laundry, putting it back exactly in its place and making sure to lock the door behind her.

On her way back to the house she gathered kindling from the box under the back verandah and paper from the paper box. She moved the basket of clothes out of the way and lit the kitchen stove. Beth made a pot of tea and because she still felt like she was trying to walk on a tiny boat that was being tossed by tidal waves she poured a cup for herself and sat at the kitchen table and gripped its sides to stop everything moving.

Gracie bounded up and down the hallway, squealing and whooping that it was her birthday, and her noise ricocheted around Beth's head.

'Wake up, everybody,' Gracie hollered as she ran up and down. Her feet thumped the floorboards and rattled the teapot on the kitchen table. She jumped into the kitchen in bunny hops, her hands up like paws, her hair in its rags bouncing in all directions, her eyes eager for the day ahead. She couldn't keep her balance as she hopped and nearly toppled over and she and Beth laughed.

'You're still in your nightgown,' said Beth, rubbing her head as Gracie hopped around her.

'It's my birthday.' Gracie smiled at Beth. Her six-year-old excitement was contagious and Beth reached out to hug her. Gracie tore into her arms.

'It's Gracie's birthday, remember,' said Edie, coming into the kitchen in her summer dressing gown, followed by Paul in his night shirt and gown.

'How could I forget? She's been reminding us all week,' Paul said and he motioned to Beth to pour him a cup of tea. But Beth just sat nursing her strange head. Edie looked at her and asked gently, 'Should I do it?' Beth nodded and ignored Edie's concerned gaze. She couldn't tell them what was wrong with her because she didn't know herself.

'Do you know what day it is, Beth?' asked Gracie, pulling on her sleeve.

'I don't think Beth is feeling one hundred per cent, Gracie, perhaps don't tug at her,' said Edie

'Umm — nope, no idea,' Beth teased.

'It's my birthday.'

'No kidding,' said Beth and then she looked at the clock and said, 'Oh my goodness, is that the time? There's hours yet before your birthday. You weren't born until the afternoon so you're not officially six until then and I have to prepare lunch. There's potatoes to peel and peas to shell and we all have to go to church first.'

Edie offered to help with the lunch but Beth wanted to be alone. She had something to figure out, though she couldn't work out what. She didn't want Edie's concerned looks and questions.

'I'm sure if I just have some quiet and another cup of tea I'll be right,' she said and hoped her brain would sort itself out. Beth was sure she was ill, otherwise she was going mad. When Edie had taken Gracie away to help her dress and Paul had gone off to his room, Beth pulled the potatoes from the sack beside the cooker and began peeling. She cut her thumb because she was watching the clock and not the knife and stood mesmerised by the red running from the cut. She came to her senses and ran her finger under cold water and tied a rag tight around it to stop the bleeding. When the potatoes were cut she started on the pumpkin and lost great chunks of the flesh as she slashed at the tough hide of the pumpkin because she was watching the clock. She shelled the peas but absently ate most of them, distracted by the aching slowness of the hands of the clock. She walked to church in a daze and didn't hear one word of Reverend Whitlock's sermon and walked home absentmindedly, occasionally bumping into fences. At one point Paul had to pull her back as she nearly stepped into the path of Doctor Appleby's new Napier motor car, the only motor vehicle in town.

It was no better when they got home. Beth had forgotten to put the leg of lamb in the oven before church so now it would be served too late and Gracie's birthday lunch wouldn't be ready until half-past two when Paul always liked lunch to be served at precisely one. She made custard for the cake but she forgot to stir it and it caught, burning on the bottom and turned into a gluggy mess with nasty brown specks through it and she had to throw it out down the back of the garden and then put oil in the saucepan and leave it to soak in the sun. They finally sat down to lunch at one forty-five and Beth served the tiny pieces of pumpkin and split what peas were left evenly between them, counting out six peas each. She felt Edie and Paul look at each other and then look at her and she shrugged her shoulders and gave them no explanation because she didn't have one herself yet.

'So your birthday lunch at last, eh Gracie,' said Paul. 'Would you like to give thanks for the food as it's your birthday?'

Gracie did and Paul stood and carved into the lamb. Blood spurted out like sauce and settled in a red pool in the bottom of the dish. Beth saw Paul look over at Edie again.

'Sorry,' she said, 'I should have put it on earlier.'

'Are you okay, Beth?' asked Edie. 'Is something wrong? Has Young Colin upset you? Papa can take to him with his umbrella if he has.'

'No, no, I just have a bit of a headache but I'm fine. I'm not going to miss Gracie's birthday for anything.' Even Beth could hear the lie in her voice. It was more than just a headache — but what was it?

Paul took the knife to the lamb again and carved around the edges.

'Perhaps it can go back in the oven for a bit, Beth,' he suggested.

'Hmm what?' she replied. Her mind was so full of fog and she shook her head to try and shake it out.

Edie and Paul glanced at each other again, Gracie looked back and forward between everyone.

'I'm okay, really, everyone. Let's concentrate on the birthday girl.'

'Beth, you look really pretty today,' Edie said. 'I think those clothes look better on you than they ever did on me.'

Beth looked down at her clothes. She was wearing the pale blue skirt and bodice that Edie had given her.

'We are really going to miss you when you finally agree to set a date with Young Colin Eales,' Edie said.

'There's no rush,' snapped Beth, and she looked at Edie's clothes, so different to what she was wearing. Edie was wearing smart office-y clothes: a grey woollen skirt, A-line and close fitting that stopped a couple of inches above her ankle, and a crisp white shirt. She had a grey suit jacket to match but she had taken it off after church. The first time she wore the outfit Paul had asked her if she didn't look a tad too manly. Edie said sharply that she looked modern and capable.

'We must have a birthday cake,' demanded Gracie.

'Of course,' said Edie, reaching over and playing with her curls. 'Birthday milk from a cow that was having her birthday the day she was milked, birthday bread from a baker whose birthday it is and birthday jam made by our own Beth on her birthday. But not till after you've eaten your meat and vegetables.'

'Well that's easy,' said Gracie, looking at the tiny serves of food on her plate. She popped the last piece of lamb in her mouth and bounced from the table and danced around them, her arms flailing wildly. Beth needed more tea to settle her stomach and she reached out for the milk but she knocked the teapot off the table and the spout broke and the handle snapped off and Gracie stopped dancing and they all cried 'Ohhh' in unison.

Edie said quickly, 'Don't worry about putting anything away, Beth, we'll all do it later, after we've had afternoon tea. Why don't you have a bit of a snooze?'

'Yes, I think you should,' said Paul. 'I know you'll survive whatever has you in a tether, but I'm not sure Lucy's crockery will.'

So Beth lay down and the others cleaned up after lunch.

The birthday cake was to be saved for afternoon tea when it was officially Gracie's birthday. But Edie knew the real reason they were delaying the cake was to wait until after Theo Hooley's inevitable visit.

Beth joined them after the cleaning up and they sat in the cane chairs in the sunroom off from the dining room. It had bay windows that stretched from the floor to the ceiling so you could either look towards the back garden or past the study to the front, where you would see Theo and his band of children as he turned up the driveway. Edie sat looking to the back garden and tried to read *To Win the Love He Sought*, but Beth knew she wasn't really reading because she hadn't turned one page in half an hour and kept looking at the clock every couple of minutes, which seemed to be taking a year to get to three.

Beth was sitting on the floor measuring Gracie for a new coat for next winter. She made sure to take into account the extra inches the child might grow over the summer, but Gracie was still very small and didn't seem to grow at the same rate as her sister's children had.

'I'm giving a speech tomorrow,' said Paul, filling the room with his voice. 'Now that we have secured an old age pension, I am agitating for a maternity payment for poor mothers so they don't have to hand their children over to orphanages.'

Beth smiled at him. The sun shining through the windows was warm and she felt lazy and drowsy from lunch. The fog in her head was thickening.

A while later Edie said, 'How long do you think he will keep persisting?'

Paul raised an eyebrow and looked at Edie over his paper.

Beth quickly looked at the ground. She didn't know why her cheeks were suddenly so hot. Perhaps she was ill after all? Her heart began to pound so loudly she was sure they could all hear it and she felt faint again. She put her hands on the floor to steady herself and she looked at the clock. At that very moment she realised that her life was spent waiting for the rose Theo left on the porch each week.

Gracie wriggled.

'Hold your arm out, Gracie, and keep still,' Beth said, but it was Gracie's birthday and she couldn't keep still, keeping still made her arms and legs hurt and there were presents wrapped in brown paper and string in the corner and one present was in a box and she had had to wait all through church and then all through lunch and now until afternoon tea time, which Paul had pronounced, because of the late lunch and Mister Hooley, would be postponed until four.

'Have you made a cake, Beth?'

'I don't make cakes for girls who don't keep still.' Beth winked at Paul.

'I don't like cake with fruit in it,' said Gracie.

'I know that and if I was to make you a birthday cake it wouldn't have fruit in it.'

'I like chocolate cake.'

'Well you might, but cocoa is four and halfpence for only a quarter of a pound tin.'

'Oh my glory!'

'It's been that for ages, Papa,' said Edie.

'No, no, no, I don't give a hoot for the price of cocoa,' he said.

'Well, what then?' asked Edie.

He rolled the paper and slapped it against his leg. 'I'm in the paper again. Can't the papers find any real news? Thank goodness they haven't mentioned my name. But in this town everyone will know it was me anyway.'

'Go on. You've got our curiosity aroused,' said Edie. 'What are you famous for now?'

'I did two cases this week that have been reported. One was a woman who wanted maintenance for her thirteen children. I did it pro bono of course. She'd never have paid the bill anyway. This woman is a prime example of why women need a maternity payment.' He paused for effect as though he was in the courtroom.

'On with the story,' said Edie.

'Well, I'll cut it short for you. She arrived at court with seven of the kids in tow looking like she'd just dragged them up from the mines. Their clothes were filthy, ill fitting and they looked terribly hungry. The husband turned up too and I had a dickens of a job stopping her from yelling obscenities across the court-room at the him, things I can't repeat, and he was yelling back that half the children weren't his so why should he have to pay a darn penny for them. Judge Murphy finally came in and said to the husband, "What's this all about?" The father said, "She's not fit to look after me kids and I reckon some of them are probably not mine and I pay her what I can."

'Judge Murphy said to him, "Well, I'm sure she says you're not fit either. How much can you afford?" and he said "Nothing" and Judge Murphy turned to my client and said, "You heard him," and dismissed the case on the spot. I felt so terrible I gave her ten bob but after that what could I do but send her on her way? And here it is in the paper, you can read it for yourselves, along with the next case, which was just as ridiculous. This stupid twit from Sydney sued the Bunch of Grapes because the victualler, my client, declined to provide him with a meal at ten o'clock at night and the twit had travelled 100 miles that day meaning the victualler was legally obliged to provide him with food regardless of the time the twit appeared at his door. Judge Murphy had no choice but to abide by the law and fine the poor publican one pound. That's city folk for you, they've got to have what they want immediately, no matter who gets put out to do it.'

Paul leant over to Gracie and said, 'And that's life as a lawyer for you, Gracie, that's your father championing the rights of the poor. The rich city folk get a pound for nought but complaining, and a mother of thirteen gets sent on her way with nothing to feed her kids.'

'Mister Cottingham, I'm sure both parties appreciated your efforts even if they didn't show it at the time,' said Beth.

Paul looked at her with soft, thankful eyes; his eyes were changing with age, losing their sharpness and becoming like mists in late autumn, incapable of storms and angry lightning bolts. His shoulders now sloped away, he was shorter and would lean heavily on his umbrella, which had become his walking stick.

'Beth's right, Papa,' said Edie. 'Who else would look after these people if you didn't?'

Gracie wriggled again and to keep her still Beth asked, 'What's your birth date Gracie?'

'November the fifth oh five.'

'What's the date today?'

'November the fifth oh eleven.'

'Just eleven, there's no O when we get to double figures. There, you can go now,' said Beth and Gracie scampered off to sit on her father's knee, her curls bouncing as if eager to leap away from her head. Paul folded his paper and put it aside.

'Give me one of your smiles, Gracie. My day is only worth living if you give me one of your smiles,' he said.

She smiled at her father and then at Beth and at Edie.

Everyone noticed little Gracie's smile and her gentleness that made them feel as though they had found where they belonged. Everyone who came to the door asked, *'Have you got a smile for me, young Gracie?'* And when she smiled they put their hand over their heart to still its thumping.

As Gracie smiled at her, Beth felt the fog in her head clear and everything fell into place. Suddenly she knew where that some-where else was that she wanted to be, and who the someone was that she wanted to be with, and she was filled with a deep sense of loss because neither would ever be possible.

Nineteen

The Smile

Which comes when least expected.

Edie's eyes travelled over the same chapter heading again and again. She really wanted to toss the book against the wall except that she had greater respect for books than that and her father had taught her to control her temper, especially when it was threatening to go feral. Her mind was on Theo's impending visit. *Please don't come, please don't come today,* she begged silently. If he came, once again she would feel that overpowering urge to leave everyone she loved and run off with him.

Every Sunday when he appeared on the doorstep a war raged inside her. On one side was Theo, on the other her sister and father. She was the rope, fraying and weakening, being pulled in both directions. Once or twice Paul had said to her, 'Why don't you go with him, love?'

And she'd said, 'You know full well why, Papa.'

'But I'm sure we could manage,' he'd say, and she'd shake her head.

There was so much that kept her at home with Gracie and Paul. Early on Gracie had been so tiny. She had struggled to grow and would gasp for breath. Doctor Appleby had said it was still touch and go and would stay that way until Gracie turned six or seven. 'She'll catch anything and everything,' he told Edie and Paul many times. And Nurse Drake agreed with him, 'She's a slow grower.'

'But she'll get there in the end,' Edie would say, and she knew she had to stay and give Gracie the best care she could. Slowly Gracie had grown stronger, though she was never the size of other children her age.

But still Edie thought of Theo constantly. Was he at his piano? Was he teaching? Was he eating enough to stay strong? Sometimes she wondered what her life would be like if she ran off with him. She knew he wanted her to. And she knew she was going to carry this love for him forever. It was a weight in her chest, a yearning that never went away. Every time Theo came to visit she wondered if she would be strong enough to resist him yet again. The thought that she might weaken one day and lose her resolve frightened her. So Edie determined more than ever that her life was committed solely and wholly to Gracie's wellbeing. She was sure this was the right choice, and when Gracie smiled at her Edie's heart filled with contentment and she knew she was atoning for what she had nearly done to Gracie. More than anything else she was doing what her mother wanted her to do and though she hadn't promised her mother she would care for Gracie she had written it as a promise in her notebook. And once something was written in her notebook, it was a done deal.

'Edie, you're awfully quiet,' said Paul, resting his chin on Gracie's curls.

'Mmm,' said Edie and glanced at her wristwatch — ten to three.

'He should be here soon,' Beth said.

Edie thought Beth looked awfully pale, 'Are you all right, Beth? You've looked a little pasty all day.'

'I'm fine,' said Beth, putting her hand over the knot in her stomach.

'I can answer the door today,' said Edie.

'No, it's my job.'

Edie was taken aback by the firmness in Beth's voice and wasn't going to argue with her. 'Thank you, Beth, these weekly visits have become so difficult for me to endure.'

'Then stop giving him hope,' said Paul and Beth at the same time.

Tears sprang to Edie's eyes. 'I don't give him hope,' she said. 'Do I?'

Beth wanted to say, *Of course you do, you let him know every week how torn you are, how tempted you are to run after him, and that gives him hope and it's not fair.* Maybe one day she would say it. Beth looked at the clock again. It was three o'clock.

'I'll get it!' Beth said and she started towards the door.

'But no one's knocked yet.' Edie looked at Paul, who shrugged.

Beth went to the front door anyway and stood behind it and waited. She knew what she was waiting for, she knew what had made her so stupefied. As soon as she heard his steps on the verandah she pinched her cheeks and flung the door open and the sun shone on her face warming her skin and everything in her world seemed brighter.

'Haven't you given up yet?' she barked as Theo stood, his hand raised ready to knock.

'Maybe — maybe not. Today may be the last day I'll ever bother you, Beth.'

'And why would that be?'

'Well,' he said slowly, 'Gracie is six today, I remember. She is past her childhood illnesses and old enough to start school come next February, so Miss Cottingham will be free of her responsibilities.'

The clouds passed in front of the sun, suffocating it, and everything in the world turned dark and grey and the thought that he might not come to the door ever again made her feel that the whole world had shrivelled up and died.

'Oh, you don't bother me. Why, you're part of the furniture now,' she said.

'But I've never been past the front door. And I really wanted to see that underground house Mister Cottingham built.'

'The underground house is for us family only. Think of yourself more as a garden gnome.'

Beth looked out into the street. 'Brought the whole town's orphans with you as usual I see,' and she waved to the children that filled the street.

Theo scratched behind his ear. Beth thought it was an endearing quality. She didn't know many men who took time to think. Colin Eales never thought, he just plunged on in — he was a boy-man really. She gazed at Theo, so close to her with only the doorstep between them. She could feel the heat of his breath. She could smell his warmth and steadiness.

He looked directly back at her, his eyes intense and melting her. The moment stretched forever until he finally said, 'I s'pose I better be seeing Miss Edie.'

'Right.' Beth walked slowly to the living room and said, 'Guess who?'

Edie sighed. 'This has got to stop.' She stood and brushed off her skirt and didn't notice Beth follow her to the front door and stand just out of sight, where she could see and hear everything that passed between Edie and Theo.

Edie held onto the door jamb and looked at him. She wanted him to speak first because she didn't trust herself to be strong. She had to finish it with him completely. Gracie was only six, and though she was growing well, she wasn't out of the woods yet.

'Seven,' the doctor had said, 'wait until she is seven.' Gracie had no mother but her and Edie reminded herself of that over and over, and of the promise she had made in her notebook.

'Where is the child?' His voice was raspy and wavering, as if he was on the edge of something momentous.

'Um, she's with Papa, it's her birthday.'

'Hmm,' he said. 'I know.'

The silence between them was threadbare and it barely held them apart. She was sure she could touch his soul if she just let go of the door jamb.

'You do love me, don't you?' he whispered finally.

She looked at him and saw all the hopes she had held in her heart six years ago. She took a deep breath and held up her chin and he saw her straightforward, no-nonsense manner that he loved.

She sighed with her whole body and scrambled inside herself for the words she needed. When she spoke it was barely above a whisper. Each word was painful and she could feel her insides bleeding.

'For six years now I've tried to ignore you in church. I've tried not to think of you at your piano, or walking each Sunday to my home. When I've lain awake at night thinking of you I've tried not to think about whether or not you are awake and thinking of me. I've tried to ignore your weekly visits and the rose you always leave on the porch. I've tried to forget your cowlick and the hair that always flops onto your brow no matter how often you try to sweep it back. I've tried to forget that annoying little habit you have of scratching behind your ear. When you play the organ in church I try not to let the notes swim into my heart. But I failed. I have loved you, Theo. I will always love you,' she said and she let out her breath and felt an enormous burden released from her.

She saw the leap in his eyes, she saw them fill with stars and his face burst into a smile.

Theo saw the love in her heart. This would be it. She would be his. Today would make all the other days, all the months and years he had waited worthwhile.

She started to speak again but he got in first.

'My last rose,' said Theo and he held it out to her. 'I have waited six years — forever. Will you become mine Miss Edith Cottingham?' He bent over and with a swirl of his arm that was almost a bow put the rose on the step.

She felt her legs give way and she clutched the door jamb even tighter to hold herself steady.

In the hallway, Beth put her face against the cold wall and fell into it.

Theo could feel the thin space between them disappear. It was pulling them together. Edie was going to fall through the door straight into his arms. Her eyes were filled with tears, her heart was crying out to him, he could hear it. He knew she loved him with the same love that had carried him through the last six years. It was a yearning that haunted them both. Her hands were white and shaking as they grasped the painted wood and he reached out and tenderly unclasped her hand, one slender finger at a time. He would set her free.

He held her free hand in his and clasped it tightly, he would never let it go. He reached over with his other hand and brushed a hair from her face, then slid his hand down her cheek to her shoulder and down her arm to her other hand. Edie was ready to plummet into him, she no longer had the strength to resist his love. He was taking her other hand safely in his when all of a sudden it was gone, and he looked down and saw the child had placed her hand in Edie's. Gracie poked her face around Edie's skirt and Edie pulled her other hand from his and clasped Gracie to her side.

'I can't,' whispered Edie, a tear spilling down her cheek, the cheek he had just touched with all the tenderness he felt for her. He looked down at the child and she looked up and smiled at him.

An angel struck his heart and split it open. He staggered back from the step. 'Ahh,' he said. Why hadn't he ever noticed before? He could only put it down to the fact he hadn't wanted to see. But now he understood what bound Edie to the house. It was not that the child needed Edie; it was Edie who needed the child. The child was the very life of the house and would never be sent away, not to school, not to a nanny, not anywhere. If she was sent away the house would stop breathing and shrivel and die.

He knew a charm had just entered his soul and he found himself bending down and picking up the rose and handing it to Gracie. Still looking at Gracie's lovely smile he said to Edie in a feeble voice that even he didn't believe, 'She can come with us. Or I can come here.'

'My father can't live without her.'

'Of course.' He could see that. He probably knew that the day she was born, and had just refused to admit it. But now he'd seen the child with his own eyes. Properly seen her. Not like all the times he'd seen her in church and hated her for keeping him from Edie. Now he'd received the gift of one of her smiles he knew there was something about her that made you feel contented and at peace with whatever life brought. His mind frantically searched for an answer. He could live with them, but she saw his thoughts and shook her head.

'You wouldn't be happy in another man's home, you wouldn't. I've made my decision, Theo. I know where I am meant to be. I'm sorry.'

He stepped away. He thought he was going to take her away, to give her freedom from the child. But she had chosen the child. She wasn't caged, she was already free.

Just like that he found himself able to let go. He wouldn't come to the door any more. He would find another way to be with her, another way to let her know his love would be undying.

Edie slowly began to shut the door on him, thinking it was finally done and he was gone. She had set him free. She had nearly abandoned everything for him. She fell against the closed door still clasping Gracie to her. She leant her cheek against the door; on the other side Theo stood with his forehead pressing against it. The door could have been a mile thick with him on one side and her on the other. They were in separate worlds now.

Theo wandered off down the side of the house. He didn't take the path, he walked on the dirt and kicked at the stones with the toes of his shoes, wondering what he'd do now; he had no plans, no ideas, no future. He hadn't thought about anything beyond winning Edie. He hadn't even thought what he would do when he won her.

He was halfway to the front gate when he heard a voice calling to him. It was a sweet voice and an unexpected voice.

'Wait, I'll marry you, I will.'

He turned and saw her in the dress that had first captured his heart completely, that skirt that had enraged everyone with its ridiculous shortness. It seemed quaintly old-fashioned now and he chuckled. He watched her ankles as they tripped along the stones, the hem of the pale blue skirt falling around her feet like clouds. She took his hand and skipped alongside him, she was faster than him and soon she was pulling him along behind her as though pulling him through life.

He let her lead the way and she took him down Webster Street and across Wendouree Parade and down the dirt path that circled the lake. He had to take little running steps to keep up with her as they almost ran along the path. He didn't see the stares or the gaping mouths of those who saw them. She kept going, pulling him along until they reached the spot the children called Fairy Land, where the tall grasses grew tall. In behind the grasses, where the earth had been baked dry and hard by the sun, she fell breathless to the ground and pulled him down on top of her. She didn't say a word, she was kissing his neck and he kissed her shoulders and then he parted her bodice and kissed her breasts and her skin was fresh and pink and for the first time since Africa he felt nourished. He laid his head on her bare breasts and shut his eyes and drank in the smell of her. He found his way under her skirts and slowly, slowly walked his fingers up her legs and inside the warmth of her body and he knew he had needed that warmth more than he had needed food. He undid his trousers and pushed her clothing aside and she drew in a sharp breath as he gently moved inside her and all the wanting, all the waiting was satisfied and in ragged breaths he whispered, 'Marry me, marry me.'

And he felt such relief in knowing she would say yes.

Twenty

The Engagement

Monday, 6 November 1911, when the
weather is the only thing that is fine.

All day Beth held onto her secret. She had told Edie she was ill and needed to spend the day in bed, but she wasn't really ill — she just couldn't look Edie in the face. So she lay in bed clutching her stomach, which filled with shame when she thought of Edie and Colin, and then with happiness when she thought of Theo, which washed the shame away. The shame and happiness crashed into each other like waves, making her seasick.

Edie was kind and said not to worry that she had missed Gracie's cake. Whatever happened it must have been important to make her disappear like that. Edie brought her tea and chicken soup, which she couldn't eat because the kindness only made her feel worse. Then at five she slipped out the back door and walked to Colin's.

Beth knew she was too early, Colin would still be at the pub, but she wanted to catch him before he got inside the house. If he got home before she caught him then she would have to knock on his door and then she would have to talk to his mum. So she paced up and down the track worn in the grass outside the house, she kicked at stones on the road, and she wondered what Beatrix Drake was doing next door and if her fella was with her. She must have been waiting for an hour when Colin's front door creaked and groaned as it swung open. She knew it couldn't be Colin and she didn't want to face anyone from his family.

It was his mum, wiping her hands on her apron. She stood on the verandah and said, 'You sure you don't want to come and wait for him inside, Beth?'

'I'll wait here,' said Beth. 'I've got something I have to tell him.'

'You can come in, Bethie, you're family, love, you know that. You don't have to wait out here, you've been out here for ages,' and she held the door open.

Beth felt guilt coil in her soul and tighten around her veins. The waves in her stomach swelled. She couldn't tell him in front of his mum and his brothers and sister.

'No, it's really all right,' said Beth. 'It's cooled down a bit now, it's turned into a pleasant evening. I don't mind waiting out here,' and she walked into the yard and planted herself on the verandah step.

'I hope what you're wanting to tell him is that you've set a date,' said Missus Eales. 'We'd all like to see that. Seeing as you're both twenty-one next year, it's a good age to marry. Why don't you come in and help with the dinner?'

'No, I'm fine, really,' said Beth.

Missus Eales sighed, 'Please yourself then,' and went back inside. Beth knew she would never see the other side of that door again. Would Missus Eales ever talk to her after tonight?

She thought about the last twenty-four hours of her life and how much had changed in such a short time and how only the two of them knew about it yet. Though soon Colin would know and then so would everyone else. Beth rubbed her arms and tried to ignore the salty brinies sloshing around inside her.

She thought about yesterday. She had heard Edie's final refusal, heard Theo accept it, and knew that he would never again come on a Sunday afternoon. He would never bring another rose and she simply couldn't live without his roses. They were the way she was going to find her new life. They were charmed, she could feel it each time she walked into the laundry. She had leant into the wall listening to Edie and Theo, hoping the wall would hold her up because she felt like she was dissolving. Then Edie, holding Gracie's hand, had walked past her and hadn't even looked at her. Did she look right through her? Or was she writing in her notebook? Beth couldn't remember but she did remember that once Edie had gone into the kitchen with Gracie, she had run out after him. There had to be more roses, there had to be more of him. She couldn't just wait, she had to make it happen. She saw him walking aimlessly, his head down as though every last bit of life he had been holding on to had evaporated away. She could see he was empty and she could fill him up, so she took the chance that was right in front of her. She grabbed his hand and then they were swept away together. The roses had worked their magic. With him she became someone else, somewhere else.

She heard Colin before she saw him. She could hear his drunken singing getting louder as he came closer. *Let me call you sweetheart …* She stood up and watched him come around the corner. He and Davo Conroy were leaning into each other, trying to hold each other up. They walked right past her, both of them giving her wide foolish smiles as they passed, and they stumbled up to Davo's gate where they untangled themselves from each other and Davo waved at Beth and she waved back. She watched Colin as he made his way back to her, holding onto the fence and singing.

He already looked like a stranger; he was somewhere she didn't belong.

'*Let me call you sweetheart, I'm in love with you, let me hear you whisper that you love me too,*' he sang and then he grinned at her, a naughty schoolboy who'd been caught smoking behind the shelter shed.

'How much have you drunk?' she asked and immediately scolded herself. What was it to her any more what he drank?

'Enough,' he said. 'Or maybe just a little bit more.'

'Colin, I have to tell you something. I have to give you something.'

His grin widened and he looked towards the laneway.

She should wait until he was sober but she couldn't wait, she had to tell him now, she had to start her life. 'No, Colin listen to me.'

'No laneway — that's okay, come on love, let's sit on our step,' he said, wrapping his arms around her. She squirmed free and stood away from him. He lunged for her again and she stepped back again and said 'Colin, no!'

'Oh, don't be like that, Bethie,' he said. 'You've seen me have a few before today.'

'I don't care if you've been drinking. Colin, listen — I have to talk to you. It's important,' and she crossed her arms over her chest. She shut herself off from him completely and he felt it like an icy gust that froze his soul. He saw the wall that had gone up between them, built in a second, brick on brick, until he knew he couldn't reach her.

She saw the realisation spread across his face. She hated herself for what she was going to do to him. She put her hand over her heart; she needed to see if it was still there.

His gaze settled on her bare ring finger and his eyes travelled back up to her unreadable face. He'd always been able to read her face but now there was nothing. There was nothing there for him and the sudden gaping emptiness inside him sobered him up.

'Where's your ring, Beth?' he asked quietly and dangerously.

She shook her head.

'Bloody hell, Beth. Bleeding hell,' he swore and kicked at the fence, splintering and smashing the thin palings.

Beth stood further away, she was afraid of what he might do.

He spun around and glared at her. 'This is some kind of game, is it? You want me to prove my love, you want me to wait for you like that Hooley idiot waits for your boss?' he spat.

She cringed at how tawdry he made it sound. It was a beautiful thing that Theo had done and Colin just never understood it, he never understood what she needed.

'It's not a game, Colin,' she said quietly. 'You know it's not. You know I ...'

He moved up close to her, his nose almost touching hers and she could smell his beery breath and she couldn't breathe.

'You don't really love me. That's what you're going to say, isn't it?'

He looked at her like he hated her. She couldn't bear his hate, it slapped her harder than if he had hit her with his fist.

'Beth, you don't love me any more, do you?'

She nodded, she couldn't lie any more. 'I love you like a brother,' she said, knowing it was lame and he stepped back and laughed. His laugh was harsh and bitter.

'Well, Beth.' He waved his hand in the air while he thought of what he wanted to say. He stepped in close to her again. 'I love you and I always will. You might think you belong somewhere else, with someone else, but you don't. You belong with me. And if you think you're going to catch that Hooley — well, know this, Beth: he will never love you. He doesn't belong with you like I do. He belongs with someone else and if you can't see that you are blind. He doesn't even know who you are, Beth, but I do. So you know what I'm going to do, Beth? You know what I'm going to do?' He stopped and spun on his heels. He said calmly, 'I'll tell you what I'm not doing. I'm not bringing you frickin roses each week, that's for sure, if that's what you're thinking. No, what I'm going to do is, I'm going to wait for you to come to your senses. Hmmm. Yes. You'll come to your senses, Beth — you'll see.' And he walked inside and slammed the door on her.

She trembled and stood shaking for some time. She heard his mother call out from inside the house, 'Is Beth okay?' and she looked towards the window and she heard his voice reply, 'She's fine Ma, just leave her be.' She saw his mother watching her from behind the curtains.

She realised she hadn't given him the ring, so she took it out of her pocket and popped it in the letterbox.

A light came on in the front room next door and Beatrix Drake stepped onto her verandah and looked at her. She looked straight back, she would feel no shame in front of that Nurse Drake. Beatrix shook her head as if she was telling a child *No, no, no, don't you do that — you know that is wrong, you know there are consequences for bad children.* Beth began to cry, it wasn't happening the way it should. She should be happy but she wasn't.

'I always knew you wanted to be somewhere else and something else, Elizabeth Crowe. I just didn't realise what you wanted belonged to someone else,' said Beatrix.

Beth turned away and cried all the way back to Webster Street, where she now had to tell Edie she was engaged to Theo Hooley.

Part Two

Twenty-One

The Battle

Wednesday, 12 August 1914, when Theo finally decides to act and everyone agrees it is long overdue.

By the twelfth of August 1914 everyone was declaring war on everyone else. Germany declared war on Russia and interned eleven Russian chess players who were attending a tournament. Because everyone knew chess was a dangerous game of war. Then Germany declared war on Belgium and France. Great Britain, taking its children Australia, Canada and New Zealand with it, declared war on Germany. Australia fired the first Allied shots from guns at Fort Nepean as the German steamer SS *Pfalz* tried to sneak out of Port Phillip Bay. Montenegro declared war on Hungary and Austria. Austria and Hungary declared war on Russia and Serbia declared war on Germany. So Great Britain declared war on Austria and Hungary. Italy and America said they were going to sit it out and see where the chips fell. And the tennis went on and Australia beat England three to two.

The world became a schoolyard brawl. The Order of the White Feather was established so that boys not willing to throw their bodies into gunfire could be shamed into it. But Theo wasn't a man who needed to be shamed into doing the right thing.

Theo stood by his window and looked at the row of trees that ran down the middle of the wide street. They invited children to climb in them and then mischievously sent them home with torn clothes; they invited lovers to carve their initials into them and then kept them even after the love had vanished. In summer they lavished the street with constant shade, but in winter they looked like skeleton trees; without their clothes they were naked and humbled.

Theo was in his flannelette pyjamas and his feet were bare and cold on the floorboards but he didn't notice the coldness working its way up his legs; he was thinking. He had been woken early by the groaning of the trees in the wind. They were determined not to let him sleep and as he gazed at their exposed branches he made his plans. He had done nothing for long enough and if he kept doing nothing he would become nothing and any love that had kept him in the world would also disappear and amount to nothing.

He thought about the afternoon when he had taken Beth down by the lake. He couldn't remember how it had happened. How had he made such an awful mistake? He had tried to remember, he had searched his mind for the details but they wouldn't come.

He remembered that he had let Edie go, he had set her free, but at the same moment he felt he had locked himself into a cage from which he could never escape. He remembered the blackness of the stones in the earth, like evil eyes scoffing at him and how he kicked at them with all his fury. He remembered a voice and he thought it was her voice. He had turned and it had been her dress and then he had been pulled along, hurried into something — and he never hurried into anything. He remembered the deliciousness of her body and how she had wrapped him up and he felt safe and at home. He remembered how his soul sang when she accepted his proposal. He remembered afterward he had sat up and been stunned to realise it was Beth he had made love to; it was Beth who had accepted his proposal, it was Beth in her dress.

It wasn't Edie. He had said that over and over to himself so many times in the last three years or so. *It wasn't Edie.*

Beth had started kissing him and telling him she loved him and that she had loved him since the first rose, and as her warm kisses touched his skin he thought maybe he could love her back. Maybe all those fights they had over nothing at the front door were love. Maybe he had been blind to his true feelings and it was really Beth he wanted after all and he would be happy.

They had walked back to Webster Street arm in arm and just walking with someone, their bodies touching, in a space no one else shared, filled him with such joy. But they got to the house in Webster Street, and he said goodbye and she called him darling and the word grated shreds from his heart and he knew instantly it wasn't the right fit.

He had seen Edie because he wanted to see her. He had only wanted Beth when he thought she was Edie and now the bars of his cage were pressing into his skin and leaving harsh red marks.

He had gone home from Beth and gone straight to his piano and played Rachmaninoff's *Musicaux Number 3* over and over and the entire house crumpled under the pain the notes sang. Lilly sat in the kitchen sobbing into a tea towel for all she had lost. She wept for the dances and the kisses in the kitchen with Peter that were never to be again. When Theo's fingers hurt he still kept playing. *Cry for me world*, he'd thought, *cry for me because I can't cry for myself.*

His insides swirled and churned; he was angry. He had given Edie six years of his life, surely that was long enough. Surely after six years it was right that he accepted they could never be together. It was right for him to search for happiness elsewhere. After he had played the music over and over many times, somewhere as the notes built and moved and shifted, his innards moved and shifted as well and they stopped churning. He felt it and stopped playing, and waited to see what would happen next. Slowly the churning began again in the opposite direction. His fingers once again struck the melancholy notes and he thought how he was being cruel to Edie. It wasn't her fault she couldn't be with him, she had the child to think of. The child whose smile brought serenity.

As he'd played he realised he had to keep loving Edie even if he had to love her from afar. He wondered what was the more honourable thing to do. Should he break with Beth and say it was a mistake? Or should he marry her? It was an important decision and he couldn't hurry it.

So he had thought on it every day for the last three or so years.

He'd told Beth they couldn't be together again as they had at the lake until they were married. He said they needed to wait at least a year to marry because Beth was too young and he couldn't marry her until she turned twenty-one. He'd thought that would give him enough time to decide and she thought he was being considerate of her age and reputation. The year came and went and in that year he visited the Cottingham home every week and they all thought he was visiting Beth. At the end of the year he told Beth they had to wait another year because it would be disrespectful and hurtful to Edie if they married too soon and Beth's guilt wouldn't let her disagree so she accepted it. And so he had afternoon tea with them every Sunday. Then he told Beth they had to wait because there was so much unrest in the world and who knew where it was heading.

Beth was furious. She said he was making her look like an idiot and why couldn't they do what they had done down by the lake again? She had yelled and stamped her feet and that made Theo only more determined to hold off on marrying her. He didn't like the way she rushed into things without thinking.

'I want to wait until we are married Beth, we shouldn't have done what we did. I want to marry you honourably; we will be together when we marry. I just want to wait one more year until things settle down in the world and we know where we are.'

'And the way you can wait — that may bloody well be when the cows come home,' she said and she looked at him with utter contempt.

'I thought that was one of the things you liked about me, Beth — that I didn't rush into things.'

She'd pushed him hard in the chest and said, 'You didn't mind rushing down at the lake.'

He couldn't tell her that the longer he was engaged to her the more he got to see of Edie. He no longer stopped at the door of the house. Now he got to sit by the fire, to sit around in the kitchen, laughing with them and being part of their family. When it was hot he got to go downstairs with them into the underground house and eat sausages and potato salad and as Beth's fiancé there was nothing unfitting about it.

If Edie was upset about the engagement she didn't show it once. She was polite and warm to him and kind to Beth and acted as though she was happy for them both. It only made him love Edie all the more. So for three years he had sat and allowed himself to imagine he was one of them and during those three years he saw how devoted Edie and Paul were to Gracie. He understood that she was Lucy's gift to them and he pushed what that cost him aside

and let their family love wash over him and let himself believe he
was a part of it.

Now, standing at the window, looking out over the street at the
grass white with frost and the bare empty trees, he realised it was
time to make a decision. He couldn't hold Beth off forever. He
had to break with her or marry her, and believing in being honourable, he knew which he had to choose.

He put on his dressing gown and slippers and walked into the
kitchen where Lilly was stirring a pot of porridge. He thought she
had put on even more weight over the last three years. Everyone
said he was becoming thinner.

'Mum, I have some news,' said Theo.

'It's so hard now the war is on,' said Lilly. 'I heard there is going
to be rationing of food. Do you think I will still be able to get
oats, cocoa and sugar? Or flour? I mean, if there's no flour, well,
you just can't bake, can you?'

'Mum, I need you to sit down because I have to tell you
something.'

She stopped stirring and looked at him. 'Well, if it's important
I better put the kettle on first, hadn't I?'

Theo sighed. He wanted to tell her now while the words
were clear in his head. Once he said the words, his plan could
begin, the words would start it. If she needed a pot of tea to feel
comfortable, then perhaps it was just as well he let her make it. He
got up and got two cups and saucers and poured some milk into
a small jug.

'The bowls, Theo,' said Lilly, 'for the porridge and plates
for toast.'

She poured porridge into the bowls and passed him the full one.

'Way too much for me,' he said.

'Oh, go on with you,' she said, 'you're skin and bones.'

She sat down and poured the tea and he reached over and spooned three teaspoons of sugar into her cup. She would need the sweetness to calm her nerves.

'Well,' she said after she had taken three sips of tea, 'I'm ready for this news then.'

'Well, Mum,' said Theo, 'I'm going to marry Beth.'

'We all know that, dear, you've been engaged for three years.'

'Well, I had to wait for her to turn twenty-one,' he said.

She raised an eyebrow. 'Since when has that been a requirement for marriage? I know you, son. I don't just cook, I can see, you know.'

Theo took her hands in his and they sat together in the silence, knowing each other, the porridge bowls between them like a shared communion.

'I know you know what's in my heart, Mum, and sometimes I'm ashamed.' Theo held Lilly's small plump hands in his own. Her hands were warm and soft like a young girl's.

She pulled one hand away and brushed his hair back from his face. 'Oh son,' she said, 'you deserve to be happy and Edie Cottingham has chosen another life. And who can blame her with that poor child to look after and an ageing father. Beth loves you, Theo — isn't that enough for you?'

'Well, Mum,' he said, 'that's what I wanted to talk to you about. I think it is enough and I am going to set a date. We will marry on the seventh of November.'

Lilly wriggled her ample bottom out of the chair and walked around the table and put her arms around him and kissed his head.

'I think it's the right decision,' she said. 'It's the only decision. You deserve a love you can actually have.'

He stood up and pulled away from her arms. 'Mum — there's more.' His voice was full of sorrow for her.

She began shaking, he hadn't even told her yet and she was trembling. She knew what was coming. He sat her down and moved the tea over towards her.

'The whole last week I have been worrying you would do this.' She was already crying.

'I know,' he said, 'you've eaten three apple cakes. Mum, come on, I have to. You know I have to.'

'But you're thirty-eight years old, Theo — they want young boys. You're not a young boy any more.'

'As long as you have at least a thirty-four inch chest and are five foot six they'll take you, Mum.' He didn't tell her that thirty-eight was the oldest you could be to enlist.

'You're my boy. My only boy,' she was sobbing and he passed her the chequered tea towel. He squatted down in front of her. 'Mum, I will be okay — you know me. I can wait out any strife.'

Twenty-Two

Gracie

Wednesday, 19 August 1914, when Gracie refuses to budge.

Gracie spun around in circles turning her pale blue dress into a parachute and then collapsed noisily on the wooden floorboards. When her head had recovered and stopped spinning she clambered up and did it again, twirling until she fell helplessly in a tangle. Shopping for material was boring for a nine-year-old girl and Beth was taking an inordinate amount of time. Gracie spun herself dizzy a few more times and then, tiring of that, she noticed the hats in the corner of the shop, so she tried on hats, and beads and ribbons, and when Mister Lacey the haberdasher looked cross at her playing with his merchandise she smiled at him, because she knew that being sweet usually always made people happy, even when they were trying to be cross.

Mister Lacey begrudgingly let her play with his stock because after all the poor child had lost her mother and her father had a lot of money and Mister Lacey knew Mister Cottingham didn't mind spending any of that money on his two daughters. But most of all because no one could deny the child simply had the most delightful smile, a smile that made you instantly stop worrying about the debtors and the suppliers and accounts that weren't paid. So anything the child did that made her smile was well worth it.

Gracie had on three hats and several strings of beads and she went to find Beth to show her how funny she looked, but Beth was engrossed in materials, carefully feeling each roll, gauging its potential for happiness, its silkiness and shine. She had already chosen lots of material that she had placed on the counter. Gracie couldn't see how she could possibly need any more. She watched for a while as Beth looked at this bolt and then that one. You couldn't possibly need that much cloth for just two dresses. She walked over and felt the silky material on the bolt that Beth was studying.

'I'm trying to do this as cheaply as possible,' said Beth, 'taking into consideration that your father is footing the bill and that there is a war on now.'

Beth put the bolt down and moved on to look at trimmings. Gracie, bored with the haberdashery shop and spinning and hats and beads, took them off and put them in a pile on top of the bolts and decided to go and wait outside where she could watch the comings and goings in Sturt Street, which had to be more inter-esting than Beth and material.

Besides, the Reverend's wife and Missus Blackmarsh had come into the shop and they kept scowling at her as though she had no right to be on the face of the earth.

'If you're going outside don't forget your coat and hat,' said Beth.

So Gracie, wondering how Beth knew she wasn't wearing her coat when Beth hadn't even looked at her, begrudgingly put on her hat and coat.

'Uh uh, gloves and scarf too,' said Beth just as Gracie was about to escape.

Gracie had to search for where she had left those, and found them under the ribbon counter. Waving them in the air to show Beth she had them, she went outside and sat on the steps. She rested her chin in her hands, her elbows on her knees, her dress and coat pulled tightly over her knees to keep them warm.

'And how are you this morning, young Gracie?' said a man who knew her. She didn't know him but she smiled anyway as he walked on and she hummed to herself the song that Edie always sang to her.

As anyone who has lived in a country town knows, the place to meet your neighbours is down the street, where you can catch up with anyone you need to if you just wait for long enough. In the country there is no such thing as a short trip to the shops just to pick up a few things. Any trip down the street will take a minimum of two hours as you must stop and chat to everyone you know. The following hour was no different for Gracie. The first people to bump into her were Nurse Drake and Constable George.

'And what are you doing sitting on the haberdasher's step in that lovely coat, young Gracie?' said Constable George and Nurse Drake patted her on the head. Gracie smiled at them and as they walked off, Beatrix leaned over and said to George, 'All her early ailments aside, Mister Cottingham is blessed with that girl. She's so pure she could be the mother Mary.'

'I'm sure you had a hand in it, dear,' said George.

Beatrix said, 'Well, I have practically brung her up so far, haven't I?'

Gracie listened as the Town Hall clock chimed three and hoped Beth wouldn't be too much longer. It would start getting cold soon. The next people she saw were Theo and his mother.

'Beth says you can't go in,' said Gracie, moving to the middle of the step to block their entrance. 'She's says it's bad luck for you to see what the bride is going to wear. She's selecting materials and stuff.'

'Well,' said Missus Hooley, 'we don't need any bad luck, do we.'

Gracie smiled at them both. As they walked off, Lilly put her arm through Theo's and said, 'When that child smiles, you know God is smiling down on the world.'

Gracie watched as some boys kicked a bottle up Camp Street and she watched as Mister Laidlaw stopped his horse and cart when the horse did a shit and got out a shovel and a potato sack and shovelled the shit inside. He saw Gracie watching and he tipped his hat.

'Miss Gracie,' he said. 'I can get good money for that shit. How's that for a laugh, eh?'

She smiled at him and he said, 'Oh, you make my heart flutter, you do. You'll have to marry me now.'

'I can't,' she said, 'I'm only nine — well, I will be in November.'

'And I had my hopes up,' he said. 'Say hello to your papa, he'll remember me. And say hello to that sister-in-law of mine. Tell her to come round. Tell her Dottie wants to talk to her.' Then he thought for a moment and said, 'He built it for you, you know.'

'I do know,' she said and he was off.

Gracie looked just like Edie, but no one saw that. They didn't notice her plain face or her jutting chin that was just like her older sister's. All people saw when they looked at Gracie was an angel. Gracie didn't care that people were always asking her to smile. It was an easy enough thing to do and she smiled gladly at people as she sat on the front step of the haberdasher's. When Doctor Appleby used to come to the house to prod and poke her and to listen to her chest, he always asked her for a smile and then he would say, 'Gracie dear, you are a gift from God himself.' But he didn't come any more unless she was really sick like when she got chicken pox.

Missus Blackmarsh walked out of the shop with Missus Whitlock and they stood on the doorstep behind Gracie. Missus Blackmarsh groaned loudly making out that Gracie was leaving no room for them to pass her and get down the steps, which there plainly was.

'Indolent child,' muttered Missus Blackmarsh, so Gracie, who normally would have leant well out of the way to let people past, sat solid in her spot. She didn't like Missus Blackmarsh one bit; she always looked like she was about to spit something out of her mouth and her bosom was too big, like an army tank clearing the way before her and her hair was like slick black tar.

Missus Blackmarsh, groaned again but Gracie still stayed put.

Missus Blackmarsh crossed her arms over her big breasts and said to Missus Whitlock, 'I told you so, I could have told you yonks ago it would never last with Edie Cottingham.'

'Beth is much more suitable,' agreed Missus Whitlock.

'Why do you suppose it's taken so long?' said Missus Black-marsh and they stepped around Gracie and trotted off down the street, their rear ends like the rear ends of two cows waddling off to be milked.

Gracie wasn't sure what hadn't lasted with her sister Edie or what had taken so long but she would ask Beth as soon as Beth finished her shopping.

Finally Beth emerged as the clock stuck half-past. 'Righteo,' she said, 'that's all I need to order there, now off to the flag-maker's.'

'What's taken so long?' asked Gracie putting her hand in Beth's.

'What do you mean?'

'Missus Blackmarsh said it had taken a long time.'

'Well — I suppose they meant that the one thing you can say about Theo Hooley is he never hurries into anything,' said Beth. 'Oh look, the florist, I completely forgot about a bouquet.'

'Can't you do it tomorrow? It's getting cold,' said Gracie and she hoisted up her skirt and coat and showed Beth the goose pimples on her legs to prove it and luckily Beth decided to take her home.

When they got home Gracie sat and drank hot milky tea to warm her up. She watched Beth cover the sunroom floor in newspaper and draw shapes on the sheets. The shapes looked nothing like a dress and Gracie would have wondered if Beth knew what she was doing if she hadn't seen Beth make clothes before. Then Beth carefully cut around the shapes and labelled them and folded them and put them in two shoeboxes. Gracie helped her carry them to her room.

'Now I have to wait for what I ordered to arrive. Three weeks. That's not too long, is it? As long as it's here by the end of October. Now tomorrow, missy, you must go to Dana Street. You have to go to school for at least one hundred and forty days a year and as it's already the end of August that's going to be a push.'

Gracie didn't particularly like school. She definitely preferred home to school, home with her father and her sister and Beth, where she imagined they all lived in a jewelled genie bottle full of soft cushions with tassels and beds for princesses, where she was safe from the cruel winds and the sharp hailstones. But the teachers were kind and the last time she went to school, which she thought was probably last week, the teacher had said she was going to show the girls how to knit socks for the soldiers from scraps of wool, and sometimes if the class had been good she read to them from *The Children's Hour*.

Twenty-Three

The Parcel

Which comes on 30 September 1914 in the afternoon post.

Gracie saw the parcel on the porch when she came home from school. She dropped her satchel on the floor and walked as fast as she could to find Beth and tell her it was there. Beth squealed and shook her hands about in the air and did a little jig when she saw it, so Gracie squealed and danced about with her. Beth took the parcel and walked down the hall and Gracie followed her, they were going to open it together, it was exciting. But when Beth got to her room she shut the door behind her and left Gracie outside and disappointed.

'What are you doing? Can't I come in?' Gracie asked through the door. She had really wanted to help unwrap the parcel; it would be as if it was her birthday or Christmas.

'I'm cutting the material and sewing the panels together one stitch at a time, praying that each stitch will be a day, no, a year, I'll get to spend with my husband.'

'Why's he taken so long to marry you? Papa says a three-year engagement is too long and unnatural,' said Gracie, mimicking her father. As the question left her lips she realised that was

213

the long thing that Missus Blackmarsh had spoken about outside the shop.

'Because,' said Beth, 'these things take time. Now go away, I'm busy making the dresses.'

'Can't I see?' Gracie pleaded.

'No one else gets to see the dress. It's very bad luck,' said Beth.

A few days later Gracie had to stand for what seemed like hours while Beth measured her and pinned a petticoat. 'Recite your times tables,' said Beth. 'That'll take your mind off standing still.'

Gracie, standing on top of the kitchen table, her legs aching, recited her times tables up to twenty-ones and it didn't help one bit.

'Why aren't you measuring the real dress on me?'

'Because I want it to be a surprise. The petticoat will tell me how big I need to make the dress.'

Gracie hoped her dress would be white satin with Chantilly lace. She hoped it would have a bow for the waist embroidered with pearls and cream satin rosebuds and that she would have a matching Dolly-Varden bonnet and a new pair of kid leather shoes from Faulls. She'd read in the paper about a flower girl who got to wear all those things.

'When do I get to see my dress?'

'It's a surprise,' said Beth.

'Go on, show me, I won't tell anyone what it's like, I promise.' Gracie hadn't had a new dress in simply ages. Papa said they all had to do without new things and put all their spare money into war bonds for the war effort. Whenever she saw the ad that said, *My daddy bought me a war bond, did yours?* she would say out loud, 'Yes he did, thank you very much.'

Papa said he was making a special allowance for Beth's wedding.

'I'll tell you this much,' said Beth, 'yours is the same as mine, only smaller. It's just the right size for a nearly-nine-year-old girl named Gracie. Now I know it's hard but keep still for goodness sake or your dress will be down at your ankles in one spot and up at your chin in another.'

Gracie beamed. She hadn't been a flower girl before. This was going to be the most fabulous day of her life. She couldn't wait and she was sure Beth would make her dress even more beautiful than the one she had read about in *The Star*.

Twenty-Four

The Disappointment

*Saturday, 7 November 1914, when
the sun gives way to the rain.*

Gracie bit her bottom lip. She bit it hard because if she didn't, tears were going to spill from her eyes; she could feel them building up, just waiting to burst free and run down her cheeks. She was going to get an almighty ribbing if she went to school on Monday, she knew that much. She might be able to change out of the dress when they got home from church. Perhaps she could wear her Sunday best for the reception at least. She felt like a clown, like the one she saw when Edie took her to Worth's Circus. He was a kaleidoscope of mismatched colours, like the socks they knitted from any old scrap of wool for the soldiers at the front. The clown was silly and she'd tried not to laugh because she couldn't see the point of him but then she found herself laughing anyway and Edie said that was the point.

It was hard not to let on to Beth just how disappointed she was.

Beth was standing with her hands on her hips, gazing at her. 'Perfect, just perfect for a war bride,' she said.

216

Gracie looked over at Papa. He was in his best clothes, ready for the wedding, and raised an eyebrow as if to say what could he do to save her, and went back to reading his paper.

Gracie looked at Edie. She looked disappointed too — surely she could help, she would see that Gracie couldn't possibly go out in public like this. This must be a joke and there was another dress somewhere.

Without any warning Edie pulled a few of her curls from their clip.

'Owww,' said Gracie.

'Just a minute, Beth, I just need to fix Gracie's hair,' and Edie pulled her down the hallway to her bedroom and shut the door. Then Edie put her hands on Gracie's shoulders and manoeuvred her so she was standing plumb in front of the mirror. Edie stood behind Gracie and trapped her curls back inside the pin. 'Remember, Gracie,' said Edie into the mirror, and Gracie looked back at the Edie trapped in the mirror, 'it's Beth's special day and it's the one day in a girl's life that she gets to have whatever she wants. After that she has to think about her husband and family first. You can do this for Beth.'

Edie was so sincere that Gracie thought she certainly could do it. She turned and smiled at the real Edie, then threw herself into Edie's arms and breathed in the soft powdery smell of her older sister–mother.

'Now,' said Edie, pushing her back to look directly into her eyes, 'Beth has decided that today, her wedding day, she is finally going to let us see what she has been hiding in the laundry all these years, and isn't that exciting? Exciting enough to take your mind off the dress?'

Even though Edie didn't really look like it was exciting, Gracie couldn't do anything but agree it was thrilling. She had always wondered what was hidden in Beth's laundry. She imagined there were wicked imps in there that Beth had trapped in the garden that must never escape or they would wreak havoc on the world. Or perhaps it was full of magic spells for love and that was how Beth had won Theo. Or maybe there were flying unicorns in there.

She put her hand in Edie's and they walked down the hall to the kitchen.

'Okay,' said Beth, who was still in her petticoats, 'do you have your flower basket, Gracie?'

Gracie went and got it from where it was sitting on her dressing table waiting for today and when she came back Beth led them to the laundry. She took a key from where it was hidden on top of the door ledge and opened the door and flicked on the light.

'Ohhh,' said Gracie, slapping her head and wishing she'd thought to look for the key up there, then she could have had a peek inside the laundry years ago.

Gracie stood for a while getting accustomed to the dim light, then what she saw took her breath away. There was jar after preserving jar lined up on the shelves in the laundry and in each jar was a perfectly preserved red rose that glimmered in the light coming through the door.

Gracie looked at Edie and wondered why Edie looked so miserable and then she realised these were the roses from Theo, the ones he'd brought for Edie.

'Oh,' said Gracie, 'these are all the roses that you didn't want, Edie.' Gracie ran her fingers along the jars on the lowest shelf. Her fingers tingled. 'They are beautiful, Bethie,' she whispered. 'It's like being in another world, isn't it?' she said. 'A world where everything is made of surprises.'

Beth unclipped the lid of one of the jars and carefully lifted out the rose as tenderly as if it was the newest thing that had been born in the world, then she shook it and the petals fell into Gracie's flower basket.

'No,' cried Gracie. 'No don't — you'll let the magic escape.'

'No, we're taking the magic with us,' said Beth and Gracie knew that Beth needed that magic. She couldn't be without it or her fairytale would stop. Beth opened another jar and another and shook them into Gracie's basket. Gracie looked at Edie but Edie was just standing there, her mouth open, and Gracie thought she saw tears in her sister's eyes.

'They do make you want to cry, don't they?' she whispered to Edie. 'With happiness.'

But Edie didn't answer.

With her basket full of Beth's rose petals and Beth now dressed and holding her bridal posy and Papa with a full dried rosebud pinned to his lapel, they set off for the church — Gracie, Edie, Papa and Beth. Papa stopped at the letterbox and looked at the sky.

'It's going to rain later — it's building up to a spring storm.'

'Will we get to the church in time? I can't get wet,' said Beth.

'We could take a cab,' said Edie.

Gracie looked at Papa and said, 'I think we should walk,' because it was Beth's day and she knew Beth would want to make it last as long as possible.

'No, we'll be fine, it won't rain for a good hour yet,' Paul decided. 'But I can smell it in the air.'

The November sun pushed back the grey clouds that threatened to undo their happiness and it warmed their skin and their hearts and sparkled off the shine of the silk on the dresses as they walked. Feeling generous, the sun let its glistening rays halo around them, making their walking together a perfect moment that could last forever.

As they passed the end of the street, the children who had accompanied Theo each week were gathered waiting for them. They cheered and waved as the bride, the flower girl, the father and sister walked past and then the children fell in behind them, forming a procession like a brass band, the boys pretending they were trumpets and snare drums, the girls pretending they were flutes and cymbals or extra flower girls as they clutched daisies torn from gardens. The women stood at their front gates and held their hands on their hearts or threw flowers from their gardens at the wedding party and the men clapped. When the procession was out of earshot, the men made obscene jokes to each other about what the groom had to look forward to after all was signed and sealed, and the women wondered what magic Beth had used to capture Theo when his heart had belonged to Edie.

Gracie couldn't look at anyone in case they were laughing at her dress. She was absolutely sure they were. She studied her feet in her best shoes. She saw the cracks in the road and fiddler beetles flying off to safety as her feet landed near them. Finally they reached the church; it was the longest walk to church she had ever had. Edie left them then and went inside and Gracie heard the music start and right after that first note the clouds opened and dropped a deluge of spring rain on the town. It was so furious that Gracie put her hands to her ears but when she stepped into the church, with its high ceilings and stone walls, the rain was silenced and all she could hear was all the eyes in the congregation watching her.

Gracie still couldn't look at anyone as she walked up the aisle, carefully placing one foot in front of the other, trying to stay in time to the 'Wedding March', just like Beth had made her practise. Beth and Papa would be behind her, she knew that from the practice. Beth would have her arm through Papa's. When Reverend Whitlock said, *Who gives this woman to this man?*,

Papa was going to say *I do* in his big booming voice that he used at work but never at home. Beth's dress was exactly the same as hers only bigger. Beth thought their dresses were wonderful, she was so proud of what she had created. As Gracie walked slowly up the aisle she wondered what their house would be like without Beth living in it any more. She wondered if they would miss her or if it would soon seem normal not to have her there. But she reminded herself that Beth said she wasn't really leaving because she was going to come each morning at nine and leave each evening at six. Gracie scattered the dried rose petals ahead of her hoping they would work their magic just like Beth needed them to. She didn't want to tread on them and break them so she threw them to each side of her instead of in front. Sealed in glass jars they had kept their aroma and as she scattered them perfume filled the air and everyone in the congregation breathed in their magic and breathed out an audible 'Ahhhhh,' as if they now had all the contentment they could hope for in the world. They looked at their spouses who they had grown weary of and beaux they had bickered with and friends and family who were irritating and gave them a little squeeze and a smile and a nod.

Gracie saw Theo Hooley standing at the end of the aisle. He was in his uniform. Each time he came to visit Beth, he would ask for her so she began to go to the front door with Beth to welcome him. He would wink at her and then ask her to smile for him and when she did he would put his hand over his heart and say, 'Gracie, you have made me a very happy man.'

She smiled at him now and he winked at her and put his hand over his heart. All the women in the church sighed, they thought he was holding his heart for Beth. They didn't know his hand was on his heart for Gracie. But Gracie knew because he did it all the time. Gracie couldn't see what the fuss over her smile was about.

She'd spent hours smiling at herself in the mirror trying to see what everyone else saw but as far as she could tell, her smile was no different to anyone else's; in fact it was worse because it was a little lopsided.

Theo winked at Gracie, such a lovely child, and then he looked behind her to Beth, his bride, who was walking next to Paul. She had her veil over her head. Then he saw Edie, sitting in the front pew next to his mother.

His mother cocked her eyebrow at him, *Come on, son, you can do it*, and she wished he had eaten the fried eggs with the thick slices of bacon she had served him for breakfast. She had saved for weeks for that bacon. He had taken one mouthful, said he wasn't hungry and left her to finish it off for him. She knew where his heart was and why he appeared to be so devoted to Beth and visited her so often. She saw him gazing at Edie sitting beside her and not at his bride who was walking down the aisle.

'You're doing the right thing son,' she whispered, 'a life must go on and it was never going to go anywhere for you with Edie.'

Theo saw his mother's reprimand but instead of making him pay attention to his bride his blood filled with shame and rushed through his body to his heart and he determined never to be unfaithful to Edie again.

Gracie moved to the left-hand side of the church, like she'd practised, and felt Beth standing next to her. She looked behind her and saw Edie sitting next to Missus Hooley, both of them in tears. Missus Hooley nibbled on a biscuit she had hidden in her white lace handkerchief. She looked around at the rest of the congregation. The women were dabbing their eyes with handkerchiefs and whispering, 'A good wedding is just what we need in these sad times.' She saw the men digging each other in the ribs with secret knowing winks.

Reverend Whitlock coughed and Gracie looked up and saw every hair up inside his large nostrils. He started his sermon.

'Well, now that we are all ready, I'll begin. This war is God's way of bringing morality and order to the world,' he said loudly, 'and just as God has sacrificed his son for us, so Beth you must willingly sacrifice your claim to Theo so he can go to the front and fight for you and your children's freedom and for Christianity and honour. It is God's divine way.'

Gracie thought of God sitting like a general with a baton and a monocle, creating wars to bring moral fibre to the world. She knew Germany had no morals because only the other day she was reading in the paper that they sent schoolboys to the front, fourteen year olds not much older than her, right into the firing line to have their hearts shot from their chests. Theo was definitely not a schoolboy. In fact he was getting a bit bald at the back where he couldn't see.

Reverend Whitlock coughed again and asked, 'Who gives this woman to this man?' and her father said 'I do,' and he sat down next to Theo's mother in the space that had been left for him.

Reverend Whitlock said, 'If anyone can see why Theo and Beth should not be wed,' and she saw her father lean forward and look at Edie as though he thought Edie might have something to say but Edie just stared straight ahead and then her father turned and looked at Laidlaw sitting on the other side with Beth's sisters and another man and she was sure she heard Laidlaw say, 'Bet Young Colin'd have something to say, eh Davo?'

The Reverend waited and even though there was some muffled muttering no one said anything loud enough for the whole

congregation to hear so Gracie turned back to look up the
Reverend's big nostrils.

Young Colin couldn't have spoken up at Beth's wedding even
if he wanted to. He had made a point of telling everyone he
was working this Saturday and he wasn't the slightest bit interested in nobody's wedding. Now his body was deep below the
earth. The mine, driven by hunger and vengeance at being raped
and carved out to its very soul, sucked in the heavy spring rain
that had come crashing down and sent the water racing down
its tunnels and shafts, chasing its prey, leaving no dark corner
untouched. Without warning the currents rushed at Young
Colin, belting his chest, throwing him into its torrent as though
he was no more than a grain of dirt. It gushed and hated and
pushed against Young Colin's ribs and cracked them into splinters that pierced his skin and his lungs. The surging water then
filled Young Colin's lungs with its icy muddiness and tossed
from him wall to wall as though he was no more than a rag doll.
It smashed his limbs against sharp exposed rocks and bruised his
skin to a purple and blue patchwork. Then the collapsing mine
buried its murderous crime and Young Colin's body deep under
the crumbling earth where it turned to dust and would never
be found.

With no one to speak out against the marriage, Reverend Whitlock coughed and continued the ceremony.

'I have a poem to mark this occasion,' he announced proudly
and unfolded a piece of paper from his pocket and began to read:

War for the end of war,
Fight that fight might cease,
And out of the cannons' roar
A thousand years of peace.

'I wrote it myself,' he said.

Gracie felt the awkward cold emptiness in the room. No one knew whether to clap in the middle of a wedding or not. She was holding a flower basket so no one could expect her to clap but then Reverend Whitlock said the groom may kiss the bride and everyone did clap and Theo leant over, lifted Beth's veil and kissed her on the cheek.

Missus Hooley pulled a biscuit wrapped in paper from her bag and offered it to Edie and Edie said, 'Oh, I'm just crying tears of happiness.' Missus Hooley raised her eyebrow and Gracie thought a dunce could see Edie wasn't happy at all. Missus Hooley took the biscuit out of the paper and handed it to Edie and Edie said, 'Oh, why not,' and took a big bite.

After everyone had eaten sandwiches and cakes in the dining room, Beth went to her bedroom and changed into her day dress: a pale blue skirt, a white blouse and a lovely matching pale blue jacket that hung loosely to her thighs. She tidied her hair in the mirror and picked up her overnight bag. They were taking the train to Melbourne for their honeymoon. Theo said one night was all they could manage on account of the war, and because it was on account of the war she couldn't argue. At least he had finally married her. At least she was now someone else — she was Missus Theo Hooley. When she came out Theo was standing talking to Paul, and she slipped her arm through his and gave him

a little squeeze and waited for him to smile at her, but he didn't, so
she held on tighter to make him aware that she was there.

Paul saw her and her bag. 'Righteo, let's see them off,' he called
to the guests, and he nodded at her and she threw her bouquet, aiming for Edie who caught it and quickly passed it to Gracie standing
next to her. Gracie held it high so everyone could see what a beautiful posy of flowers it was and then she giggled and said, 'I'm too
young to be the next married, Beth — you should throw it again.'

'Oh, I don't think so,' said Beth. 'I think you can only throw it
once, it doesn't work the second time.'

Beth was hurt that Edie didn't want her bouquet and had passed
it to Gracie. She reminded herself that Edie hadn't wanted Theo
and she had and she had nothing to feel guilty about. She hoped
Edie would still find someone she did want, even though she was
approaching middle age and it wasn't likely. But Beth would feel
so much better if Edie had someone.

Beth looked at Theo but he was somewhere else so she nudged
him and he smiled at her, but she knew he still wasn't really looking at her.

She hugged Edie and Gracie, Paul and Lilly, and her sisters and
nieces and nephews and Laidlaw.

'Well, let's see them off,' said Paul and everyone walked to the
station, and on the platform Beth hugged everyone all over again.
She even hugged Nurse Drake. Theo helped her onto the train,
but he still hadn't really looked at her and she felt his indifference
like a slap across her cheek and it turned her skin hot and pink.
They stood in the doorway and waved and called goodbye to
everyone and she saw his eyes light up as they rested on Edie as
she stood on the platform next to her father, and for just a moment
Beth's heart sank to rest among the sharp stones on the railway
track and she heard Colin's words: *He will never belong with you.*

The conductor blew his whistle and the train pulled out and she toppled into Theo with the jolt and everyone laughed and cheered for them. Theo straightened her up and said, 'Righteo,' and walked to a compartment. He pulled open the door for her and then shut it so they had the compartment to themselves. She sat by the window and he sat next to her and she leant over to kiss him and he turned and kissed her cheek first.

'Bloody hell,' she said and he screwed up his face in distaste. 'You told me I had to wait until our wedding night before we can you know — do what we did down the lake, so we can consummate our marriage properly as husband and wife. Then you make me wait three bloody years and now we are married you don't want to kiss me?'

Theo stared straight ahead; he wouldn't have a war with her.

She sighed and crossed her arms over her chest.

'I set the date because I leave on Monday,' he said finally, looking at her as though he didn't know her. 'I wanted to do the right thing. This way we can ease into things — take our time to get used to married life.'

Beth couldn't speak. Something inside her just bottled up and the lid closed down fast.

'So when do you have to be at your barracks?' she asked at last, keeping her voice flat and cold.

'Well,' he said, 'it was supposed to be three this afternoon but they have let me have until six on account of the wedding.'

'So I'm supposed to spend my wedding night on my own?' she wailed.

'At least we will be married,' he said. 'Isn't that what you wanted? Besides, you will get to see me off on the ship if you come to the dock on Monday morning — all the other wives will be there, I imagine.'

'A proper husband and wife have sex,' she said. She was red in the face. She knew he couldn't even look at her.

'And we will,' he said, 'when I get back and we can settle down to a proper family life. Everything in its right time, Beth. I would be a terrible husband if I took the risk of possibly leaving you pregnant and having to raise a child on your own with a war on. It's better this way. We can start a family when I get back.'

Family was a word that always caught her heart. He saw her soften a fraction and said, 'In the meantime you will live with my mother. You're a proper member of the family, and she'll look after you, I promise.'

Twenty-Five

The Mortification

*Sunday, 8 November 1914, when George thinks
it's time for a bit of a chat with Beatrix.*

George told Beatrix the news about Young Colin. He had held
onto it until after, in case the news upset her and she didn't want
to give him any loving on account of it. So while they were putting their clothes back on he told her casually, like it was nothing
at all, and she turned and looked at him square on, holding her
petticoat up in front of her bare chest like George had never seen
her bare chest, hadn't been nuzzling her breasts just twenty minutes ago and swearing they tasted like honey and cream.

She said, 'I'm telling you, he called that collapse on himself. He
knew the mine was too wet. And all that rain yesterday. These
last three years he's been that distraught at Beth's running off to
marry Theo Hooley. He's had a death wish on him, that boy. He
brought it on himself. I've seen it many a time and I know what
I'm talking about.'

George said, 'Hmmm.' He stood up now he was dressed and
tapped his baton against his hand and said, 'I'm just going to chat

with Davo two doors down while you get some grub up. Can I borrow your brolly?'

George asked Davo if management was at fault. He hoped to God they were — he really wanted to get the greedy buggers. They sat on two upturned milk crates on Davo's front verandah out of the rain, which still poured down in torrents, and had a smoke and stared out into the narrow street.

Davo thought for a while and finally said, 'Young Colin had been going down shafts he knew to be dangerous, to places other sensible men wouldn't go. For this to happen on the very day of her wedding, most likely at the very moment she was pronounced married, I reckon he willed the earth to keep him down there in the black where he couldn't see or feel nothing. The boy was like a son to me, George, and that is my honest opinion, mate.'

George went back up to Number 9, shook the rainwater off the umbrella and flicked it off his shoulders onto the kitchen floor, making Beatrix scowl. He told her what Davo said and sat down to the afternoon tea she had laid out on the table — drop scones and oat biscuits. It would have been sponge cake and date loaf if there wasn't a war on.

Beatrix said, 'Well, Georgie, I have to agree with Davo, not that I'm an expert on mines or anything, but what I do know is human behaviour, and some things are just too much for anybody, even a strapping young lad. Some things just make life seem not worth living.'

Monday, 9 November 1914, when there is a fine account
in the paper.

Gracie went out in the rain in her nightdress and grabbed the papers from the front lawn and went back inside with them. She wiped the wet grass off her feet on the doormat and shook her hair.

'I got them,' she called, 'before they were ruined.'

She had both *The Star* and *The Courier*. She went into the kitchen where Edie and Paul were sitting at the table. She plonked into a chair and opened the first paper.

'Careful,' said Edie, 'you've got it in the milk jug.'

'Oh,' laughed Gracie and she shook the soggy corner so that drops splattered over the table. Then she tore through the pages of *The Star* and found the wedding page. She hoped beyond hope that Beth's wedding wasn't written up with her name in it. But luck wasn't on her side.

'Read it aloud,' said Papa.

She looked at Edie.

'Go on,' said Edie.

'Yes, let's hear it,' agreed Papa.

So Gracie pushed her chair back and stood up and read the words slowly as nine year olds do.

A Patriotic Dedication, reported by Clarence Watty

A quiet but otherwise interesting wedding was celebrated at Dawson Street Baptist church on Saturday morning at 10 a.m. when Captain Theodore Wilson Hooley of the Australian Armed Forces married Elisabeth Mary Crowe of Webster Street. The bride entered the church to the strains of the 'Wedding March' on the arm of her employer, Mister Paul Cottingham, who gave her away. The church had been prettily decorated for the occasion by Mister Cottingham's two daughters.

The bride had made her dress out of the colours of the flags of the Allies. The bodice was royal blue, and panels of the dress imitated the Australian flag and the Union Jack alternately. A novel feature was a floral 'V' she carried as her bouquet, expressing all our hopes for the future and as a compliment to the bridegroom.

The flower girl, Miss Gracie Cottingham, also of Webster Street, was dressed in a replica of the bride's attire, completed by a bow

appliquéd with the stars from the Southern Cross tied around the bod-
ice. The presents were numerous and included a cheque from Mister
Cottingham. The bride's present to the groom was a signet ring. The
groom's present to the bride was an aquamarine necklet. The groom
and bride left for the train station amid showers of confetti before the
groom left to join his battalion and made ready to leave for the front
the next day.

'Well, it only took her three years but she got him,' said Paul. Gracie
saw him look at Edie and whisper, 'Did you wish it was you?'

Gracie was suddenly still. She knew she was hearing an adult
conversation and that more was being said behind the words. Paul
and Edie both looked at her, as if suddenly remembering she was
there, and she smiled at them both.

'No,' said Edie. 'What do I want with the worry of a man
away at war?' She was lost in Gracie's smile, which always filled
her with a sense of being in the right place. Then she got up and
put more water in the kettle and while she was turned away from
them she took her notebook out of her pocket and wrote:

Ninth November Fourteen
Plan — Help Theo at war.

Twenty-Six

The Comfort Pack

Wednesday, 26 May 1915, when love is sent across the sea.

The first list of Gallipoli casualties appeared in the Ballarat papers on the third of May 1915. From then on the lists of dead boys grew longer each day. The attack on the Turks on the fifth of May was a disaster, as were the attacks on the sixth, seventh, eighth and ninth of May and all the other days of May and the lists of dead boys continued to grow longer and the advertisements urging more young men to go and die also grew. Mining reports of new shafts sunk and good stone quarried and advertisements for new fabrics were jammed in tiny spaces between all the news of the war. *Buy war bonds* the ads cried. Send little luxuries to the front. Send your sons to the front. Women were encouraged to keep knitting, buy buttons, hold fetes and pack up comfort packs to send to the soldiers. Germans were notified that they must attend the police station to register their details, including their date of birth, current address and occupation. The Royal Agricultural Show was suspended but Dame Nellie Melba sang at the Coliseum Theatre in South Street with all proceeds to the Red Cross and the trams waited to take the concertgoers home afterwards.

Notices of the dead, missing and injured were printed in thin, neat columns, sometimes with a photo and an obituary — a young man from Box Hill, another from Fitzroy, two from Hampton. Soon the local papers didn't have room for the dead boys from far away and gave preference to local lads. The pages were filled to the brim with notices of boys from town and the surrounding areas — a lad from Sebastopol who was ruck on the football team, a captain from Garibaldi with a baby, a chap from Black Hill who was youth leader at the Methodist church. Heroes to the last. Crisp, clean words suggesting tidy, painless deaths.

Everyone thought the war would be over quickly — by Christmas, the experts had said, and the boys would be back home in no time. Mothers comforted themselves with this thought; they dreamt of their sons walking in the door and laughing about what a good lark it had all been and how the government had let them see Europe for free. Everyone agreed God was on their side, just ask Reverend Whitlock or Father O'Malley. But now Christmas had come and gone and the war drove on like an insatiable beast.

The town had not seen one bullet, one bomb, one Turk in his weird little hat, but the town would never be the same again.

Every day Edie scoured the newspapers to make sure Theo's name wasn't there, and in Ligar Street Beth and Lilly did the same. When it wasn't there Edie thanked God for answering her prayers and Beth and Lilly hugged each other and Lilly put on the kettle and got out the biscuits.

Lilly and Beth had finished their dinner and cleared away the dishes and now Lilly was putting together a package for Theo as she had done every week of the six months he had been away. She had the box up on the kitchen table and Beth was sitting at the end of the table knitting green socks for the soldiers who were going to face a cold northern winter.

Lilly picked up the string to tie up the box and asked, 'Have you got a note you want to pop in, Beth, before I tie this up?'

Beth became flustered, her cheeks went pink and her ball of wool rolled off the table onto the floor. In fact, Beth looked as if she had been caught off guard in an embarrassing situation, which didn't make any sense to Lilly at all.

'Of course,' Beth stammered, picking up the ball of green wool from the floor. She dropped her needles onto the table and the ball of wool rolled onto the linoleum again where it remained as Beth disappeared into her room. Lilly had assumed Beth and Theo would write to each other regularly, growing their love through words, but as it was always she who collected the mail she couldn't help but notice that Theo only wrote to both of them, *Dear Mum and Beth*, and she wrote long letters back *with much love always from Beth and Mum*.

She could only wonder why her request had made Beth so uncomfortable. Maybe it was the distance, and she thought of when Peter had gone away to cure himself and how she had been devastated and closed herself off from the pain in her soul so she could keep doing daily tasks like cooking for Theo when all she wanted to do was crawl inside herself and wait until he came back. *We all have different ways*, she thought, maybe Beth and Theo didn't know how to bridge the physical space between them and needed some motherly help. Lilly looked at the box filled with a fruitcake soused in whisky so it wouldn't go off, Anzac biscuits made without eggs for the same reason, a jar of apricot jam, a pair of socks, a woollen beanie and a woollen vest for warmth that she had knitted for Theo and thought he could hide under his uniform. She was trying to think if there was

anything she had forgotten to put in when Beth came back with
a sealed envelope.

'That didn't take long,' said Lilly sadly, hoping that Beth would
have written pages and pages to Theo.

'Not much of a writer,' said Beth crisply.

'You should put on lipstick and kiss it,' said Lilly.

'Really Mum!' squealed Beth and the two of them giggled.
'I don't have any pots of lipstick.'

'No — no neither do I,' said Lilly, wishing she did have such a
thing, it might make her feel brighter in these dark times. 'I have
a beetroot though.'

So Beth pressed her lips to half a beetroot and then to the letter,
leaving a crimson print on the envelope and she held it with the
tips of her fingertips like a tainted thing and let it flutter into
the box. Lilly quickly tied up the box to keep the beetroot kiss
from escaping.

'Paul was grumbling again today,' Beth said as she lifted the
box onto the floor. '"It isn't right to employ a married woman
and if you must keep working for us, Beth, you will only do so
Monday to Friday,"' she mimicked Paul's voice.

'Well, I like having you around on Saturdays and Sundays,' said
Lilly. 'And you needn't work at all if you don't want to. Theo and
I are quite capable of supporting you.'

'So you keep saying, Mum, but working keeps me sane.'

'Well, as long as you're happy, dear.' Lilly thought how lonely
she would have been if Beth hadn't come to live with her and she
wondered if Theo had married Beth just so she would have company while he was away. Maybe he had and Beth knew and that
was why they didn't write to each other. She scolded herself and
quickly pushed the thought from her mind. That would be a terrible reason for her son to marry. Cross at thinking such a thing,

she grabbed a lemon biscuit to push the thought away and instead turned her mind to Maud Blackmarsh.

'You've done a world of good for that girl, Lilly,' Maud had said to her earlier in the day as she peered over the fence into Lilly's place as if looking for a secret.

Lilly looked around her garden but couldn't see anything that hadn't been there before.

Not finding any secrets, Maud had stared pointedly at Lilly's house. Lilly had got Theo to paint it a lovely cheery yellow some years back.

'Are you going to repaint that house?' she asked, not hiding her distaste.

'Not while there's a war on, dearie,' Lilly said and walked inside, leaving Maud standing at the fence.

Lilly glanced at Beth, sitting up the end of the table again, the click-clack of her knitting needles making a soft comforting rhythm. The girl had grown, her breasts now fell soft and round, her stomach and hips spread out with generous friendliness. She was no longer the slip of a girl she had been when she married. She was what a wife should be: a safe place, a solid woman to come home to, able to make a man feel that his life was grounded and secure.

She thought her Theo would be happy to see Beth filled out. Beth had needed new dresses as her old ones became too tight, so Lilly had sewed them for her. Beth said, 'Geez, Mum, no one has made dresses for me since I was little' and then had given her a hug, which made Lilly feel that she really had gained a daughter. The two of them got into a groove of living together. Lilly did the cooking and when Beth got home from her work in Webster Street Lilly would make sure to have something ready and wait-ing on the stove, and when Beth had eaten the mains there would always be something sweet to top it off, like some pineapple cake or honey joy biscuits. After dinner they would sit in the lounge room near Theo's piano and knit socks, scarves and balaclavas for the soldiers or make comfort packages to send to the men with tinned delicacies that wouldn't rot on the long journey to the other side of the world, like condensed milk, tea — anything that they imagined the men wouldn't be able to buy from stores at the front. And every week Lilly made a special care package for Theo filled with her cooking.

Sunday, 30 May 1915, the day before the Australian Imperial Forces change the rules to accept shorter men.

Edie was reading an article calling for more boys and men to fight for freedom. The rules for enlistment were to be changed starting tomorrow. Now you could enlist from the ages of eighteen to forty-five and you only had to be five feet two inches tall. '*The war needs you. Wives — let your man defend your honour,*' she read out to Paul. He was writing on a pad of paper in his lap. His hair was greying and his brow more furrowed but he still insisted on righting wrongs when he could.

'Hmmm,' said Paul, 'five and a half thousand boys. That's how many are needed each month alone to replace the dead. Spring Street is talking about holding a referendum next year on conscription. How can we force boys to walk head on into death?'

'I don't know, Papa,' said Edie, 'but I will do what I can to help the ones who have gone,' thinking of the one solider she wanted to help most. She folded up the paper and put it in the basket. 'Well, Papa, I am going to leave you to your speech because I'm going to go on with my own little project for the boys.' She walked down the hallway past the portraits of those who had gone before that inevitably filled her bones with the sureness of death, and felt as if she had eaten something rotten. She held her breath for a moment, her arms clasped tight across her chest, hoping and praying that Theo was safe.

Gracie was already in the kitchen, sitting at the table writing. The kitchen had become a packing room. There were three towers of cardboard boxes piled four and five high. One tower was empty boxes that wobbled and threatened to fall over, the second tower was boxes that sat heavy and firm on top of each other, full of brown glass jars that Edie had bought from the grocer. The third tower was filled boxes, glued, tied up and addressed, ready to be sent to the Comforts Fund, who would then send them on to the soldiers. Edie, Paul, Gracie and Beth when she was there, had to manoeuvre around the boxes to get to the stove or the pantry, but no one complained because it was all for the war and their sacrifice of a kitchen was nothing compared to the sacrifice of women who gave their sons and husbands.

Edie squeezed sideways between the table and the boxes until she got to the other end of the table. She took a cardboard box from the top of the empty box tower and put it on table. Then she reached for a newspaper from the pile that sat under the table and scrunched up the sheets of newspaper to make a nest on the bottom of the box. Next she took the top box from the tower of glued boxes, sat it on a kitchen chair and opened it, sliding a knife under the flap to unseal it. She put the box on the floor at her feet and took out a jar of Bovril. The brown glass jar was round and bulbous at the bottom like an onion, with a short neck shut tight with a screw-on lid. The words *Bovril Limited 8oz* were embossed in the glass like braille. Edie shut her eyes and ran her fingers over the raised letters that felt like scars on the smooth glass. She rolled the jar up in two sheets of paper in one direction and then two sheets of paper in the opposite direction and laid the jar with its protective newspaper in the carton on the nest of scrunched paper. She kept going until she had filled the carton with twenty-four jars of Bovril facing each other head

to head, in four layers of six jars, and then she took the pot of glue
from the stove and pasted the flaps of the box down. She cut a good
length of string, strung it right around the box several times in both
directions and tied it tight. Finally she took a sheet of plain brown
paper and a pen and wrote *To the Australian Comforts Fund, Ballarat
City Branch* and glued it to the top of the box. She heaved the box
into her arms and carried it to join its brothers, the tied-up boxes,
all filled with jars of Bovril. Then she started a new carton, another
twenty-four jars to be sent to the men at the front.

'Who are you writing to, Gracie?' Edie asked as she scrunched
up paper for the bottom of the new box.

'To Queen Mary. I'm telling her about your boxes of Bovril.
But this is the third time. I want my writing to be neat.'

'Well, as long as she can read it I expect that is all that will matter. Can you pass me some newspapers from under the table and
save my old back from bending over again?' She wasn't going to
ruin Gracie's fun by telling her that her letter would most likely
never even get to the Queen. Hardly any letters were getting
across the oceans, let alone a letter to the Queen. If it did get all
the way to the Queen no doubt it would be read by one of her
many aides who in all likelihood would toss it out.

'Gracie, you need to do it without all the bouncing. I've told
you before if you keep bouncing every time you move you will
bring all the boxes tumbling to the floor. They might even crash
on top of you.'

Tomorrow Laidlaw would come and collect all the boxes that
were ready to go.

'Why is Bovril good for the soldiers?' Gracie asked so she could
write it in her letter.

'Like I said before, because "vril" means "an electric fluid" and
bovine means "cow", so it's called Bovril. The electrical quality
of Bovril maintains your bodily fluids in their natural equilibrium

and the meaty beef provides strength for the liver. Bovril can cure diseases that are common in the trenches, where the men don't have access to a good hot cooked meal like you and I have. If you don't eat meat every day you die and the electric quality of Bovril means it is better absorbed and therefore better for you. There,' said Edie, 'so far I have sent enough Bovril for sixty-two thousand cups of broth for the soldiers.'

Gracie wrote *My sister has sent sixty-two thousand cups of Bovril* in her letter to the Queen.

'That will keep them in good health as they fight for our freedom on the other side of the world. Pass me another newspaper,' said Edie.

Gracie reached down and pulled up a wad of newspapers and something on the top sheet caught her eye.

'Don't sit there and read it,' said Edie, 'pass it over.'

'Listen to this, Edie,' Gracie said, *'Cadet's Last Message,'* then waited a moment for Edie to absorb that before she went on:

'The warship Leon Gambetta *went down. Seven officers seized Admiral Senes, who ran out of his cabin clad only in his nightshirt, and forcibly lowered him into a launch, but the boat capsized and all were drowned. As the last boat was making for the shore, long after the* Leon Gambetta *sank, it passed a cadet — the last living object in the water. It was impossible to take him aboard, as the small craft was already crowded; so the boat forged slowly away from the boy, who gasped, "Never mind lads! Give a kiss to my mother for me."'*

Gracie put the sheet of newspaper down on the table and smoothed out the creases with her hands. 'I can't let you scrunch up that sheet, Edie, it would be like scrunching up the boy's memory.' She looked up with tears in her eyes. 'That would have been an English boy?' she asked.

Edie nodded, she could feel the tears filling her eyes, too. She passed the kitchen scissors to Gracie. 'Here,' she said, 'cut out the article and we will glue it to the wall and that way we can remember his sacrifice.'

She watched Gracie carefully cut around the article, then Edie lightly smeared some glue across the back of it and pasted the article to the wall and they both stood and looked at it and wondered how a boy could be so brave. They stood side by side in silence, united by their own helplessness in the face of the boy's courage. What could they really do to save these poor boys' lives?

'I'm going to marry a brave English boy,' Gracie said finally.

'Good heavens,' said Edie. 'Why?'

'I just think,' said Gracie carefully, knowing she was putting bricks in place in her life that, once assembled, could never be moved, 'that if the English are that brave it might be a good idea.'

Edie tapped Gracie's nose. 'You've got at least ten years before you marry anyone.' And Edie reached for a jar of Bovril and held it out to Gracie. 'Kiss it for good luck,' and Gracie did so and Edie hoped that Theo would get that jar of Bovril as she wrapped it and put it in the box.

She wondered again if Theo was safe. She tried not to mind any more that he had got over his love for her and married Beth. In her notebook she had written:

Plan — Be happy for Theo and Beth even if I'm not.

And she really tried. She would remind herself that she loved Beth like a sister and so she could only wish good things for her. She told herself that she couldn't be angry with Beth because Beth hadn't chased Theo, they had found each other because of her. She had said no to him, rejected his love, so how could she expect him to give up his life for her and not to make a life with anyone else? And if he was going to make a life with someone else, she would rather it was with Beth than, say, Vera Gamble.

But when Beth announced they were engaged so soon after she had said no once and for all, it had cut her heart to pieces. The week after that he walked Beth home from church, leaving her and Papa to walk about half a block behind. She watched as Beth hung tightly onto his arm as if the faintest breeze would pick him up and blow him back to her. On the other side of him was Gracie, holding his hand and pulling him in different directions as she skipped and hopped. Edie could see he was paying more attention to Gracie than Beth but she didn't wonder why. Gracie would command anyone's attention. At the corner of Webster Street and Drummond Street Papa had leant over and patted her arm and asked meaningfully, 'Are you okay?', pointing his umbrella accusingly at Theo.

'I changed my plan, Papa, and now I must wear it,' she said, and hoped she was wearing it well.

Then, as well as walking Beth home from church, Theo had started visiting during the week. Edie knew his knock on the door like the back of her hand and for a moment her heart would skip and she would have to remind herself that it wasn't her he was calling on. Sometimes while he was visiting they found themselves alone in the hallway together — she might have been going to her bedroom and he to the study to see her father — with no more than their breath between them and they would stand like that forgetting where and who they were until her father appeared and said something like, 'Theo, come and look at this.'

When Theo spoke to her she felt a mashing pain in her chest. He spoke kindly, as if she could be anyone and certainly not someone he had fervently loved for years, and she spoke to him as though he was nothing to her other than Beth's fiancé. But her heart was a pulpy mess.

Edie knew she had two choices. She could take bitterness and slowly shrivel, or she could love him privately, secretly, in her heart. Whenever she so much as glanced at Gracie and Gracie looked up at her and smiled, she knew that Gracie loved her more than anyone else in the world, even more than Theo had loved her, and she knew that she returned that love and that her decision was the right one. So she had watched as Beth had filled Theo's stomach with her roast pork and his eyes with her prettiness and bantered with him in a way Edie never had and she became convinced that he was much better off with Beth. She would never have loved him as Beth did, because her true love would always be Gracie.

If she did love him she should want the best for him, and that was Beth. But she still yearned for him. So she made a plan to help him and packed Bovril to keep him safe while he was in the trenches.

'Pass me a jar of Bovril, Gracie, I can fit in one more jar.'

Gracie passed over a jar and neither of them noticed that a tear for the English boy that had been sliding down Gracie's cheek had spilt onto the label and smudged the ink.

Edie took the jar and wrapped it in newspaper and put it into its bed in the box with its brothers and sisters. She glued the lid down, tied the string and reached for the paper and pen to address the box. As she held the pen mid-air she stopped and thought for a moment. Then did something she had never done before. Instead of just writing *To the Comfort Fund*, she wrote:

To the 8th Battalion
Australian Imperial Forces
C/o The Australian Comfort Fund

Twenty-Seven

The Afternoon Tea

*Saturday, 4 December 1915, when all the town
can hear Gracie yell.*

Edie asked Gracie to check the afternoon post. Gracie sighed but she put down the scarf she was knitting and did it anyway.

Edie smiled at the scarf looped onto the large wooden size-eight needles, full of holes where Gracie had dropped stitches and then picked them up again several rows later. It looked more like a fishing net than a scarf but she would help Gracie fix it up and it would still keep some poor soldier's neck warm.

'Though with all those colours he's likely to become a sitting duck,' she said to herself. She picked up the needle and held it up and the scarf hung down like an abstract tapestry. The wools were different sizes and colours, the edges meandered in and out like waves, but the scarf sang with all the determination and enthusiasm that children put into their creations. Edie could hear it and she hoped whichever soldier got the scarf would hear it too. She rubbed the soft wool against her cheek. Suddenly the scarf's song was drowned out by hollering coming from out the front of the

house. Edie dropped the scarf back onto the table and ran, her
heart thumping, to the front door. In his study, where he was
writing a speech in support of the election of Vida Goldstein as
the first woman in parliament, Paul heard the yelling and put his
hands to his ears. He rushed out into the hallway where he nearly
collided with Edie.

'Come on,' said Edie, 'that's Gracie — something must be
really wrong.' Paul ran out of the house behind Edie. Nothing
could happen to Gracie, it just couldn't. She made Edie's life
whole. Gracie's voice rang out in high-pitched squeals and the
men preparing the lake for the upcoming aquatic carnival to raise
funds for the Red Cross dropped their tools. The folk walking
around the lake enjoying their Saturday afternoon stopped still
in their tracks and people up and down the street dropped their
cups of tea and their books and ran out of their houses. Jack Puce
dropped the screwdriver he was using to hang a new photograph
of the boys. Daphne Puce dropped the apple she was peeling for
the crumble and it rolled along the floor and under the table.
Arthur dropped the cricket bat that was really an old paling and
Geoffrey dropped the tennis ball they were using as a cricket ball
and they ran to the street with John following behind to see what
the noise was all about and who had died. Laidlaw, Dottie and
Beth dropped the bread they were rationing to the swans and the
swans flapped and greedily gobbled the meal that was now a smor-
gasbord. The three of them ran towards the Cottingham house
leaving the swans to fight it out. Nurse Drake, hiding in the tall
grasses in Fairy Land, shook herself off George, held out her hand
to yank him up and together they ran toward the Cottingham's.

Edie saw the crowd gathering as she ran down the driveway
towards the letterbox. Her heart had stopped now, she was sure
of it. Gracie had to be in the middle of all those people. Had she
been hit by Doctor Appleby's car? He always drove like a maniac,

tearing along at at least twenty miles an hour. No one would have a chance if they got in his way. Had a snake or a spider bitten her? There were tiger snakes that made their way into people's backyards — she was forever telling Gracie to keep an eye out over summer, and there were red-backs that hid in letterboxes. What if she had killed Gracie by sending her to the letterbox? Had Gracie fallen and smashed her head on the hard road? All these possibilities raced through Edie's mind and they all ended with a vision of Gracie sprawled bleeding and dead. She pushed her way through the throng and Paul followed close behind.

And there was Gracie in the middle of the crowd of neighbours, jumping up and down, flapping her arms in the air and holding onto an envelope. As soon as Edie saw Gracie's face she knew that all the noise was excitement. Some of the other children started jumping up and down and squealing too, even though they had no idea what about. So Gracie wasn't dead or injured, she was well enough to be bouncing as always, and the noise she and the children were making was building. Edie looked at her father for help. Paul put his hands in the air and called for silence like a judge in an unruly courtroom. Everything became quiet and Gracie stopped jumping. Edie put her arms on Gracie's shoulders to keep her still.

'Now what's all this fuss? Are you hurt? Are you injured? Tell me quick.'

'I have a letter from the King and Queen! All the way from London!' Gracie flapped the envelope in front of Edie's face and the paper brushed against her nose making her blink. Edie felt an enormous relief that Gracie was okay and all this fuss was over a letter. But she looked hard at the girl, she wasn't bleeding and dead but perhaps she wasn't as rosy as she could be and she was far too short for a ten-year-old girl. She needed more tonic and perhaps some cod liver oil.

'I'm okay, Edie, stop worrying,' said Gracie. 'Didn't you hear me, a letter from the Queen!'

Gracie broke free from Edie's clasp on her shoulders and jumped up and down some more.

Edie said, 'Well, there's certainly nothing wrong with you health-wise.'

'It's a letter from the Queen,' Edie said to Paul and he laughed, 'Yes, it is apparently.'

'Look, look, it's come in the afternoon post.' Gracie flapped the letter again and the north wind tried to tug it away so she scrunched it tight and stood puffing in front of them.

Jack Puce said, 'Oh, this is exciting, we all need a bit of good news. It's got to be good news, hasn't it, if it's from the Queen?' and Daphne Puce said, 'My aunt got a letter from royalty once,' but no one heard her.

Beth, who had arrived puffed and had been bent over and holding onto her knees, said, 'Go on, Gracie, open it up.'

'How do you know it's from the Queen?' asked Daphne Puce.

'It's got the royal insignia on the envelope, see, a red crown stamped on and everything,' said Gracie. But she was holding the envelope so tightly no one could see anything.

'For goodness sake come in out of the hot sun; come inside and then you can read it to us,' said Paul, 'if you can smooth the crinkles out of it. Come on, everyone, into the dining room. Laidlaw,' Paul said, 'come on, you know your way in, lead on.'

'Everyone?' asked Edie.

'Why not?' said Paul.

'Why not indeed.' Maybe he was right, maybe this was just what they all needed in the middle of the war — a letter from the Queen.

Everyone else thought this was the best news anyone had had in many a month — they were going to get to go inside the famous Cottingham house and all because of a young girl and her letter. So Jack and Daphne Puce acted as if they had been inside the Cottingham home so often it was no fuss to them. But others, some from Soldiers Hill, some from Newington, and a few miners from East Ballarat and their families who were all out for the free entertainment the lake offered, were now getting so much more. They poured past the boarded-up door they had heard about and into the Cottingham dining room to see Gracie's letter.

Edie looked at all the people squashed into the dining room. People were taking off their hats and enjoying the coolness of the Cottingham's big home. Her gaze lingered on the mining families and their waifs, the mothers without husbands and the children without fathers who had gone to war. She was standing next to Paul who was talking quietly to Laidlaw. Laidlaw was telling Paul he had signed up but hadn't yet told his wife. Edie thought it was awfully unfair how men felt free to make decisions by themselves but women felt they had to ask permission. Gracie was standing next to her, ready to read her letter. She saw the expectation in people's faces, that the letter contained something bigger than their lives.

'We should all have tea first,' she said to Paul. Following her gaze to the children's hungry faces he said, 'You know what, I think we might all go downstairs where it's even cooler and then we can really take the time to enjoy this special letter.'

No one could believe their luck. They were going to see the famed underground house. Now it was Laidlaw's turn to be cocky. 'I built it with my own hands,' he told everyone many times.

Edie wasn't sure how they were going to make afternoon tea for so many people.

'I need our Lord Jesus,' she whispered in Paul's ear, 'to turn a single loaf of bread into many.'

'I'll help,' said Beth.

'See — he heard your prayer,' Paul said.

Edie didn't know how she was going to do it but she pulled out all the china, the good and the everyday, and Daphne and her boys ran next door and got her everyday china and her three aluminium teapots, her milk and a loaf of bread and a pot of jam. Beth put on the kettle and filled three saucepans with water for the six teapots Edie had managed to find in the cabinets.

'Don't put out the sugar,' said Beth, 'no one will expect it with the rations.'

'Sensible,' said Edie.

She found cups for the adults and glasses for the children and even with Daphne's contribution they were still short but it worked out because some of the people who had been picnicking around the lake had their own cups.

Then Edie, Beth, Dottie and Daphne carried trays with the tea, milk, glasses and teacups downstairs and it took them three trips each and on the final trip Edie saw that sandwiches, cake and biscuits had appeared on the downstairs dining room table and she looked at Paul.

'Oh yes, people have opened up their picnic baskets,' said Paul.

'Isn't it lovely,' said Gracie, beaming.

'Well, this is much more fun than the lake,' Laidlaw said to Dottie.

When the food was gone and the tea was drunk Edie nodded at Gracie. 'I think it's time for this letter then.'

'At last,' she said, as though the wait had been more than she could bear and people laughed as she slowly peeled the envelope open.

'Wait,' said Paul and he got off his chair and moved it over for Gracie to stand on so everyone could see and hear her.

'It's not every day you get a letter from the Queen,' Edie said.

'I have to do it carefully, I have to make sure I don't tear it,' said Gracie, her fingers trembling.

'We'll still be waiting this time next year at this rate,' said Paul and everyone chuckled.

'I want the moment to last forever,' said Gracie and she looked at everyone watching her as she pulled out the letter.

Paul picked up the envelope as it fluttered to the floor and turned it over. 'That's the royal insignia all right. Who'd have thought?'

The letter was on thick creamy paper, folded into three equal parts. Gracie carefully unfolded it.

She held it up and showed it to everyone like her teacher did with picture books, making sure even those crammed in the corners of the room could take time to see. Everyone took a deep breath. Even if it hadn't had a message on it, the letter was magnificent.

At the top of the page were two lions: a golden lion wearing a crown and a lion on the other side wearing red pants. The lions stood in a field of green grass and white flowers. Between the two lions was a large gold and red crown, from which hung a banner, and they were all encircled with a blue wreath.

When everyone had seen how beautiful the letter was, Gracie began to read:

Dear Miss Cottingham,
I wish to mark by this personal message my appreciation of the service your sister has rendered your Country. I have read of the cases of Bovril your sister is sending to the soldiers in the trenches.
I can fully realise how comforting your sister's work must prove, especially during the cold and damp weather, and I heartily congratulate your sister on the happy thought which prompted her to initiate such a useful project.

Your parents must be very proud, firstly of your sister, who is able to put the needs of our soldiers who fight for our freedom uppermost in her mind, and secondly they must be proud of your so unselfishly commending your sister to our attention.

Yours sincerely,

Mary R, 1st October 1915

Gracie passed the letter to Paul. Edie was dying to read it for herself but because the letter was about her, she held off; she didn't want to seem vain. She got up to start clearing some dishes, pretending that she wasn't concerned about the Queen's letter and that she wasn't completely puffed with pride and there weren't any tears in her eyes and her heart wasn't completely and utterly spilling over with the love she had for Gracie. As she looked over at her sister, Gracie beamed at her.

'Even the Queen recognises how kind and generous you are, Edie. We should have it framed, Papa.'

Edie looked at everyone looking at her, 'It's only a letter,' she said, uncomfortable being the focus of everyone's attention.

'It's only Bovril,' said Paul, 'but if it saves even one young man's life, it's pure gold.'

Edie thought of the man whose life she wanted to save. Was Theo getting her Bovril? Would a hot cup steaming with love save him and bring him home safely?

After everyone had thanked Paul for his hospitality and began to file back up the stairs, Edie saw Laidlaw whispering to Gracie and she wandered over pretending to clean up where she could hear.

'He built it all for you, love,' he whispered, and Gracie whispered back, 'I know' just like she had when he said it in the street.

Then she said, 'Built what?'

Laidlaw said, 'This magnificent underground house that is the talk of the town. He built it for you to keep you cool in the hot summers when you were but a wee thing.'

Gracie looked around the room, at the flickering fairy lights strung along the tops of the walls, at the photo of her beautiful mother on the wall, at Edie who had been her real mother.

'Really?' she said, and Edie nodded and Gracie smiled her smile and Laidlaw flicked one of her curls.

When everyone was back in their own homes sitting on their verandahs drinking beer or fanning their faces in the cool evening breeze, they all agreed it had been a delightful afternoon and completely unexpected and what a sensible idea an underground house was, but best of all was the letter.

Fancy that, the town getting a letter from the Queen.

As Christmas was approaching, everyone agreed that practical gifts were essential given the war and not too much tinsel. Lilly sent her regular weekly gift box to Theo: she put in a Christmas cake, some shortbread and a jumper she had knitted in the colours of the flag. Lilly didn't know that her packages to Theo went missing more often than not and that the soldiers complained that the packages went from Australia to London and back again and God only knew how many months they spent traversing the globe before they were likely to reach them.

Part Three

Twenty-Eight

The Soldier

Friday, 17 December 1915, Cape Helles, on the Sea of Helle, Turkey, where the blood of men and boys turns the sea red.

Theo was squatting at the bottom of a trench, his feet sunk into the river of mud which seeped over the tops of his boots and oozed around his toes. His hands were knotted tightly over his stomach. He was sure he had eaten nothing for months except hard tack biscuits and black tea. The Turks' trenches were forty feet away. Sometimes the Turks threw raisins or sweets that Theo didn't recognise into the Australian trenches, and in return Theo threw his cigarettes back to them because he didn't smoke anyway.

Theo was so hungry that his stomach had shrivelled into a hard stone inside him. There hadn't even been tins of that God-awful Maconochie stew, which was no more than watery soup with slices of turnips and carrots and a sludge of greasy fat at the bottom of the tin. He threw those to the Turks too, good riddance to the muck, in exchange for raisins but right now he would even eat Maconochie, he would even eat it cold, which once would have made him vomit. He would eat it right now straight out of the tin with his fingers if he could get some and the Turks would have to

go without. He could feel the sides of his wrinkled stomach chaf-
ing against each other. He could put his fingers around his arm and
they met. Using his bowels made him cry out with pain because
everything inside him was so hard and dry. There was jam to eat
but the moment he opened the tin millions of flies descended into
it and he ate them as well and they buzzed around his mouth in a
panic at suddenly being caged, crashing into his gums, the roof of
his mouth and stinging as they collided with his tongue.

Theo reached into his pocket for the tin of strawberry jam.
It was runny, you'd have to look hard to find any fruit in it. His
mother would have tossed it out saying, 'That'll never win me
any prizes at the Ballarat Show.' He stood up and hurled the jam
to the Turks then he quickly squatted down and waited and sure
enough a few minutes later they threw back a brown paper bag.
It landed in the mud and he dived on it before it sank or drifted
away in the muddy river. He tore open the soggy paper and inside
found four small parcels wrapped in greaseproof paper. He peeled
the paper away from the first to find something, he didn't know
what, but he put it in his mouth, and then the others one after
the other and let the sickly sweet taste trickle down his throat. He
didn't notice that he was eating some of the paper as well. All too
soon the memory of it was gone and all he could think about was
the hunger and dream of what would end it. Apricots. He hadn't
seen a tin of apricots in months. What he would give for a tin of
apricots. Sometimes the Turks threw apricots stuffed with some
creamy white substance, he thought maybe it was sweet cheese or
milk. He wished they had thrown some of those.

Theo wiped his sticky hands on his greatcoat, which only
glued the fibres of his coat to the stickiness. Dobson stumbled past
him, splashing mud and knocking into him then banging against
the rock and timber walls of the trench, groaning pitifully and

holding his stomach, so Theo staggered to his feet, put his arm around Dobson and helped him to the latrine.

'Tell me a joke, Dobson,' he said, trying to make taking another man to the lav seem normal. Dobson always had a joke. Theo could never remember them when he wanted to tell them himself. In one ear and out the other.

'Did I tell you the one about Dad and Dave?' mumbled Dobson. Theo could barely hear him.

'Nope,' said Theo.

'I'll tell ya when I've dumped a brick,' said Dobson.

Theo helped him unbuckle his pants and left him to it. But Dobson took so long that Theo forgot him and wandered off until an hour later when he went to use the same latrine.

'You still here, Dobson!' he cried, seeing Dobson still sitting over the pail. But Dobson didn't answer. His vacant eyes looked past Theo to some other world. He was stone dead. Theo walked away and left Dobson to his peace.

Later in the day Theo watched as Dwyer, who reckoned he was nineteen but looked not a day over fourteen if he was lucky, ran past him screaming.

'I really am nineteen,' Dwyer had said when he first arrived.

'Yeah? What year were you born?' They'd laughed as they watched him stumbling over the math in his head and they laughed so hard they fell over.

'Fourteen,' someone suggested.

'Nah, give him the benefit of the doubt.'

'Yeah, maybe he looks young for his age. Maybe he's fourteen and a half.'

But now Dwyer ran past Theo with bits of him missing. 'Hey Dwyer, you've misplaced your arms,' Theo screamed at him.

But it was a silent scream.

Theo looked up as the skies opened fire on him. It raged and pelted down around him mercilessly.

God had thrown his lot in with the Turks. Theo was sure of it.

Saturday, 18 December 1915, when nowhere in
Australia gets as cold as here.

It was so cold his clothes froze onto his skin and the trenches filled with rain, while he slept fitfully and dreamt of his mum's apple upside-down cake. When Theo woke in the morning there was a thick layer of ice sealing bodies in chilly, watery tombs.

Theo watched as the ice melted in the midday sun and bodies silently floated past him like the wooden sailing ships he'd played with as a boy.

Theo survived it all. He was a survivor, and he knew how to wait. If he waited long enough this would all be over. A bit of icy cold water wasn't going to get him. The Poms hated soap and water — not that there was any soap to be had. But Theo didn't mind water. The word among the ranks was that they were all going to be evacuated soon, might be weeks, might be days, might be only hours. They said some had gone already. No one had come for Theo — they knew he could survive.

'Take the young boys,' he said to the bodies floating by. 'They need their mothers.'

It was supposed to be a secret that they were going, though everyone knew. Theo didn't want to go anywhere with the taint of this wretched place still on him. He peeled off the soggy great-coat and ripped off his torn, dirt-encrusted shirt. He leant against the timber and rock wall of the trench and tried to pull off his boots, but he couldn't. They were caked on with mud and filled with water. He tugged several times and nearly fell so he gave up and plunged himself in.

'Get out of the water, you bloody Aussie bastard!' A British soldier waved his arms at him. 'You're all mad you lot — you know that, don't you!' he yelled. 'Sergeant says he can't do a thing with you lot, you're so undisciplined!' The soldier turned and laughed as though there was someone standing right next to him. 'Let's just hope we never get attacked at night, 'cause you'll never get the Aussies out of their beds,' he said to his invisible friend.

'Top blokes during the day,' the soldier answered himself.

'Too right! Never said they weren't. Just said at night the dead can't wake 'em.'

Remembering Theo, he yelled, 'You lot need to get out of the water! It's contaminated, you blooming twit!'

But Theo didn't listen. He was a survivor. A bit of water wasn't going to do him in. He scrambled about like a pubescent boy in the Yarra. He thought the Turks were looking down on him from high up on the cliffs next to God. He forgot their trenches just feet away.

'Anyway,' he yelled to the soldier, 'everyone knows you Poms are dirty bastards that never wash.'

Theo scrubbed at his chest with his knuckles until his skin was raw and bleeding. He'd get this place out of his system if it killed him.

The soldier watched him. 'Your lips are turning blue. You're going to catch pneumonia.'

Theo finally clambered out of the water onto some dry ground on the trench wall, huffing and heaving. He was closer to the British soldier now. He tried to dry himself with his wet greatcoat, then pulled on his wet shirt and put his hands in his shirt pocket. He pulled out a damp photograph. It was small and dog-eared.

'My wife,' he said, and held the photograph up for the British soldier to see.

'How'd an ugly old codger like you get a sweet young thing like that? And who's the sweet little lass beside her?' the soldier said and Theo thought the soldier was looking straight through him as though he was a ghost

'Stupid blighter, you shouldn't have been in the water,' said the soldier and then he was gone — poof. There was a noise and the bugger disappeared.

Monday, 20 December 1915, when the Turks turn a blind eye.

The pain ripped through Theo's gut. It came without warning. It was so bad that Theo thought it must be a bullet, though he didn't see how when he was inside the trench. He looked for blood, he slapped his hands all over his body. He checked to see if he still had all his limbs. Another razor-blade of pain coursed through his abdomen, splitting his stomach into shards. He crawled up the ladder and out of the narrow trench and collapsed onto the dusty ground. The pain ripped through his body again, it reached up to his brain and down to his toes, it was thorough and didn't miss one bit of him and everything became a black nothing. When he opened his eyes, his eyelids hurt. His eyes were two peach stones stuck in his head, rough and stinging, his mouth was a raw gaping hole and his stomach chafed on rusty blades. He didn't know where he was or how long he'd been there.

'It's all right, we'll have you at a hospital soon,' said a voice and he recognised the accent. Some Pommy bastard. For a moment Theo thought it was his Pommy bastard. The bastard who had stood on the top of the trench.

'Who are you?'

'Rose.'

'Roses are for love,' Theo said. 'Didn't work, though.'

'Well, it's Rosenberg, really. Reuben Rosenberg — but I don't usually tell people that. Don't know why I just told you, for that matter.'

'Who are you?' Theo asked again.

'Royal Flying Corps.'

'What're you doing down here then? You should be off shooting those bloody Huns,' he rasped.

'We're evacuating, remember — it's all spare hands on deck. I land, fill up and fly off. I wait to my next shift, I can't sleep so I see what I can do to help and I run into you, you silly bugger. You get to go first today, seeing you're sick. I've called for the ambulance cart.'

Theo listened to the sounds around him. He could hear the noises of war, the guns pelting death, the screams of orders and fear. He felt so disappointed and cheated. For a moment he'd thought he was somewhere else. Then there was silence.

'Blimey it's cold.' Theo felt his body begin to shiver. Just a little at first, but soon it became uncontrollable and rattled him as if he was a toy in a child's hand.

'Weather's making things tough, that's for sure,' he heard the Pommy voice say somewhere off in the distance, 'but we'll have you out of here in no time.' It was a soothing voice that lulled Theo into stillness. He was sure the war was just a dream inside his head and it had faded. It was an almighty relief. He was so happy it was over, he was sure he was making a fool of himself and crying. He felt extraordinarily tired. He wanted to sleep and not wake up till he was home. He could hear the lullaby of the surf in the distance and he suddenly felt that all he wanted was to fall asleep to its song.

He shut his eyes and murmured.

'Who can you see?' The voice was so gentle that Theo wanted to please it, so he took a deep breath and even though it was agony to speak he answered.

'I know that if I could see her one more time I'd be all right.' His voice was little more than a croak.

The far-off voice said, 'What did he say? Sometimes I can't understand you Aussies with your accents.'

Theo didn't answer any more. The voice was no longer in his world.

Twenty-Nine

Reuben

When something important is lost.

Reuben Rosenberg had been in the prime of his life when he'd enthusiastically signed up for the war. His chest had been full of vigour and courage. His limbs had been strong; his eyes were clear and saw everything he wanted or needed to see. He could see German Fokkers before they'd even left the clouds. His hair was dark, proud, thick and wayward; it spoke of rebellion, which the girls really loved, and when they took the photo of him for the newspaper — *Our Heroes of the Sky* — he'd stood in his fur-lined leather flying helmet and held himself as though posing for the head of a coin. He inspired all he touched and spoke to. His voice was rich, timbered, fitting for a hero; his nose was slightly curved and roman and his lips were soft and full. He was old enough to know how to seduce women of any age and young enough to have the boyish charm to do it, and he was a fighter pilot, a celebrity, and that made the girls want him regardless of any charm.

'I'm just a humble pilot, one of a new breed,' he always said, pleased that he wasn't conceited like some, and he would be ready as the girls melted into him.

His family home was in West Coker, a small village two miles out of Yeovil. It didn't have its own railway station, you had to go to Yeovil Junction for the train, but it did have three pubs, a town hall, a post office and St Martin of Tours Church, which everyone called St Martin's. The church had eight bells and an organ that had cost five hundred pounds when it was bought a good thirty-five years ago in 1885, so just imagine what it was worth now. West Coker was farming country, it was undulating hills that sloped to rivers on whose banks dairy cows idled away their days.

Overseeing West Coker sat Ashgrove House, bought by Reuben's grandfather, who had contributed most of the cost of the church organ even though he never stepped foot inside the church. Unfortunately the contribution of the organ bought him a smaller level of acceptance than he had hoped. Some locals were never going to accept Jews in Ashgrove House. The house stood three storeys high with two double-storey wings; it had five ponds and a rose garden and three hundred acres behind large brick and stone gates. Beyond the grounds of Ashgrove Hall the family's land was tenanted out to farmers. Reuben thought that if it didn't rain all the time and his parents weren't there, it would be quite a lovely place.

On weekends when he had leave, he and his mate Holmes would find a dance to go to. Reuben would stand in the entrance of the dance hall as his eyes adjusted to the dim light cast from the hanging lamps hand-painted with scenes from Japan or China. There would be a vocalist on the stage singing 'It's a Long Way to Tipperary' but slow and low and mournful, like jazz. There would be a band wearing suits behind the singer, and behind them wafts of white curtains like the clouds he flew in. There would be a pianist at a grand piano and tables with drinks and sandwiches and staff serving in tails. Mothers would sit at linen-covered tables along the sides of the hall sipping tea and sherry and keeping an eagle eye on their daughters to protect them from men like him.

Reuben was fantastic, standing at the top of the steps in his uniform, a cigarette held suggestively between his lips, his eyes hinting at the immorality he was so eager to share with any young lady who had no chaperone in sight. He would see the young women glancing furtively at him as their dance partners twirled them about. They could sense the danger in him. He was irresistible. Soon the young women gathered around him and when the pianist stopped playing he would walk over to the piano and the girls would lean their delicate elbows on the piano top, sip their sherry, their lips wet and slightly parted, and Reuben would tell them flying stories with such vigour that the blood rose to the young ladies' cheeks as they gasped at the peril he faced daily as he fought the Huns. The mothers would eye him warily from their perches along the walls. The fathers who huddled together discussing the turns and twists of the war didn't notice him entrancing their wide-eyed daughters and the men glared at him jealously.

'I love the forbidden,' Reuben would say quietly to the girls, and they would gasp at his daring and then he would talk about flying and they would be calmed because that's what his words did to people. His voice was mesmerising and the way he told stories took the girls to another world where there were no rules and the skin on their arms turned goosepimply and their heads were filled with thoughts of what a man like Reuben Rose could do and at least one of them would disappear into some dark corner to give him hope before his next flight.

Reuben didn't view the war the same way Theo did. Reuben didn't see the panic and fear. It was all about victory to him, conquering the skies and glorying over his enemies. Life came easily to him, and success fell into his lap. There was never any thought that he might not win. The Australians were beaten, worn out; some had given up and were waiting for death, some threw themselves into the sea pleading for the Turks to do them in right there and then. Reuben's optimism slapped them in the face. He was a champion. They weren't. He was another careless heavy boot stomping the ground over their graves. The Australians could sense his blindness and kept their distance.

Reuben crouched over the dying Aussie. His flanks began to ache so he sat in the mud beside the man who was trembling uncontrollably, his entire body vibrating on the ground, his teeth rattling in his mouth. There was no hope for him, it didn't need a medic to tell Reuben that.

'What's your name?' he asked gently.

The man didn't answer so Reuben carefully lifted off his dog tag and saw *T Hooley* etched into the metal. 'What's the T for?'

'Oh, her smile,' whispered the man, barely alive.

'Whose smile? Have you got a message you want me to pass on to your wife?' He yelled at the men rushing back and forth through the mud, 'What's his wife's name, for God's sake?' There was no time for the dying. Reuben shouldn't really be bothering, either. There was too much to be done and it all had to be done quietly. They didn't want the Turks to know they were leaving. Soon it would be Reuben's turn to go back up and distract the Turks in the seaplane while men filed silently onto ships like ghosts.

The dying man reached out and grabbed his hand.

'Whose smile can you see?' asked Reuben.

'It'll be his mother,' said a passing soldier. 'We all see our mothers. We all cry out for our mothers. Thank God they can't see us. They'd put us to bed with a good spanking for getting in this much strife!'

Reuben looked at the dying soldier. He was older than him, maybe by twenty years or so. He felt a tug in his gut; a feeling that he and this soldier could have been friends in different circumstances. From what he could tell the man had a genuine face. He tried to imagine the face fatter, with colour, smiling. He tried to imagine sitting at the club with the man, raising their whisky glasses together and toasting the King; the King and to the King's wife and the King's good health and the King's good victory and all the King's soldiers.

The dying Aussie smiled, but not at Reuben, and said, 'Edie.'

'Edie. Is that your wife?' Reuben asked.

Suddenly, Theo grabbed Reuben by the collar with his two bony hands that were thin like a skeleton, and he drew him close. He whispered in Reuben's ear, 'If you find Edie tell her I'm sorry and if you see little Gracie — well, if you see little Gracie ask her to smile and you'll never want anything else.'

The foul smell of the man made Reuben want to vomit.

'Leave him alone. He's deluded. It's just as well; better not to know you're dying uselessly in a God-forgotten battleground,' someone yelled.

Reuben was still leaning close as the dying man whispered, 'Edie,' again.

'But I thought it was Gracie,' said Reuben and gave up asking questions and just cradled the dying man, who obviously wasn't even going to make it to the hospital ship. He sat in the dirt and the caked blood and stroked the dying Aussie's matted hair. The poor blighter was seeing the secrets of life that you only saw in death. Finally the ambulance cart arrived. No one saw the wheels roll over Theo's dog tag, burying it beneath the red dirt.

'Here, try and give him this and we'll be back in a moment,' said the stretcher-bearer, who had a boy's face, round and fresh. Reuben watched as the boy took a dessertspoon of Bovril from a jar and put it in an enamel tin mug.

'The label is smudged,' said Reuben.

The kid looked at the jar. 'Won't change the flavour none,' he said and poured hot water into the mug from a thermos. He stirred it three times with a dirty teaspoon and handed it to Reuben.

'What's your name, lad?' called Reuben, but the stretcher-bearer and the medics were gone so he held the mug to Theo's lips and tried to feed him some of the liquid without spilling too much down the man's front. At first Theo spluttered and coughed and sprayed the stuff everywhere and Reuben had to dodge the spittle so he didn't catch the man's germs.

Then there was silence everywhere apart from the muffled comings and goings of the men.

'The Turks have stopped firing,' said Reuben. 'They're letting us leave.'

Part Four

Thirty

The Grave

Saturday, 22 January 1916, in Ballarat, when Milton
Blackmarsh has given Lilly a rabbit.

Beth knew that she needed the preserving jars. She needed them so her heart wouldn't disappear. She could feel her heart dissolving inside her. If it dissolved she would become hard, she would be a sheet of glass and everyone would see everything inside her. They would see she had no heart and they would see all her guilt. They would see she had caused two deaths. She got up from the bed and looked through the curtains at the trees and she wondered how many times Theo had stood in this spot, looking through this window at the same trees. Had they whispered to him? Because she was sure she could hear them whispering over and over, a polyphonic chant. She saw the sun just breaking as it entered the day, its light dappled and soft through the leaves. The sun was deceitful and would turn on them, scorching everything it touched by afternoon. She quietly dressed, pulling on the clothes that were nearest, her black skirt that she had worn a week ago at Theo's memorial, her white shirt. She held her boots in her hands and made her way down the hallway to the kitchen door and stood in the hallway before peering carefully into the kitchen like a child playing peek-a-boo. She had hoped Lilly would still be asleep, but no such luck. Lilly was already up and dressed and whipping batter in a bowl. Beth stayed out of sight, peeping occasionally into the kitchen to check what Lilly was doing, and when Lilly was distracted by the whistling kettle Beth took her chance and snuck past the kitchen, then quietly opened and shut the back door. She sat on the back step and pulled on her boots, lacing them badly and knotting them. They would be a pain to undo later. Then, even though there was no need, she tiptoed through the grass to the garden shed. She pulled the latch and switched on the light and there it was waiting for her.

'Ahhh, you,' she said, and she took Lilly's wooden wheelbarrow and put her hands firmly around each handle with its peeled red paint and pulled the barrow outside, then she realised she would need padding so she left the barrow alone in the middle of the lawn, snuck back into the house — it was harder because she was wearing her boots and she tried to time her steps with the beating of Lilly's spoon against the china bowl — she snuck back past the kitchen as Lilly added fruit to her batter and beat it within an inch of its life — she got the quilt from her bed and some bath towels from the linen press and snuck back outside again and put them in the barrow. Saying 'Shhh,' over and over to the barrow as it creaked and groaned, complaining at being woken so early, she pushed the barrow down the side path and out the front gate and didn't see Lilly watching her from the window. She pushed that heavy wooden barrow all the way to the Cottinghams. The barrow made a ridiculous amount of noise as it was pushed over the rough roads and it caught purposefully on stones and ruts to spite her and she had to use all her strength to heave it over them.

The north breeze, which would work its way up into a suffocating north wind by lunchtime, annoyed her by blowing her hair in her face, and with both hands pushing the barrow she couldn't brush her hair away. Just over Doveton Street Beth tucked her hair behind her ears, took off her jacket and put it in the barrow with the blanket and towels. It was still only eight in the morning when she got to the Cottinghams and wheeled the barrow around the back to the laundry, wiping the perspiration from her forehead with the back of her hand. She reached inside the door and flicked on the light.

The preserving jars were exactly where she had left them, each standing in its place with its sisters. Beth stood and looked at them. It was like seeing an old friend you could take up with right where you had left off. She took the first jar carefully in her hands and ran her fingers over the glass, then laid the jar on the blanket in the barrow and turned to the next preserving jar and, making sure she had a layer of blanket between it and the other jar, she placed it in the barrow. She handled the jars cautiously, meticulously, like placing a baby in a cot. Each jar had to have a blanket layered around it to protect it from crashing against the others and breaking.

As she reached for another jar she felt Edie behind her. Edie stood in the doorway watching her and for a moment Beth felt like a thief. They had belonged to Edie, these roses, he had given them to her, but it was Beth who had cared for them and she needed them now. She hoped Edie would see how much she needed them.

'We heard the noise coming down the side of the house,' Edie said.

'Must you take them, Beth?' asked Gracie, coming to stand beside Edie.

Beth turned, still holding a preserved rose safe in its glass coffin. Through tears she looked at Edie, then Gracie, and then at the jars. No, Gracie would never disappear and Edie would never disappear. They were solid people; their feet were firmly on the earth, whereas Beth didn't know who she was. Everything she had ever had belonged to other people. She had nothing of her own.

'Would you like me to help you?' asked Gracie.

'No thanks, I have to do this myself.'

'I'll at least get you more blankets,' said Gracie, and she went to get some.

Beth looked at Edie, haloed by the morning light as she stood in the doorway in her nightdress. She looked older and worn. Beth could see pain and loss in Edie's soul, she had always seen it but had ignored it. Beth felt guilt rush through her and her cheeks burnt crimson.

'I loved him. I truly did. I loved him from the moment he stood on the doorstep with that first rose behind his back. But now he is dead and perhaps you are right, Edie, when you say people's paths are laid out for them. Perhaps Theo's path was to love you from afar and perhaps my path was to marry Colin and I didn't do that, so instead I've sent them both off to their deaths.'

Tears fell from their eyes; they were in the same river now, united in their shared grief.

'No, Beth, don't say that. War is a horrible thing,' said Edie. 'It takes men without any consideration, it doesn't look into their souls and leave the good ones, it just flails about downing whoever gets in its way. And Colin took risks he shouldn't have. You can't blame yourself — that is too much guilt for a person to bear.'

Beth knew Edie was right about the war but that didn't stop it being her fault that Theo and Colin were both now dead. She would never love another man. Her love sent men to their deaths one way or another.

Gracie came back with the blanket from her bed and the one from Edie's bed. Beth saw Edie nod to Gracie that she had done the right thing. Edie went and got their wheelbarrow and they filled it with preserving jars as well. Finally Beth placed the last preserving jar in her barrow and tucked them safely in their new bed with more blankets.

'Just hang on,' said Edie, 'just wait while we throw on some clothes.'

Beth nodded. She had thought she needed to do this alone but she realised she needed to do it with Edie. They had both loved him, so they should do this together.

Beth, Gracie and Edie walked back to Ligar Street. They walked slowly because the barrows were heavy to push and because they didn't want to break the glass. They stopped every couple of blocks for a rest. When the barrows jammed on a stone or a rut, the three would carefully lift the barrow over the obstruction and then continue. Gracie offered to take a turn pushing but Beth and Edie wouldn't let her, so she carried a jar. It made her feel better to lighten Beth and Edie's burden even a little bit. Sweat ran down Beth's and Edie's faces, but neither of the barrows were as heavy as Beth's soul. The hard work made her heart pump so she could feel it in her chest and know it was still there. When she got to the house she left Edie and Gracie standing guard over the preserving jars in the front yard. She needed more equipment for the task ahead. The sun was warm but she could see angry clouds coming in from the distance and she hoped it wouldn't rain until she had finished. Beth went into the garden shed and clasped the spade by its neck and went back into the front yard. When she decided she was plumb in the middle of the yard, without a word she started digging. She dug and dug and didn't hear Lilly come and stand next to Edie and Gracie. After an hour of digging Beth had made a hole in the ground about two feet deep and two feet wide. She flicked away the sweat from her forehead and neck with her hand. The four stood in silence and stared at the hole.

'I'm knackered,' said Beth. 'I can't dig any more but I reckon that will do. You're the gardener, what d'you think, Mum?'

'Looks good to me,' said Lilly, still not knowing what the hole was for.

Beth reached out for the preserving jar Gracie held and Gracie put it gently into her hands. She unclipped the lid. The jar breathed a sigh of relief as the air inside was released; they all heard that breath in the silence and let the rose perfume seep into them. Beth read the date on the label out loud, then with the jar in one hand, she carefully pulled out the rose with the other and squatted and laid the rose in the grave. Edie gasped and put her hand on her heart to stop it leaping after the rose. Gracie steadied her so she didn't topple over. Lilly wept silent tears that wet the ground where the rose lay.

Beth read the date on the next jar and laid its rose into the hole, and another, and with each jar Edie saw her and Theo's love being buried in the ground forever and Beth saw that all she had hoped for would never come to pass and Lilly saw that her son was never coming back and Gracie saw there was too much pain in the world.

'Do you think he died for nothing?' Beth asked, her voice weak and small. She began to shake because she believed that he had died for nothing, she'd taken him from Edie's love and he hadn't even consummated their marriage. There was no child, nothing of him to remain in this world. Nothing to comfort them. Gracie put her arms around Beth and held her tight.

'Don't even think it,' Edie said. 'It would be too awful to even think it.'

Beth opened the last jar, read the date on it and placed the last rose in the grave. She looked at the other women. Her job was done.

Theo's body was lying in some distant place, a strange country that grew trees that Beth had never seen and where foreigners that he had fought would stomp over his grave with no concern that below their shoes was the story of a life. But here at least his roses would be buried beneath familiar soil and no one would trample on this spot.

'Wait,' said Lilly and she went inside the house.

She came back and knelt down, not minding her dress turning black at the knees in the freshly turned soil, and she carefully placed a fruitcake and the sheet music for Chopin's Prelude in E Minor on top of the roses, her tears pouring onto the music and the cake.

Beth, Edie, Lilly and Gracie scooped the black earth back over the roses, the cake and the music with their hands. They did it gently so that nothing under the earth would be disturbed or broken and they all spilled tears over the grave and their tears mingled together and watered the buds below.

When they had cried out all their tears, Lilly looked up with red swollen eyes and dirt-stained cheeks and said, 'It's still early I expect but Milton gave me a rabbit he caught so I have rabbit stew inside. We could have it on toast for breakfast or lunch, whichever it's closest to.'

The others nodded, suddenly aware of how empty they felt. Lilly's food might be just the thing to fill the space inside them. They ate until they felt they could go on with life, though it would never be the same life without Theo.

Thirty-One

The Train Trip

Monday, 24 January 1916, when Beth changes course.

Beth put on the black skirt and her white cotton shirt, her stockings and shoes. It was awfully hot and the stockings were already sticking to her legs. She went into the kitchen where *The Courier* was laid out on the table with Theo's photo large and clear at the top of the third page. He looked out at them as though he could just step out from the newsprint and walk to his piano, as though at any moment they would hear the notes ring out. But he was stuck under the heading 'Ballarat and District Heroes', next to an article headlined 'Troops Have All Done Splendidly' and just above an advertisement for the Women's Peace Army. '*We war against war*', the women cried out from the page, and their cry was loud in Beth's ears.

'I'm going to frame it,' said Lilly, who was sitting at the table, still in her nightgown, tracing the photo with the lightest touch, hoping it could materialise into her Theo.

Beth turned the paper around and read the advertisement for the Women's Peace Army, then she got the scissors from the drawer and cut out the photo of Theo and handed it to Lilly and when Lilly was busy filling their bowls with porridge, she cut out the advertisement for the Women's Peace Army, folded it twice and tucked it in her pocket.

When Lilly sat down Beth got up and walked around the table and wrapped Lilly in her arms.

'I'm leaving,' she said quietly. 'This isn't my life, this isn't where I need to be.'

'When did you decide that?' asked Lilly.

'Just now,' said Beth, as surprised as Lilly. 'I just decided right now.'

'When are you leaving?' asked Lilly.

'Today — now.'

'Is there anything I can say to stop you?' Lilly gently held the photo of Theo as if holding his soul in her hands.

'I don't think so,' said Beth.

'Why don't we have a cuppa and some more porridge and think about it?'

Beth saw Lilly wipe the tears from her eyes. Beth had to be strong, so she shook her head. She had to do it now or she might change her mind. Lilly put the photo down and she touched Theo's newsprint cheek one more time. She stood up and hugged her.

'You can come back any time. You know that — any time.'

Beth nodded, holding back her tears.

'People are always leaving me,' Lilly whispered but Beth didn't hear her as she was already walking to her room. She dragged her suitcase from under the bed, the same brown suitcase, still tattered at the corners, still with someone else's name embossed in the worn leather, that she had carried all those years ago when she had trotted along behind Nurse Drake to start work at the Cottingham's. The case screeched as the studs on the corners dragged along the floorboards. Beth put it on top of her bed and opened it. Lilly stood in the doorway and watched her. Beth knew Lilly was trying not to cry and she could feel her own tears threatening to spill out. She would miss Lilly, but she couldn't stay here with Theo's ghost and all the things that hadn't happened. She hadn't ever really been Theo's love, she hadn't really been married or really been a wife. She hadn't really been a part of the Cottingham family and she wasn't really Lilly's daughter and this wasn't really her home. She had thought it could be, but she knew now it wasn't.

Beth folded her three dresses and stacked them on top of each other in the leather case. She put in her winter coat, gloves and scarf. She put in her two nightdresses and thought how all these clothes, the dresses and the nightdresses, had been made for her by Lilly. She put in her stockings, camisoles and her hairbrush. Then finally Beth got her tins of money from where they were stacked inside her wardrobe. In 1910 the currency had changed and Paul had paid her a pound a week instead of a sovereign. She had changed all her saved half sovereigns for shillings at the State Bank of Victoria, ten shillings for each half sovereign. Then each week when Paul gave her the new pound she had it changed into twenty shillings and gave ten to Dottie and kept the other ten in her tin. When she had collected too many shillings she changed them into pound notes because they were easier to store. She had purchased little things here and there over the years, gifts or underwear and stockings, preserving jars, but she never needed much. All her meals had been provided by the Cottinghams and then by Lilly, all her dresses had been Edie's and then Lilly had sewn clothes for her. So in all that time she had saved and her savings now amounted to two hundred and thirty-five pounds rolled into cigarettes and bound with a string bow. She counted it every Sunday night. It was enough for board, food, clothes, everything she could need for a year at least, longer if she lived frugally. Then she looked at Lilly standing in the doorway, trying to hold in her loss so it didn't undo her. She was a mother with no children and

Beth thought there was nothing sadder or more desolate in the world than a childless mother.

Beth wondered if she was doing the right thing. How could she leave Lilly? How could she be so cruel? She started to take the clothes out of the case but Lilly said, 'Go on, love, you can always come back and visit. It's only a train ride.'

'You're right,' said Beth, 'you're right. It's only a train ride,' and she put the clothes back in the case.

Beth held a roll of pound notes out to Lilly but Lilly tucked her hands tightly under her arms.

'No, love, I don't need your money. You won't be getting a wage from the Cottinghams any more.'

So why am I leaving? Beth wondered. Because she was twenty-five years old and maybe it was time she looked after herself.

'Go on — take it. I can get compensation,' said Beth, 'for being a war widow. Seventy-eight pounds a year until I remarry.'

But still Lilly held her hands tight under her arms and clamped her mouth shut and shook her head.

'I don't need your money. I had a very prudent husband, he was much older than me and he made sure Theo and I would never want for anything when he was gone.'

Beth walked back to the bed to lock up her case and with her back to Lilly she pushed one of the money cigarettes under her pillow for Lilly to find later.

Beth picked up her hat and put it on, she picked up her handbag and her case and kissed Lilly on the cheek and then she threw her arms around her and hugged her tight.

'Go on, love,' said Lilly. 'You can't stay here with me. It's no life for a young girl.'

Beth linked her arm in Lilly's and they walked silently to the gate. Then Beth walked down the street, past Missus Blackmarsh collecting her milk.

'Where are you headed to, young lady?' asked Missus Blackmarsh.

'Away from small town gossip,' said Beth and she walked on before Missus Blackmarsh could think of an answer. As she walked she could feel Lilly standing and watching her from the letterbox, and so many times she nearly turned back. But who would she be if she did? As she walked past the trees and buildings she had known all her life she didn't think she was leaving forever, and she reminded herself that this wouldn't be the last her town would see of her. She would just be a couple of hours away. She walked to Paul's office in Dana Street to tell him she wouldn't be coming to work today or any other day. She took a deep breath for courage because so much of her wanted to stay with everything that she knew and the people she loved. When she reached Paul's office she almost jumped up the front steps and came to a standstill in front of Bert Johnson, who nodded over the counter to her.

'Is he in his office?' she asked.

Bert was fifty, too old to join the war. Paul's six younger clerks had all signed up and gone. They knew Jensen wasn't coming back; Georgie was, but with most of him missing, and Fred was coming back, too, but his mind wasn't. The office felt empty to Beth, as if it was full of ghosts, not people. It had once been a flurry of busyness, constant chatter and bulging files bursting open and paper fluttering through the air like feathers as clerks hurriedly crashed into each other and tried to collect the papers up again before Paul noticed. Now there was only Bert and Archie, and Archie was even older than Bert and sat at a desk yelling down a phone.

'You're in luck,' said Bert. 'He's only just arrived and hasn't got anyone with him.'

She walked through to the back of the office and nodded at Archie on her way past.

Paul looked up from his desk. 'Beth,' he said and got up and pulled out a chair for her. His dignity and composure made Beth wish, as she often had, that he was her father.

He took the suitcase and put it in the corner without asking why she had it. *He knows I'll tell him when I'm ready*, she thought. Then he took her hat and hung it on the hook next to his own.

She sat firmly in the chair so it could ground her to the earth. He perched on the edge of the desk in front of her and waited.

She realised she was going to have to speak first and said, 'I'm going to Melbourne.'

He nodded, and she knew he understood why she had to leave.

'I need a reference,' she said.

'Of course, Beth,' he said. 'You won't have any trouble getting work. I hear that with the shortage of young men, women are being employed in all sorts of jobs now. I might have to employ a young woman myself,' he smiled. 'I doubt Archie can hear a word anyone says to him.'

He walked around his desk, pulled a sheet of letterhead from his desk drawer, sat down in his large leather chair and began writing. Beth looked out the stained-glass window and wondered who she would become in Melbourne.

Eventually he said, 'That should do it,' and put down his pen and gazed at her.

'Will you say goodbye to Gracie and Edie for me? I don't think ...'

He came around the desk and put his hands on her shoulders. His eyes were kind and fatherly, and she couldn't stop the tears any longer.

'You've been part of our family, Beth, for twelve years or so. We will miss you and I am sure our paths will cross again,' he said. 'Don't cry, dear.'

'I'm only going to Melbourne,' she whispered. 'It's just a train ride.' She swallowed her tears.

'So it is,' he said. 'But a different life and — a different Beth, I suspect.'

He walked back to the desk. 'It's dry now,' and he folded the letter and reached in his drawer for an envelope. He slipped the reference in and handed it to her. Then he took her in his arms and hugged her.

'Let me know who you become,' he said.

He picked up her suitcase. 'Well, come on then. Let's get you to the station.' He reached for her hat and put it on her head.

'Johnson,' he called as they went past the front counter, 'I'm just taking Beth here to the station.'

They walked to the station in Lydiard Street and she asked him three times to make sure he said goodbye to Gracie and Edie.

When the train pulled in she hugged Paul again. 'Tell Edie I'm sorry for everything,' she whispered and she got on the train before he could answer. She watched from the doorway of the train as she was pulled away and he drifted out of sight until all she could see was the plume of steam from the train clouding over everything in her past. Then she found an empty carriage. She put her case on the seat and shut the door so she could be alone. She sat opposite the case and stared at it. It was all she was. She lifted the window to let a breeze in and opened the envelope to read her reference and a fifty-pound note fell out. She smiled at Paul's kindness. It was generous, nearly an entire year's pay. The flock of sheep on the note turned and looked at her and she put them safely away in her bag. Then she put her head out the window and let the wind blow the hair from her face and sting her eyes until they watered. She settled her head against the back of the train seat and half dozed, the occasional jolt banging her head hard against the timber panel at the top of the seat, waking her with a sudden whack. Each time she would rub the back of her head and doze off again until the next jolt.

The train pulled into Spencer Street Station and Beth stood on the platform overwhelmed by the noise and the rush. She hadn't ever been to Melbourne and she didn't know which way to go. There were people going in all directions so she followed the largest flow of people and found herself standing on Spencer Street looking up at a street sign that said Collins Street. Men hurried past, sometimes bumping into her and muttering *Sorry love*, sometimes bumping into her and nearly knocking her off her feet and not apologising at all. A group of twenty or so soldiers in uniform stood on the other side of the road, then together they crossed like a herd of oncoming cattle and she found herself swamped by them as they surrounded her and then moved on without a backward glance. Pedestrians played Russian roulette with the horse-drawn cabs and motor vehicles. Trams rang their bells as they played follow the leader up the street and down again.

Beth felt the heat rising from the asphalt footpaths melting the bottom of her shoes. There was not a tree in sight. Massive advertisements stared at her willing her to buy Velvet soap, Brasso, and Milo cigarettes *exclusively for women — a delicate aroma of pureness.* The noise lifted out of the footpath, scrambled across the road and bashed hard against her ears. She pulled her hat down harder and wriggled her toes, which were swelling in the heat. She pulled out the folded newspaper advertisement and checked the address. Yes, she was in the right street. Then she checked the numbers of the buildings to see which way they were going and once she was sure she was going in the right direction, she headed off. She lugged the case, changing it from one arm to the other as each arm got tired and she was amazed that not one man came and offered to carry it for her as they would have in Ballarat. She nodded hello to people as they came towards her but no one responded and soon she stopped. She was aching all over by the time she'd walked five blocks and she put the case down and stopped to catch her breath. She was at the number she was looking for.

Three young women stopped and smiled at her. They all wore city dresses, shorter than hers and more fashionable. One of the women had red hair tucked up under a sailor hat and a skirt and top cut like a sailor's outfit. She looked so incredibly modern. The other two had on simple brown skirts and shirts and were wearing French berets. Beth thought she looked so obviously just-off-the-train-from-the-country. They looked at her and smiled as if they knew her and she smiled back as they disappeared into the building. Beth hoped they were headed to the same place she was.

She left her case propped against the building and walked out into the road and looked up. The building was five storeys tall and on each floor had verandahs with ornate bannister railings. She leant back and saw the turret at the top and then someone yelled, 'Watch out, love!' and hurtled past with their horse and cart and she quickly got back on the footpath. She checked the number again just to make sure, picked up her case and walked up to the front door, which was guarded by two massive columns. She whispered 'please' as she walked through. There was a wide foyer and she looked at the carved timber scroll on the wall listing the building's occupants in gold lettering. Her destination was on the ground floor and as she walked up the passage she could hear the chatter of women before she got to the open door.

The three women she had seen outside were standing in a circle chatting with two others. The red-haired one saw her and put her teacup down on a nearby table and walked over.

'Come on,' she said, linking her arm through Beth's as though they were sisters, 'we're always looking for new members. I was hoping you would be one when I saw you outside. I'm Clara, by the way.' Beth thought Clara was about ten years older than her, maybe she was thirty-five. Her red hair was defiant and coils of it sprung out from under her cap. She was about Beth's height and with Clara's arm linked through hers and Clara leaning into her in such a pleasant way, surely they could become friends. The room was larger than it appeared from the doorway and was filled with chattering and teacups rattling on saucers and politics being argued. There were trestle tables laid out with teacups, enormous aluminium teapots and milk jugs just like morning tea at church. Beth could do with a cup of tea and Clara poured one for her, putting in too much milk.

'Cake?' Clara asked. 'We've got some somewhere. I don't think anyone's put it out yet.'

Beth wanted to say that she hadn't come for cake, she'd come for a new life, to be someone new, but she just said, 'No thanks.'

A massive green, white and purple silk ribbon ran almost the length of the wall opposite her and above it was a sign that said WOMEN'S POLITICAL ASSOCIATION. On the other wall was a sign that said WOMEN'S PEACE ARMY. Smaller signs were scattered about on the other walls: WOMEN WAR AGAINST WAR, VOTE NO MUM OR THEY'LL TAKE DAD NEXT, EQUAL PAY FOR EQUAL WORK.

Beth could feel the women's need to be listened to. They felt invisible, like her. Like her they wanted to be someone. Beth took a deep breath. A man hammered away on a typewriter in a far corner of the room. He looked over at her, nodded, and went back to his typing. She wondered what sort of women had a man working for them. What sort of man was willing to work for women?

'He's our secretary,' said Clara. 'We have many men members, more than you might imagine. Some men believe in the emancipation of women and certainly in our current goal of ending this war.'

Beth sipped her milky tea. Clara held out a case filled with gold-tipped ladies cigarettes and Beth took one to be polite. After all, this was going to be a new Beth, so why shouldn't the new Beth smoke like any sophisticated city girl?

'And who have you got here, Clara? A new recruit for us?' Beth thought the woman holding out her hand was older than Clara, maybe in her late forties. She had lovely thick dark hair and even darker eyes. Beth tried to imagine her younger and thought she was probably very pretty when she was young. The woman looked like she had been a housewife all her life, someone who had brought up her family and was now a grandmother. She wasn't the sort of woman Beth had expected to see here — she seemed too ordinary, too nice. There were no edges to her, her softness made Beth feel at home.

'Here, dear,' the woman put a pamphlet into her hands. Beth looked at it: *The Woman Voter.*

'But don't we have the vote?' she said.

'Yes,' said the woman, 'but we have no rights. I always say that the position of women is the barometer by which a society can be measured. A society truly rises from barbarism when women have true equality. Adela, come and meet our new recruit,' she called to a younger woman who excused herself from the two women she was talking to and came over to join them.

'What we want now is for women to vote against conscription at all costs. We must fight for peace and stop this bloodshed of our boys. There would be no war if women ran the world. Don't you think …?'

'I do think and my name's Beth,' she said, and she thought of Theo buried in foreign dirt and she had to agree that saving the boys' lives was something worth fighting for.

'Where are you from?' asked Adela, who was perhaps the same age as Clara. Adela had none of the softness the older woman had. Beth could feel her astringency, it was there in her clipped words and the way she held her shoulders back, as if she was ready to fight the world.

'Ballarat,' said Beth and both the other women laughed.

'Oh, we've both spoken in Ballarat, haven't we, Vida?' Adela said to the older woman.

Vida. Beth remembered Paul writing letters in support of Vida Goldstein. This had to be the same Vida, surely.

'I think my employer wrote letters in support of your election to Parliament. Paul Cottingham.'

'Oh yes — he invited us to speak in Ballarat. He's a wonderful supporter of women's rights. It was just a shame he was the only one in Ballarat to do so. We didn't go down too well there, did we, Adela?' said Vida.

'Ballarat is like that,' said Beth, feeling traitorous as she so easily distanced herself from her home. 'It can take a while for things to change. People are suspicious of new ideas.'

And she thought how Paul supported women's rights but wouldn't let Edie work. He said that wasn't a matter of rights, it was a matter of privilege and as Edie had privilege she needed to leave jobs for women who didn't.

'Yes, well, you're our first and only Ballarat recruit apart from Paul. You'd think the spirit of the Eureka Stockade would have lived on, wouldn't you?' said Vida.

Beth shrugged. 'People got shot in the stockade.'

'How long ago did you come from Ballarat?' asked Adela.

'I arrived an hour ago,' said Beth, and all the women laughed and she laughed with them.

'Goodness, child,' said Vida, 'where are you staying?'

'I don't know,' said Beth truthfully. She hadn't thought that far ahead.

'She's staying with me,' announced Clara. 'I have a spare room.' She smiled so warmly at Beth that Beth heard herself say, 'I'd love that.'

'Are you going to join us this afternoon? Do you think you're up to it?' asked Adela. 'What do you think of your new house-mate, Clara? Is she up to it?'

Clara looked into her eyes and Beth thought what beautiful green eyes she had. They were like green leaves after rain.

'What do you think, Beth? Do you think you're up to being a protestor?'

Beth didn't think she was, but nodded anyway. She had nothing else to be and nowhere else to go.

'Good,' said the women. 'We have a demonstration on in Spring Street this afternoon. You can come.'

'I won't get arrested, will I?' Beth asked.

'Quite likely,' said Adela. 'It happens all the time. Do you want to subscribe to our paper, *The Woman Voter*?' She nodded at the pamphlet in Beth's hand.

'She can read my copy,' said Clara, saving her.

By afternoon Beth was signed up and wrapped in purple, green and white ribbons, holding a placard that said BRING OUR BOYS HOME and marching up and down outside Parliament House on Spring Street. While the other woman protested against rising food prices and men ruling the world, Beth stood beside Clara and railed against Theo's death and Colin's death and the tears flowed down her cheeks and she felt alive.

Thirty-Two

The Friendship

Thursday, 1 September 1916, when Edie discovers something unexpected.

The clouds had hovered low and grey for days, rumbling irritably, discontented with their lot in life, menacing everyone and jangling nerves in the process. The wind been blowing bitterly just because it could and the old men said to each other that at least they weren't at the war, where it was sure to be worse than this. The boys who had returned from the war thanked the gods that all they had to do was live with this God-awful ball-freezing weather, which could never be as bad as the cold in Turkey. The women said to each other if it was this bad for them, what must it be like for the poor boys still at the front? So they must put their chins up and face the iciness head-on. Old ladies struggled pointlessly against the wind until they gave up and went home to sit by the fire. Then, as if God had snapped his fingers, the wind shut its mouth, the clouds quietened and the town was still. Something new was about to be born.

This is the earth before it snows. A profound quietness descended and nothing stirred to disturb the hush.

Through all this weather — the hot summer that had come before and the balmy autumn and now through the rain and sleet of winter and the icy stillness of snow — a tiny shoot of green had shot up in the middle of Lilly's front yard. It had survived.

Edie had determined not to go out into the cold, but at one in the afternoon she changed her mind, put on her coat, hat, scarf and gloves and got her umbrella in case it rained. She told Gracie to keep on with her homework because she would be back very soon and to put another log in the stove. As soon as Edie was gone Gracie pushed away her homework and started drawing unicorns and fairies dancing on rainbows.

Edie walked to Lilly's house and by the time she got there the snow was falling. She went around to the back and called out, 'Cooeee,' as she banged on the back door. Lilly came to the door rugged up in a thick cardigan. Despite the bulk of the cardigan Edie could see how thin Lilly had become. Edie had seen Lilly at church on Sundays but until now hadn't noticed how much weight she had lost.

'You need some coca-wine — a wonderful mix of cocaine and wine that is perfect for fatigue of the brain and the body,' said Edie, stepping quickly out of the cold into the warmth of Lilly's house. 'I'll get you some.'

'What are you doing out in this weather?' asked Lilly.

'Oh, I was just wondering,' asked Edie carefully, 'if I could take a clipping from the front yard.'

'But it's snowing. It's a wonderful thing when you're inside and looking out at it through a window standing by a warm fire. But it's not as lovely as it looks when it's soaking you through.'

Edie shook the snowflakes from her jacket as she took it off. 'You know, I don't know why I had to do it today of all days.

I suppose we don't know if this weather will clear up. I mean, I would rather snow than hail and sleet, which is what we've been getting till now and — Well, I just have to do it. May I? May I have a clipping?'

Lilly had a kind face. Peter always said her face had the kindness of an angel. Her grey hair was tucked loosely into a bun low at the back of her head. Her eyes had gentle folds of age around them but if you looked closely you could see the filmy cataracts of loss. She ushered Edie into the kitchen.

'Of course you can, dear. If you first have a cuppa and a piece of cake with me. You must be freezing.'

The kitchen was snug and warm and filled with the smell of warm cinnamon and nutmeg and just-baked cake.

'Hmm, did you know I was coming?' she asked.

Lilly giggled. 'You know how much I bake.'

Edie took off her hat and gloves and put her umbrella on the table. Lilly filled her with hot cake crusted with cinnamon, butter and oats. It was called German cake but Lilly couldn't call it that now they were fighting the Germans so she called it potato and cinnamon cake because of the amount of mashed potato in it. She filled Edie's teacup with hot steaming tea and pushed over the milk and sugar. Lilly watched as Edie ate the cake and as soon as Edie finished her piece, Lilly cut another and put it on her plate. Watching Edie eat the cake made her feel less hollow.

'You haven't eaten your first piece,' said Edie, 'and here you are giving me another.'

'Oh,' laughed Lilly, and cut off a piece with her spoon. She had no one to eat for now, so most of the time eating was something she just forgot to do. As they lifted the warm cake to their mouths the scent of the cinnamon on the oat crust wafted around the kitchen, making it smell warm, as if they could hear the muffled voices of children playing in the next room.

Lilly wiped her fingers on her apron and stood up from the table to get some sheets of newspaper from the basket beside the stove and put them under the tap. She handed the wet newspaper to Edie, 'To wrap the clipping,' and handed Edie her sharpest knife.

'Do you know where to cut?' she asked.

'I do,' said Edie.

'It's grown extraordinarily fast.'

They both put on their coats, hats and scarves and shoved their gloved hands in their pockets to keep them warm and walked out into the falling snow in the front yard. The sky was white, the trees were white with fresh clean snow and the yard was a carpet of pure white snow except for the brilliant green of Theo's rose bush, which had already grown to almost full size and stood with no snow on it at all. They stopped in the silence of the snowing earth and listened. In the stillness that swirled about them they heard the rose bush singing, like whispers on a floating feather.

'It seems to just keep on growing,' said Lilly. 'I don't think it's stopped yet.'

Edie bent down and gently took a lower branch and cut a stem from it. Lilly was pleased she cut swiftly and clean; she didn't want the rose bush to suffer.

Maud Blackmarsh came out, pulling her scarf down from over her nose, and said, 'Ooh, are you getting a cutting? Can I have one, too? You have to tell me where you got that rose bush, Lilly. I have never seen a bush grow so quickly, it just sprang out of nowhere.'

Lilly looked at Edie and they both knew that the bush hadn't sprung from nowhere, it had sprung from love. She couldn't give a cutting to Maud, and looked to Edie for help.

Edie remembered Missus Blackmarsh once saying she was plainer than a bowl of porridge, and as she looked at Lilly she saw

Lilly shake her head just enough, so that Edie knew what she had to do.

'We don't know how this bush grew, Missus Blackmarsh. It was a miracle. It was grown of love and so we are very sorry but if we gave you a cutting it would only die.'

Missus Blackmarsh pulled her scarf back over her nose and huffed off, slipping and sliding on the snowy ground.

Edie giggled. 'I didn't know I had it in me,' she said and Lilly giggled with her. Edie stood and carefully cut into either side of the clipping, not deep, but enough to let roots grow from there, then she gently wrapped it in the damp newspaper. The snow kept falling and the children who weren't at school had run squealing out into the street and were already throwing snowballs. The ones who were in school were pleading with their teachers to let them run outside and before the teachers could answer they were already outside, their faces to the heavens as the snow fell on their noses and eyes.

'Come on,' said Edie, and she put her arm through Lilly's, put up her umbrella and walked with Lilly to Webster Street, carrying the clipping as though she was cradling a baby. Lilly waited on the verandah, out of the snow, while Edie ran inside and found one of the preserving jars and took Gracie's knitting needle from her wool bag. Edie came and stood on the verandah next to Lilly and finally chose a spot in the middle of the front garden. Lilly stood over her with the umbrella as Edie pushed the needle into the soft wet earth, then she turned on the garden tap, but it was frozen up and nothing came out except a whining, gurgling complaint, so she went to the kitchen and filled the jar with water from the kettle and then filled the hole with water. She removed the lower leaves of the cutting and placed it into the hole and packed the earth back around it. Then she got the preserving jar and placed it over the cutting to protect it from the frost and snow. She stood

up, holding out her cold dirty hands and looked at the clipping
for a while. Then she said, 'Stay for dinner,' and realised she really
wanted Lilly to stay. They were bound to each other by their love
for Theo.

'Well, I guess I have no one to go home to,' said Lilly and
Edie saw her eyes shine a little as they lost a fragment of their
loneliness.

In the kitchen Lilly made an impossible pie and Gracie ran back
and forth getting the ingredients she asked for and dipping her
finger into the mixture when she thought Edie wasn't looking.
Each time she did it Lilly winked at her. Edie cooked ox tail broth
and they all sang together badly — except Gracie, whose voice
was true and rang out over theirs hiding all their mistakes. Paul
came home from work at six and stood in the kitchen doorway.
Edie looked up at him and shrugged and smiled. They'd made a
fine mess in the kitchen and dishes, vegetable scraps and cooking
utensils were scattered everywhere.

'My gosh,' he said, 'I could hear the voices of angels singing
from the street.'

'We have a visitor staying for dinner,' said Gracie, her mouth
covered in coconut shreds.

'Ah Missus Hooley hello — welcome,' Paul said and Edie
thought Lilly actually blushed like a girl and she said, 'Please, you
must call me Lilly. Or Lil — my husband used to call me Lil or
Lillian but he only called me that when he proposed — Oh, but
I shouldn't have said that.' Edie had never heard so many words
from Lilly at once.

'Lilly,' said Paul and walked over to her and took her hands in
his, not even seeming to notice they were covered in flour. Edie
wondered what was wrong with him as he held Lilly's hands just
a little too long to be polite and she coughed to remind him and
said, 'Lilly has made impossible pie for dessert.'

They ate in the kitchen that was filled with steam and comfort from the smells of the cooking and warmth from the stove and Edie found herself listening as Paul and Lilly chatted on and on about everything and nothing at all. Paul told Lilly all about his latest political interest and how he was trying to get Beth to bring her new friends Vida and Adela back to Ballarat and how the conscriptionists must not win and how they planned to launch their campaign next month on the sixteenth at Alfred Hall and the boys must not be forced to give up their lives and he Paul would be standing with the unionists on this. Lilly told him all about the onions she was pickling and her Piccadilly mustard and her champagne jam except of course at the moment she couldn't put champagne in it as it wouldn't be right when there was a war on and the wonderful competitors she saw perform at the South Street Eisteddfod every year. Edie thought Paul couldn't possibly be as engrossed as he appeared because he never listed to her when she talked about cooking, he just said, 'You make it, dear, and I will eat it.'

At eight Edie reminded Gracie it was her bedtime and Gracie complained and said, 'But if it keeps snowing there won't be any school tomorrow,' and looked at her hopefully.

'Half an hour longer,' said Edie and Gracie smiled triumphantly.

Paul said, 'You two girls can go and do whatever you want to do. Lilly and I are fine here chatting,' and he smiled at Lilly and she smiled back and he added, 'I'll see Lilly safely home in a cab.'

Edie threw him a questioning look and he looked at her steadily in return. So she took Gracie's hand and Gracie groaned because it meant she was going to bed after all and Edie stopped at the kitchen door and gazed back at Paul and Lilly sitting engrossed in each other's words. Edie sighed, she felt bothered by her father's attention to Lilly. It was as if he had been lit by something, and he was happy about it, and she had to admit that if Lilly could do

him this much good over one meal then she would have to invite
her for dinner more often. After she had tucked Gracie into bed
she went to her writing desk, took her notebook out of her pocket
and she wrote:

First November Sixteen
Plan — Make Papa happy. Invite Lilly for dinner every Friday night.

And she knew that once it was written in her notebook it happened, unless she wrote a new plan that cancelled it out.

Thirty-Three

The Kiss

Saturday, 11 November 1918 — no planting today.

Sixty thousand Australians were killed in the four years of the war. Three thousand nine hundred and twelve had left the wide streets of Ballarat where they had played cricket on Sunday afternoons, stopping mid-game to let traffic go past; where they had swung on lampposts after a few, or carried their mother's shopping, griping when she stopped to chat because they wanted to get back to their mates. Of those Ballarat boys, eight hundred had died, never to return to have that drink at the Bull and Mouth now it was all over, or to marry that girl who had been waiting so ardently, or to say, 'See I told you that you were worrying over nothing,' to their mums. The five hundred girls employed at the Lucas clothing factory sold cloth dolls and held fetes and asked management to hold a portion of their wages each week for a special fund. The money would build an impressive heroes' arch to announce the beginning of Australia's first Avenue of Honour. The money would pay for the trees to form the avenue. The girls had approached Mister Smith, who was head of the Art School, and he had drawn up a design and an architect's plan. The arch would span the width of the road, and was to be crowned with a rising sun and flanked by two large columns. Over the past year the girls and the townspeople had forgone their walks around the lake and instead spent their weekends planting elms, ashes, oaks, maples, alders, birches, limes and poplars.

The result would be thirteen miles of trees on either side of the main road out of town. A tree for every man and woman from Ballarat who had answered the call and gone to war, planted in order of when they enlisted. Each tree had a plaque with the soldier's or nurse's name and number. The avenue would be a small way to honour the dead, who made up more than a tenth of the town's population, and it would also honour those who had returned. The Lucas girls started a trend that swept the country and towns everywhere began planting avenues of honour. But everyone knew the idea had begun in Ballarat with the Lucas girls. Three thousand nine hundred and twelve trees were to be planted. It was nearly finished — just a few more Saturdays and the job would be done.

But there was no planting today.

The Lucas girls were with everyone else, jostling in the middle of town at the intersection of Sturt and Armstrong Streets outside the Town Hall, whooping and hollering and hugging. The war was officially over.

The crowd spread all the way from Drummond Street down to Grenville Street. The Town Hall bells rang over and over. Whistles blew and the brass band played and everyone whooped and hollered and the noise could have been heard in Bacchus Marsh if the townspeople of Bacchus Marsh hadn't been making their own cacophony. Boys swung girls they didn't even know over their arms as if they were about to tango and kissed them as though it would be their last kiss. The women Beth had recruited into the

Women's Peace Army smiled satisfied smiles and acted as though it was their efforts alone that had ended the war. Women who had been working wondered what would happen to them now and whether they would still be able to have jobs and earn their own money. Boys grabbed the twirling streamers flying from the roof of the Town Hall and tied each other up and yelled grandly that they had captured the enemy. Girls took strands of broken streamers and danced around lampposts as if they were princesses or tied streamers in their hair. Mothers gave thanks to God that some sons would be saved, if not their own.

The soldiers were the heroes of the hour and were patted on the back so often they got hand-shaped bruises up and down their spines. No shop owners argued when the soldiers told them to close up and celebrate. But the tram supervisors insisted the trams keep to schedule, though how they could when Sturt Street was blocked from one end to the other by the throng and the soldiers stepped onto the trams and took the controllers' keys and hid them so the trams were forced to stop and the conductors happily joined the party. The police later had to negotiate the return of the keys from where they were stashed at the Soldiers Institute. Hats flew in the sky like escaping budgerigars and the brass band played 'Pack Up Your Troubles in Your Old Kit Bag' and everyone sang along at the top of their lungs and then the band played 'It's a Long Way to Tipperary' and everyone knew the words to that one too. Then they went back to 'Pack Up Your Troubles'.

Edie held thirteen-year-old Gracie's hand tightly as they were bumped along in the crowd. She looked over her shoulder regularly to make sure Gracie was okay as bodies pressed against bodies in the throng and bells and whistles shrilled in her ears. Her blood rushed through her body making her cheeks flushed and her eyes bright. She couldn't help smiling and laughing, swept up

in the joy that encompassed the entire town. The happiness made
Maud Blackmarsh lean over and kiss Milton Blackmarsh firmly
and lingeringly smack on his lips and she hadn't done that in a
good twenty years. When she finally pulled away he went back
in for another kiss. Happiness ran through the earth and into the
mines making the gold nuggets sparkle and if miners had been
down there they could have plucked them from the earth with
their fingers. But the miners were drinking beer in the street and
clinking glasses with each other and cheering the girls who gave
them kisses, even if they were married. The happiness filled the
trees and the sun held back its heat, making it an extremely pleasant day to spend on the streets with everyone else in town. The
band started playing 'Tiger Rag', men grabbed whichever girl was
nearest and swung them wildly, pulled them in tight and then
swung them out again and people pressed back to make room for
the dancers. Edie and Gracie were swept away from each other.
Edie frantically looked for Gracie and caught a glimpse of her
laughing as a boy twirled her in his arms.

Suddenly Edie was swung out and in and then the soldier who
had danced her away took both her hands in his and his feet tripped
here and there in the air and she tried to keep up. He swung her
out and his fingers waved in the air, he swung her in and under
his arm and out again. He pulled her to him and clasped both her
hands in his, their fingers entwined. He spun her around and his
chest was pressed to her back as they danced, her feet not quite
touching the ground as he carried her weight.

Then she was facing him again and she could see all the happiness she had ever known caught in the blue shine of his eyes.
When the music stopped they bent over, laughing. Before Edie
caught her breath he pulled her to him, took her face in his hands
and gently kissed her lips. She was thirty-two and had never been

kissed like this and she never wanted it to stop. Without thinking she gave herself to it and when he finally pulled away, a soft sigh escaped from her heart and he heard it and smiled, as though he knew all there was to know about her.

That knowing smile pulled her to her senses and she put her hands on her hips and tried to look offended.

He didn't apologise, he leant in and whispered in her ear, 'You looked so beautiful,' and he took her hand and shook it vigorously. 'Virgil. Perhaps I should have introduced myself before I kissed you,' and he laughed. Above the noise and music and bells, he yelled, 'What the hell,' and pulled her to him and kissed her again and she didn't think another kiss could be better than the first one but it was and too soon it was over and he was standing back and she tried to steady herself. He handed her a card.

> *Mister Virgil Ainsworth*
> *Lessons in Motor Vehicle Driving*
> *Attend 305 Windermere Street*

'My new business,' he shouted over the noise as he walked away. 'I lose the uniform next week. I could teach you.'

Edie stood in the middle of the crowd, no longer hearing the noise or feeling the people jostling against her. It was just her, standing in the middle of nowhere, holding his card.

Suddenly Gracie, puffing and red in the cheeks, was standing in front of her and that pulled Edie back into this world.

'What are you grinning at?' she asked. 'Stop it, Gracie. Stop that right now.'

But Gracie couldn't stop giggling and smiling at Edie.

'I saw it all,' she said between her chuckles.

'There was nothing to see,' said Edie, and she took her note-book out of her skirt pocket and slipped the business card inside.

Away from the crowd, watching everything but not a part of it, Paul turned and softly kissed Lilly and she closed her eyes and shut out the rest of the world.

She couldn't remember the last time she'd been kissed like this by a man. It must have been thirty-one years ago when she was thirty-three, when Theo was just twelve years old. It must have been the morning her gentle Peter, who she had married despite her parents' protests, despite everyone telling her she would be nursing him in his old age, had tenderly placed his hand against her cheek and kissed her goodbye on the front verandah. He had walked to the bank in Lydiard Street where he was the manager and when he arrived, his chest, which had never fully recovered from the consumption, filled with fluid and drowned him and he never kissed her again.

Now Paul was kissing her and it was making her tremble and she could feel the warmth of his lips on hers. He pulled away and she opened her eyes and saw Maud Blackmarsh staring at her open-mouthed and she remembered Edie standing up to Maud in her front yard and how good that felt, so she put her arms around Paul's neck and kissed him back and hoped she remembered how. Somewhere inside her was the person she had been when she ran away to marry Peter. She could almost touch that person and she wanted to stay in this world that was just her and Paul with her lips on his long enough for her to grab hold of who she had been. She hadn't been that person for a long time.

Paul pulled away from her but he was looking at her kindly. His eyes were moist and glistening, as though he was finding himself, too.

'Let's get away from this raucous party. Let's go for a walk around the lake,' he said.

Yes, she thought, *let's stay in our own world.*

He took her arm in his and placed his hand over hers. 'I'm sixty-four, Lilly,' he said as they walked. 'I'm thinking I'll retire next year — well, partially retire. I'll keep a watch over things at work but maybe I won't go in every day. Maybe I'll take a trip away. Maybe we could go together? Somewhere where only we two will know who we are.'

She couldn't answer him because she was still trembling and she didn't trust her voice. For two years Lilly had been having dinner with the Cottinghams every Friday night. She would arrive at four and help Edie and Gracie prepare the meal. Now that she knew Edie, she could see why her son had loved the girl so much. She was filled with a dignified compassion for others that she had inherited from her father. If Edie had any sorrow that she hadn't married Theo, or any bitterness that Beth had married him, she never showed it even once. All Lilly saw was her love for her family, her single-minded commitment to mothering Gracie and caring for Paul. If Edie thought anything was a threat to either of them, her chin went up in the air, her feet dug into the ground and she became immovable. Lilly had seen it when Old Mister Crocket at Queen's Anglican College had, after many threats, finally given Gracie the strap for singing while doing an exam. Gracie had come home in tears and said that she hadn't even realised she was singing, it just happened. Edie's chin had gone up and her eyes had narrowed at the injustice of this crime against Gracie. She dropped the potato she was peeling and stormed off down to the school, leaving Gracie to be comforted by Lilly. When she came back she said she had spoken with the headmaster and threatened him with all the legal ammunition at Paul's disposal if they ever touched Gracie again.

And Gracie — well, she was just a delight. The girl seemed to have a permanent smile glued to her face. Even when Lilly's heart was bitter and scorched that she had lost Peter and now Theo, Gracie would smile at her and she would feel her heart softening and she would find herself smiling back. If you are smiling at the world, how can you hang on to resentment? Gracie was thirteen now and would be finishing school next year, and Edie had her chin in the air about that, too. She was angry that Paul wouldn't let Gracie take a job. He was sticking to his guns that while he could support the girls, there was no need for them to go to work. He said they had a social responsibility to leave jobs for the people who needed them and couldn't survive without them and that was even more important now there were going to be returned soldiers needing work. So that was that.

Six months after Lilly had started having dinner at Webster Street on Fridays, Paul had started coming home from work early on Fridays so they could play croquet together on the back lawn before dinner. If it was cold or raining they stayed inside and played snakes and ladders, climbing ladders of self-denial and kindness and falling down snakes of depravity and unpunctuality. Soon he was leaving work at lunchtime on Fridays, meeting Lilly at Ligar Street and walking with her to Webster Street. They played rummy and snap and his hand sometimes landed on hers and he'd leave it there and gaze into her eyes until she said, 'I got there first. I just beat you fair and square, Paul Cottingham.'

Then she would join Edie and Gracie in the kitchen and she'd cook him a different cake each week and they all ate together in the kitchen. After dinner he always took two slices of her cake and she felt filled up and nourished and didn't eat any herself because she wanted to leave it all for him. What was unsaid between them smouldered away quietly, keeping them warm. Now it had been said and she was afraid everything that had been so wonderful and so unexpected would change.

They walked up Sturt Street towards the lake in silence. Truth be told Lilly wanted to sit down, have a cup of tea and maybe an Anzac biscuit, which would be fitting today, and mull things over. They reached the lake and sat on one of the slatted benches in the shade of a tree. The sun filtered through the leaves, putting its arms around them, and they sat in its warmth. They watched the swans bicker while the ducks cajoled their nervous offspring into swimming further on the lake than they had before. A group of swans skittered across the water, building up speed until they took flight and soared victoriously into the sky.

'You wouldn't think such heavy birds would be able to fly so gracefully, would you?' he said.

'No, not at all,' she agreed.

'You are coming to dinner tonight?' he asked anxiously.

'But it's not Friday,' she said.

'I hope you'll come Friday as well and several other nights too.'

'Oh yes,' she said. 'I thought you might like a lemon meringue pie. I haven't made one since before the war. Missus Blackmarsh gave me some eggs from her chickens, so why not use them on something extravagant.'

They walked hand in hand to Ligar Street to collect the eggs, then to Webster Street, where Lilly picked lemons from the tree in Paul's backyard. She squeezed the juice into curd and whipped egg whites into gentle white clouds while Paul spent an hour taking the boards off the door to Lucy's room. They came off much faster than they had gone up.

Thirty-Four

Lisbet

Saturday, 8 May 1920, West Coker, England,
when Reuben cannot forget Theo.

Reuben had a splinter that was festering deep inside him. It was the loud hum of the plane engines, the explosions of metal and bodies, the rage and sorrow that tore a man apart. The voice of God constantly nagging, reminding him life was finite, and the voice of the Devil asking if he could live with mortal life and its disappointments. God challenging him to make use of what he had and the Devil tempting him to throw life back in God's face. Or were they the same voice — God and the Devil? The voices and noises crashed in his head, fragmenting into shards like the thinnest glass shattered on the floor. Reuben remembered the cart taking the dying Aussie away from him. The man's breath had been hot on his face and he must have caught something from him because after he'd touched that man everything changed for him.

It was in the moment of death, when the boy with the cart had finally come back and they had loaded the silent body onto it. As the wheels of the cart had started to roll away over the dirt, the man had opened his eyes and looked at Reuben, trying to tell him something. Reuben had run to the man he knew only as T Hooley and put his ear against the man's lips, waiting for a whispered secret of life, the secret you only knew too late, in the moment of death. But T Hooley whispered no secrets to Reuben and Reuben stood, disappointed, and the man seemed to take his last breath so Reuben banged the side of the cart to go on. As the cart rolled away Reuben felt something rush from him after the man and the cart. He was sure it was his soul. That night the voices and the nightmares began. He was officially diagnosed with shell shock, and given a few weeks to recuperate. Then he was declared fit for duty once again and was sent back into the circus until the next time, when he could take no more of it. He spent the rest of the war like that, in and out, in and out.

'I shouldn't have come back,' he said to Holmes. They were sitting in his father's study in Ashgrove House, in the dark. The light from the moon glinted off the whisky bottle but their faces were hidden in shadow. They were drinking his father's best whisky and smoking his cigars. His father Doran and mother Lisbet had gone to bed.

'But you did come back,' said Holmes.

'What?'

'You did come back, Reuben,' said Holmes, and he puffed white smoke into the night.

'Why, do you suppose?' asked Reuben, and they leant forward, as if searching the darkness for some deep truth.

'You came back in one piece, to boot,' added Holmes, 'and everything's going ahead.'

'I heard things are going to get bad. There could be a civil war, like the French, if there's not enough work.' Reuben spoke without any hope for the future, his future. He took the cigar box and offered another to Holmes, then took one for himself and bit off the end. He lit it with his RAF-issue lighter and passed the lighter to Holmes.

'Rubbish. Where did you hear that nonsense? From an accountant, I'll bet,' snapped Holmes, and held his glass out in the moonlight for a refill.

Reuben filled his glass until the whisky slopped over the top and spilt onto Holmes's fingers.

'Cheers,' said Holmes, licking up the spilt whisky.

The war had made life so utterly dreadful for so many people. How could worse possibly be coming? Worse just wasn't possible, but Reuben knew worse was coming, he could feel it inside him. The voices in his head told him. They told him over and over and never shut up. All the optimism and glory had been shot out of him. His soul had been shot out of him, and this was what was left.

'My father is at me to find a job. I tell him that I'm leaving a job for some more needy fellow,' said Reuben.

'We had the war to end all wars and now it's time to get in on the action. Buy stocks, property, whatever you like. It's all booming. Get focused,' said Holmes. 'You don't have to work if you don't want to, but for God's sake get yourself a wife, Reuben. There's plenty to choose from — more of them than us thanks to the war. There must be some piece of skirt out there you haven't yet seduced that you could settle down with. Look at me, Reuben, I'm married and happier for it.'

Reuben raised a sceptical eyebrow. Holmes had married his family's choice of bride, not his own, and spent more time between other women's legs than his wife's.

'Before the war, a fellow of standing was expected to be a gentleman of leisure; but things have changed, Reuben. Get a wife and then think about a job — that's what I have to say on the matter.'

Feeling that he'd done his bit and shown Reuben the way forward, he stood up. 'I think I'm done in.'

'I must find it,' mumbled Reuben, 'then I can create instead of destroy.'

'What's that? Oh that thing you keep mumbling about — that thing you say is in your head? Have another whisky, Reuben — that'll fix your head.'

Reuben put his glass down and started to get up. He glimpsed one of the maids scurrying past the door. He wondered why she was about the halls so late, perhaps she was waiting for him. She wouldn't be the first maid to hide in a dark corner, her back pressed to the wall, waiting for him to pass. It was close on midnight. Reuben smiled. Being with a woman was the only time he felt like his old self. When he was with a woman and his skin was hot and moist, his muscles hard and unyielding, his breath ragged and urgent, he forgot everything and it was bliss. He forgot he was in a nasty hotel, or pushing her up against a cold stone wall in a dark and dreary lane, or letting her share his bed in his timbered room. He forgot her but most of all he forgot those damned voices and the explosions in his head. For the moments he was with a woman, he had silence — pure, beautiful, rare silence. He slapped Holmes on the back.

'See you in the morning, Holmes — you know your way to the guest bedroom.'

When he heard Holmes's footsteps recede up the stairs and his door close, he made his own way up the staircase. As he went up the second flight the maid was coming down it. It was unusual to see a maid on this staircase, the servants had their own stairs, but everything had changed since the war and Reuben had drunk too much and was too exhausted by life to question it. His eyes settled on the starched apron stretched over her breasts. She blushed and

lowered her head in a way Reuben found irresistible. He made
sure that he brushed lightly against her body as they passed each
other and smiled to himself when she gasped. He kept going but
she was delicious and sweet and he needed her, so he turned and
she was waiting for him.

He took her hand and led her to his room and once inside
the room he lifted her up and laid her on the bed. As soon as he
started to make love to her, to taste her, to kiss her, the screaming
of dying men, the explosions of bombs, the images of flying earth
and flesh died away, and he had peace. But as soon as he'd had her
and had rolled away to light a cigarette, those ruddy voices were
back and with them came the guns and the barbed wire and the
body pieces and he felt miserable again. He sat on the edge of the
bed and shoved his fingers in his ears and shook his head. She sat
behind him and put her head on his shoulder, and that was when
he remembered that he'd better ask what her name was, because
he was, after all, a gentleman.

'Alice, sir,' she said, straightening her uniform.

'Alice, sir,' he repeated, and he kissed her on the cheek and
pulled her to him so that she was folded into his lap and she put
her head against his heart and the quietness drifted back in and she
thought that he must love her to kiss her so sweetly.

'Marry me, Alice,' he whispered, and she smothered him in
kisses saying *yes* over and over.

*Saturday, 9 October 1920, when Reuben's future is
discussed at length.*

'You're marrying to spite me,' said his father, pacing from one end
of his study to the other. Reuben's mother, Lisbet, sat staring at
the ground. Reuben thought what opposites they were: his father

pacing and prowling, ready to pounce, and his mother barely moving at all.

'Yes, yes, I suppose I might be, but what does it matter? I eventually have to marry someone and this someone is carrying my child, so that seems a good enough reason to me.' It could work, he thought, people married for less. Maybe the chatter of a wife would drive away the voices in his head. Maybe the gnawing futility would disappear.

His father fired up a cigar and passed one to him. His mother wasn't offered a cigar — or whisky, for that matter. Doran had poured one for himself and one for Reuben, but assumed Lisbet, being a woman, wouldn't drink during the day even if the occasion called for a stiff shot. But Reuben knew, because his mother had told him one night after she'd had several sherries, that when Doran was out of the house she snuck into his study, took a fat cigar out of its silver case, poured herself a whisky and sat in his favourite chair overlooking the garden and pretended everything was hers to do with as she wished.

Reuben watched as Doran paced from the floor-to-ceiling bookshelf on one side of the room to the stern portrait of his father on the other and back again.

'You've been back from the war for, what? Nearly two years, and in that time you've done bugger-all. You don't even have proper interests.' Doran growled and puffed out smoke, making a noise like a horse.

Reuben thought bugger-all was a strong word to use in front of his mother.

'Well, Doran, you have to remember that Reuben does have one particular interest,' said Lisbet and smiled to herself. She was pleasantly shocked that she came out with the innuendo. She didn't know she had it in her, and Reuben couldn't help but smile back at her. So often he thought he had the sum of her, but when she said unexpected things like that he wasn't so sure.

'At least he's got his body in one piece. It's only his head that's defective,' Doran said.

'I am here in the room, you know,' said Reuben.

'Doran, you're talking about our son,' his mother scolded.

'He's a grown man, Lisbet. For God's sake he's nearly thirty years old and he's been melancholy for a good year and more now.'

'But I've heard some men came back worse than Reuben, not only parts of their bodies damaged but their brains gassed to nothing but vapour. They just wander aimlessly around London. They don't even know who they are or where their homes are. I'm told this all the time. There are boys out there whose mothers would have been better off if they hadn't come back.'

'Thank you, Mother,' said Reuben.

Doran put his hands in his pockets and looked out the window at his gardens. Reuben watched as he rocked on his heels.

'You're quite right, Lisbet. He's not that bad, I grant you.' He turned to Reuben. 'I daresay we could get some reasonable girl to settle down with you, a solid girl from a good family, preferably a good Jewish girl who might want you to go back to your proper name instead of this Rose business.'

Lisbet sighed. 'I don't know, Doran. Reputable fathers don't want their respectable daughters anywhere near him. Reuben's always been what you'd call a ladies' man. If this girl has his child — our grandchild — what does it matter? She can always convert. Give him something to do, Doran.'

'I suppose he could manage the tenants.'

'Once again, I am right here.' Reuben stood up to meet his father head on. 'And I am not managing the tenants. I'm not the slightest bit interested in the land or the tenants' cottages! I'm not doing your inspections. I'm not poking my nose into other people's cupboards.'

'Damn it!' snapped Doran. 'We're not talking about other people's cupboards, we're talking our cupboards, our rooms, our own property. Our cottages and barns. We have to make sure it's all being kept properly. I'm not asking you to do something dirty. In fact, I'm not asking you to do anything at all. Do what you like. Maybe I shall even cut you off.' Doran's cheeks and ears were sizzling and his skin was moist with anger. He snorted again, his nose flared, and then he let the emotion go. The effort had worn him out and he sat down next to Lisbet, who patted his hand ten times, as if she knew that was how many pats it took to console him. She looked at Reuben.

'I suppose you should bring this girl and her family to dinner. We should meet the mother of our grandchild. Friday?'

'It's Alice,' said Reuben.

'Alice?' said his mother, and Reuben watched her piece it together. 'Our Alice from the kitchen?'

'Our Alice,' said Reuben.

'Get me a whisky,' said Lisbet, 'as you should have in the first place. And a cigar.'

Alice brushed her long auburn hair a hundred times, the way she'd heard you were supposed to do. She really should get it cut chic and short like the new fashion, but Reuben said he loved her long hair and had buried his head in it and taken deep breaths as if they would give him life. She took her hair in her hands and wound it into a loose bun at the back of her head. Defiant wispy bits immediately fell to the sides of her face. She looked at herself in the mirror. They said she was pretty. Not beautiful but pretty, and Alice preferred pretty to beautiful. Pretty was more inviting, pretty was humble. Alice was a humble girl. She never expected anything that she hadn't worked for, and she never tried to be centre of attention. She put her hands on her waist; it was thickening with the life growing inside her. She touched the skin on her face and put her fingers on the freckles on her nose and cheeks. She touched her lips, where Reuben had kissed her.

She and Reuben agreed they would each tell their parents on the same day, at the same time. Her parents were excited about the opportunity that had opened up for her. All they could see was her living a life of comfort at Ashgrove House. What more could they want for their daughter? All she could remember was the song in his voice and the soft warmth of his mouth. She was sure in the moment he kissed her that he loved her deeply and she tried to hold onto that. He had whispered in her ear and his breath made something come alive in her, his voice was soft and lilting like an old folk song about love and she closed her eyes, sure the whole thing was a dream. He had lifted her up in his arms and held her there as though she was no effort for him and he would carry them both and forge a future for her. She had seen him a couple more times after that, when he had found her going about her chores and desperately pulled her into a dark corner of the house as though he had some awful disease only she could cure.

'Are we still engaged?' she breathlessly asked him between kisses, and he pulled back and looked at her as if he had forgotten he had asked her to marry him, then remembered, and being a man of his word, he said, 'Yes, yes of course.' And she felt so wonderful that he had chosen her. Because she knew his reputation, they had warned her when she began work at Ashgrove House: 'Don't get caught with Reuben on the stairs — you won't be the first and you won't be the last.'

Thirty-Five

The Conversation

Wednesday, 9 April 1921, when Reuben talks back.

Alice sat propped up by pillows in the bed and held the baby she had given birth to three hours earlier. He began to mewl and look about for a breast, his tiny mouth trying to latch on to anything. She looked about the room, there were only women in there — herself, her mother-in-law and the nurse — so she started to unbutton her nightgown the way her mother had told her to. Her mother said it was easier to do than it seemed, that the baby would do all the work. But Lisbet jumped out of her chair and pulled her nightgown closed over her chest.

'No, no, dear, we'll get him a bottle. It's far more … hygienic. And that's why we have Nurse — she knows the percentage method.'

'That's right,' said the nurse, jumping up from her chair. 'It's a very precise mix of orange juice, honey, evaporated milk and cod liver oil. That baby will be fat and healthy in no time.' Lisbet looked up at the nurse, who scurried out to prepare the formula.

Lisbet leant over and whispered in Alice's ear, 'Only the workers breastfeed. You're a Rosenberg now, dear.' Alice didn't know whether to feel scolded for doing the wrong thing or pleased to be included as a Rosenberg. Lisbet fussed over her pillows but only succeeded in making her uncomfortable. Then Lisbet took the brush from the dressing table and began to pull it through Alice's hair. Alice was relieved when Lisbet gave up and rang the bell. The maid appeared and Lisbet said, 'Mary, bring Alice tea and toast and a boiled egg.'

Lisbet sat on the edge of the bed and together they gazed at the brand-new life that bonded them.

'You must be so happy, dear,' said Lisbet.

'Yes,' said Alice, and she held the baby tight against her chest until Mary came back and set up the tea, egg and toast on the bedside table. She had brought enough for Lisbet as well.

'Have my parents been called?' Alice asked, looking at the limp toast. She didn't think she could eat, her stomach was numb and she was extremely tired. She wanted her own mum; neither the egg, the tea nor the toast.

'They should both be here any moment, your mother and your father,' said Lisbet, pouring herself tea and dropping in a slice of lemon, making the tea slosh over the side of the cup. 'Oh bother,' she said and left the saucer with its pond of tea behind on the table.

'Where is Reuben?' Alice asked and she saw Mary, who was standing waiting to be dismissed, back into the corner of the room, blushing and looking at the ground.

'Oh,' said Alice. Everything in the room turned grey as bitterness settled inside her and dropped a seed in her belly. The seed sprouted and grew into a thorned shoot that coiled around her heart. *You're not the first*, she wanted to say to Mary, *and you won't be the last, but you can never be his wife. That will only ever be me.* But she said nothing and swallowed the bile that rose in her throat.

'How long have you been here?' Alice asked Mary.

'Just a few minutes, ma'am.'

Alice heard the tone, the you're-no-better-than-me tone. Mary kept her eyes firmly planted on the ground, her palms pushed against the wall.

She can't look me in the face, thought Alice. 'No, I mean how long have you been working in this house?'

'Just a few days, ma'am.'

'When, exactly?'

'I started two days ago on Monday, ma'am.'

'That long,' said Alice. The thorn that had been resting against her heart pierced her and she felt the blood ooze out of her heart.

The door to the bedroom flung open and Reuben paused dramatically in the entrance, his hands gripping either side of the doorframe. He let his body hang there for a moment, a cigarette resting between his lips.

'Here I am,' he said.

He is beautiful, thought Alice, but she saw Mary's face lighten and saw the glance that passed between Reuben and the maid. She said, 'Speak of the devil.' Reuben chose to ignore the jibe; he would be the noble one and it hurt her even more.

Reuben strode into the room. 'Let me see my new son.'

Alice held the baby up and Reuben tossed his cigarette into the soupy saucer his mother had discarded. He took his son and held him at arm's length.

'He's not a bottle of wine, you can hold him close to you, Reuben,' said Lisbet.

'My glory,' said Reuben, still holding the infant out in the air.

'You don't like him?' Alice felt the tears building in her eyes. After all she'd been through, all the months of carrying him, all the months Reuben wouldn't sleep with her for fear it would hurt the baby, the nights he was away and she knew he wasn't alone because when he came home in the morning and she leant in to kiss him he would smell of strangers. Not to mention all the hours of pain delivering him, and now Reuben didn't like him and suddenly she didn't like the baby either — he was the cause of this nasty growth inside her, he was the reason Reuben hadn't wanted her all these months and she rubbed her belly, which felt bloated with something that didn't belong. She watched Reuben carefully and saw tears appear at the edges of his eyes.

He looked at her and said quietly, 'I can see his soul, Alice.' Reuben's beautiful voice quavered. In barely more than a whisper he said, 'I can see straight through to his soul.'

Alice didn't know what he was babbling about but she saw Reuben's eyes changing, their colour deepening, and brimming with tears. He looked down at her kindly, as though he could really see her. She felt a glimmer of hope. Maybe the baby would change everything. She rubbed her belly again, which began to feel less full, then held out her arms to reclaim her baby. But Reuben continued to hold him at arm's length, where he rested precariously in the perch of Reuben's hands.

'I can see your soul too, Alice, and yours, mother,' Reuben said. He looked at the maid. 'I can see your soul too, Mary. I can see all your souls glimmering with flickering wings, ready to take flight. Only held back by your own fear.' He looked back at the son he held awkwardly in his hands. 'But his soul, his soul is fresh and true.' He looked down at his chest. 'But I can't see my soul. Mine is gone.'

Alice couldn't take his nonsense any more and she cried. Her husband ignoring her, her husband being unfaithful, these were things she could find a way to deal with, but her husband babbling about souls like a madman was incomprehensible and she was afraid. The birth of their son had made his brain ill and she cried out when Reuben fell to his knees on the floor beside her. He flopped down there with a jolt, the baby still in his arms, and she thought for a moment he was going to ask her forgiveness for his infidelities. His eyes were pleading, but he didn't speak to her. Instead he said, 'I am yours. You have spoken in a way I can hear.'

To Alice's immense relief he stood up and handed their son back to her. He began to walk towards the door but stopped.

'Don't name him,' Reuben ordered. Alice held the baby tight, worried Reuben might take him again. She wasn't going to let Reuben have him. Not in this state. But Reuben dashed out of the room.

'Well,' said Lisbet, 'what the hell's got into him now?'

Thirty-Six

The Prince

*Sunday, 8 May 1921, when everyone in
Australia has been charmed.*

He was twenty-six and a prince when he visited, and there really
wasn't a better age for a prince to be. Prince Edward had set foot
on Australian soil on the second of April 1920 and spent fifty days
in a shower of confetti, eating barbequed sausages wrapped in
bread and dripping with tomato sauce that ran down between his
fingers. He ate every barbequed sausage as though it was the first
he had ever tasted, and he ate them in every corner of the country,
sometimes a dozen in one day, and still he smiled like a prince. He
drove around waving at millions of people for hours in glorious
motor vehicles. The women were delighted with his good looks
and English accent and they pushed and scrabbled just to touch
him. The men were impressed when he went bush for a spot of
kangaroo and emu hunting. In the crowds men reached over the
women and whacked him on the head with rolled-up newspapers
and even though the whacks were sometimes too hard and hurt
his head, still the prince smiled. Sometimes he wore his uniform
and sometimes he wore civilian clothes, a long coat and a boxer,

but whichever outfit he wore, the women held their hearts and looked to the sky, thanking God for him.

'He's so tall and gloriously handsome,' they sighed.

'If only I could marry him,' they wished.

'He can only marry a royal, you twit, and a virgin to boot,' laughed the men.

So the women contented themselves with being in his presence. If they were close enough to touch him with the tip of a finger they cried, 'I touched him!' and fainted, to be carried away by the medics.

When his railway carriage overturned in Western Australia the Prince emerged leisurely and unscathed from the tangled metal and wood, his cocktail shaker in one hand and the papers he was about to sign in the other. How much more princely could a prince be?

Gracie wondered if he was her brave Englishman and she was his Cinderella, but he smiled for the cameras, thanked the Australian people for their tremendous sacrifices in the Great War and hopped back on his boat and sailed back to his castle, bruised from all the prodding and red-eyed from all the confetti that had caught in his lashes.

But the Prince paved the way, he made a track in the ocean for British immigrants to follow. Australia said it needed Sons of the Empire to protect the country in case of another Great War — those bloody Huns could never be trusted. The British wanted a bit of time in some sun, away from constant drizzle, and so the situation suited everyone. The turbine-powered steam ship the *Ormonde* could bring immigrants from London to Melbourne in the record time of just forty days; when it arrived in port it threw down its gangplank and, like a dam wall breaking, it flooded the nation with eligible Englishmen, any one of whom could be Gracie's hero. In the past year some of them had found their way to Ballarat and attended the Baptist church. Gracie would feel a tingle of secret excitement wondering if this one was hers with the unruly hair and the cheeky grin, or perhaps that one with the tall straight back as though he never put a foot wrong in life. But none of them were hers. She knew that because the moment she was introduced to them the excitement died like a match going out.

Gracie was getting dressed for church, and she was doing it quickly because it was chilly. She put on her one-piece silk camisole. She wanted a longline elasticised corset like Edie's, but Edie said corsets were for older women like her and not for young girls of fifteen like Gracie. She pulled on her white Holeproof stockings that were anything but hole-proof; Edie said she should put her gloves on first and that way her nails wouldn't tear her stockings but she never remembered to do it. She eased the stockings up over her legs carefully so that she didn't put a ladder in them. She clipped them at the top to her garter. Then she slipped on her blue shift dress with its long sleeves and white binding that hung to just below her knees and tied the belt which hung loosely on her hips. Then she tied the matching short cape about her shoulders. She reached for her camel mary-jane shoes and sat on the edge of her bed and buttoned the strap at the sides. She stood in front of the mirror and even with the shoes she was still only four feet and eleven inches tall and wished Edie would let her wear a higher heel so she could at least get to five feet. Her friends Mabel and Thelma called her Shrimp. She didn't mind because she was a shrimp and nothing could be done about it until Edie approved heels, and even then she would still be a shrimp. She brushed her poodle bob hair; she never needed to have her hair finger-waved like Mabel and Thelma did, her abundance of unruly natural curls did all the waving she needed without help. Then she trapped her hair in her camel cloche hat with its little white cotton daisies sewn on the side. Last of all she took her camel velvet cape lined with gold satin from its hook in her wardrobe and she was ready for church. Perhaps today she would find her Englishman?

Edie waited for her by the front door and Gracie thought Edie always looked so modern. Edie had her hair Dutch bobbed and had tucked it under her green cloche hat which had a large red satin rose sewn onto the side. The rose was beautiful and Gracie was sure it whispered love into Edie's ear. Gracie would have liked a rose on her hat but Edie had said, 'Oh dear, you are too young for such loud decoration, you have to let your natural beauty shine. Whereas at my age I need all the distractions I can get.' Gracie thought Edie was very beautiful no matter what she wore or what age she was. Edie's stockings were white and her shoes were cream leather pumps with a large red button on the side strap. She wore a green pleated jersey skirt that sat low on her hips and hung midway down her calves.

When Edie had first shown her the outfit Gracie had said, 'You could go shorter, you know,' but Edie said, 'Not at my age, dear.' Edie had tucked her cream blouse into the skirt with a belt sitting loosely over her hips.

From her collar hung a green tie that matched the skirt. Over the blouse and the skirt she was wearing a green woollen cardigan and on the lapel of the cardigan was another beautiful red silk rose that sat near her heart. Oh, she did look so terribly smart, thought Gracie.

'Won't you be cold out like that?' she asked. Already the puddles were iced over in the mornings, the water was freezing lumps in the taps and the icy wind turned bare noses blue at the Doveton Street intersection.

'I'll put a coat over. Where's Papa?'

Gracie went to look for him and found him in his bedroom fussing over his tie.

'Oh Papa,' she said, walking over. She fixed his tie and looked around for his bowler hat. It sat waiting on the bed and she popped it on his head. 'Don't you think it's time you got a new hat? And don't you think it's time we got a motor vehicle?'

'Never,' he said, 'to both,' and touched her nose like she was still a little girl. Gracie walked towards the doorway but he didn't follow.

'What have you forgotten?'

'Ah,' he said, and picked up his umbrella.

Back in the hallway she said to Edie, 'I tried.'

'What did you try?' asked Paul.

Edie replied, 'We need a motor vehicle, Papa, and I need to learn to drive it.'

'We have feet for walking and good men to drive cabs. Besides, do you really think motor vehicles could replace a good honest horse that doesn't break down? Horses are reliable. I hear these motor vehicles are a constant expense due to regularly not working. Don't look at me like that, Edie, it's nothing to do with you being a woman. It's to do with keeping jobs for cab drivers who do it hard enough already.'

They took a cab to church so that Paul could prove his point, picking up Lilly on the way.

Gracie sat in the hard pew next to Edie and ignored her every time she dug her in the ribs because she wasn't listening to the sermon. She had no interest in what Reverend Whitlock had to say; she preferred to see if there were any new English faces in the congregation. But when Reverend Whitlock's voice suddenly changed from being low and controlled to high and trembling, Gracie looked up at the pulpit and gave him all her attention. Reverend Whitlock's sermon was intended for one person in the congregation and that person was her papa sitting on the other side of Edie next to Lilly.

Reverend Whitlock was looking down on her papa and no one else as the words flew from his mouth like glass arrows that cut through the air and hovered above Paul's head. Paul's eyes were dark and his mouth tight. She could see he was furious, but he didn't seem shocked, and turned and shrugged his shoulders at her. He'd been expecting this. The Reverend thought he was safe behind his pulpit so he pointed his long scrawny finger at Paul and left it lingering in the air. Gracie saw her papa sigh; the Reverend was no more than a nuisance, an insect that wouldn't go away. Paul folded his arms over his chest, and that was never a good sign. The Reverend railed, he flailed his arms in the air as he wailed about the evil of communism. The new Australian Communist Party was a threat to Australia to equal the Germans, it would lead to a new war, the workers would rise up against the leaders and the only result would be social upheaval. All communists, he said, looking straight at Paul, were servants of Satan. It was the duty of every Christian to hunt out the Reds and banish them from the church and the country.

Everyone in the congregation knew he meant Paul.

After the Benediction Gracie sat stunned as the congregation filed out. Maud Blackmarsh walked straight past and accidentally trod on Paul's foot. Her eyes were dark little slits and she said sorry with not once ounce of regret in her voice and Gracie knew she had done it on purpose. When most of the congregation had gone out onto the porch Gracie stood up.

'Oh dear,' she said.

'Yes,' said Paul. 'Oh dear indeed.'

They went outside but were left huddled in their little group of four and only a few brave people dared to nod at them or tap Paul on the shoulder and say quietly that they would catch up with him during the week.

'Why don't we have morning tea at home this week?' Gracie suggested, and she peered at the tin Lilly was holding.

'Rock cakes,' said Lilly.

So Gracie linked her arm through Paul's, kissed him on the cheek to show him she was proud of his stance for the poor and whispered in his ear that she wanted to be just like him. Edie and Lilly linked arms on the other side of him so the four of them took up the entire pathway all the way home.

Edie sat at the table, opposite Gracie and Lilly. They were all watching Paul pace. It was like watching a tennis ball bounce from one end of the court to the other as he went back and forth from the fireplace to the window.

He waved a rock cake in the air. 'I wondered how long it would take the Reverend to hear that I am a founding member of the Communist Party,' he said. 'Along with Adela Pankhurst and our own Beth. Of course Adela's baby was at the inaugural meeting too, so I suppose it's a founding member as well. I bet it was old Maud Blackmarsh who told him. I'm ropeable, you know, not about Reverend Whitlock, I couldn't give two hoots what that stick-insect has to say. I'm angry about the plight of the returned soldiers, and no amount of preaching from Whitlock is going to help those poor blighters. Of course I joined the Communist Party — what decent man wouldn't?'

'A lot, it seems,' said Edie. 'But I'm sure you and Adela Pankhurst and our own Beth are capable of finding more members — even in Ballarat. For goodness sake sit down and have some tea before it's cold.'

'He forgets that I am also on the School of Mines Repatriation Committee and the Soldiers Housing Fund.' Paul took a vicious bite from the rock cake and waved it in the air again and crumbs flew from it and settled on the carpet. He thought for a moment. 'I'll certainly be voting for Adela if she stands for parliament. I will, you know. And I think it's time I started a Ballarat chapter of the Party — then I won't have to keep taking the train to Melbourne for meetings down there. Perhaps I could get Beth to come up for the first meeting. We need the same here as in Melbourne. We need communal kitchens and free books.'

Edie felt a rush of resentment come from nowhere and run hot through her veins. She remembered him telling her so vehemently that no daughter of his would work while he could support her. But Adela Pankhurst could stand for parliament and get his support, Beth could help him start Communist Party meetings, but his own daughter couldn't work or drive a motor vehicle because that would embarrass him.

'Does that mean it's okay for me to work now?' she asked.

'Yes, yes,' he muttered. 'Do whatever you like,' as if it had never been an issue for him.

'Well, I might like a job in your office. Or I might take driving lessons.' She smiled at Lilly and Gracie and Gracie smiled back. She knew where Edie was going. Yes, thought Edie — that would trip him up.

But he ignored her and kept pacing.

'Papa, take off your jacket, the room is warm enough with the fire. Sit down and finish your tea,' said Gracie.

'Yes, do,' said Lilly. 'Then we'll have lunch. I've made a blackberry pie for dessert. I made it with those blackberries we picked yesterday.'

'I picked most of them,' said Gracie.

'You mean you ate most of them,' laughed Edie.

Edie was glad her father had a friend in Lilly; she had made him rounder, certainly in the stomach area, but in his mind and soul too. When he was with Lilly, they sat quietly by the fire reading. Paul went into the office three days a week, the other days he often spent with Lilly.

Paul sighed, took off his jacket and draped it over the back of the chair so it wouldn't crease, and sat down. Edie knew he would eventually calm down; he never liked to be angry in front of them. He saved it to fight for his causes — causes that needed his anger.

'The war is well and truly over and what are we left with? Have our boys had the spoils of a victory? No, they have not! Instead they've walked the streets like lost souls looking for the afterlife!' Paul flipped a slice of bread onto his plate. Edie winced at the whack of the bread knife as it hit the china plate instead of the bread.

It was reading the paper yesterday that had got him riled up in the first place. Edie had seen him turn stony as he read, his brow furrowed. He'd been stewing all night and then Reverend Whitlock had put the icing on the cake, blasted man.

'What has been done to help their repatriation?' Like a schoolmaster Paul pointed his finger at Edie, who shrugged.

'A fat lot of nothing!' he answered for her.

'Listen to this, girls, Lilly, just listen!' Edie liked being called a girl. Now she was thirty-four it was only ever her father who still called her a girl. Paul stood up, got the paper out of the basket and scrambled through the pages for the section he wanted.

'Here, listen to what the politicians are saying about our boys, who only a short while ago were our heroes:

"The public are shocked to hear accounts of soldiers said to be walking city streets destitute," said local MP Mister Davies. We at The Courier do not know if there is any proof to this bold statement. "There are some men," said Mister Davies, "that no amount of effort will help. They are unfortunate beings with neither initiative nor application. Such men go from pillar to post pathetically. There is plenty of work on the land for a returned soldier who has perseverance. But many are nothing more than the worst type of human being, they are sluggards!"

'It's a fickle society we live in, girls, where one moment you can be a hero and the next,' he looked at the paper again to remind himself, 'and the next, a sluggard!'

Edie returned his gaze with a blank face; she didn't know what he wanted from her.

'Well, what are we going to do about it?' he demanded.

'Volunteer for the soup kitchen,' suggested Edie. She pulled out her notebook and flicked to the last page where she had written:

Twelfth November Eighteen
Plan — Learn to drive. Get lessons from Mister Ainsworth.

Now her father had given her permission for driving lessons. *Do anything you want,* he'd said, and so she jolly well would, and she'd jolly well buy a nice shiny vehicle as well.

Monday, 16 May 1921, when Edie runs an errand.

From 1917 approximately fifteen thousand cars were imported into the country every year. By 1920 a quarter of the vehicles on the roads were motorised and this number would grow every year until 1927 when the motor vehicle overtook the horse. Roads

were hurriedly rebuilt to accommodate them and the popularity
of the new vehicle with young men gave police an opportunity
to come into their own, and they relished their new task of fining
any driver they considered to be driving furiously. With the speed
limit at fifteen miles an hour the police had plenty of ticket-
writing to keep them busy. As the numbers of motor vehicles
being purchased grew, the price fell sharply and a new Chevrolet
now cost £545 — a handsome sum, still, but not out of reach for
the wealthy. Not out of reach, Edie knew, for Paul.

On Monday afternoon Paul said he was going to pop into
the office and see how they were all going. He wouldn't be doing
much, he said, he wasn't going to interfere in anything, but Edie
knew that as long as the business carried his name, he would interfere in everything. Geoffrey Coutts of what was now *Cottingham
and Coutts* would just have to grin and bear it.

Edie was glad he was going to the office because she had her
own special errand to run and as soon as he had vanished into the
cab she went and told Gracie she would be gone for an hour or so.
Edie put on her hat, gloves and coat and walked to Windermere
Street, the address on Mister Ainsworth's business card. Number 305 was a cream-coloured single-fronted cottage with a bay
window that looked out onto a neat little front garden of native
daisies and boronia. A clambering rose that still had a few golden
blooms scattered among its green foliage covered the arch over the
front gate, which opened onto a path leading to the tiled patio and
leadlight front door. It was a sweet little cottage and she thought
a man who kept a cottage as pleasant as this would probably be
an organised teacher. Or perhaps there was a Missus Ainsworth
who looked after the little garden. She rang the cow bell that
hung beside the door and soon she heard footsteps coming up
the hallway. She had never forgotten the Victory Day kiss but she
hoped he had well and truly forgotten it and wouldn't mention

it if there was a Missus Ainsworth. Men and women were kissing wildly and indiscriminately on that day so surely he wouldn't remember her.

The door opened and he stood in front of her. Slowly a smile spread across his face.

'I expected you to turn up one day,' he said. 'You took your time.'

'Mister Ainsworth,' she said, 'if there is one thing to know about me it is that nothing in my life happens in a hurry and I have learnt to be patient.'

'I still knew you would eventually turn up.'

'Why?' she asked.

'Because I saw your eyes light up when I mentioned driving lessons. I think that excited you more than my kiss.'

'I'll say it did. The kiss I don't remember at all.' Her burning cheeks belied her words and she prayed he wouldn't notice.

'Is that so?' he said.

He knew she was lying and it made her indignant. He should have the decency to at least pretend to believe her.

'It's all right,' she said, 'I was mistaken. I thought I wanted lessons but I've changed my mind,' and she stepped down off the porch and was halfway up the path when she heard him call from the door.

'I'll pick you up in the motor car at 3 p.m. sharp. I know where you live.'

It wasn't a question so she didn't answer. And she realised there couldn't be a Missus Ainsworth or he wouldn't have been so forward. She was relieved, and her stomach, which had been whizzing around like the wind was caught inside it, settled.

She walked home dying to tell everyone that she was going to learn to drive, but she said not one word to anyone except Gracie, who smiled and said, 'Papa won't like it, not one little bit — but it will be good for him,' and passed her a silverside and mustard sandwich.

'What's this?'

'You need to eat before your lesson,' said Gracie.

'Oh no, I'm far too nervous to eat,' said Edie, so Gracie ate the sandwich and Edie sat at the table drawing invisible pictures with the tip of her finger and watching the clock.

At fifteen minutes to three Edie stood in front of the mirror in the entranceway and fluffed her hair. Then she squashed it all down again under her green cloche hat. She put on her coat and scarf and put her gloves in her pocket and walked down to the kitchen.

As though she was doing something perfectly routine, she announced, 'I'm off for my driving lesson. Mister Ainsworth should be here directly, and soon I'll be able to drive us anywhere we need to go.'

'If Papa ever agrees to buying a car,' said Gracie.

'Oh, it will happen,' said Edie.

Gracie was reading sheet music for songs she wanted to learn. 'What do you think of "I'm Forever Blowing Bubbles"?' She held the music up for Edie to see.

A horn beeped at the front of the house. 'Well, that's me — wish me luck.' Edie kissed Gracie on the cheek, walked back down the hall, checked herself one more time in the mirror (though she wasn't sure why), then she took out her notebook and wrote:

Tenth May Twenty-One

Plan — Purchase a motor car. One that gleams and reflects the white clouds in the sky.

The horn beeped again and she tucked her notebook back into her bag and walked down the front path that had been pebbled recently to cope with the new motorised delivery vans — tyres sank too far into the mud in winter, which only made Paul comment that they wouldn't have needed to have the driveway done if the world had just stuck to horses, which were perfectly capable of taking them wherever they needed to go in adequate time.

She almost skipped along the path and the pebbles crunched under her shoes, making crackling music.

Virgil was parked in the driveway. He leant on the bonnet of his two-seater Morris Crowley, his arms crossed over his chest, smiling. His smile was lopsided and made him look like a boy who had got up to some mischief, mischief like kissing her. She'd make sure that didn't happen again. She sensed he was a man who didn't mind breaking a few rules. As she felt her heart thump against her ribs she realised it was a very appealing quality in a man and a shot of electricity ran through her to her fingertips.

The car was a glorious blue and the sun bounced off it in impish sparks. Edie couldn't help sweeping her gloved hand along the bonnet and saw the reflection of the clouds in the gleam. This was the type of vehicle she needed. She noted that Virgil was wearing a knitted vest that matched the colour of his motor — and the colour of his eyes.

'All ready?' he said.

'I think so,' she said, letting her hand linger on the bonnet in the sun. 'It's very kind of you to give up your afternoon with so little warning.'

'Well, first of all you're paying me, and secondly I didn't have anything more pressing to do this afternoon, Miss Cottingham.' He spoke as though she was the only thing in the world that mattered to him. She heard the meaning in his tone but let it fly right by.

'Well, I'm very pleased because I am eager to learn to drive and my father will send you a cheque,' and she could hear her voice sounding strained and nervous. She decided it was the automobile making her nervous and not the teacher, she was nervous about being behind the wheel of an enormous vehicle, its fury in her control. That's why she was anxious and it was showing in her voice. She coughed to clear her throat. 'And please let's not call each other Mister and Miss.' She hated being called Miss, it didn't fit her. Miss was for young girls like Gracie.

He laughed. 'Yes, well, I suppose we have been on more intimate terms.'

She was hoping he wouldn't bring that up. Her cheeks glowed hot so she looked at the ground and the black ants like spilt tea leaves scurrying around the white pebbles.

'I'll just back it out into the street,' he said. 'Backing up can be a bit tricky for a beginner. Edie?' he said and she looked up. He was looking straight into her eyes. 'Edie, I'll just back it out and then you can take over.'

'Yes, of course.' She couldn't stop thinking about that kiss. He walked to the front of the car. His hair was thick and shimmered in the autumn sun. He walked with his shoulders straight and back — still like a soldier, she thought. He cranked the motor and it rattled to life with a bang that startled her. He backed the vehicle out of the drive and into the street and left it running as he got out and indicated for her to sit in the driver's seat.

She got in awkwardly. She had wanted to look graceful but she caught her dress on the rim of the door and he had to lean down and untangle it for her, his head almost touching her knee. Then he shut the door, walked around to the other side and sat down in the passenger seat. Suddenly she was aware they were in a small private world, so close they could easily be touching.

Then they were touching. He had taken her hand and put it on the gearstick, and she could hear her heart thumping in time to the thumping of the car's engine. He leant right over and pointed to the pedals.

'Left foot on that one, that's the clutch, that's right. Now right foot on that one, yes good, that's the brake. Now don't take your feet off until I say,' and he pushed her hand on the gearstick and the car grunted and groaned. 'That's first gear, and we will only be going into first gear today. Now take your foot off the brake and put it on the pedal on the far right, that's the accelerator. Take your foot slowly off the clutch but at the same time put the other foot slowly down on the accelerator, like a pulley — as one goes down, the other goes up,' and he moved his hands in the air, one hand the weight, the other the pulley. She did as he said and the car made a sickening grunt and stalled.

'Never mind,' he said and pushed the gearstick back into neutral. He told Edie to keep her foot on the brake and he got out and cranked the engine again.

'Now Edie,' he said, sitting back in the passenger seat, 'let's go over everything again very slowly.'

'Do you think I'm too old to learn something new?' she asked and wondered where the question had come from. He would think she was pathetic and she wasn't.

'Nonsense,' he said. 'And I'm not going to teach you if you're going to talk rubbish. We haven't even started. Now put your hand on the gearstick and your foot on the clutch pedal — the peddle on the left. Let's run through the gears just so you're familiar with the feel of them before we begin, but all I want you to learn today is first gear.'

He put his hand over hers again and moved the gearstick into first and after three tries she finally made the car lurch forward in painful noisy leaps before it stalled. By the end of the hour-long lesson she was able to bunny hop all the way to Drummond Street.

He was patient, especially when she made mistakes, like forgetting to use the clutch. Or when she stalled by trying to take off in third instead of first. She thought he probably got that patience from his time in the war. He just chuckled at her mistakes and his laugh was a quiet laugh that was sincere and deep, as if he was having some private little joke with himself. She liked that sureness about him, it was a quietness that reminded her of her father and made her feel less nervous. At the end of the lesson she made an appointment for the next one.

Thirty-Seven

The Last Straw

*Wednesday, 6 July 1921, when the heavens play a trick
on Lisbet in West Coker, England.*

A tapestry covered nearly the entire wall of the foyer of Ashgrove House. It depicted the prophet Elijah rising up to join God. Lisbet and Alice sat opposite Elijah as he stared down at the earth he was leaving behind. '*Good riddance,*' he was saying to Lisbet, '*you thought I was barmy with all the voices I could hear, but there you are stuck on the earth while I, the crazy one, am being lifted to the heavens.*' Lisbet would have liked it if Reuben was a prophet and the voices in his head were God speaking to him, but she feared that even if he was still alive, he was just plain old brain-addled from the war.

'Oh dear,' she sighed, thinking of how Reuben had disappeared. They had not seen him since his son's birth. He had taken the Daimler and several days later the police had found it miles away with no petrol and no sign of Reuben. They were all in a panic. She had lived through Reuben going off to war and he had survived, she had lived with his wild ways, but she couldn't live with him now dying in peace on home soil. Why he had run off like that? Had the responsibility of a child broken him?

341

Was he deranged like other returned soldiers and she just hadn't been willing to face it? She sat and waited, occasionally patting Alice's hand as she sat beside her cradling the still unnamed baby. At first Doran had got daily updates from Chief Detective Inspector Glover on the police search, none of which were reassuring for Lisbet, but as time wore on the Inspector came less often. Now he came each Wednesday morning to deliver his update. So as they did every Wednesday morning now, Lisbet sat and stared at Elijah, who mocked her, and Alice sat beside her with the baby. Despite Ryan telling them he would call them the minute the Inspector arrived, they waited here in the foyer. When he arrived they would stand and follow him into Doran's study like pupils following the teacher. There they would come upon Doran sitting behind his desk, waiting like the school principal for his underlings to report to him — or in this case, the Inspector.

The Inspector arrived at ten o'clock, his usual time, and as Ryan took his hat and coat Lisbet and Alice stood ready to follow him into the study where Doran was waiting. Lisbet was going to have her say and so she had asked Esther to put morning tea out for the Inspector and to make it quite lovely. When Ryan appeared in the study pushing the trolley of cake and tea just as they were sitting down, Doran waved them away.

'Not necessary, the Inspector won't be here that long.'

But Lisbet said, 'No no, bring it in. I'm sure the Inspector would love a piece of Esther's sponge cake and fresh clotted cream.'

The Inspector smiled. 'You've made my day.' Already he was tasting the sponge and cream and Lisbet smiled at Doran and he conceded at once. Chief Detective Inspector Glover was already on his second slice of ginger sponge. 'Very good, very good,' he muttered, 'my wife can't … very good.' When he finished the sponge he wiped his hands on the serviette and took a good slurp of his milky tea and looked directly at Lisbet.

'He's definitely alive, you know. There's no body, and that's a good thing. If some foul play had occurred there would be a body by now. He's out there somewhere.' He said it very matter-of-factly and Lisbet was pleased. He wasn't trying to console her, he really thought Reuben was out there somewhere. Lisbet watched the Inspector carefully. He wriggled uncomfortably in his seat, there was something else he had to say but he didn't know how to say it, so she held Alice's hand for strength and waited.

Eventually he said gently, 'It's not uncommon for the returned men — to do something like this.'

'What about his friends?' asked Doran. 'Ah, Houston ... or Haines.'

'Holmes,' said Alice. 'His friend is Charlie Holmes.'

'Surely he's heard from him?' said Doran.

Inspector Glover shook his head sadly. 'We've spoken to him, sir.'

Lisbet got out her handkerchief to mop up the tears. Her heart was crying for her son, he could be anywhere out there, wandering the English countryside without food or shelter, lost in mind and body. She asked the only being she thought could ensure his safe and speedy return for assistance.

Alice sat at the huge dining table playing with the cutlery. Reuben had gone mad and deserted her, she was sure of it. He was never coming back. Resentment dug its roots into her veins and muscles. She tried to shoo away the pictures in her mind of what he was doing because whatever she imagined involved other women.

He was off somewhere having a grand old time leaving her to deal with his family, the worry and the baby. Her face darkened.

'He'll be back. Reuben knows his duty,' said Lisbet, bringing her back to the table.

Is that what I am, a duty? Alice wondered. As if Lisbet could see her thoughts, her mother-in-law said, 'You lay in his bed, dear, and from the gossip I've heard it was quite a nice one.'

And aren't I paying for it, thought Alice. She looked over to Ryan, who was standing against the wall but he didn't meet her gaze. Alice hated the way he called her ma'am now instead of 'young Alice' like he had for most of her life. She and his daughter Jocelyn had been good friends. 'Why do you call me ma'am?' she'd asked when no one else was around. He said it wasn't proper to call her anything else now she was a Rosenberg. But sometimes he would wink at her and they would find a private spot in the house and have a good yak and she would ask after his wife Marj and he would ask after her mother and father and they would gossip about all the village people and it would seem just as if they were both back in the village until someone interrupted them and she became ma'am again. Alice looked at Doran sitting at the head of the table, where he always sat. He looked hollow, as if everything inside him had drained away and all that was left was a shell. He had looked like this since the day the baby was born and Reuben had fled. Opposite her, Lisbet was holding up, thought Alice, *like me, but that's all we're doing, just holding on waiting to see if he ever comes back.*

Esther had made roasted squab pigeon, which she cooked every Monday and which Alice didn't like, but first came the soup. Alice watched for Doran to give Ryan the nod he was ready to start the meal and there it came, so discreet you would miss it if you weren't looking for it. Ryan didn't nod back but acknowledged the nod by carrying the soup tureen towards the table. At the same moment Ryan stepped forward, Reuben burst through the doors. Ryan jumped. The lid fell off the tureen and clattered across the floor and under the table. Tomato soup sploshed into a red pond on the floor. Alice gasped and began to stand but Lisbet motioned for her to stay seated, so she plopped right back down. Lisbet was right, they shouldn't overreact, they didn't know his frame of mind. They should stay calm. So Alice bit her lip and watched as he strode across the room.

'Father,' he said, and nodded to Doran.

He kissed his mother on the cheek before making his way around to the other side of the table and kissing Alice's lips. She was so surprised she pulled away. He hadn't kissed her like that in many, many months. Pleased, she smiled at Lisbet, who mouthed, 'I told you so.'

'I hope you're off to a fancy dress,' said Doran.

'Are you leaving again?' gasped Alice. She wiped the kiss from her lips, rubbing hard. He disappears for weeks, months, then he turns up when he knows they would be eating and is promptly off to some party — and his next girl, no doubt! She should have noticed his clothes when he came in. Her belly was full of disappointment that she couldn't rub away no matter how hard she rubbed.

Reuben smiled at them all and when he was sure he had their absolute attention he announced, 'I have discussed it all with God, I have seen men's souls and I have done enough killing. Now I have been called to save men and create God's kingdom on earth.'

Doran laughed harshly — the camel's back was broken.

'Oh Reuben, I do hope you're playacting,' said Lisbet, her voice faltering.

'No, he's not!' said Doran, slamming his hand on the table and making the cutlery jump. Alice flinched.

'Look at him, for God's sake! Look! He's wearing a white dog collar and a black suit.' Doran pointed at Reuben. 'You're in all seriousness, aren't you, Reuben? You've converted! I knew it was coming when you shortened your name.'

Reuben nodded and sat down opposite his father at the other end of the table and lifted his soup spoon as though everything was perfectly normal.

Ryan had mopped up the soup from the floor, set a place for Reuben and poured what was left of the tomato soup into shining bowls, first Doran's and then Reuben's.

'Thank you, Ryan,' Reuben said as his soup was poured.

'You're welcome, sir,' said Ryan and he raised his eyebrow at Alice, who shrugged. She had no explanation for Reuben's behaviour so it was no use looking at her. Reuben had never thanked Ryan before. Reuben smiled at everyone and Alice felt reassured. Perhaps her husband was going to be okay.

Soup spoons chimed against the silence as they dipped into the china bowls.

'I'm Pastor Rose now,' Reuben said.

'Past what?' snapped his father.

'Pastor. I've joined the Baptists. I've been baptised, immersed.'

Lisbet gasped. 'Oh Reuben! I've prayed for you to come to your senses, I've prayed for your safe return, but I never prayed for you to be a Baptist!'

Doran pushed his soup bowl aside. Soup slopped onto the table and began a painful drip onto the floor. He scraped his chair noisily on the floorboards; the sound sent shivers down Alice's spine.

'I should have known you would do something truly stupid one day. I should have seen it coming. I should have been tougher with you. It all started when you changed your name.'

'Well, don't get too worked up yet because there's more,' said Reuben.

They all stopped eating and waited. Everything inside Alice was still. There were too many changes happening too fast. What other change could Reuben possibly bring into her life?

'We are moving to Australia. That is where God has called me to serve. My wife, my child and I are going to Australia.'

Doran threw his napkin on the table and stormed from the room, slamming the door behind him. The force of it made Alice jump in her seat. Lisbet, she saw, was determined to remain calm. Alice tried to copy her; she took deep breaths and rubbed the pain in her belly.

'Wasn't your bar mitzvah enough religion, Reuben?' Lisbet said quietly.

'Lovely soup, Ryan, please tell Cook,' he said.

He looked kindly at his mother. 'I know this is hard for you, but if it makes you feel better it's not that I am no longer a Jew. Christianity is a sect of Judaism, really. It's just that I am a Jewish Christian. I have welcomed the Lord Jesus into my heart. I have not turned my back on Judaism, I have just taken Christianity as well. I have completed who I am. I don't know why Father is so upset, we've never been religious, but now I am, so I suppose I am more Jewish.'

'A Jewish Christian,' Lisbet repeated.

'Such people do exist, you know. I am not alone.'

Alice thought of their baby up in the nursery. Did this mean he didn't have to be brought up Jewish now?

'So will we be baptising our baby as a Christian at St Martin's?' she asked hopefully. She would much prefer that they did.

'No,' he said. 'Baptists don't baptise babies.'

She heard Lisbet sigh with relief, but she groaned with anxiety. If the baby wasn't Jewish and he wasn't baptised, then he was nothing. If he died like so many children did with childhood diseases that always seemed to lurk in the doorway of the nursery, he wouldn't go to heaven. How could Reuben do this to her on top of everything else? How could he do this to their child?

She glared at Reuben but he looked back as if everything between them had always been pleasant and sweet, as though she was his much-loved wife and he had always been her faithful devoted husband.

'Alice, how do you feel about being a pastor's wife?' Reuben could have been asking how she felt about a picnic on Sunday.

She felt an overpowering urge to hit him, so she sat on her hands. Her mind reeled with the implications of what he had done and what he was saying and how he was moving her to the other end of the world. Then slowly she realised there was a pay-off. It came to her like the tiny light of a match. It struggled for a moment to take hold but soon her mind was burning. She had heard about Baptists. Her friend Izzy had been a Baptist and she was no fun at all. If he was a Baptist he couldn't drink any more or go out carousing. He couldn't dance or gamble. He couldn't smoke and, most of all, if he was a Baptist it would mean that he couldn't sleep with the maids any more. If they were in Australia he wouldn't be the celebrated fighter pilot or a Rosenberg from Ashgrove House. The girls wouldn't fall into him because he would just be an ordinary church pastor.

'Baptists don't drink or gamble, do they?' she asked nonchalantly; she wasn't going to show him how much she cared.

'Alice, I am a man of God now. I live a life worthy of God.'

'Yes, but does that mean you won't drink or gamble or — or anything else?' she asked firmly. She wanted to see how sincere he was. It was possible this was just some elaborate joke to get at his father. He loved nothing more than upsetting his father and she'd never been able to work out why.

'Reuben, does that mean you won't drink or gamble or — anything else?' she asked again slowly.

'Alice, I am a man of God,' he said again. 'I won't gamble or drink — or anything else.'

They both knew what *anything else* meant.

A smile grew inside her and came to her lips. 'Well then, it seems I don't have much choice in the matter, do I?' She looked at her soup because she couldn't remove the smile from her face. Her life had suddenly turned around. She was going to have a husband who would be true to her, who would be reliable and honest. Yes he would be religious but she felt she could live with that so much more easily than what she had lived with so far in her marriage.

Reuben got up from the table and walked around to her. 'I have a name for the baby,' he said putting his arm around her shoulders, his head pleasantly resting against hers.

That cheered Lisbet up. 'Really, Reuben? A family name, I hope. Perhaps Silas or Meyer?'

'Wycliffe. I'm calling him Wycliffe after the great Protestant martyr.'

His mother frowned. She'd never heard the name before and it took her several goes to get the spelling right.

Alice liked the name. It had a ring to it. She repeated it several times.

'Mother,' Reuben said, standing tall, 'I am alive and I am going to be a better man. Surely that's all that matters.'

'I'll try to focus on that but I do think I'm going to miss the old Reuben.'

Later that night Reuben came into Alice's room and whispered love into her ear. She never asked him where he had been or what he had done in all those months he was missing. She didn't want to know. She was just glad that at last she had a real husband.

Reuben had run from the house a madman. He had stood in that room with his new child in his hands and seen everyone's souls: Mary, who he had taken in her tiny cast-iron bed in her maid's room, her soul was open to him, wanting more than he could give; his mother's soul, yearning for a life she hadn't had; Alice's soul, damp and crinkled with disappointment, growing something unhealthy; his baby's soul, fresh and new. He saw what he had done to all of them. He rushed down the stairs and he saw Ryan's soul as Ryan opened the front door for him. Ryan, who was so faithful in his service but really hated them all. He saw Pevensie's soul full of bliss as he bent over the roses, his soul intertwining with the earth. He saw the souls of the trees, fluttering, shimmering, speaking to the angels.

In his head the voices pounded, 'Talk to us, Reuben!' Over and over they called. The guns boomed and the earth split open and barbed wire tore at men's flesh.

'I'm talking! Let's discuss this reasonably. Just tell me what's next!' he yelled over the noise.

He took the car, cranked the motor and drove until the petrol ran out. It was night by the time he stopped. The voices continued to yell at him as he rested his head on the steering wheel and fell asleep.

'Reuben, talk to us,' called the voices of God and Satan. Behind the voices he could hear the bombs exploding and men screaming for their mothers. In the morning he abandoned the car and walked with his hands over his ears, trying uselessly to block out the clamour. He had no idea how far he had travelled or where he was. He just walked. He would go into the first synagogue he came to. Maybe in a synagogue God and Satan would tell him what was next. If they would just be reasonable, maybe he could do a deal with them and they would leave him alone. He stumbled through a field and saw a small timber chapel. It had an awning over the door and two plain windows at the front and sat alone in the field on the edge of the village as though someone had left it for a moment and forgotten to come back for it. Apart from the cross perched on its roof like a weather vane, it was little more than a timber barn. Reuben walked through the long grass and up the front steps and tried to open the door but it was locked. Reuben hated God and Satan then for keeping him out, they were being so unreasonable.

'He hates us,' said Satan to God.

'Sometimes,' said God.

How dare they bring him all this way only to lock the door in his face! He swore and banged on the door with both fists. He banged louder than the bombs, louder than the screams of dying men, but not louder than the voices of God and Satan.

'You're going to punch a hole in my door,' came a new voice.

The sounds of dying men and an irritable God and an overbearing Satan faded off into the distance. He turned around. The man was tubby and had a baby face. Reuben couldn't trust someone who looked so innocent; who looked too young to have experienced the war.

'You're not a rabbi,' said Reuben.

'No, I'm not, son,' said the man, whose voice was old and fatherly, 'but God can still speak through me to ease your burden. I know what the war does, I know the burdens you carry. I've heard many confessions.'

Reuben looked at the man's clear young eyes and realised they were set in an older face. His eyes travelled from the man's face to his chest, and sure enough there was his soul, red and fervent, eager to spread the word. The man was in fact very elderly and had experienced many wars and many deaths.

'Just let me go and get the keys for the chapel. I live next door in the manse,' said the Reverend, indicating a cottage about three hundred yards away.

'No! I can't wait. Now! I need to finish this now! I can't stand a minute longer of this,' demanded Reuben. The Reverend looked worried; was he dealing with a madman? Should he call the police to take him away? Reuben felt the Reverend's mind turning over, deciding whether to run for the constable.

After a long moment of consideration, the Reverend said, 'Why don't you kneel there on the steps?'

And Reuben did. He hoped the man knew what he was doing; he had to stop the racket in his head.

'You have to repent of your sins,' the Reverend said.

'All of them?'

The Reverend nodded. 'Even those during the war. God does not distinguish.'

Reuben thought of the war and wondered if what he had done constituted murder. He suspected it did and didn't answer.

'Just close your eyes and repent of everything you can think of,' said the Reverend. 'Make sure you mean it. Confession and repentance are the keys to salvation. You must turn away and never sin again.'

So Reuben confessed his sins. He thought he would be confessing his fornication, but God and Satan whispered, 'No, we don't want your fornication. Confess to us your pride. Confess to us that you use others to fulfil your own needs. Confess to us your lack of responsibility towards those who love you. Confess your desire to destroy instead of create!' Reuben did, and it took so long the Reverend's legs got tired and he sat on the step next to Reuben, his hand resting on Reuben's head.

Hours later when Reuben had finished repenting, he looked up at the Reverend and tears were streaming down both their faces. Reuben listened and all he heard was silence, then slowly and quietly came a voice. It was just the one voice, off in the distance: the soothing, gentle voice of God. Satan had done his work, taken the dying and left. Reuben felt his chest and it was light. He looked down and saw his soul and it was flying, freed from its cage. Reuben didn't notice the pain in his knees from kneeling so long on the hard steps until the Reverend reached out his hand and helped him to stand.

The Reverend took Reuben home for lunch and while they ate Wensleydale cheese sandwiches and drank tea he told Reuben about the state of human depravation and the ignorant practice of infant baptism. He showed Reuben verses from the Old Testament and the New Testament that proved salvation came through faith, and Reuben learnt them by heart. That night he showed Reuben to his spare bedroom and they started again the next day and the day after that and after many weeks, when the Reverend had taught Reuben all he needed to know, he took his small flock of thirty villagers down to the pond behind the chapel on a Sunday afternoon. The flock sang 'All to Jesus I Surrender' as they stood on the banks of the pond, far enough back that their shoes wouldn't be ruined in the mud. They watched as the old Reverend with his shaking arthritic arms pushed Reuben's body under the icy cold water with all his might. Reuben went into the water with his brown soul and his special white clothes and came up from the water with his clothes brown from the mud but his soul white as snow. At least that's what Reuben believed.

Thirty-Eight

The Tests

Monday, 29 August 1921, Ballarat, when no one likes a test.

June could be chilly but this was Arctic. The icy ghosts of men escaped out from the mines that had closed two years ago, and the town was filled with a cold that was unusual and silent.

Edie, Gracie, Lilly and Paul had taken a horse-drawn cab from the shops. 'I keep telling you there is no way in the world motor vehicles will outdo reliable horsepower,' said Paul several times. When the horse pulled into the drive they ran inside and slammed the door shut on the cold. Edie said, 'You could catch your death out there,' as she put her basket of shopping on the kitchen table.

'Are you having another lesson? You'll need to rug up. You should take a blanket for your knees,' said Gracie.

'It's my driving test today,' said Edie, and she felt sadness wash over her.

Edie thought of Virgil's lovely blue car, which led her to think about his lovely blue sweater and his lovely blue eyes. She would get her father to buy a Morris Crowley like Virgil's, so she would be used to it, but it would have to be a four-seater. Virgil's was a two-seater. She looked at the clock. It was 2 p.m. and her test was at three. Virgil was picking her up. She didn't know if it was Virgil or the lessons she had liked the best but either way they just had to go on because she spent all week looking forward to her lesson. It was something she was doing for herself.

Lilly and Paul had gone into his study, chatting away with each other, oblivious to Gracie and Edie who walked down to the kitchen. Gracie filled the kettle with water, Edie got out the cups and saucers and made sure the pot was empty from the last lot of tea.

'I really enjoy my lessons, you know,' she said to Gracie.

'Why do they have to stop?' said Gracie, pointing to the tea caddy that was out of her reach. Edie stood on her tiptoes and lifted it off the mantle.

'Well, I'm going for my licence and once I pass I won't need to have lessons any more.'

Gracie put two teaspoons of tea leaves into the pot. 'So don't pass,' she said, and they both smiled.

At half-past two Edie stared at herself in the hall mirror. She studied the fine lines around her eyes and mouth and wet her finger and ran it over her eyebrows. She was thirty-five years old and she laughed at her younger self who had stood in front of this mirror and thought she was too old to get a husband at nineteen. That young girl had no idea how old she would become. Edie realised how silly she had been, but now she really was old and there was absolutely no hope of a husband and a husband was something she no longer wanted. So why was there this tug on a string whenever she thought about it? She shook her head then pulled her green cloche hat firmly over her hair and down to her eyebrows; she tied a red scarf around her neck and put on her coat and gloves. Then she followed Gracie's advice and grabbed the crocheted knee rug that Lilly had made. She opened the door and jumped because Virgil was right behind it, waiting for her. He had an open umbrella, 'In case it rains between here and the car,' he said, holding it out. She peered at the threatening grey clouds and put her hand out into the air that was thick with wetness.

'Are you nervous? Don't be nervous,' he said. 'You're an excellent driver. I would put my life in your hands any day.'

'Thank you, Virgil,' she said and wondered if she had the courage to fail her test as Gracie suggested.

She drove to the police station in Camp Street and waited in the car while Virgil went in to get Old George who would test her driving. She wasn't nervous about her driving skills at all, but when Constable George looked at her, his face full of uncertainty, she played the part and quivered as though she was racked with nerves.

'Miss Cottingham, I'm not sure about this at all. I haven't tested a woman before,' he said, opening the passenger door.

'You'll be right, sergeant,' said Virgil, leaning on the car bonnet. 'I'm a good instructor.'

Old George got in and sat next to her instead of Virgil. The car groaned and sank under his weight.

'All right then,' said George, 'show me you're safe.'

Edie drove up Mair Street to the lake and drove around the lake at five miles an hour. When they crawled back into Camp Street still at five miles an hour and she parked outside the station, Virgil was standing there, his arms crossed over his chest, slowly shaking his head.

'Sorry,' said George from the window of the car. 'She's a danger on the road, she's too slow. She'll hold up the horses.'

'Really?' asked Virgil and he looked at her as though he couldn't work her out. She drove perfectly well with him.

'I'll give her some more lessons, George, and we'll try again.'

Monday, 12 September 1921, when Edie tries again.

Edie had two more lessons and Virgil booked her for another test. On the next test Edie pulled out into Camp Street, went left up Mair Street, left into Lydiard and right into Sturt. She drove up to Drummond Street and Constable George said, 'All right, I've seen enough, you can take us back now.' So she drove back to the police station and she did it all perfectly and Old George stretched back and relaxed into his seat and Edie began to manoeuvre the car to park it outside the police station and she backed into the fire hydrant so that water spurted in a fountain from the earth and a dent like a broken egg sat in the rear silver bumper bar. She and George scrambled out of the car.

Old George shook his head and said, 'I knew it. There are some things it's just not right for a woman to do.'

'Oh, I didn't mean to put a dent in the car,' said Edie, and Virgil whispered, 'But the fire hydrant was on purpose?'

'Well, that's a fail in my book,' said George, pleased to have his theories confirmed. 'I better ring the fire department about their hydrant,' and he went back inside the police station leaving Edie and Virgil staring at the hydrant and the dent.

'Ah well, we all have bad days, don't we, Edie?' said Virgil, as though he didn't think the accident was anything to do with a bad day at all. 'I'll give you another two lessons to get your confidence back and we'll test again.'

*Monday, 26 September 1921, when the third time
should be lucky.*

A fortnight later Edie was sitting the test again and at the end of the test she ran into a tree and put a dent in the front bumper bar.

'This is costing your father a pretty penny,' said Virgil.

George and Virgil shook their heads at the tree and Virgil looked at the back bumper bar and then at the front and said, 'At least they match.' He looked at Edie as though he was starting to work her out and asked, 'Another bad day, I take it?'

She shrugged her shoulders.

'You're ruining my business,' he said. 'No one will think I can teach.'

She was filled with guilt then.

Monday, 10 October 1921, when Edie loses a friend.

So a fortnight later there was nothing for it, she had to drive properly. Old George said he'd be blowed but by gum she was safe to drive. She went inside and stood at the counter and Old George issued her a licence and Virgil and Old George shook hands as though the accomplishment was Virgil's in managing to teach a woman to drive. Edie was rather pleased she finally had her licence, even though she was going to miss the lessons terribly and still had to get Papa to agree to purchase a vehicle. She couldn't help herself and reached up on her toes and kissed Virgil on the cheek and he looked at her and said, 'Thank you.' She let the soft tone of his voice rest on her skin and she knew she was forgiven for purposely failing.

Edie and Gracie, Paul and Lilly had afternoon tea to celebrate Edie's successful test. They sat around the kitchen table with the stove door open for extra warmth.

'We must order the automobile, Papa,' said Edie passing Paul the cake tin. She had forgotten what was in there. 'I think it's shortbread.'

'You do it and I'll write the cheque. Buy whatever you think is best. I've never driven so how would I know. I don't even know why you need a car when everything is practically in walking distance,' he said taking two biscuits.

That was the problem — ever since she started her lessons he had been saying that he would write a cheque but when Edie tried to get him to actually sit down and write it he suddenly had to check with his accountant, who he called 'my money man', or he couldn't find the chequebook or he was just too busy to worry about it now. Edie took a deep breath, she didn't want to say this but she felt the time had come.

'We need a motor car, Papa, because everything might be in walking distance but you have trouble making that distance these days and think of poor Lilly, she finds it even harder than you.'

Edie looked over at Lilly, who was counting stitches on the cardigan she was knitting for Paul. Doctor Appleby had told Edie and Paul confidentially that Lilly's heart wasn't strong. Paul scowled and Edie braced herself.

'There is nothing wrong with a cab. It keeps men in work and there isn't much of that around,' he said firmly and then asked, 'Where's my umbrella?'

She sighed. If he wanted his umbrella he was getting worked up and if he got worked up he would pace up and down with his umbrella lecturing them as if giving a closing speech.

'We need a motor, Papa.' She looked to Gracie for help.

'Edie's right, Papa,' Gracie piped up and handed him his umbrella, which was right by his chair. 'They say that horses will be a thing of the past within ten years.'

'Bah,' he said. Paul pushed the umbrella into the floor and manoeuvred himself to a more upright position.

'Motor vehicles are faster, safer and warmer,' said Edie. 'You can get to Melbourne in a day.'

'Or I can take the train and get there in half a day,' said Paul.

'Motor vehicles don't get ill, don't leave manure everywhere, don't need feeding and in the end, Papa, they are much cheaper than keeping a horse.'

'What do you think, Lilly?' asked Paul, completely unconvinced.

'I think it's a different world and if the girls want an automobile and you can afford it, I don't see the problem.'

Paul scowled. 'I don't want you killing yourselves in some silly accident.'

'Oh Papa,' said Edie, 'that's why I've had all those lessons from Mister Ainsworth. Everyone says he charges a little more but he is the best.'

'He can't be very good if you had two accidents going for your test. It cost me a fortune between the lessons and those accidents.'

'Papa, it won't be a fast car — will it, Edie?' Gracie smiled at him.

'I can fight one of you but no sane man would take on three females — especially one who smiles like that. But promise me you won't do any more than ten miles an hour.'

'Fifteen,' said Gracie. 'That's the speed limit, isn't it, Edie?'

But Edie was already thinking how there would be no more lessons and she felt enormously sad.

Thirty-Nine

The Picnic

Sunday, 6 November 1921, when Edie is a mess of trembles.

Gracie turned sixteen and to mark the occasion she'd prepared a special gift for Paul, Lilly and Edie, but it wasn't quite ready on her actual birthday, which had been yesterday, so she had told them she would give it to them after church today. Edie had no idea what it would be and when she tried to pry it out of her, Gracie only smiled back.

'Do we have to share it?' asked Paul.

'Yes,' she'd said.

Edie knew Gracie had been preparing the gift for months. Sometimes when Edie had gone to the shops or out for a walk she'd asked Gracie if she wanted to come and Gracie said she had things to do and Edie knew she was working on her secret project.

Edie watched as Gracie carried kitchen chairs one by one into the sitting room and placed them side by side in front of the lounge chairs. She wouldn't let Edie help but when she had three chairs lined up in a row as if in a concert hall, she let Edie into the sitting room and called for Lilly and Paul to come too.

Edie sat beside Paul and Gracie nodded her head, pleased they were being quiet and giving her their full attention. She ducked back out into the hallway.

'Today, ladies and gentleman,' she called from the hallway, 'all the way from Webster Street, Ballarat, a once-only appearance at Webster Street, Ballarat.'

They clapped and Gracie walked into the lounge room. Edie smiled at her as Gracie nervously pulled at her dress as though she couldn't get it to sit right.

Well now, Edie had heard Gracie sing at church, where her voice mingled with everyone else's, she'd heard her sing in the kitchen where her voice mingled with boiling pots and steam and Lilly's voice and her own, but she'd not heard Gracie sing alone since she was little. She watched Gracie intently, ready to tell her she was brilliant even if she wasn't.

Gracie took a deep breath and began.

When she finished Edie sat looking at her. She knew she should say something but she couldn't find any words.

'It wasn't any good, was it?' Gracie asked.

Edie wiped the tears from her eyes. 'Each note was soft like a rose petal landing on my skin.'

Paul and Lilly wiped the tears from their eyes and agreed. Paul said, 'Well, how about another? I could sit here and listen to you all day.'

The knock on the door stopped Gracie as she began to sing again. Edie stood up without even thinking about it. It sounded just like him, but it couldn't be him because he had died somewhere foreign.

The knock came again.

Edie began to move but Gracie was quicker and flung the door open.

'Ah, I'm Mister Ainsworth.'

'I know — you're looking for Edie,' said Gracie and she turned and grinned at Edie. 'The driving instructor,' she said. Edie gave her a good dig in the ribs for her pointed tone and her cheeky smile.

'Hello Virgil.'

'I thought you might like to go for a spin, no charge. Just to keep your practice up. We don't want you backsliding and crashing into anything else. You need to keep up your practice until you get your own vehicle. Or perhaps your sister might like a lesson?' He looked at Gracie. Then he brushed his hands through his hair and it flopped onto his brow.

'Yes, that would be very nice,' Edie said. 'How thoughtful of you. I'll just get my coat and hat.' Edie brushed past Gracie and almost ran to her room. 'I'm ignoring you and your giggling,' she said to Gracie, who'd followed her and stood in the doorway watching. Edie threw her lingerie out of her drawer until she found the lipstick in its metal container. She'd sent to Melbourne for the Helena Rubenstein invention not knowing if she would ever have the opportunity to use it, but thinking if she had it, then a reason to use it might come to her. The automatic lipstick promised to give her lips a cupid's bow with no need for a template or fussy shaping. She had ordered Red Geranium, which the ad said was vivacious and could take five years off a woman's face.

'Can you go and see if he wants to come in?' she said to Gracie to get rid of her.

Edie put the lipstick on as directed but it didn't work. There was no bow, just her own lips but redder. She opened the matching compact and smudged a circle on each cheek with the crimson puff, then she licked her handkerchief and tried to remove some of the red and spread the rest of the rouge out over her cheeks so she didn't look like a clown. She looked at her dress, it wasn't a good one, and she wished she had worn her black crepe de chine, which she made her look slimmer and younger. She ran the brush through her hair and puffed it out with her hands. She stood back to see what she looked like, decided it was the best she could manage in such a short time and she went out to meet him. He was sitting on the step waiting for her, his hat swinging in his hand. Goodness, had she taken so long that he needed to sit down.

'Where's Gracie?' she said.

'Oh, I told her I was fine to sit here and wait for you,' he said. She saw his eyes take her in, he noticed everything about her, and he saw the lipstick, the blush and the hair. *Well, he better not think I did it for him.* But she knew he did think that.

She said, 'Shall we go then?'

'I think so,' he said, 'but you were going for your coat and hat and you don't have them.'

'Oh,' she said and ran back inside and pulled her coat and hat from the hallstand.

Once she was in the driver's seat he instructed her to go up this street and down that street and she realised they were driving to St George's Lake. When they got there, she pulled up in front of the lake and stared at the gum leaves as they floated on the wind and then settled on the water like boats. She watched them intently as though they were the only thing in the world that needed her attention and not the man sitting so close to her in the compact compartment of the car where she could feel the warmth of his breath.

Realising he was waiting for her to speak first she said, 'Gosh, it's quite cosy in here,' and felt him looking at her.

He turned her face towards him and smiled that slightly crooked smile that happened all over his face. She followed his gaze to her hand resting on her leg, then his hand rested over hers. He left his hand like that for a few moments, letting her get used to the feel of it. His skin was warm and his hand encompassed hers completely.

When he leant over and put his lips on hers, his were soft and giving and it stopped too soon.

'Now, why would you want to do something like that, Virgil?' Her voice was barely more than a whisper.

'Edie, you know full well why.'

'But I'm old.' She really was, she was thirty-five.

'Oh, Edie,' he laughed, 'not as old as me. Come on, let's walk around the lake.'

He got out of the car and reached behind the seat and pulled out a basket. She got out of the car and he held out his hand for hers. She hoped he didn't notice the tremors that were happening in every part of her, and felt the firmness of his hand holding hers as they walked halfway around the lake in silence. He stopped, pulled the rug from the basket and laid it out for her. When they were both sitting side by side he poured her some hot tea, which she held in both hands. Even though the tea was hot and satisfying, it didn't warm her as much as her contented heart. When she had finished the tea, he took the cup from her and kissed her again and she was sure that she could hear Gracie's pure voice singing 'I'm Forever Blowing Bubbles' all the way from Webster Street and that the people sitting around the lake or canoodling in their cars stopped to listen to the sweet voice that hung in the air.

They walked around the rest of the lake back to the car; they talked about the foliage and the crimson rosellas who flew away when they drew close, the red of their feathers like fiery comets flying through the green of the bush. Virgil drove her back home and all she could think was she was thirty-five and she'd just been kissed for the second time in her life and both times by the same man. Every now and then Virgil looked over at her and she heard that quiet private chuckle that he had.

Sunday, 7 May 1922, when Edie tries to be a modern woman.

Edie and Virgil had been taking Sunday afternoon drives for six months and on this day the wind was blowing from the south and an icy blast almost blew Edie off her feet as she walked down the driveway trying to hold her skirt and coat down. Virgil was leaning on the bonnet, smiling as he always did, waiting for her. As she reached him the wind blew some of his hair into his face. She studied that hair, the way it flicked in the breeze just over his eyebrow, until she reached up and gently moved it away from his face. She got in the car, he shut the door and she took a deep breath while he cranked the car. When he got in she passed him the date loaf.

'From Gracie,' she said.

'Ah, Gracie,' he said and smiled. 'Smells amazing,' and he put it in the glove box.

They drove out to Mount Buninyong. They couldn't get up to the summit in the car because the road wasn't finished, so they got out where the road came to a sudden stop.

'It's not too cold for you, is it?' Virgil asked.

'No use living in Ballarat if you can't cope with a bit of cold weather,' she said.

Virgil grabbed the picnic basket and she took the rugs and they walked up the zigzag trail that had been worn through the bush by other picnickers. At the top they walked down into the basin, a dip where they were protected from the wind by the manor gums and messmate trees. She spread out one blanket and the other they shared over their knees. He poured them both hot black tea and they sat side by side, their fingers clasping the warm enamel cups, and listened to all the things they couldn't see. Then Virgil stood up and ran up and down the side of the crater several times. Edie laughed, she loved the way he threw himself into things and took risks that she wouldn't. He still had the eagerness of the boy he had been. He wasn't afraid of appearing foolish, he didn't think about what people thought of him. He just loved life and whatever it gave him and she loved him for it.

He saw her studying him and he stopped and pulled her up to him.

'I care very deeply for you, Edie,' he said at last, 'but I just don't know if I'm the marrying kind. You'd be happy being my companion, wouldn't you?'

She looked at him with his wild hair, the way he grabbed life and laughed his way through it.

Companionate marriage. On her last visit to Ballarat Beth had told her that companionate marriage was what it was called when you did everything a married couple did except actually get married. Beth said it was the modern thing to do in Melbourne, other than being a divorcee, which was the most modern thing.

'Some women,' Beth had said, 'lie and say they are divorcees just to make themselves seem more exciting and exotic.' Edie found it hard to believe. In Ballarat divorced women lied and said their husbands had died in the war because of the shame of it.

Edie had said, 'Well, neither of us are able to do those things, we aren't modern Melbourne women,' and Beth had looked at her strangely, as if she wanted to say more but couldn't. Edie didn't know of any women in Ballarat who would be brave enough to be companions — not openly, anyway.

Now, here on Mount Buninyong, to her utmost surprise Edie heard herself say, 'Most modern girls prefer to have a companion than marriage,' echoing what Beth had told her. 'And I've always tried to be modern.'

Perhaps his offer of companionship was the best she could ever hope for and she should take the love being offered to her. But she wasn't sure she meant one word of it. It didn't sit easily as she said it, and she knew she really yearned for more, for something more solid.

'This was once an active volcano,' Virgil said, holding her closer. 'This is actually a crater.'

She leant her head against his beating heart to see if she belonged there.

'Do you think the mountain is dead or is it just lying dormant, waiting to be awakened again one day?'

He took her face in his hands and kissed her and she gave herself to it, remembering that she always liked his warm kisses that tingled down to her toes and made her feel young. Then she trembled.

'Oh, you're cold,' he said.

'No,' she whispered, 'surprisingly I'm not.'

He unbuttoned her woollen coat and slipped it off her shoulders and arms and he carefully folded it and put it at the corner of the blanket. Then he removed her cardigan, folding it and laying it on top of the coat. He kissed the top of her head and slipped her silk shirt up over her arms and he folded that and put it on top of her other clothes. She should stop right here and now. She had always believed that sex was for marriage, but then she thought *I am thirty-five years old. I am old enough to make my own decisions and my own life and to be a companion.* He sensed her hesitation and kissed her again and she forgot her qualms as he undid the zip on her skirt and it fell to her ankles. Then he picked her up and carried her over to the rug and laid her down gently, as though she had no weight at all, pulling her folded clothes to form a pillow under her head. He pulled the other blanket over them both and over their heads so they were in their own world. He pulled aside her silk chemise and kissed her breasts and she arched her back, reaching up to him. He trickled his fingers up her legs and inside her and a moan from somewhere deep in her soul was released and he smiled at her and moved on top of her and softly into her and she moaned again as he moved in gentle sweeps until he moaned himself and collapsed over her.

She lay there in the darkness of the blanket. Realising she couldn't breathe, she pulled it back and looked at the clouds and they laughed at her as they went on by with better things to look at. She thought, *Well, that's that. I'm a companion.*

He pulled her back under the blanket and kissed her hair and cheeks and his kisses were delicious and sweet and she felt so safe, she wanted to sleep in his arms, but he got up on his elbows and she had to move aside as he pulled his arm out from under her and pushed back the blanket to reach over into the picnic basket. He dangled a fig above her mouth. He lowered it so she could take a bite and said, 'Are my kisses as good as this fig?'

'Hmmm,' she said. 'I'll need another bite of the fig to be sure.'

He laughed and lay back down beside her and they pulled the rug in tight to trap their warmth and lay like that for a long time, occasionally pulling out sandwiches and fruit from the picnic basket.

As it came close to five the weather dropped several degrees more as it always did and Edie shivered and even the blanket and Virgil weren't enough to keep her from feeling the cold. He got up and pulled her to her feet and they dressed. They drove back in silence and he walked her to the door and kissed her goodbye. As she walked inside she hoped Gracie and Paul wouldn't see that she was a different person.

Forty

The Beach

Wednesday, 28 March 1923, Fitzroy, Melbourne,
when Reuben tries to save Alice.

The house in Gore Street, Fitzroy, was a small single-fronted cottage. It had a picket fence that was sweet and suggested grander things but instead enclosed eight feet by ten feet of brick paving that constituted a front yard and even less in the backyard. The house had a small hallway one person wide, running the length of it to the galley kitchen at the back. You needed to be in a good mood to use the galley kitchen because if there were two people in there it was impossible to move without bumping into each other. The kitchen contained a small table pushed hard up against the wall so you had to walk sideways to get past it. It had a wash-basin and a cooker and an ice chest and two shelves high on the wall over the cooker. It looked out over the tiny backyard where two small children were playing with the dirt that ran between the brick paving, scooping out what they could to make into hills for their stick motor cars to drive through.

Alice and Reuben were in the kitchen and Alice wasn't in a good mood. She stood at the table peeling potatoes. Reuben sat at the end of the table, right in the corner of the kitchen which was where he wanted to be, hoping he could stay out of the firing line. He didn't hold out much hope.

'Australians have strange ways,' Alice said loudly.

There's no need to yell, I'm right here, he thought.

'They blurt out all manner of private information and they don't even blush, and they do it all within the first fifteen minutes of meeting them. They tell you all their intimate details, and the intimate details of their neighbours, and I'm sure if they don't know what those were they'd make them up. Urgh.' She threw down the potato she was peeling and Reuben winced as it broke into pieces and scattered across the floor. He got down under the table and picked the pieces up. They couldn't afford to waste food like that. Alice ignored him and she picked up another potato. He held onto the valuable pieces he had picked up.

'They squawk like hens, the women do — that accent puts my teeth on edge. They call by without making an appointment, even on a Sunday afternoon. They put my kettle on the stove before I've even had time to offer them a cup of tea myself — oh, which of course doubles for a meal as well as a drink — and they whinge constantly about everything, especially their politicians. And this bloody heat!'

Reuben winced again. He didn't like her swearing. It wasn't right for a woman to swear and not at all fitting for a pastor's wife. He knew where she was going when she got worked up like this. It always went the same way: first her complaints about the new country and then her complaints about him.

'And we've got no money. You're not providing for us. Surely that is your first responsibility,' she slammed the pot filled with potatoes and water onto the cooker.

'We're living by faith, Alice,' he said, as he always did.

She scowled at him. 'Well, you mustn't have much faith then because we are hungry,' she said cruelly.

Her words hurt and he braced himself for more, 'I'm waiting for God to lead me to my flock,' he said, reaching over and the putting the broken pieces of potato into the pot. He didn't even have to leave his seat. 'God hasn't deserted us. The door just isn't ready to be opened yet. Remember, Alice, when God shuts one door, he invariably opens another.'

'Since we got off the boat, all I've seen is God shutting doors. We're stuck in this grimy city, where we're so close to the neighbours we can hear every argument they have and, even worse, we can hear every time they make up.' Reuben winced for a third time. 'If I put my hands out I can touch both sides of the house at once,' she said.

He started to say that was an exaggeration but thought better of it.

'Look around you, Reuben. This isn't what you promised me. Look at what we have: no land, no acres, no trees, no horizon, just a kitchen table, an ice chest, a bed, two kitchen chairs and some fruit boxes for the children to sit on and now there's going to be a third.' She counted off the items on her fingers.

'I still get invited to preach when the Baptist Union can find a spot for me, and they've given us this house. I think they are being very welcoming all things considered,' he said. Sometimes he was invited to be a guest preacher at Collins Street. At other times he travelled by train to Sandringham or Mount Martha as an interim preacher when their usual pastor was away. He would be paid his travel costs and a small fee for giving the sermon and someone would invite him to their house for lunch before he returned on the train. News of his skill as a preacher was spreading among the churches and he was getting more and more invitations. He was sure that soon a church would invite him to be their permanent pastor. He spotted a potato that had rolled onto the floor and under the cooker. He bent down and retrieved it and handed it to Alice. The potato was gnarled and green. She dusted it off and looked at it as if he had handed her poison.

'I'm so tired of eating vegetable broth because that's all we can afford to make. It makes my stomach churn.'

He felt sorry for her then because it was true. She could only keep liquid down — she couldn't stomach any actual vegetables. She complained all the time that there was something else inside her besides the baby and it was killing her. The doctor had taken him aside and told him she was fragile, and added, 'I'm speaking physically and emotionally and mentally, Reverend.'

Alice said what was inside her was making her vomit and she was vomiting into the toilet often; he assumed it was because of the pregnancy, but he remembered that with the first pregnancy she hadn't vomited all the time, at least not that he knew of. Back in England she had blossomed with the pregnancy, she had been round and full and her skin was golden and her hair shiny. He'd had to keep away from her, it was all he could do to resist her because he didn't want to risk any damage to the baby while she was pregnant, so he'd gone to London often. But now she was thin and pasty and her bones protruded and her hair hung lank to her shoulders. There was a sharpness to her that hadn't been there when he had asked her to marry him.

'We don't belong here, Reuben,' she said. 'This isn't what you promised me.'

He sighed. 'I didn't promise you anything, Alice, from what I remember.'

'But you were a different man then, it was going to be a different life.'

'And you were a different girl then who was happy with whatever the good Lord gave her. Where has that girl gone, Alice?'

'Just like the Irish,' she said, holding up the misshapen potato. 'When poor, eat potatoes.'

'Everyone's poor at the moment, Alice. There are men lined up outside the Collins Street church for handouts, men lined up outside government offices hoping for a scrap of work for the dole. Wages are going down not up. The paper says it's only going to get worse. It's probably exactly the same in England.'

'Not in Ashgrove House it won't be, I promise you that. Do you think your father is eating rotten potatoes?' She picked up the knife to cut what white segments she could from the potato.

'We aren't starving yet!' He slammed his fist on the table and instantly regretted it. He hated losing his composure. It wouldn't help matters at all, in fact would only make things worse.

The knife slipped and Alice cried out and grasped her bleeding thumb in a tea towel. The cut hurt and bled, oozing a stream of her anger.

'Quick, put it under water,' he said. He reached to hold her hand up and take her to the tap, but he bumped his head hard on the shelves. She glared at him. She blamed him for the cut but he wouldn't take it, he didn't make her cut herself. He rubbed his head and sat down again.

'We're not starving,' she said holding her thumb tight in the tea towel that was turning red with her blood, 'because we owe money to the grocer and the butcher and everyone else you can think of and they let us get away with it because you're Reverend Rose, so they trust you to pay it back. Why can't you write to your parents for some money?'

Reuben sighed again, he would control his temper no matter what unreasonable thing she threw at him, 'God is looking after us, Alice, not my parents. When I turned to God I turned my back on my worldly inheritance. How can I serve my flock if I'm not one of them? How can I tell them to trust God if I don't? How can I tell them that Jesus looks after the poor if I'm not standing with them? Anyway, I have some good news that should cheer you up. I've been asked to go to Queenscliff next July. Apparently it's a lovely seaside village.'

'Like in Cornwall?' She dropped the tea towel to the floor and wiped her hands on her apron, leaving a fresh bloodstain. She had never been to Cornwall but she had heard there were lovely coastal villages that the rich visited. When she married Reuben she'd hoped he would take her there.

'I expect so,' he said. 'It's the seaside anyway and you'll like that. You're always saying you miss the country air. Their pastor is going away for three weeks and we can stay in the manse the entire time and I will get paid a full stipend for the three weeks. We can all go. It will be doing God's work combined with a holiday.'

'A holiday,' she said.

'Yes,' he said. 'So that should improve things, don't you think?' He certainly hoped it would.

'It will be winter.'

'We can rug up.'

'If only life could be fixed with a simple trip to the seaside,' she said bitterly, and turned to put her thumb under the tap.

Forty-One

The Shadow

Friday, 11 July 1924, Melbourne, when a ruckus occurs.

'She's added Walsh to her name now,' Beth said to Clara.

'Who?'

'Adela Pankhurst. She married a fella from the union in seventeen and they've got several children. She's left the Communist Party. Paul is furious. And disappointed, I think.'

They had come straight from work, still in their uniforms and were standing next to each other at the back of the Fitzroy Town Hall Reading Room. The room was only meant to accommodate a hundred people but Beth was sure there were already at least a hundred and fifty crowded in to hear Adela Pankhurst Walsh. The seats were all gone when she and Clara arrived. It was stuffy and women were fanning their faces with pamphlets. There were only a handful of men scattered among the audience.

Adela came out of a side door and everyone applauded. She stood behind a podium and gripped its sides tightly. She waited for quiet and then nodded to a man at the side of the room who held a baby girl in one arm and the hands of two young children with the other. Beth thought he must be her husband, Tom. Adela was dressed in a very smart suit that Beth thought looked quite expensive.

Turning to the crowd, Adela bellowed into the silence, 'I am going to form a new organisation. This will be a revolutionary organisation that will combat the evil of communism ...'

'That's even more of a turnaround than I expected,' Beth said to Clara and someone said, 'Shhh.'

'... and uphold the Christian way of life and family,' Adela yelled. 'Australia will be a great member of the British Empire. We will bring an end to the current industrial strife and restore goodwill and cooperation to industry. We will be deeply committed to ending communism and to furthering charitable work. We will hold regular tea parties for the wives of unemployed men, and children's meetings. Women, you must think about what your new-found employment is doing to the men of this country. Men who spilled their lifeblood over the whole surface of the earth, whose bones are strewn thick beneath every sea in the interests of future generations. Think of how you are draining their initiative from them, stealing their rightful places as providers and protectors! Are your men at home melancholy, turning to drink and gambling? Of course they are! Because of you women who insist on working!'

Beth could feel her blood boiling. She took a deep breath and yelled, 'Adela Pankhurst Walsh you are a traitorous piece of work! Rights for women! Rights for women! Rights for women! Let women work!'

Clara joined in right away and a few other women joined in on the third 'Rights for women,' but Beth was immediately identified as the ringleader and two burly men nodded at each other and before she had time even to close her mouth she found herself lifted off the ground as the two men grabbed her by the arms and escorted her from the meeting, not caring they were hurting her arms, tearing her dress or dragging her good shoes along the ground. Clara came running out after her.

Beth was deposited on the steps of the Town Hall under its six massive columns like a bag of rubbish.

'Did they hurt you?' Clara cried, then she turned on the security men. 'How dare you manhandle her like that! Look at the size of you and look at the size of her.'

Beth had suffered far worse, having been jailed overnight several times in the past few years, but she wanted the men to be ashamed for being on the wrong side and nodded as Clara railed.

Beth brushed the feel of the men's hands off her arms and, when she felt Clara had railed long enough, she said, 'Don't worry, Clara, I'm fine. I just can't believe Adela. One minute fighting for women's rights and now she's got a husband and children of her own, suddenly women should be in the kitchen and nowhere else.'

'Let's go home,' said Clara, 'and not think about her any more.' She tucked her arm into Beth's and squeezed it and Beth smiled at her. Beth gave one last death stare to the two security guards and they walked arm in arm to Flinders Street station and caught the train home to Port Melbourne. From the station they walked to the little single-fronted cottage they rented in Princes Street. Every five minutes Beth said, 'I just can't believe her,' and Clara would reply, 'The bitch — she beggars belief.'

Beth had moved into Clara's little house in Port Melbourne on her very first day in Melbourne and had never moved out. Beth felt at home living with Clara, and she felt at home with herself. She liked being an independent modern woman, it made her feel real, and now she wanted that for all women. She had the passion of the newly converted. Beth collected the afternoon mail from the letterbox and Clara opened the front door and Beth took off her coat, hung it on the hook and led the way down the narrow hallway to the kitchen at the back which looked over a tiny backyard just big enough for Beth to grow some herbs. She had nine pots of herbs lined up around the fence — nasturtiums, peppermint, parsley and chives, watercress (which was a pain because it had to be replanted so often but was so lovely in sandwiches), arthritis herb, which she made into pots of tea for Lilly who needed it for her joints, comfrey for wounds (Edie had told her to grow that), lavender for the beautiful smell, and rosemary for roast lamb.

'I'll pop the kettle on. Or would you prefer something stronger? I think we have some Cutty Sark left.'

'Both, thanks.' Beth sat at the table and flicked through the mail. 'Bill,' she tossed the envelope onto the side table, 'Bill,' toss, 'bill,' toss, 'bill,' toss. 'Oh, I don't recognise this one.'

She turned the envelope over, held it up to the light and tried to read the postmark. She opened it and took out the letter inside and as she read her heart pounded against her ribs like a jabbing stick and her skin turned white.

'Beth, what's wrong?' said Clara.

'It's from my husband.'

Beth dropped the letter onto the table but it fluttered to the floor. Clara grabbed it and read it.

'But he's dead,' Clara said.

'Apparently not.'

Beth was numb; she couldn't feel anything, nothing at all. She pinched her skin but no, she felt nothing; she bit on her tongue, nothing; she slapped her arms — nothing. Clara handed her the warm whisky and Beth gulped it down. She could feel it as it burnt all the way down her throat.

'More,' she said hoarsely, the whisky still caught in her throat. Clara poured her another one and Beth motioned for her to fill the glass to the very top. She wanted a decent dose. So Clara filled it to the top and handed it to her and Beth downed it in one.

'How could the bugger come back from the dead?' Clara asked.

Beth watched Clara pour herself a whisky and follow suit, swallowing the lot in one go. Clara refilled their glasses again.

'Is he going to want you back?' asked Clara. Beth could hear the tremble in her voice.

'What? No. I don't know what he wants,' said Beth. 'He just says he is alive, that it has taken him a while to find me and he needs to talk. Which is a laugh because talking is the one thing Theo can't do. But there is no return address.'

Beth looked at Clara. Her eyes were blue pools of sadness and her red curls had lost some of their bounce and hung unhappily around her face. Beth knew that Clara was not saying the one thing she wanted to say: *Don't leave me, Beth, don't go off with him.*

'Come on, let's have some more of that whisky, hey?'

Beth and Clara forgot about dinner but finished off the whisky and fell asleep in the lounge room sprawled over the couch and each other.

Saturday, 12 July 1924, when there is another ruckus.

Beth woke, rubbed her throbbing head and stumbled to the kitchen where she held up the Cutty Sark bottle, swore at it and put it down again. As she did so she saw the time on the kitchen clock.

'Bloody hell. Oh sweet Jesus.' She ran back into the lounge room and woke Clara. 'Come on, we're going to be late.'

The girls washed and threw themselves into clothes. Beth brushed out her short orchid bob and looked at her patent leather shoes that were scraped from being dragged along the ground when those nasty bullyboys had thrown her out of Adela's speech.

The leather had torn away making them look old, even though they were new. She threw them to the floor with a sigh and put on her sensible pumps and grabbed her coat and scarf. She stood at the door waiting for Clara to catch up.

'The signs,' said Clara. Her red curls flew everywhere and made Beth smile. Clara ran back inside to get the signs, then they ran and got puffed and walked until they could take running steps down Princes Street to Stokes Street, thanking their lucky stars they were only going to another street in Port Melbourne and not somewhere across the city.

They found the house they were looking for. People were already gathered on the street and in the small front yard. Their four comrades stood conspicuously to one side, objects of speculation as to who they might be and why they were there. Beth and Clara joined them.

'We're only waiting on Franny and Collette, but they are always late,' said Evelyn.

'This is our third in the last fortnight,' said Beth. 'They are becoming more and more common as things get worse. The last one wasn't successful — let's make sure this one is. Let's save this poor destitute family.'

The women patted each other on the back. They had protested at a cottage in North Melbourne and another protest in Richmond. The North Melbourne one had nearly got them all arrested.

The front yard had filled with people willing to brave the cold for the sake of a bargain. Someone had lit a fire in a 44-gallon drum on the pavement and some men stood around it laughing and slapping each other on the back. Children squeezed between the men to light sticks that they waved about, flicking embers onto the cold tar of the road, where they quickly died. Women chatted quietly and looked over at Beth and her comrades suspiciously, as if they were going to upset everything when all they wanted was a bargain. The men sent scowls Beth's way and dreamt of the beer they would have at the pub as soon as this malarky their wives had forced them along to was over. Three policemen arrived and immediately picked Beth's group as the day's problem and tapped their batons menacingly in their hands, glaring at Beth and the other women and muttering, 'Bloody suffragettes, bloody man-haters.' The biggest copper had put his baton in its loop at his side and swaggered as he approached Beth, each foot landing heavily on the ground as though he was a mountain struggling to walk because of his sheer bulk, a mountain moved by nothing other than his own will.

'We're here to do a job, missy,' he said standing too close and looking down on her. 'These people have to be evicted and their goods sold. Sherriff's orders and we won't be taking any interference with the law lightly.'

He didn't wait for an answer. Beth was relieved, because her insides were quaking. She watched him move towards a portly, well-dressed man who she assumed was the landlord; they seemed to be discussing how things would proceed.

Beth handed her sign to Evelyn and walked up the steps of the cottage to the verandah. She put her hands in the air to get everyone's attention. Her comrades clapped and a man yelled, 'Sing us a song, love.' The group of policemen laughed loudly encouraging the crowd to heckle her and all the men sniggered.

'Go home you stupid hussy or I'll have you locked up!' said the big policeman but Beth just stared him down and said loudly, 'Lock me up then! At least in jail I'll be fed — unlike these poor blighters! At least on these cold nights I'll be warm, unlike these sad souls.' And she pointed to the family huddled forlornly by the side fence — the father who had given up and the mother whose clothes were wet with tears and the three terrified children who didn't know where they would be sent next.

The policeman shook his head. While he conferred with his colleagues, Beth yelled to the crowd squashed into the tiny front yard and spilling onto the street.

'If any one of you dares bid on one tiny item that in truth belongs to this family, you will rot in hell. Any one of us could be in the position of this poor family. Have Christian charity and refuse to buy any of the goods that belong to them when they are auctioned today. If you do bid on them, you are in fact stealing. I beg you — step into their shoes and do as you would have them do to you. If you wish to donate to their rent, my friend Clara has a hat open and ready. Everything put in shall be passed to the family.'

The small crowd was easily swayed by the last thing that was said to them and, wanting to sleep well that night, they cheered. Beth smiled and nodded. Then the landlord stood up on the porch and elbowed her aside and started the bidding for a rather lovely but worn bridge chair at an extraordinarily low price. One man, egged on by his wife, started to raise his hand but Beth glared at him and he put it down quickly. No one dared bid on the side table or the set of dented aluminium saucepans. Finally, after trying to sell a set of cooking bowls and a set of kitchen chairs, the landlord had no choice but to return every item to the destitute family. With the auction a failure, the crowd dispersed, dropping the coins they had planned to spend on bargains into Clara's hat.

The family thanked Beth for saving their worldly chattels, few and tattered as they were, and for buying them a few weeks reprieve with the rent. Beth glanced sideways at a shadow under a tree; earlier the shade had blocked him from her view. Now she saw him waiting for her to finish saying goodbye to the family.

They looked at each other for some moments. He stayed rooted to the spot, waiting for her to come away from her friends. Finally she approached him and they regarded each other cautiously for some time before he said, 'I've looked everywhere for you, Beth.'

'Took your bloody time then,' she said. 'It's 1924, you know. I thought you were dead. For nearly a good eight years you've been dead, Theo. In fact I think legally you are dead after seven years. Yes, you're dead.' And with that she started to walk off.

'Beth.' She stopped. She couldn't pretend he was dead when he was standing flesh and blood in front of her. She considered him again. There seemed so much to say and nothing at all to say. She realised she wasn't ready to deal with an alive Theo. This time Theo would have to wait for her.

'I can't talk to you today. Come and meet me after work,' she said. 'On ...' She wondered how much time she needed and then thought, *Oh bugger it*, she might as well get whatever was going to happen between them over and done with. 'Meet me after work at the Coles Variety Store in Smith Street, Collingwood — Clara and I work there,' and she looked over at Clara who was watching her and Theo and looking like her world might disappear.

'I need some time to think. Come Monday the week after next, at six, and I'll listen to what you have to say for yourself while you walk me to Flinders Street station. You'll have forty-five minutes. I'll ask Clara to take the tram so we can be alone.'

'Monday week at six.' He lifted his hat and turned on his heel like a soldier and walked away. As soon as he was out of sight Clara came running over.

'Are you all right?' she asked.

Beth smiled at her. 'You know, Clara, I am better than I thought.'

Monday, 21 July 1924, when a walk is taken.

She saw Theo waiting when she came out of the store. He was leaning against the verandah post, his hat balanced at an angle on his head, one leg crossed over the other. People will think he's my lover, she thought, and wondered how long he had been waiting. Knowing him, probably since ten in the morning.

'So you sell nothing over two shillings, huh?' he said as she approached.

'Sorry?' she said.

'The sign,' he said, and pointed.

'Yes, and it's so successful they're opening another store soon. I'm going to be a department manager. The rest of the world might be getting poorer but Coles isn't.'

She realised that small talk wasn't going to save them from the big talk, so she took a deep breath and said, 'Have you seen Edie? Have you told her you're back from the dead? What about your mother? Have you told her?' Her voice was accusing. She hadn't meant to sound so angry.

He shook his head.

'You're my legal wife, Beth. I had to tell you first.'

She stopped walking and looked up at him. 'That hasn't really meant a whole lot, Theo, has it?' She could hear the hostility in her voice. 'Besides, I'm not sure we're married when you are dead.'

'Well, I'm here to change that,' he said gently.

Beth gave Theo the forty-five minutes she promised him. Anyone looking at them would have seen a man and woman walking oblivious to the rest of the world, talking as though their futures depended on it. By the time they had got to Flinders Street station he had said all he needed to say.

Beth caught the train from Flinders Street and walked to Princes Street deep in thought. When she knocked on the front door Clara opened it and held the door ajar with her arm stretched out, creating a barricade. She was in her nightgown, her face was fresh without a trace of the makeup she had worn to work, and her red hair glowed like embers in light from the hallway. Beth could see she had been crying. She stood there not letting Beth in.

'Well?' Clara said eventually.

'If you make me a cup of tea I will tell you,' said Beth.

'No, you tell me now and I decide if I let you back in,' said Clara.

Beth put down her bag. 'He said he was willing to pick up our marriage and give it a try if I insisted but that I should know he will always love Edie.'

'Well, I don't s'pose you can fault him for honesty,' said Clara, still barricading the entrance.

'So,' said Beth slowly, watching Clara's angst as she drew it out, 'I said to him that I wanted a divorce. I said "Theo, I've learnt who I am and it's taken me a long time and it turns out I am strong and independent and I like being on my own. I have someone else who loves me,' she said and looked meaningfully at Clara, 'and if I was going to be with anyone I would probably be with that person. But right now I want to just be by myself. So Theo, please do get a divorce. I just ask that you be the guilty party. Because you are, really, in a way, aren't you? You never loved me. In fact it's quite the in-thing to be a divorced woman, I think I shall like it immensely. Some women pretend they are divorced because it's more exciting than being unwanted and single but I will be the real deal. You do all the work and I will sign anything

I have to and we will both be free to be who we want." And he said, "Getting an annulment from the judge is quicker." He was never one for saying much. And I said, "I thought I was a widow, which is rather a sad thing to be. But I was looking forward to being a divorcee." No don't look like that, Clara. I said fine, an annulment then.'

'You said all that?' asked Clara standing aside.

'Well, that was the gist of it. I may have said a lot more than that. The strange thing is that he asked me not to tell anyone else he was alive. He made me promise.'

Forty-Two

Lilly

Friday, 25 July 1924, when the afternoon doesn't pan out.

It was three in the afternoon and Lilly was walking to Webster Street. She had a basket filled with butterscotch rolls for after dinner. They were still hot and she was cocooned in the smell of buttery sugar escaping through the tea towels in which the scones were wrapped. As she began to cross the big intersection at Sturt Street her breath left her. She undid the top button of her coat and pulled her scarf loose and bent over and gasped for air. The pain ran through her jaw and neck and she grabbed her arm, which hurt nearly as much as losing Theo.

The schoolchildren on their way home pointed at the old woman standing in the middle of the road holding up the horses and motor vehicles. George, who was retired now but never stopped feeling he was a policeman, saw her fall to the road and ran as fast as he could, yelling for others to get the ambulance as he kept running. Beatrix, who had been walking with George, waddled over as fast as she could. She pushed George out of the way and loosened Lilly's coat and cardigan and shirt all the way until she had bared

Lilly's undergarments to the world without a care and pumped her chest and then held Lilly's nose and breathed into her mouth.

'You're amazing,' said George, admiring her at work.

'Once a nurse, always a nurse,' she said between pumps. She was tired but she kept going until the ambulance truck arrived. George got up off his knees and reached out his hand to help her up and she watched over Lilly as they lifted her onto the gurney and into the brand spanking new ambulance.

'Well, that will be a tale to tell if she lives,' said George, standing next to Beatrix as they watched the truck pull away.

'She's the first to ride in the new motorised ambulance,' Beatrix said, still red in the face from her efforts.

Lilly was looking for Theo but she couldn't find him anywhere. She looked up and down the streets and went to the house and called for him in the backyard and looked in his bedroom. She found Peter sitting by the kitchen table in a singlet and his undershorts reading the paper. He looked up and smiled at her. 'Ah Lillian, my sweet rosebud.'

No one had called her Lillian since her wedding day, when the minister said, 'Do you Lillian Mary Heathrow take Peter Theodore Hooley to be your lawful wedded husband?' and she had smiled at him with all her body and said, 'Oh yes I do.'

'He's old. You'll only get twenty years with him if you're lucky,' her mother had said.

'Well, I'd rather twenty happy years than fifty miserable ones with someone else,' she'd replied.

Peter put the paper on the table and patted his knee and she sat on his lap and he kissed her and everything she had been missing so deeply came rushing back and she never wanted to leave this place.

It was the yelling that interrupted her kiss. It was most unpleasant and unkind and she would tell the intruder so in no uncertain words.

'Lilly,' said the voice, 'Lilly, who do you want us to call?'

She opened her eyes and blinked in the harsh lights they were rudely shining right in her eyes. Slowly her pupils adjusted and she saw Young Doctor Appleby standing over her, his face only inches from hers, his antiseptic breath making her queasy. The terrible realisation came to her that she wasn't in her home with Peter, she was in the hospital, and she felt bereft as everything warm flooded from her and was replaced by everything cold.

She looked at the young doctor's face. He didn't care the way his father had. Around her were the cold grey and white walls of the hospital and the harsh lights still glaring into her eyes and the white starched apron of the nurse who was looking intently at the doctor.

'I couldn't find Theo, I looked everywhere. I found Peter but Theo wasn't there, he wasn't with Peter,' she said and Young Doctor Appleby looked at the nurse.

'Who do you want us to call?' he asked her again.

'Does she have anyone, sister?' he asked the nurse.

Lilly had to think hard, it was exhausting. Finally she smiled and said, 'Call Paul Cottingham.'

Forty-Three

The Tree

*Sunday, 3 August 1924, when Maud
Blackmarsh is remembered.*

Lilly lay tiny and almost invisible among the pillows in the cast-iron hospital bed. She was breathing heavily and dreaming of everyone she loved. When she forced her eyes open she could only just see out the window from her bed. On the other side of the window was a struggling sparse rose bush. She tutted, it was not like her rose bush or Edie's rose bush. Her rose bush had grown into the largest rose bush anyone had ever seen and almost filled the entire front yard. When young couples thought she wasn't looking they came and carved their initials into its thick trunk.

The rose bush that Edie had planted in the Cottingham front yard was not nearly as large but it had the reddest roses you ever saw. They were the colour of heart's blood.

She remembered Maud Blackmarsh, who claimed to be the rose expert, saying to her that Edie's rose bush had the reddest roses because it was watered with tears and love. But no, that wasn't Maud, she wouldn't say something as lovely as that. No, it was the man who had visited her yesterday. Maybe he had said that. He said something else too, something about her rose bush growing into a tree because a bush wasn't big enough to hold a mother's love. Then her mind wandered again and she remembered other things Maud had said. When Beth had married Theo, Maud had said, 'Oh that Beth is much more suitable for Theo than the Cottingham girl would ever be.' When Beth went to Melbourne, Maud had leant on the fence and said, 'I tell you, Lilly, Beth only married Theo in the first place to spite Edie, not because she loved him. It's all very well for the rich to have staff,' she said, 'but they can never trust them. Staff are the bane of their lives. That's why the Cottinghams never employed anyone after Beth. And that's why Edie's rose bush has the superior flower.' But Lilly thought Maud talked a lot of rubbish about things she knew nothing about and one day soon she would tell her so.

Lilly was hot and she wished someone would bring her some water. The man who came yesterday had, he had gently held the cup against her dry cracked lips so she could sip at it. He had placed one hand behind her head, supporting her as she drank, and she had felt his strong hand holding her and she felt safe.

She really wanted some water now. The rose bush outside the window needed water too, its leaves were dry and cracking. Lilly's rose tree never wanted for water. She knew it had grown so large because it was watered with a mother's love, which covers a child to the ends of the earth, just like the man had said. And she hadn't just watered her rose bush, she had fed it tea for nitrogen and phosphorus, and scones for sugar, and leftover lamb stew for protein. In fact she had fed that tree everything she would have fed Theo if he had been home. Maud Blackmarsh had laughed at her feeding the rose tree all those things, but she only laughed until the tree grew strong and tall and far greater than any rose bush should be. It was Theo's rose tree.

As she thought of Theo tears filled the corners of her eyes. The man who had visited her yesterday had said he was Theo, but she knew he couldn't be because her Theo had died at the war. She had the telegram and the cloth badge they gave to war widows and mothers. The man had held her hands gently like Theo used to do at the kitchen table. He'd said, 'I'm back, Mum, and I'm so sorry I haven't come sooner.'

She wanted him to be her Theo, so she had patted his hand and said, 'It's okay love — you're here now.'

Then he had said, 'I never gave you roses, Mum, but I know you loved me with a love that is too big to be contained in a single bloom. You loved me in every meal you cooked, every cake you baked, every shirt you ironed. I knew your love in every mouthful of Irish stew, in every bite of cinnamon cake, in every starched and ironed handkerchief.'

She forced her tired eyes open and looked and saw that it wasn't yesterday the man visited her, it was today, now, and ghost or not he was indeed her Theo. Her tears fell and ran in streams through the creases of the pillows. He carefully lifted her up and held her and they stayed like that until the doctor came and interrupted them.

'Don't go,' she said as he got up.

'I won't go far — I promise,' he said.

Edie, Paul and Gracie were visiting later than they intended because Edie had been longer than normal getting back from her weekly drive with Virgil. Paul and Gracie were ready to go when she walked in the front door.

'Sorry, sorry,' she said. 'I forgot the time,' and she thought of how she had spent the afternoon wrapped in Virgil's arms on the rug in front of the fireplace in his lounge room. She got the motor vehicle keys and drove them to the hospital in their lovely Morris Crowley. It was sky blue, like Virgil's, and when it had just been polished you could see the stars in the night sky in its reflection and during the day it looked like it had been painted with clouds reflected from the sky. Paul sat in the front seat and held tight to the glove box in front of him. He didn't like being in the car when she was driving. No matter how many times she told him that she'd never intentionally hit anything, he always sat braced for an accident and said, 'There's always a first time.'

They walked through the front doors of the hospital. Edie nodded to the nurse at the nurses' station and headed down the corridor to Lilly's room. Young Doctor Appleby stepped out of nowhere into the corridor, giving them all a bit of a start.

'Can you follow me, please?' he asked.

'All of us?' asked Edie, thinking he might want only Paul.

'Yes, all of you would be best.'

He held a door wide and Edie followed Paul and Gracie into an empty consulting room. The room was stark, with just an empty wooden desk and two chairs. The only other furniture was the examination gurney covered in a white sheet. It's an omen of what is to come, Edie thought, and hoped Paul was prepared. Doctors don't take you into a quiet room for good news. They all waited politely while Paul used his umbrella to ease himself down into one of the chairs. When Paul was settled Edie looked at Young Doctor Appleby to let him know Paul was ready for him to begin. The doctor leant back against the gurney and it moved, making him lose his balance. He righted himself and folded his arms over his chest.

'She's not improving. We think her heart has been damaged too severely. It's most likely time to say goodbye.'

'Goodbye,' repeated Paul.

There was silence. The doctor didn't offer anything further and Paul got up out of the chair. His face was set. Edie could see he was making it clear he didn't need to hear any more.

'I'd be just as happy to see the real Doctor Appleby, you know. I'm sure he would be just as good as you, it's only the mind not the body that matters,' Paul said as he made his way out the door. Young Doctor Appleby looked at Edie for help and she shrugged. He was her father and everyone knew that when Paul Cottingham was set on something there was no use arguing. If he thought Young Doctor Appleby wasn't a patch on his father, then what could she do? Every time they saw Young Doctor Appleby her father said this to him. But the real Doctor Appleby had been retired for a good ten years and only went into the practice to make sure his son hadn't moved anything and get a cup of tea from the nurses. Gracie was smothering a smile and Edie looked at her severely. She better not break into a giggle. Gracie thought it was hilarious that the man was called Young Doctor Appleby given he was bald, fat and forty.

Paul was already several paces down the corridor when Edie and the others emerged from the room. Paul turned and walked back to them. He put his finger against Young Doctor Appleby's chest and said, 'You should know her heart has survived far worse than this.'

Edie thought he said it as if he was reprimanding a six-year-old. Young Doctor Appleby must have felt it because he blushed. Paul then turned to Gracie and said, 'His father, the real Doctor Appleby, said you wouldn't survive, you know,' and she looked at Edie.

'It's true,' said Edie. 'He said you were too weak to survive. But you were stronger than he thought and you proved him wrong.'

'You can't trust them. They're all quacks.' Paul turned his back on Young Doctor Appleby and stalked off to Lilly's room. Edie took Gracie's hand and followed her father. Young Doctor Appleby had said Lilly had suffered a heart attack and there was nothing to be done, but Edie didn't believe that for a moment and read everything she could find about healing the heart. She scoured the chemist for the latest treatments and she finally came across belladonna. She read that nothing regulated the heart like belladonna.

She had already been treating Lilly for a number of years with coca-wine, a wonderful mix of cocaine and wine with the alcohol cleverly removed so as not to cause drunkenness. Without it, who knew, Lilly might have been in worse shape than she was. Goodness, she might not have even lasted this long. One dose a week she'd told Lilly, but she knew that when the pain in Lilly's heart was too great Lilly sometimes snuck an extra dose or two. But how could she not when her heart was cracked in two and both halves were filled with pain? One half for Theo and the other for her husband. But now Lilly needed something stronger. Yes, she would get Lilly some belladonna tomorrow. Lilly looked lost among the clouds of white sheets and pillows on her bed and the brutal greys and whites of the walls around her. She was asleep and Edie thought that was probably best, to let her body rest. They wouldn't wake her, they would let her be. Edie kissed her forehead, then she gazed out the window at the dying rose bush and perched on the low windowsill. Paul sat in the only chair, which he pulled up close to the bed, and took Lilly's hand and gently stroked it. Gracie sat on the end of the bed. Edie took out her notebook and wrote:

Third August Twenty-Four
Plan — Buy belladonna extract and heal Lilly's heart.

She tucked her notebook away in her pocket. Lilly opened her eyes and looked at Paul and Edie saw the quiet love pass between them. They had a calm knowledge of each other; they never tried to be anything other than who they were and loved each other for it. Edie felt a pang in her heart and the emptiness that had been in her as a young girl cracked open just a little further. She wasn't a modern girl, she wasn't being who she wanted to be with Virgil. She took out her notebook again and turned to an earlier page:

Seventh May Twenty-Two
Plan – Virgil Ainsworth: we are companions.

She had written that after the day at Mount Buninyong when he had made his proposal and she had accepted. But she had never made any other plans about Virgil. How could she make plans when he had made it clear that plans were the one thing he really didn't want? He said he couldn't live with another person and she had never spent a night with him. He said inside he would always be the lonely soldier and she was his only comfort. Edie told herself it was a good thing they were opposites and opposites are good in a relationship to balance each other out. Edie thought about all the plans she had made in her life. Sometimes a good plan took time but once made, once written in her book, it happened. Well, it had all happened except that very first plan — the plan to marry Theo.

Edie looked up from her notebook. Lilly was properly awake now and whispering something to Paul. He leant in close, putting his ear against her lips to hear her, then he sat back, obviously shocked.

'What's the matter?' Edie moved over to sit next to Gracie.

'Papa, what did she say?'

'She said Theo came to see her,' said Paul.

'You don't believe it?' said Edie. She whispered, 'It's what her heart wants to be true.'

'Of course I do,' said Gracie. 'I believe her. Lilly's never once told a fib.'

Edie didn't know why but she suddenly reached for Gracie's hand and held it tight.

Forty-Four

The Stranger

Sunday, 10 August 1924, when Virgil sees a menace out of the corner of his eye.

Edie wet her finger and ran it along her eyebrows that she'd had plucked that week in the new fashion, thin and rounded, and wished she hadn't because it had hurt so much when the woman at the salon had said it wouldn't hurt at all. She ran her finger along the outline of her mouth and saw the fine lines appearing at the edges of her lips. Acknowledging that there was nothing she could do about her lines and she just had to live with them, she unleashed her hair from its clip and it fell around her face in a delicate halo and rested on her shoulders. She put on her favourite green cloche hat, even though it was starting to get worn, and pulled it down tight, forcing her hair into obedience. Her light silk coat was hand-painted with Japanese ibis and matched her silk skirt; both were light and completely wrong for a cold day in August but they were Virgil's favourites on her. Then she waited for his knock.

When she opened the door he was wearing his blue vest, her favourite on him. He held it out from his body and said, 'I'll have to throw this old thing out one day, you know.'

'But it matches the car,' she said.

'Yes, well, that's going to have to be replaced one day too. They don't last forever, you know.'

'For goodness sake don't tell Papa that.'

Virgil drove to the Arch of Victory at Edie's request. He thought it was a dismal place. All those trees struggling in the Australian weather reminded him of the war and death. A spindly tree with a name plaque seemed poor consolation to the mothers who had lost their sons and daughters. He knew there must be a tree with his name plaque but he had no wish to see it. But Edie wanted to go, so he went. They got out and walked through the trees, winding in and out of them, reading out the soldiers' names on the plaques. The trees were different heights and ages. Some of the trees were dying, the foreign species that couldn't cope with Australian heat or the winter frosts, and they were being replaced with elms and poplars.

Edie stopped at one tree and suddenly he felt she'd gone far away. He looked at the soldier's name. It wasn't anyone either of them knew, as far as he could remember.

'I'm glad it isn't one of the dying ones,' she said quietly.

'Who is it?' he asked.

'Lilly's son,' she said and the words hung between them like a wall and he had no idea why.

'You never mentioned Lilly had a son.'

'No.'

Virgil could sense she was moving away from him and he had no idea how to bring her back. 'What's up?' he said.

'Nothing,' she said, but he knew it wasn't.

Virgil put his arm around her and tried to dance her up through the trees, taking her in his arms and twirling her. He would dance her out of her melancholy mood. But she wouldn't join in and pulled away.

'I'm sorry,' she said, 'my mind is with Lilly. She said some strange things in the hospital. I expect she was just a bit delusional.'

'Would you like me to take you home?' he asked.

She shaded her eyes against the winter sun to look up at him. 'No,' she said, 'kiss me instead.'

'I'll do more than kiss you, Miss Cottingham.'

'Oh, that wicked glint in your eyes makes me forget everything.'

He kissed her and left his lips glued to hers as they walked awkwardly back to the car and she giggled more than kissed. They only parted when they got to the car and he held the door open for her and she got in the passenger seat. He drove to Windermere Street. He kissed her again and kept kissing her all the way up the path and out of the corner of his eye he saw a man watching them from the corner of Urquhart Street, his features hidden by the shade his hat cast over his face. Virgil suddenly felt the need to keep Edie become more urgent. He fumbled with the lock and pushed the door open, rushing her inside and up against the wall. Without waiting till they got to the bedroom, he struggled with her clothing, desperately undressing her, doing it as quickly as he could before she vanished and he never had another chance. He made love to her up against the wall in the hallway, the pictures rattling on their hooks and the floorboards vibrating beneath them and at the end they both collapsed on the floor and laughed and he nearly had her back with him.

He took her hand and took her into the bathroom, lit the water heater and ran the warm water and then he got in and pulled her in on top of him. They lay like that as the water rose around them and when they were completely immersed Virgil made love to her again.

'I'm glad I found you, I'm glad I have love in my life,' she said, kissing him, but he still didn't feel safe.

When the water turned cold they got out and got dressed and he drove her back to Webster Street. He knew as soon as he pulled into her driveway that the man sitting on her verandah was the same man he had seen in the street and he felt he had just lost something he hadn't quite ever possessed.

Forty-Five

The Bovril

When Edie is in a quandry.

Her father was sitting next to him, a glass of water in his hand. Gracie sat on the other side of him.

Edie recognised Theo instantly and put her hand to her heart. She couldn't feel it. Her heart had stopped beating; it had frozen.

'It can't be,' she said.

She turned to Virgil. 'I'm sorry but I have to go and I can't invite you in. I'm sorry.'

Virgil looked at the man on the verandah and back at her and she saw his eyes fill with worry — or was it sorrow?

'I have to go,' she said urgently and got out of the car. She shivered and wrapped her arms around herself. She watched as Virgil backed out and drove away and when the last speck of the brilliant blue of his car had disappeared she turned and walked towards the verandah, forcing one foot in front of the other when she really just wanted to collapse.

'Look Edie,' her father called out. 'Your Bovril saved him after all.'

Edie looked at her sister, her lovely face poking up above her scarf and under her wide-brimmed felt hat. Even though it was winter Gracie looked like spring. Gracie turned and smiled at Theo and he put his hand on his heart and thumped it on his chest in time to his heartbeat and Edie remembered him doing that when Gracie was little.

'Where were you?' she asked him.

'I was saved, Edie, by your Bovril and an Englishman.'

'Hah,' said Gracie. 'Those brave Englishmen. It's always the brave Englishmen.'

'Well, I wouldn't even know his name,' said Theo, speaking slowly and quietly, 'but he did save me. I remember his voice, it was gentle like a song and I remember him pouring hot liquid down my throat and later they told me it was Bovril that some Australian woman was sending to the troops. The only thing was, I lost my dog tags at some point, and so when they were found lying on the beach they assumed the rest of me was dead and washed away in the sea. So they sent the telegram. But I woke up on a hospital ship bound for England and it took an awfully long time for me to become well. Then they sent me out to East Africa with the English soldiers, and army efficiency being what it is, no one bothered to list me as now being alive or to send a new telegram. When I told them I was dead they laughed and said, "Some days, mate, we all wish we were dead and with this war we may well get our wish." I just couldn't tell anyone back home I was still alive in case I didn't make it out of Africa; I couldn't make you and my mother go through it all again, so I thought I would wait and see if I survived, which I did, and I got a job working on a farm, which it turned out I was quite good at, and I kept meaning to write but I just couldn't face what I had created here at home. I had to wait for the right time to sort it all out.'

Gracie and Paul looked at him wide-eyed and open-mouthed and finally Paul said, 'I think that you just said more than you have said in the entire rest of your life.'

'And in all that time you didn't think to let anyone know you weren't dead?' snapped Edie. She could barely look at him. How could he have let her, let his mother, think he was dead all these years?

'I couldn't, Edie,' he said. 'I didn't think I had anyone to come back to.'

'Maybe Gracie and I have something to do inside,' said Paul.

'Do we?' asked Gracie. 'Because I want to hear what happened to Theo.'

'Yes, I think we do,' said Paul and Theo helped Paul up from the step and Paul patted Theo on the shoulder like he would a son who was just leaving after his weekly visit, as if Theo had never been away all these years, as if they hadn't thought he was dead. As if he'd merely popped down to Melbourne for a spot of business.

Edie sighed crossly. Paul raised his eyebrow at her and handed her the water glass and she gripped it tight as if it might hold her up, or as if she might throw it at Theo or at her father for patting him like the prodigal son returned.

'I invited him in. He says he won't come inside,' said Paul. 'He says he can't come inside until he's spoken with you. So speak with him, will you, because it's getting dreadfully cold out here.'

'So, Papa ...' Gracie said when they got to the kitchen, leaving Theo and Edie outside. She knew more was happening than Theo simply appearing from the dead, that was a miracle in itself but she had expected it and wasn't surprised and didn't know why Paul and Edie were surprised. Lilly said she had seen him.

She put the kettle on. 'There's obviously a story here. Why hasn't Beth come with him?'

'It's a long story, Gracie.' Paul sat in the kitchen chair. 'It's a love story but not one about a man and a woman, though that's part of it — it's a love story about two sisters and a father.'

She put her hands on her hips and stared down at him. She wanted more and she would get it.

'All right, judge,' he said. 'I don't know what he's doing here without Beth. Yes he married her but it was always Edie he loved, but you were too young to know that.'

'Did Edie love him?'

'Immensely, but she didn't want to marry him and Beth did and that's what happened.'

'Why didn't she want to marry him if she loved him?'

Paul thought for a moment and said, 'Because Beth loved him too, and you know your sister, she always puts everyone else's needs first.'

'Well, we must find out what he is doing here and where he has been. Perhaps something has happened to Beth and he's come to tell us, did you think of that? We can't leave Edie out there alone.' Gracie started towards the door and Paul reached out and stopped her.

'Alone is exactly what they have never had and need,' said Paul. 'So make me that tea you promised.'

Theo stood in front of her, his hat in his hand. The cold wet air settled on his greying hair, the moisture turning it silver. Edie looked hard at him, trying to see if he was the same person. His hair was longer than he used to have it and more wayward, there was no oil in it to hold it down and it looked as though an old aunt had ruffled it. His moustache was gone and his chin was sturdier; the lines on his face were weathered. His eyes and mouth had fine lines around them as though they were always ready to smile. He stood there tall and proud, almost challenging her to reject him, and she realised he was much stronger than he had been when he was young, and he had the face of a man who had worked hard. She looked at the ground, then back up at him, and it was as if she was nineteen again and she began to melt into him. Then she remembered she was nearly twice that age now and there was Virgil.

'I am old,' she said. Her voice was barely there.

He didn't laugh at her.

'You have never been more beautiful,' he said, and the quietness was theirs.

They stood in it for some time. His eyes were still the kindest eyes she had ever seen. He was fuller, though, and she laughed.

'You've actually put on some weight.'

He looked down at his belly and smiled at her. It was the same smile she remembered, the smile that knew all about her stubbornness and her desire and her loss and loved her anyway.

'Edie, I always have and always will love you with every part of me.'

'I have met someone,' she said slowly and cautiously, so he could hear all that she meant by it. He seemed completely untroubled by this. A fly landed on his arm and he brushed it away along with her words.

'We belong with each other,' he said. 'It turns out I am a farmer and quite a good one. I am also good at saving money and I have bought a small plot at Scarsdale. I'm thinking raspberries and herbs. I want you to come and live with me in Ligar Street. I'll give the house a lick of paint.'

'Yellow?'

'Yes, if you like.'

She thought about how far she had travelled and who she had become. She wasn't that nineteen-year-old girl any more.

'I can't,' she said.

'The girl I know can do anything,' he said. 'She can make her dress ridiculously short despite all the busybodies, despite Missus Blackmarsh and Vera Gamble gossiping about it.' She smiled and he went on, 'She can turn her back on her desires because her love for her family is all that matters to her, and she can save a man's life with a cup of Bovril.'

He waited.

'Have you seen Beth?' asked Edie.

'I have. I had to — it was the right thing to do.'

'Oh,' said Edie, and everything inside her began swirling.

'I wouldn't have come if we couldn't be completely free,' he said. 'Beth has her own life and it doesn't include me. We're having the marriage annulled. We never consummated it after the ceremony.'

'Oh,' said Edie.

'Beth wanted a divorce — she thought it sounded more exotic.'

'Oh yes,' said Edie, 'she wants to be a divorcee.'

'But it turns out an annulment is quicker and easier with the judge. The hardest part was proving I'm still alive.'

'Couldn't you just walk in there and show them?'

'I had to get the army to write that they had made a mistake and to list me as not dead and the army doesn't like to admit to mistakes.'

'Would we be … companions?' Edie asked, looking down at her feet.

'Good heavens no,' he laughed. He took her face in his hands. 'Edie, I want you good and proper as my good and proper wife and no other way.'

'I don't know,' said Edie, her mind cluttered with images of Virgil.

'I'll wait,' said Theo. 'You know I can do that. You know I will wait for you forever, Edie.'

Everything she had felt for him as a young woman came pouring back into her soul. But she didn't know if it was real or a memory.

Forty-Six

The Room

Wednesday, 27 August 1924, when ghosts are faced.

When John Appleby Junior appeared for his morning visit he found Lilly sitting up on the bed dressed in a sunflower dress that looked like spring, a straw hat on her head with a ribbon and that old Mister Cottingham sitting on the chair beside her.

'You can discharge me now, young man. There is nothing wrong with my heart,' she announced.

'Maybe not, but you'll catch your death if you go out in that thin dress,' he said. Blast these old patients of his father's who never treated him like a full-grown man and a doctor in his own right. 'I'm the doctor,' he said. 'I'll decide if you go home or not.'

The old woman smiled at the old man as though they would humour him if he insisted on it. He pulled out his stethoscope and listened to her heart over and over, from the back and from the front to make sure.

Finally he said, 'Well, it's a miracle beyond my understanding. You can go home if you can find something warmer to wear.' She started to get up from the bed and he said, 'And provided you have someone to look after you every hour of the day.'

'Where is Theo?' Old Cottingham asked her.

'He's coming and going, he says he has things to arrange and that he doesn't know when he will be here or there,' said Lilly.

'Well,' said Paul, 'the doctor's right.'

'Thank you at last,' said John but they merely looked at him as if he had rudely interrupted an important matter and continued without him.

'You can't go to your own home where you'll be alone. You can have Lucy's room and I won't hear a word about it.'

John thought the old man must have been a formidable force when he was younger. The old lady submitted immediately to his decision and John would have too had it been required.

Paul wondered if he had just made a mistake. He had removed the boards from the window and doors many years ago but still none of them ever went into Lucy's room.

When Paul arrived home with Lilly, Edie and Gracie had a day bed ready for her in the sitting room beside the fire.

'She has to have plenty of rest,' Paul said and he looked sternly at Lilly and said, 'Doctor's orders.'

Then he took Edie and Gracie into the hallway and Edie wondered what he needed to say that couldn't be said in front of Lilly.

'Now I need you girls to clean out your mother's room for Lilly to stay in.'

Edie didn't think she'd heard properly.

'Edie, I need you to get your mother's room ready for Lilly.'

Edie could feel herself staring at him like an idiot, as though she didn't understand the question.

'Sure,' said Gracie and she pulled Edie down the hallway to the room that was never opened. Gracie had grown up with that room boarded up and had just accepted it. When she had asked about the room she had seen Paul's and Edie's faces stricken with pain and she soon realised it was better not to ask and just let it be. If she asked Beth about the room Beth would also become quiet and tell her that it was not her place to tell her. Her father had taken down the boards on peace day but still no one went inside.

Edie stood at the door of the room as if afraid to go in.

'Are you okay?' Gracie asked her.

'I haven't been in here for nearly nineteen years,' said Edie. 'It was our mother's room and I think Papa was just so broken and sad at losing her that he couldn't cope with the thought of anyone coming in here till now. I feel that when I walk in there I will find all the ghosts I don't want to see.'

'Well,' said Gracie, 'maybe you will find ghosts you do want to see, ghosts that will bring you comfort. But I will go first and scare all those horrid ghosts away so only the benevolent ones are left.'

Gracie walked in and pulled back the curtains and sunlight filled the room. It shone on the perfume bottle on the dressing table and on the gold thread in the bed cover and Gracie was overcome by the thought that here were all the things that had belonged to the mother she had never known. Her mother had touched and loved these things. Gracie smelt the perfume and opened the cupboard and buried her face in the clothes and she realised that they didn't really mean anything to her because Edie was her mother.

'Come on, Edie,' she called. 'It's quite lovely and not at all scary.'

Edie walked in and looked about her. The room wasn't at all musty, it smelt of her mother, she could hear her mother's voice singing. Or was it Gracie? She realised they sounded exactly the same. She touched the perfume bottle and held it to her nose and memories of her mother's smell flooded into her, then she opened the drawer and touched the silk underwear, now so incredibly old-fashioned, and remembered how soft her mother's skin was.

'She loved you, Gracie,' she said.

Gracie said, 'I know,' and believed it because Edie said it.

Edie sat on the bed with a plop and a dust cloud filled the room. They both ran out laughing.

'Oh, we have some work to do,' said Gracie, but Edie grabbed her and held her tight and whispered that she loved her over and over. When Edie finally let her go, Gracie said, 'What do we start with? The dusting or the floors?'

'The bed.' They both agreed and within hours the room was clean and fresh. It still had Lucy's things in it, and when Edie touched them she thought how right her mother had been to make her promise to care for Gracie.

Forty-Seven

The Notebook

Sunday, 31 August 1924, which isn't as pleasant as expected.

Edie couldn't think straight about anything at all. Theo had said he would see her at his usual time, which she took to mean three on Sunday afternoon, when he used to come each week with his rose. Which was the exact same time she usually went for a drive with Virgil and she just couldn't bring herself to tell Virgil not to come around because that would make him curious and she would have to answer a lot of questions about Theo. She and Paul and Gracie were sitting in the kitchen. Lilly was resting in Lucy's room.

'Look at this, Edie,' Paul said, holding a rolled-up newspaper in the air so she couldn't see anything at all. 'Not only did Reverend Whitlock spout all that rubbish from the pulpit this morning but he has a piece in yesterday's *Courier* claiming that those — and we know here he means me — fighting for a forty-four hour week for workers are extremists attempting to undermine the economic stability of the state. He only got the piece printed because he's retiring, and for that reason alone I am going to be the bigger person and let him have the last word.'

'Well, there is a first time for everything,' said Edie.

Edie heard the knock on the door at three and went to open it, not sure which man she would find. It was Virgil. He stood hat in hand and looked at her hopefully.

'Virgil, hello,' she said, as though he was a friend she hadn't seen in months. 'Why don't you come in for afternoon tea?' Why was she talking to him like that, sounding so formal?

'Afternoon tea? Why not.'

So she took him into the dining room and left him there while she went back to the kitchen and asked Paul and Gracie if they could entertain him for a moment. Edie went to her bedroom and paced and took out her notebook and flicked through the pages and put it back in her pocket.

Gracie came in and said, 'Are you going to come and see him? He's come for you, after all. Why aren't you going for your usual drive?'

'Ohhh,' said Edie. 'You're right.' And she followed Gracie back into the dining room and was relieved to find that Paul had engaged Virgil in a one-way conversation about the working week.

Ten minutes later the next knock on the door came and she rushed to make sure she got to it before Gracie.

'You're late,' she said to Theo.

He smiled. 'Am I? Late for what?'

She didn't know and motioned for him to come inside.

'I'll just see my mother first,' he said.

Edie watched from the door of Lucy's room as Lilly, who had been having a rest, got up and threw her arms around Theo, saying over and over that she never once believed him to be dead.

She left them and went back to the dining room where Virgil was waiting for her with Gracie and Paul. She had no idea how they filled the next fifteen minutes until Theo walked in.

Edie saw Virgil's face darken when he saw Theo.

'Virgil Ainsworth, this is Theo Hooley,' said Edie and Virgil stood up and the two men shook hands too vigorously.

'Virgil is staying for tea and cake too,' Edie told Theo.

Theo didn't react. To Edie he seemed calm and unreadable — or was he so sure of his future with her that Virgil was just a hiccup to him? She couldn't tell and it bothered her because as far as she was concerned she hadn't made any decisions.

She looked to Paul and Gracie for help but they were trying to wipe the grins from their faces. Paul pulled himself together first. 'We should go to the kitchen,' he said. 'It's more friendly.'

So they all sat around the kitchen table — Gracie, Paul, Lilly, Theo, Virgil and Edie. Gracie kept looking at Edie and then at Theo, then at Edie and then at Virgil, trying to see which coupling worked best and Edie scowled at her to stop. But Edie found herself gazing at Theo and then Virgil and then Theo, trying to compare the two men and realising she couldn't because they were cut from different cloth and it would be unfair to try.

Gracie made tea and put out scones and got the good china. Paul kept grinning at Edie and she knew it was because he was enjoying every minute of her discomfort at being stuck between these two men.

Virgil talked about automobiles, and when it became obvious Theo knew nothing about automobiles, Virgil got fired up and talked about drum brakes and ignition starters. Theo talked about Africa and coffee beans and growing raspberries that do well in the frost, unlike most things, which Virgil knew nothing about. Paul and Gracie watched on, raising their eyebrows at Edie every now and then as if this was all her fault. Edie was indignant. She hadn't done this at all, she hadn't made Theo come back eight years too late.

When Virgil prickled and sat up straighter in his chair to try and be taller than Theo, Paul defused everything by talking about the forty-four hour week again, which he was adamant was needed to protect the health of the workingman and the predicted financial collapse which nobody but he believed would actually happen, and Gracie sat grinning like this was the best entertainment she'd ever had. Edie had never had two men fight for her and didn't know what to do. She didn't want to hurt either and was a fluster of upset. Her tea went cold in its cup and whenever anyone asked her a question all she could manage was 'Hmmmm.'

When the scones were gone and the afternoon had gone as well, both men tried to be the last to leave but eventually Edie saw it dawn on Virgil that nobody could outlast Theo and he got up and said, 'I must be going.' Glaring at Theo, he added, 'I don't want to wear out my welcome.'

Edie walked Virgil out to his car, where he stopped and took her hands in his and, hoping Theo was watching, said, 'I think next week we might go for a drive on Saturday afternoon instead of Sunday,' then he leant in to her and whispered, 'and back to my place afterward,' but she leant away from him even though she didn't know why and when he tried to kiss her, his lips landed on her cheek. He slammed the car door when he got in and it made her flinch.

When she went back inside Theo was deep in conversation with his mother in Lucy's room. By the time he came out Edie was in the kitchen with Gracie and Paul washing the dishes.

He stood in the doorway. 'Lovely scones,' he said. 'I'm off, I won't be back for a fortnight, I have things I have to organise,' as though he had not the slightest fear that Virgil might get the advantage during his absence.

Saturday, 6 September 1924, when Edie knows.

A week could be a very long time. It could take from one Sunday afternoon to the following Saturday and a whole life could be lived in the middle.

At three Virgil arrived at the door. The weather, being stubbornly changeable and unreliable in autumn, surprised everyone by being pleasant. Virgil suggested they drive to Lal Lal and Edie, who couldn't concentrate on anything, would have agreed to go anywhere he wanted.

They walked around the racecourse and discussed nature and trees and birds and Edie thought neither of them said one word to each other that they actually wanted to say. After they had walked more than she wanted to they meandered back to the car and Virgil said, 'Do you want to come back to my place?'

Edie said, 'I would like to but I need to get home to help care for Lilly,' even though Lilly was up and about now and probably putting dinner on and needed no care at all. Suddenly she felt guilty she'd put him off like that with a lie and added, 'But you could come in for some tea if you like,' realising it was a poor consolation and wasn't at all what he wanted from her.

'If I like?' he said bitterly and he got in the car and forgot to get the door for her so she opened it herself and got in the passenger seat. They drove to Webster Street in silence, and the silence continued even after he had parked outside her house. Some minutes later she realised she was waiting for him to say something and he wasn't going to and was probably waiting for her to say something. She didn't know what to say so she reached for the door handle and said, 'I've never seen you lost for words before.'

'I am lost for words. Edie,' he said and he reached into his pocket and pulled out an envelope. He gave it to her and said, 'I should have done this when you wanted me to.'

'Oh,' said Edie and she turned it over in her hand.

He got out and walked around and opened the door for her.

She got out of the car and he put her arm in his and walked her down the driveway. The pebbles were out of tune under her feet. She couldn't find her mind, or any other part of her. Every time she thought she'd found just one thread to hang onto, it floated away on the breeze until it was just out of reach.

At the door he took her face in his hands and kissed her and she remembered how sweet his kisses were, and the feeling of losing something when they stopped.

She realised that Theo had never kissed her.

Virgil pulled away and smiled. 'I've never forgotten our first kiss.'

'You didn't even ask,' she said.

'No, I didn't,' he said, laughing. 'I saw a pretty girl and I took her,' and she watched him walk back down the drive in his blue vest with his blue eyes.

'Darn it,' she said again, leaning against the kitchen table as she opened the envelope and read Virgil's letter.

'What does it say?' asked Gracie.

'Don't bother her, it's obvious what it says,' said Paul.

'It's a marriage proposal. Now I have two,' said Edie.

'Oh,' said Lilly, hoping Edie would choose Theo.

Edie flopped onto the chair and buried her head in her arms on the table and thought of the irony of life and how as a young girl she had desperately wanted just one proposal. Back then she would have imagined having two offers being exciting, but it wasn't, it meant there was a choice to be made that could change everything. It meant someone was going to be hurt and she was going to be the cause of it. Paul and Gracie reached over and wrapped her in their arms.

'What will you do?' asked Gracie, putting her head against Edie's.

Edie looked at her. 'Nothing. It's my own stupid fault; I shouldn't have let this happen. I will choose neither. I can't leave you and Papa. I never could and I never will. I won't accept either of them.'

'Bloody hell!' said Gracie.

Edie was shocked, which was exactly what Gracie wanted.

'Of course you can leave us. I can look after Papa perfectly well and we have Lilly now too, don't we, Lilly?'

Lilly looked at Paul and he nodded. 'She's not going anywhere.'

'Oh yes,' said Lilly. 'Yes, you do have me.'

Gracie stood as tall as she could, which wasn't very tall, so she stood on the chair and put her hands on her hips. 'Edie, you have been the best mother a girl could ever want but I can look after Papa and I have Lilly who will feed us both and make us fat, won't you?'

'I imagine Gracie can look after us,' said Paul, 'though I don't need looking after.'

'But Gracie needs her own life,' said Edie, and then she realised what she had said. 'Gracie, I never regretted it, not for a moment.'

'It's okay, Edie. I will follow my heart when my Englishman arrives.'

'Gracie, you don't know how life is going to turn out,' said Edie.

'I do know,' said Gracie stubbornly. 'I love you, Edie, and if you don't follow your heart I will never smile again and you know what that would do to Papa.'

'I have noticed every gentle wrinkle around his eyes and committed them all to memory,' said Edie and she smiled and knew her decision.

'Well, it's settled then,' said Paul and he thumped his umbrella on the ground firmly, as if it was a gavel in the courtroom finalising everything, and it made the floorboard quiver and the table bounce.

Lilly topped up the teapot with hot water and Edie took a cup to her room and sat down at her dressing table and replied to Virgil's letter and then she took out her notebook. She had one empty page left and she wrote:

Sixth September Twenty-Four
Plan — Marry him.

Forty-Eight

The Widower

*Monday, 15 September 1924, when Reuben finds
a little redemption in Ballarat.*

Two weeks he had been in Ballarat and the gossip about him had
spread from the Arch of Victory to Bakers Hill and from Mount
Buninyong to Black Hill. He hadn't even given his first sermon
yet. But the gossip about the new pastor was all any one talked
about. Some of the women said his wife had left him and run back
to England, some said that she had gone completely bonkers and
was in an asylum, some said he had done her in and then everyone said, 'Nooooh — he couldn't. He's a man of God,' and the
person who had said it would laugh awkwardly and say they had
only been joking. But one thing everyone knew was that the new
pastor was English, handsome, and his voice made you feel like
you could fly away. What's more he had three little tykes and he
needed a woman in his life.

Reuben was well aware of the gossip about him that filled the
streets of Ballarat. He had walked up to people too quickly and
overheard things; he had seen the way the women looked at him
and he knew when the women came to the door of the manse,

married or not, they were offering him more than the steaming
lamb casserole they held out under his nose. He remained stoic
and dignified through it all, ignoring the women's attempts to
lure him. He was so relieved to finally have his own church and
he was well aware that, apart from the fact he was no longer that
man, any untoward behaviour on his part would raise the ire of
the church deacons. And weren't they a bunch of stuffy old men
who constantly told him that he didn't understand the workings
of a small Australian town. Hah — nobody understood the workings of small rural towns like those from small English villages.
He had a thousand years of village gossip in his blood.

Monday was Reuben's day off but he was so glad to have his own
church that he didn't mind when his flock came to see him. They
could come any day of the week so long as he got paid his stipend
and could feed the children — but now he could see why Alice
had been so worried, why she had nagged him endlessly about the
money. Food was so expensive and money was so hard to come by
and a pastor's stipend, even full-time as he had now, was small.

When the knock on the door came he stood Martha and
Wycliffe in front of him and said sternly, 'Now, you have to be
good, not a sound, and look after your brother.' They both nodded and agreed they would be good so he went to the door and
opened it to two women. The younger one was short, he was
sure if he stood right up against her she would barely reach his
elbows, and the older one was not much taller. He'd seen them
in the congregation on Sunday, when he had sat through Deacon
Blackmarsh's effort at a sermon, but he didn't know who was who
yet. He ushered them into his study, 'First door on the left,' he
hurried them along and blocked their view so they wouldn't see
the hallway.

The women stood in the study. 'Gracie,' said the older woman,
nodding at the younger one, 'and I'm Edie.'

He indicated the two chairs in front of the desk. The chairs were shabby and he suddenly felt embarrassed offering them. Then he saw the study with their eyes: it was dark and dank. He didn't like the study or the rest of the house, which was filled with the previous pastor's choice of furniture. Everything felt old and tired to him, but he was too poor to replace anything. He had just got all of them seated when the screaming started. It was loud and high-pitched, like children being beaten, or a cat tormented by schoolboys. The women were shocked, their eyes wide.

'It's the children making a racket in the kitchen,' he said above the noise. 'I will just be a minute, please sit, I won't be long.' He heard the older sister whisper to the younger one, 'Missus Black-marsh says he's a widower, left with three littlies, the oldest only three and a half and the youngest a baby still at just thirteen months.'

Reuben stood at the door of the kitchen and took in the war zone that confronted him. Wycliffe and Martha were upending bottles of peaches and sauce over baby Wesley's head. 'We baptise you,' they were laughing, 'we baptise you,' and tomato sauce and preserved peaches poured over Wesley in a thick red waterfall. The preserved peaches and the tomato sauce were gifts from some of the women in his congregation, but all he could see was good money he would have to spend replacing the food going down the drain. His temper was already lost.

'Wycliffe! Martha! What is the meaning of this? I can't trust you to look after your brother for two minutes and not only are you wasting precious food but you are being sacrilegious while you do it!'

He was too harsh. Martha burst into tears and looked at him with sad, lost eyes. Tears streamed down her face making tracks in the sauce that was smeared over her cheeks. Wycliffe sulked. Reuben tore his hands through his hair. This was his life now, trying to manage the children, trying to hold a job to feed them, trying to keep his faith.

He only ever said Alice had died. He never told anyone that they had gone to Queenscliff, that he had expected it to make everything better, that she had been so consumed by disappointment that in the middle of his sermon she had got up, handed the new baby to the woman sitting next to her and quietly walked out. They had found her clothes neatly folded in a pile on the beach, her shoes sitting side by side on top, but they had not found her. Not in the days nor the weeks that came after, and he hoped that the sea had carried her back to England. The churchwomen in Melbourne had tried to help him, they pitched in and cared for the children while he arranged the funeral, but then he had told them one by one that he didn't need their child-minding and their house-cleaning because he needed space to make decisions. He couldn't hear anything other than the rushing of waves and needed to listen in silence and find out what should be next. Should he give everything up, write to his mother to ask for the passage home and get back on the boat?

One night he heard the children thank God for him as they said their bedtime prayers, and he knew he had to stay strong because he was all they had now. But he couldn't pray himself and he couldn't hear God's voice, which was just as well because he was angry with God and sometimes with Alice. He had had enough death in the war. Why did God think it was okay to send more into his own home? Or was it the other side of God? Was it Satan who had sent him more death? Either way he wouldn't stand for it. How could Alice do this to him? Leave him alone with the children?

So he'd written to his mother. He sealed the envelope and put it on the kitchen mantle to post the next day and just as he had the children in their coats ready to leave the house (and that alone had taken him an hour to manage) for the post office, Mister Wallace, the secretary at the Baptist Union, had opened the picket gate and walked up the path. Reuben told the children to take off their coats and go inside and put the baby in the cot while Mister Wallace told him that a church in a country town was considering him as a replacement for their minister who had finally retired after far too many years in the post.

Three days later Mister Wallace came back again to tell him that the deacons had decided on him and that he could go as soon as he felt ready. Mister Wallace told him there would be a double-storey brick manse and a regular weekly stipend. There was a public school around the corner for the children, just over the road, really, in Dana Street, and that would keep them out of his hair most days, though he had no suggestions regarding the baby.

The letter home didn't get posted and Reuben decided this was God talking to him and looking after him. Perhaps he would forgive God and they could get on with things. He packed up the house in Fitzroy Street and packed up the children and took the train to Ballarat.

Two weeks later it was clear the decision had been a mistake. Nothing was better at all. Reuben squatted on his haunches in the middle of the catastrophe in the kitchen, put his head in his hands and cried. Even though he and the children had only been in the manse a fortnight, Martha had already scribbled on the walls of the hallway with black crayon — large sweeping circles that she said were angels taking her mama to heaven — and nothing that he had tried would remove it. Wycliffe was sullen and moody and wouldn't speak. Wesley whimpered and just never stopped. And he himself was the centre of unwanted gossip.

Seeing their father in tears for the first time in their lives the children sobered up. Wesley stopped whimpering and sat open-mouthed, licking sauce from his face. Martha stopped crying and wiped her tears, spreading sauce further across her face. She and Wycliffe put their saucy, sticky arms around his neck, spreading tomato sauce and peach juice all over his suit and his tears washed away his temper.

'Come now, Martha, I need you to look after the little one,' he said gently.

'But how can she when she is barely more than a baby herself? Is she two? She looks just over two.'

He turned and it was the younger sister. She walked over and picked up Wesley and didn't even seem to bother that the child was covered in sticky saucy mess.

'You go and talk to my sister about her wedding and I'll fix all this up,' she said and smiled at him. Suddenly he knew that he was where he was meant to be. He was filled with contentment and his life didn't seem so bad. He could manage it, he could find his way. He stood up and towered over the short girl. How old was she? Seventeen? Nineteen at best — a child still. He used to take girls like her and fill them with his lust. Then he banished the thought. He couldn't become that man again. He watched, his hand gently on Martha's head as Gracie got a cloth from the sink and ran it under the water, then still holding Wesley on one arm, she came back to him and she reached up on her toes and wiped the sauce from his shoulders, his collar, and last of all his cheek.

'There,' she smiled, 'you just look like a normal father who loves to play with his children.'

'Thank you,' he said.

'Well,' she said, 'my sister is waiting — off you go.'

For the first time in his life Reuben felt that a female had the upper hand and he started to protest, but seeing the determination in her face, the pursing of those lips that only a few minutes ago had filled the room with their smile, and feeling that really she was much taller than him, he put his head down and did as he was told.

When he got to the office the sister was waiting patiently, not a scrap of irritation in her, as though waiting was something she was quite expert at.

'I'm sorry,' he said, 'the children.'

'Oh, Gracie will sort them out,' she said.

'Hmm,' he said, realising that despite any real evidence he was sure she was right.

'So you are getting married?'

'Yes,' she said. 'Can it happen on the ninth of November?'

'Any reason for that date?' he looked in his diary.

'No none at all — just that it's a Sunday afternoon.'

'I don't know if I can do it on a Sunday,' he said. 'There are two church services — one in the morning and one at night, as you know. It's most unusual.'

'We only ever go to the morning service. Couldn't it be done at three in the afternoon?'

He thought of the sister and the quietness that was filling his house. 'Has she murdered them?' he asked and they both laughed. 'Sunday afternoon it is then. You will need to let me know what hymns you would like in the service — the week before will do. Perhaps you and your fiancé can come and see me that week.'

'Yes, that would be fine,' she said and he stood up.

'We better go see what your sister has done to my children.' They walked back into the kitchen and found Wycliffe and Martha clean, in pyjamas and eating fruit at the clean table. Wesley was in the kitchen sink being bathed.

Gracie turned and smiled at them. 'All set for the wedding then?'

'Your sister's smile,' said Reuben to Edie, and he held his hand over his heart.

Later that day Reuben piled the two youngest children into the pram, Wesley sitting on Martha's lap and Wycliffe balancing on the axle at the back, and he wheeled them all to Ligar Street, where he was told he would find the church organist painting his house. He wanted to make sure that the hymns he had chosen for his first service were ones the organist knew.

He saw the man up the ladder, splashes of yellow paint dripping down his overalls, and called out to him. The man held onto the ladder with one hand and turned and waved with the other, still holding the paintbrush, dripping yellow paint over the garden.

When Reuben saw who it was he almost fell to his knees. Even though he was older, and had filled out, Reuben knew him the minute he saw him because he had seen him so often in his dreams and nightmares. When Theo had clambered down from the ladder and stood the paint tin safely on the grass, Reuben could wait no longer and he wrapped Theo in his arms and held him tight, wet paint and all.

'You saved me,' he said.

'Ah no, I think you saved me,' said Theo.

'No, it was you who saved me,' said Reuben.

The two men sat for hours on the verandah, saying nothing while the children played around the tree in the front yard and the baby slept in the pram.

'Is that a rose tree?' asked Reuben.

'It's a long story,' said Theo, 'for another day.'

Later that night Reuben swore that he would never question God or his ways again.

Forty-Nine

Sunday Afternoon

*Sunday, 10 November 1924, at 3 p.m., when
the sun shines love on the world.*

The sun was kind and sweet and a warm glow settled on the earth
making everyone feel sleepy and pleased with themselves. The musk
ducks played in the tall grasses and children splashed and made as
much noise as they could in the shallow muddy waters. A slight
breeze blew and everyone agreed that all this talk about the econ-
omy could be left to the politicians and bankers and the ordinary
folk could go on with the important things in life like visiting the
lake, getting married, having babies, drinking tea and beer and finding love, which was often right in front of them and not hiding at all.

In the morning Gracie, Lilly and Edie had gathered the most
beautiful roses from the rose bush. They sat at the kitchen table
and carefully removed the thorns from each stem and then they
tied the stems together with red ribbons to create two posies.

At three Edie stood in the entranceway in her new cream silk
dress. It had lace at the neck in a V shape and lace trim on the
hems. The sleeves hung loosely to her elbows and the dress was
tied with a wide sash at her hips. It hung to just below her knees.

She was wearing cream-coloured stockings and camel pumps. She had a wide-brimmed white hat and Gracie tucked a rose from the bush into the cream ribbon tied around the hat and the rose sat there, its red even richer, like glowing embers against the white of the hat.

The sun shone through the leadlight windows and Edie stepped into the beams and let them turn her arm into a rainbow and she whispered her wish.

Gracie had on a new dress too; it was blue like the summer sky with white lace trim and a white sash at her hips. Her cloche hat was pale blue to match. Paul was wearing his suit with a rose in the lapel and one in the band around his boxer. Lilly was wearing pale yellow with a matching hat that matched the new yellow of her house in Ligar Street. The cab arrived to take them to the church and Paul, Edie and Gracie sat in the back seat squashed together and Paul sat in the middle of Edie and Gracie and patted each girl's hand and Lilly sat in the front.

As Edie walked up the aisle, her arm in Paul's and Gracie walking ahead of her, she saw Theo standing waiting for her. She knew the tiniest details about him, she knew them the same way she knew how to breathe the air or knew the thoughts in her heart and she realised that though they had not been together, they had never been apart.

'It's a beautiful day for a wedding, Miss Cottingham,' he whispered as she reached him and he leant forward and she felt his lips press tenderly against hers and Reuben said, 'Not yet,' but he continued kissing her anyway and she remembered that girl who had stood under a tree waiting for his kiss and she was that girl.

Acknowledgements

The biggest thank you and love to the following people who have provided me with support, love, advice, gin and tonics and time to assist getting this book off the ground: Linda Funnell, Selwa Anthony, Linda Anthony, Peter Bishop, Annabel Blay, Jo Mackay, Peter Neal, Asher Leslie, Seth Leslie, Indea Leslie, Zane Neal, Maia Neal, Kylie Mitchell and Clara Edwards.

talk about it

Let's talk about books.

Join the conversation:

 on facebook.com/harlequinaustralia

 on Twitter @harlequinaus

www.harlequinbooks.com.au

If you love reading and want to know about our
authors and titles, then let's talk about it.